Planet B

Jasper T. Scott

Anthem Press

Copyright © 2022 Jasper T Scott

All rights reserved.

No part of this publication may be reproduced, distributed, or transmitted in any form or by any means, including photocopying, recording, or other electronic or mechanical methods, without the prior written permission of the publisher, except in the case of brief quotations embodied in critical reviews and certain other non-commercial uses permitted by copyright law.

This is a work of fiction. All of the characters, names, incidents, organizations, and dialogue in this novel are either products of the author's imagination or are used fictitiously.

Cover Art by Christian Bentulan

https://coversbychristian.com

Content Rating: PG-13

Author's Guarantee: If you find anything you consider inappropriate for this rating, please e-mail me at JasperTscott@gmail.com and I will either remove the content or change the rating accordingly.

Swearing: Brief instances of strong language
Sexual Content: Mild
Violence: Moderate

Acknowledgments

A big thanks goes to my editor, Aaron Sikes, my proofreader, Dani J. Caile, and to all of the advance readers who helped me polish this first edition. In particular, my gratitude goes out to: Gaylon Overton, Bob Sirrine, Gwen Collins, Lisa Garber, Gaylon Overton, Jim Kolter, Wade Whitaker, Howard Cohen, Mary Kastle, Dave Topan, and Davis Shellabarger.

And finally, many thanks to the Muse.

PART ONE: INTERVENTION

Chapter 1

September 22nd, 2069 AD

Alice Rice stood up from her telescope and shifted her weight for a better stance, listening to the old boards of the deck creak beneath her feet.

"I wanna see!" her nine-year-old son, Sean, said pressing in eagerly beside her.

"Patience," Alice replied. She bent forward again and made small adjustments to the focus, marveling at the hazy white band that gave the galaxy its name. A warm breeze blew, carrying with it the fresh, loamy smells of the forest. The trilling of frogs and the chirping of crickets filled her ears. To her, the woods of Maine in the summer were pure bliss. Going camping there with her husband and son was as close to paradise as Alice had ever found on Earth—*not that I've ever been anywhere else,* she amended with a wry smile.

But her imagination was fertile ground for more exotic paradises to flourish. As an astronomer, she spent most of her time thinking about what else could be out there. With the sheer number of stars and exoplanets that orbited them, the existence of places more idyllic and habitable than Earth was practically a given. And yet, alien life still hadn't been discovered. *Or discovered us,* she thought.

"Can I see?" Sean asked, bouncing on his toes.

"Hang on. It's almost ready."

"You said that ten *minutes* ago..."

Alice made a final adjustment and then withdrew from the eyepiece to regard her son. Nine years old and already looking like a little man. Where had the time gone? It felt like she'd blinked and the swaddled bundle nursing in her arms had become this lanky man-child standing before her. He had his father's brown eyes, but her oval face, button nose, and blond hair. "Go on, take a look," Alice said.

Sean took a quick step forward.

"Careful," she chided. "Don't bump it."

"I won't. Wow... what *is* that?"

"That's our galaxy, the Milky Way. Stars and dust thousands of light years away from us."

"Wow," Sean said again.

The screen door of the cabin creaked open and her husband, Liam, stepped out. "Am I too late?" he whispered, his eyes gleaming darkly in the starlight. He had two wine glasses in one hand, and an open bottle of Merlot in the other.

"Right on time," Alice said, smiling as he eased the door shut.

Alice looked back to her son, watching with a growing smile as he marveled at the stars. It reminded her keenly of her own childhood, growing up in rural Maine with her friends, and her grandfather, who had introduced her to her first telescope.

"Here you are," Liam whispered, handing her a glass. Alice raised it for a sip. Smooth and red. Not too dry, not too sweet. Definitely a Merlot. Liam's arm slid around her waist, pulling her close, and the two of them stood by the wooden railing, watching as their son gawked at the staggering beauty of the universe. Out here, in Baxter State Park, far from the light pollution of the cities, the sky was crowded with jewels. Alice admired them wonderingly as she sipped her wine.

Sean withdrew from the telescope. "What else can we see?"

Before she could answer, a bright flare of light appeared, dazzling her eyes.

"What was *that?*" Sean erupted.

Alice recovered with a frown. "Probably just a meteor..." But the flare was still shining brightly, gradually shrinking down to an oversized point of light at least as bright as Venus.

"Is it going to hit us?" Sean asked.

"It's not burning up, or is it?" Liam asked.

"I don't..." Alice hurriedly set her glass down on the railing. She used the finderscope to line up the object before peering through the eyepiece and bringing it into focus.

"What is it?" Liam whispered breathlessly.

For a long moment, Alice couldn't speak. She wasn't sure what she was looking at, and then when she realized what it must be, she still couldn't frame her thoughts into a coherent sentence, because what she was seeing didn't make any sense.

"Alice?" Liam pressed.

"It's... a planet," she finally said.

"A planet? Which one?" Liam asked, stepping closer to the telescope.

"I don't—I don't know," she said. "Maybe it's Venus? Or..." But she knew that was wrong. She could clearly see Venus as she pulled away from the telescope. It was hanging low in the western sky. This object was a bright, greenish-blue orb. No planet in the solar system looked like that with an optical telescope. Nor would any asteroids. She needed to get a closer look.

"Mom? What's wrong?" Sean asked.

"Nothing, sweetheart."

Whirling away, Alice almost knocked the tripod over in her hurry to reach for the bag of eyepieces sitting on the porch beside her. She stooped down and withdrew her phone, using the light of the screen to rifle through the bag for the right focal length. She picked the four millimeter one and a three times Barlow lens to increase the zoom to four hundred and fifty times. Her hands shook as she hurriedly changed the eyepieces. Alice glanced up periodically to check that the object was still there.

It was impossible to miss, even with the naked eye. Shining with a steady greenish-blue light, it was far bigger and brighter than Venus.

Bending to look through the telescope once more, Alice stared at the blurry green-blue orb and played with the focus wheel to sharpen the image. Her heart thumped hard in her ears, so loud that it drowned out the chirping of the frogs and crickets.

Her heart rate spiked sharply as the image cleared. It was definitely a planet. A planet with the white swirls of clouds, the freckled blues of lakes, and bright, verdant greens everywhere else.

"This is impossible," she breathed.

"What is?" Liam asked, sounding almost annoyed from the suspense.

Alice stepped back on trembling legs, and gestured helplessly to the telescope. Liam set his wine glass down beside hers and looked into the eyepiece. A sharp gasp tore from his lips. "What on Earth?" he gasped.

"Looks a bit like Earth," Alice replied. "Greener, though."

Sean wrapped his arms around his mother's waist in a fierce hug. He might not know how to say it anymore, but he was scared.

Alice laid a hand on his head, her fingers stroking absently through his hair. Liam turned from the view to look at her with wide, gleaming eyes.

"This must be some kind of mistake. Maybe there's something stuck to the lens?"

Alice snorted and gestured to the new star in the sky. Except that it wasn't a star at all. "It's right there. You don't need the telescope to see it."

"Right..." Liam trailed off, quietly gaping at the sight. "But planets don't just appear out of nowhere, Alice! There has to be some explanation. You're the astronomer. What is this?"

Alice slowly shook her head. "That flash of light we saw. Maybe it was a star going nova, and this blue-green orb is the expanding cloud of gas that it left in its wake?"

Liam hesitated. "You think so?"

But even that explanation fell short. The image was too sharp. Too clear. A blurry blue-green smudge of gasses could be explained away like that, but not this: an opaque, sharply defined sphere with *clouds* could only be one thing.

Her next best explanation was that this was a dream and she was fast asleep inside the cabin after staying up too late and drinking too much wine with Liam.

"I need to get back to New York," she said.

"I'll start packing," Liam added, retrieving their glasses in one hand and heading for the door.

"Good idea," Alice replied.

"But we just got here!" Sean complained. The screen door banged shut after Liam as he stumbled inside.

"Go with your father. Hurry," she said, prying her son's arms away from her waist.

"Are we in danger?" Sean asked, looking back at her as he went. A light flicked on inside the cabin as Liam started packing.

"No. I don't think so. But this *is* an emergency." And that was really something for an astronomer to say.

"Okay." Sean hurried inside, and Alice spun back around to look at the glowing light in the sky. Still shining steadily. She'd half-expected it to have vanished just as mysteriously as it had appeared.

She had to get back to her lab in NYU. But first, she had to find out more about what was going on. Alice thumbed her phone to life and said, "Call Julio Acosta."

"Calling Dr. Julio Acosta," a pleasant robotic voice replied.

By now thousands of people in the western hemisphere had already seen the same thing, and with countless observatories and high-powered telescopes on this side of the globe, surely someone already knew more about this than she did.

Her mind was bursting with questions as the phone rang. How far away was that planet? Where had it come from? Was it in a stable orbit around the sun, or just passing through? What was that flash of light that had preceded it, and why was it *green?*

Chapter 2

6:00 AM, September 25th

An incessant buzzing noise pierced Layla Bester's awareness like a jackhammer. She swatted at the air, then felt her smart watch vibrating against her wrist.

"Alarm off!"

The lights swelled gradually until they reached half their normal brightness. "Good morning, Layla," a pleasant female voice said. "It is six AM. Your coffee is waiting for you downstairs in the kitchen."

"Thank you, Alexa."

Layla didn't get up right away. She lay there, staring at the ceiling barely four feet above her head. That reminded her of times gone by, of sleeping in her parents' RV when they'd gone camping in Vermont. At first she'd thought it would be cozy and nostalgic. Now she wasn't so sure. It was one thing not having a lot of space when you had the great outdoors right outside. Then again, she supposed that New York City was a certain kind of outdoors.

And rentals in Brooklyn Heights weren't cheap. She'd jumped at the chance to lease a brand-new ten by ten smart loft in the Acropolis, one of the city's newest and most secure apartment buildings. But tiny living was a big adjustment, even now that she was on her own again. Neil and Jess had seen to that. Damn them both. A knot rose in Layla's throat, and her eyes burned, but she refused to cry another tear over it.

She should have been on her honeymoon right now, sitting on a beach in the Caribbean, sipping cocktails. Instead, she was going back to work two weeks early.

It never ceased to amaze Layla how many U-turns life took. Seven years ago she'd met Neil in jail—she, the arresting officer, he, the perp's lawyer—and now she was right back where she'd started: a single cop working the streets of New York. They'd had so many other plans. She was going to resign. Take a year off, then settle down and start a family.

Thank God she hadn't resigned.

Smelling the pot of coffee downstairs, Layla crawled out of bed—literally crawled—and made her way down the ladder to the first floor. She poured a cup of the dark brew, and walked two steps from the kitchen to sit in the mini loveseat by the apartment's only window. The glass was currently dark and opaque, set to its tinted privacy mode.

"Window clear," Layla said, and watched a dizzying urban sprawl fade into focus as she sipped from her mug. The coffee was black and bitter, and it burned her tongue, but it poked a welcome hole in her fog of sleep and navel-gazing, so she took another sip.

Her AR glasses were on the table, right where she'd left them the night before. Layla slipped them on, and said, "Alexa, play the news."

"Playing NYCN."

The glasses overlaid a feed of a pretty blonde-haired news anchor sitting behind a desk in the top right of her field of view.

"Nassau county protests continued late into the night with residents chanting—" The scene cut to protesters thrusting both physical and virtual signs in the air like pitchforks and shouting, "—Build Nassau a wall! Build Nassau a wall!"

The feed cut back to the news anchor. "Mayor Lacy Durham had this to say in a statement to the press—"

Mayor Durham appeared behind a lectern, bombarded by flashing lights. "Rising sea levels are a concern for everyone, but sea walls are not a magic bullet, and they are prone to catastrophic failures. Our current relocation policies and incentives to move residents away from the coastal areas are both cheaper and—"

"Pause," Layla said. The mayor's face froze in a contorted expression, dragging a crooked smile from Layla's lips. "Minimize." The window disappeared from her glasses. Layla settled deeper into her seat, pulling her feet up to sit sideways and watch out the window as air and ground traffic crowded a dreary canyon of skyscrapers: crimson ribbons on one side, white the other. The sun was just coming up, casting all of it in a rosy light and illuminating the solid gray wall at the end which kept the rising sea levels from swallowing Brooklyn Bridge Park. Growing bored with the view, Layla said, "Alexa, read me national headlines about the climate crisis."

"Okay...

"California Experiencing Worst Fire Season in State's History.

"Worsening Drought Pushes Bread and Produce Prices To Record Highs.

"Cattle Dying From Texas to Montana as Heat Wave Continues.

"Red Tide Thickens.

"Hurricane Hanson Promoted to Category Five.

"Hanson to Make Landfall in Less Than 48 Hours.

"Lousiana Evacuations Slowed by End Times Protesters.

"A New Planet, a New Hope? Astronomers Cry Wolf."

"Stop," Layla said. "Read article from last headline."

"Okay... Doctors Alice Rice and Julio Acosta of NYU claim to have discovered, and confirmed, the existence of what some are calling *Planet B*. A newly discovered exoplanet that's a near analog of Earth and seemingly even closer to us than Mars. Yet Doctor Rice cautions, *Planets don't suddenly appear out of nowhere*, adding that the data has yet to be peer-reviewed, and that we shouldn't jump to any conclusions until we know more. *Just three days ago, I was stargazing with my son in Maine when I saw it appear with a flash of light,* Alice recalls. Countless observers from around the country all saw the same thing. With theories for the planet's inexplicable appearance ranging from the apocalyptic to the divine."

"Stop." Layla frowned, wondering if she could trust any of what she'd just heard. Maybe Alexa had lost her mind again, and this article had been pulled from a gag feed. It had to be a joke. "What's the source of that article?"

"The source is NYU News."

Layla blinked and slowly shook her head. They must have gotten the numbers wrong. Bad math. A rounding error. Something.

Her watch and glasses vibrated, and a caller ID appeared on both, along with an attractive head shot of the caller; thick black hair, a strong chin, a black suit, and a checked blue tie to match his eyes. Neil Forester.

Layla scowled, and debated rejecting the call. "Answer."

A vid-feed of Neil appeared on her glasses, faithfully reconstructed as a digital avatar of himself that was nearly indistinguishable from the original. Sensors and cameras in his AR glasses and watch tracked his movements and facial expressions.

"You look like you just woke up," Neil said, leaning back and sipping a fancy cappuccino from Kelly's behind his big cherry-wood desk, his back turned to an impressive view of Manhattan.

"And you look like you haven't gone to sleep," Layla countered, noting his bloodshot eyes and the wrinkles in his suit and tie.

"The Marino case had me pulling an all-nighter. Listen, Jess, I—"

Layla's blood pressure spiked, and her pulse thundered in her ears.

"Shit. Sorry." He set his cappuccino down and rubbed his eyes. "I meant to say Layla. I've been thinking about that whole love triangle of ours. Jess must have been on my mind."

Layla smiled tightly. "What's this about, Neil?"

"I hate how things ended," he said.

A muscle jerked in Layla's cheek. "You slept with my best friend. How the fuck did you think it was going to end?"

"It was a long time ago," Neil argued. "We'd just started dating, and we'd never really said if we were exclusive."

"We'd been dating for five months! Exclusivity was implied. And Jess said you tried to hook up with her again after that. *She* was the one who turned you down."

"Look. I know I messed up. But I can do better, Layla. Just don't do this. We had so many plans! New Jersey. Three kids. Hell, we even had names picked out for our dogs!"

"If it makes you feel better, even if Jess hadn't told me, it would have ended the same way when you found some other slut to sleep with."

"Layla, seriously? She's your best friend."

"Not anymore."

"You weren't even friends with her when we slept together. You met Jess through *me!*"

"Just think about how fucked up that is, Neil. You introduced me to your lover."

"One time. It was *one* time. One stupid, drunken night."

"With intent to repeat. You're not marriage material, Neil. Face it."

He scowled at her. "If that's how you feel, then you should at least give the ring back."

Layla's mind spun. "Is *that* why you're calling?"

"It was thirty-five thousand credits! If you want to talk things over and think about it some more, I've got no problem with you keeping it. But if you've already made up your mind, then that ring doesn't belong on your finger."

"Fuck you, Neil." Layla made a swiping gesture, ending the call. She got up and crossed to her closet to get dressed. Thanks to him, she was about to arrive late to the precinct. Not the best precedent to set for her first day back on the job.

Chapter 3

9:00 AM

"MAKE A LINE! HANDS where I can see them!" Tom Smith stood behind the other inmates from C Block, waiting to get out into the yard.

We're like dogs to them, Tom thought. He eyed the fat, curly-haired prison guard, Murphy, as he strolled by, wagging his finger at each of them as he made a head count. *They feed us, walk us, tell us when to sit, when to lie down...*

He caught a backward glance from one of the other prisoners—Fango Morales, or *Solo*, as he was nicknamed thanks to his obsession with Star Wars. Tom smiled thinly at him and lifted his chin, as if he had something special planned for their yard time. He didn't. But that didn't mean he couldn't front like he did. Can't show weakness in prison, and this one was maximum security, so head cases like Fango were everywhere. *You don't get into Sing Sing for white collar shit.*

Fango smiled back, flashing a golden tooth. Fango had it out for him ever since he'd arrived. Tom remembered getting cornered by Fango and a pair of his buddies, because, as they'd put it: they were going to make him their black bitch. Tom had beaten them all within an inch of their lives in thirty seconds flat, with nothing but a few bruises for his trouble—but he'd also received six days in the hole. When he got out, he'd received three months free membership with the Bruthas. Of course, Fango had never forgiven him for that humiliation.

"All accounted for," Tom heard Murphy report to Chief Hanes.

"Let's go, people!" Hanes bellowed. "Sixty minutes, starting now."

Everyone filed out into the sunny blue-sky morning. Tom took a deep breath of summer and listened to the sweet melody of birds chirping. His eyes drifted shut and he sighed. Freedom. That's what it felt like. A fleeting taste that elicited faded memories of lying in the summer sun on a creaky wooden dock, of trees rustling, and swimming in the lake at his grandfather's farm. That was before his old man got locked up for dealing. Before his momma had to take two jobs in the city just to put food on the table.

Years later, he'd done the same to put himself through school, eventually getting his masters in paleontology. And that was where he'd met his late wife, Tamara. Tom winced as her smiling face flickered through his mind: sparkling brown eyes and smooth ebony skin wrapped in sheets and beams of sunlight.

It almost didn't matter anymore that she'd been unfaithful. Could he even blame her after he'd spent six months away on a dig in Australia? The other side of the world, and thanks to the time zones they'd barely even had time to call or chat. What he wouldn't have given just to see her happy. But life had darker plans for her. For both of them.

Tom's eyes cracked open to see everyone splitting off into their usual groups. Gangs by any other name. And they were defined exclusively by the color of the inmates' skins.

Does that mean we're all just as racist as Fango? Tom wondered as he followed the rest of the African-American inmates to their side of the yard where they promptly began *spinning* laps.

Most walked in silence, while a few quietly traded intel and stories about other inmates and the guards. Tom drifted to the back of the group, wanting some alone time. When you're caged in close quarters with a thousand plus smelly, noisy, disagreeable assholes, you begin to appreciate whatever solitude you get. Tom threw his head back as he walked, taking in the vast blue wonder of open sky.

Walls, walls—everywhere but up. God, why didn't you give me wings?

Tom's gaze came back down to see that he was catching shade from Fango and the rest of *La Familia*, or the *Fammies* as the Bruthas liked to call them. Maybe Tom didn't have anything planned, but Fango and his buddies looked like they did.

Ordinarily, Fammies knew better than to pick a fight with him. The Bruthas were the biggest, meanest gang in Sing Sing. But as it happened, Tom was overdue on his membership fees. Some prisoners got money regularly deposited to their accounts by family or friends on the outside. Tom was one of those lucky few, still financed by his momma after ten years. She might just be the only one left in the world who still believed he was innocent.

But getting money was a double-edged sword. Those who had it were obliged to share, or else they were on their own. Tom was supposed to keep half of anything he got for the Brutha's leader, Roach, to administer. But he'd secretly been saving up, holding out how much money he really had, and last month he'd made the mistake of splurging to buy himself a new pair of kicks from the commissary.

Feeling suddenly vulnerable, Tom picked up his pace, getting closer to the Bruthas walking ahead of him. As he spun his second lap, he noticed that the Fammies were right behind them, with Fango in the lead. The man flashed another golden-toothed smile. Tom frowned and looked back to the fore. *Big Boy* and *Hazer* glanced back at him, the latter looking apologetic—and then, as if it had all been choreographed ahead of time, the Bruthas peeled off, heading for the shade of the trees at the far end of the yard. A group of Fammies went jogging past Tom, forcing him to stop and back up against the fence to avoid being blindsided by one of them. They encircled him in such a casual way that it looked almost as though they'd adopted him as one of their own.

Fango melted out of their ranks, grinning darkly at him and cracking his knuckles. He was big for a Fammy. Bald and six-foot-nothing with more tats than skin. He was built thick across the chest and shoulders, with just enough fat on him that he could throw his weight around. By contrast, Tom was lean and ripped, and probably a good twenty pounds lighter despite being two or three inches taller. "Looks like it's just you and me now, *Romeo,*" Fango said.

That was Tom's nickname. He'd earned it when people found out that he'd been locked up for supposedly killing his wife and her lover.

Tom glanced behind him, checking for the nearest guard tower. The Fammies were standing too close, so it wouldn't be easy to pick him out from that tower. By the time they realized something was up, it would be too late.

But there was one silver lining: only Fango was coming at him. The others were just standing around, blocking sight lines from the guards.

Tom rolled his head and shoulders, then put up his fists. "Let's see what you got, Fammy."

Fango's grin vanished, and he produced a metal shank from his sleeve.

Where the hell did he get that? Tom wondered. It looked like a piece of scrap metal.

Fango closed the gap between them in two quick strides. Tom saw an opening, and took a swing. Fango ducked and jabbed with the shank. But Tom caught his arm and deflected the attack. He made a play for the weapon, but Fango danced back out of reach, withdrawing sharply and slicing Tom's palm open before he could get a good grip.

Tom hissed between his teeth, feeling that side of his hand growing hot and numb. He checked the injury briefly. Deep enough that he'd need stitches.

"You're gonna pay for that," Tom gritted out, dripping blood into the scrappy grass and dirt.

Fango said nothing. He came in slashing in broad strokes with the shank. Tom evaded each swipe of the blade, ducking and backpedaling—until he ran into some of the other Fammies—getting kicked in the ass and the small of his back.

He went down hard, landing hard on his hands and knees and stirring up a cloud of dust. He saw the shank gleaming in the sun, and the hateful sneer on Fango's face as the blade swept toward his throat. He threw up his hands, but it was too late.

Tom cried out in terror, realizing that this was it. He felt someone pushing or pulling him back, and Fango stopped suddenly, blinking in confusion as the blade flew out of his hand.

Then a flash of light erupted between them, dazzling Tom's eyes.

--:--- AM/PM, September --

TOM BLINKED HIS EYES open to find himself staring up at the sky. Bright and blue and filled with scudding clouds. *What the...* had the guards used some kind of new crowd control weapon on them?

Tom sat up quickly, ready to fend off a fresh attack in case Fango had already recovered.

Fango was sitting up across from him. They were lying in a field of tall, bright green grass, with no sign of walls, fences, guards, or any other inmates.

Tom's jaw dropped.

Fango's did, too.

They weren't in Sing Sing anymore.

Their eyes met across a gap of maybe ten feet.

"*Que chingada?*" Fango muttered.

Tom didn't know exactly what that meant, but he could guess. "What the fuck, is right..."

Fango jumped to his feet, aiming his shank like an extension of his finger. "What did you do?"

"Me?" Tom roared, indignant.

"Am I dead? Did you kill me, you little bitch?"

"You're the one holding the knife," Tom pointed out. "Maybe you killed *me*." That was a disturbing thought. Was this heaven? Wonder and hope swirled together, filling Tom's chest with a breath of the sweetest air he'd ever tasted, fragrant with a woody, citrus smell—like oak and lemongrass.

Fango's eyes darted away, bugging out of his head as he gawked at their surroundings. The field was surrounded by tall trees on all sides, but sprawled down to a sparkling blue lake to Tom's left. The far side of the lake swept up into towering, snow-capped mountains.

The air felt colder than it had a moment ago. Not too cold, but definitely colder. Birds were still chirping, but they didn't sound familiar, with whooping cries and trilling calls that echoed in fading swells. An animal that sounded like it had swallowed a pipe organ—deep and rumbling—roared from the trees. Tom found his gaze glued to that forest, listening to the groaning bellows of the creature. *A bear?* The trees began to shiver and shake in time to *thudding* footsteps.

"What is that?" Fango whispered.

"What makes you think I know?" Tom countered.

The jury was out on whether or not he'd woken up in heaven, but this definitely wasn't New York.

And those trees looked *strange*. But what was it about them? Too tall? Too green? Almost like a jungle, except there weren't any jungles in America. At least, not on the mainland.

The thunder of those heavy footfalls grew progressively closer. Whatever was in there, it was headed their way.

"We'd better get out of here," Tom muttered.

Fango led the charge, running in the opposite direction from the trees, up a grassy hill. Tom hesitated briefly before tearing after him. They might have been enemies in prison, but out here, with God-knows-what chasing after them, they stood a better chance together than alone. *If nothing else, that bear will have someone else to eat while I get away,* Tom thought grimly.

Chapter 4

12:32 PM, September 25th

Preston Baylor sat in his penthouse overlooking Central Park, sipping a cappuccino and watching the news on his AR glasses. Every feed ran the same story, which lent credence to an otherwise impossible tale.

A new planet had been found, and it lay even closer to Earth than Mars.

There was simply no way that could be true. He of all people would know. As CEO and founder of the Space Development Group (SDG), he knew more about the solar system than practically anyone else. Local space had been mapped thousands of times by hundreds of different telescopes, and he'd personally sent missions to half a dozen planets and moons, along with a few mining and prospecting runs to the belt. SDG had been instrumental in establishing the Mars Colony, and they'd been sending annual resupply missions ever since.

With all of that activity and attention on their cosmic backyard, the thought that an entire *planet* could have been hiding in plain sight was simply impossible.

But that didn't preclude other possibilities. What he needed was a look at the data coming back from the telescopes now aimed at this so-called *Planet B*.

"Alexa, call Alice Rice from NYU."

"You do not have an Alice Rice in your contact list. Would you like me to add her number for you?"

Preston grimaced. "Yes. Search NYU Faculty Directory."

"Searching... Found, one Dr. Alice Rice, professor of Astronomy at New York University. Comm number not listed. Would you like me to try something else?"

"Call New York University."

"Calling..."

Preston waited while the call rang through the speakers in the frames of his glasses. An attractive young woman appeared on the lenses, smiling brightly at him.

"Hello, Mr. Baylor! It's an honor to speak with you, sir. I'm a huge fan of you and your family's work!"

Preston waved away her praise. "I'd like to speak with Dr. Alice Rice."

"Of course... one moment, let me see if she's available."

The woman tapped away on a keyboard beyond his field of view, and imagery flickered brightly across her glasses.

"It looks like she's in a work conference at the moment. If you like, I could take a message for you, or ask her to call you back when she's—"

"Is she on campus?"

"Yes, sir."

"Good, then I'll go see her directly. Thank you for your time."

"But—"

Preston ended the call. He stood up suddenly from his living room couch and spun around to find Terry, his butler bot, gliding in with his lunch—lobster mac and cheese with a green smoothie. The bot was the latest model from Andromax: gleaming silver and black, with two legs, a rubbery white face and two disturbingly life-like blue eyes.

"Here you are, Mr. Baylor," Terry said, smiling as he set the tray down on Preston's backlit onyx dining table.

"Sorry, Terrance. Something came up. Give it to Buck."

"The dog has already eaten, sir."

"Then save it for my dinner!" Preston called back.

"Yes, sir," Terry replied.

Preston barely heard the bot. He was already halfway to the front door. Just before he reached the entrance of his penthouse, he had another thought, and turned back the other way, heading for the floating staircase in the living room. Fighting his way through traffic to reach the university would take a while. His air car would be much faster.

12:48 PM

LAYLA STOOD IN THE yard of Sing Sing Correctional, taking a statement from one of the guards, Murphy Carson.

"I noticed the commotion over there, by the fence." Murphy pointed. "I was just about to sound the alarm when I saw this flash of light. And then they were gone. A bunch of the guys started shouting, screaming about the end of the world..." Murphy trailed off shaking his head. He looked like he was about to be sick. "I don't know how they did it, but by the time I got there, they were gone. We did a roll call. Counted everyone twice. And both times they came up missing."

"By *they*, you mean Tom Smith and Fango Morales?" Layla asked.

"Yes, ma'am," Murphy said. His head bobbed, making the fat rolls bunch beneath his chin.

Warden Joseph Snyder pushed his AR glasses higher up on his nose. The images flickering across the lenses made it look like he was watching the news. She could imagine why. The entire city—no, the *world*—was busy losing its head over this Planet B thing. It was big news. Maybe the biggest ever, but as far as Layla was concerned, it didn't matter how near or far that planet actually was. She lived *here*, and dealt with crime here. Not in outer space, on some alien planet that was probably millions or trillions of miles away.

Layla frowned and glanced at her partner, José Cortez. He was short, but fit, with a well-trimmed beard and thick black hair to match. Jose shrugged. "Let's go take a look over by the fence," he suggested.

"Sure thing," Officer Murphy said, leading the way across the clumpy field. He stopped beside the fence and pointed to a spot where the footprints in the sandy track around the fence were smudged beyond all recognition. "They were right here when they vanished."

Layla went over to the fence and grabbed it in both hands. She rattled the chainlink, checking for signs of sabotage. It hadn't been cut. She walked down the length of it in both directions, shaking the fence and checking the posts to make sure they were all still firmly planted in the concrete. Everything seemed to be in order. After that, Layla walked around the area, stomping her foot.

José sidled up to her after about a minute of that. "What are you doing?" he whispered.

The warden was looking at her like she'd lost her mind.

"I'm checking for tunnel entrances," she said, loud enough for the warden to hear. He did.

"You *really* think they could dig a tunnel *here*, in plain sight of all the guards?"

Layla walked right up to him. Joseph Snyder straightened his back. He was a tall, thin man with pinching brown eyes and thinning gray hair swept back from his forehead. She crossed her arms and regarded him with a wry smile.

"All right. Then how do *you* think they got out of here?"

"Three days ago, a planet appeared in the sky where there was nothing but empty space before. One of the astronomers who claims to have discovered it says that she saw a flash of light before it appeared. Now, two days later, another burst of light blinds a dozen of my guards and more than a hundred prisoners, taking with it two hardened criminals. You don't see the connection?"

"So... your theory is that a planet abducted them?" Layla said.

"Don't be ridiculous. My theory is that the two phenomena are connected. That is all." With that, the warden cast his eyes skyward.

Layla frowned and joined him in looking up. All she saw was a pale blue sky, cotton ball clouds, and the sun glaring down. To all appearances, it was a day like any other, and nothing was amiss. But the warden's words chased up a confusing collection of memories, muted and faded with time.

It was the eleventh grade. She was fifteen years old and living in Middleton, New York. The school took a field trip to the Sterling Hill Mining Museum. She spent the day with her classmates, pretending to be interested in the fluorescent mineral displays, while actually using the cover of darkness to make out with her boyfriend, Axel Harper.

Then, when it came time for lunch, she went to the bathroom, while he went ahead to grab a plate of food for her. When she came back, Axel Harper was missing. The teachers went crazy, running around, asking everyone who'd seem him last, but no one knew where he was. Pretty soon the mine was swarming with police. They questioned her thoroughly, but she was barely coherent through her sobs. Their parents were called, and then the busses took them home early.

To this day, Axel's disappearance was an unsolved mystery in Middleton. And in part, the trauma and horror of that day had contributed to Layla's decision to become a detective.

"If an entire planet can suddenly appear in an empty vacuum, why can't a pair of inmates vanish into thin air?" Snyder asked. "Everything we thought we knew about the universe has been called into question."

Layla brought her gaze back down to Earth with a scowl. "I want all of your security footage from the yard from the last two days up until the moment those prisoners disappeared."

"Of course," Snyder said. "Anything else?"

"Yes. I want to speak with the prisoners who were closest to them when they disappeared."

"That will be *La Familia.*"

"La who?"

"The Latino gang. They had Tom and Fango surrounded to keep the guards from seeing them fight."

"The prisoners were fighting each other when they disappeared?" Layla asked, her brow furrowing. Up till now, she'd assumed that they'd been working together to escape.

"Yes. Didn't Officer Murphy tell you?"

Layla glared at the curly-haired guard. He drew himself up, pulling some of his prodigious belly into his chest. "I didn't think it was relevant," Murphy said.

"Everything is relevant!" Layla snapped at him. Looking back to the Warden she added, "Let's go see La Familia."

"Of course. This way." Snyder began cutting back across the yard to the cell blocks.

"Who pissed in your coffee this morning?" José whispered to her as they followed the warden.

Layla flicked a scowl at her partner, and he held up his hands in surrender.

"Easy tiger. Rawr." A grin lit his face, and his brown eyes sparkled mischievously.

"Fuck off, Cortez."

Chapter 5

1:57 PM

ALICE RICE SAT BESIDE her colleague Julio Acosta at the desk they shared in one of the conference rooms at NYU. Julio was hunched over, his elbows propped up with his head in his hands as he stared at the data on their virtual screens. His scraggly black beard and hunching posture made him look even smaller than his five-foot four inches normally allowed. Curly black hair matched his beard, just as his pudgy cheeks matched his belly. Julio was a brilliant man, but unfortunately his intellectual prowess was not equaled by its physical counterpart.

Both of them wore their slightly more cumbersome wide-field AR glasses to make it easier to see and manipulate the virtual screens on the wall in front of them.

Right now they were looking at the latest numbers from the Square Kilometer Radio Array (SKA) and the Event Horizon Telescope (EHT), as well as actual imagery from the Galileo and the Carl Sagan Space Telescopes. Each set of data told a slightly different story, capturing readings across different wavelengths of the electromagnetic spectrum.

"See that there?" Julio whispered, gesturing to the imagery from the SKA and EHT. Both telescopes had captured images in the radio spectrum, which Alice and Julio had then resolved into visible light. The images showed a bright speck that was Planet B in the center, and just above it was an even brighter speck, designated Rigel Kentaurus—otherwise known as Alpha Centauri. That star repeated again, a little higher up and dimmer than before, and again... and again...

"Remarkable..." Alice whispered.

"What's remarkable?"

Both of them turned, and Alice saw a vaguely familiar man standing in the open door to their office. At least six feet tall, with an easy smile, ruddy cheeks, green eyes, and mid-length blond hair. He wore an expensive suit, but no tie. Alice could have sworn she recognized him from somewhere, but her brain was too busy wading through a sea of shock to catch up and put a name to the face.

"Am I interrupting?" the man asked, stepping into the room.

"Yes, this is a private meet..." Julio started to say. Then his jaw dropped, and he shot out of his chair. "Preston Baylor! What are you... how..." Julio cleared his throat and straightened his tie. "It's a pleasure to meet you, sir!"

"The pleasure's all mine," Preston said. He strolled over to the wall with their virtual screens on it. "May I see?" he asked, and drew a pair of glasses from his jacket's inside pocket.

"Yes, of course!" Julio replied, hurriedly inviting him to share their screens. Alice approved the request as the billionaire slipped his glasses on.

"It's a mirage," Preston said after a moment. "Rigel Kentaurus appears four times. Each time farther away and dimmer than before."

"Correct," Julio said. "Can you guess what's causing it?"

"A black hole?" Preston ventured.

"Yes!" Julio replied. "Very good! Yes. It's caused by the immense gravity. Light gets trapped in an orbit around the black hole. Some of it circles endlessly, while the rest escapes after completing just a few orbits."

Julio pointed to the first mirror image. "One orbit." Then to the second. "Two orbits." And finally to the third. "Three orbits. There should actually be an infinite series of mirror images, but we can't see the others, because they're too dim. The more times the light orbits before escaping, the dimmer the cloned images will be."

"Fascinating," Preston said. The virtual screens scrolled off his glasses as he turned to look at Alice. "So what does this mean? Could it explain how Planet B appeared out of nowhere?"

"Maybe," Alice admitted. "But only under very specific conditions."

Julio blinked and his eyes widened as realization dawned. "That would mean..."

"That it's a wormhole," Alice finished for him.

"But this is incredible!" Julio cried. "We've never even found a wormhole before! They're purely theoretical structures."

"Not anymore," Preston said.

The three of them looked back to the screens.

"How far away is it?" Preston asked.

Alice shook her head. "The wormhole? Or Planet B?"

"Both."

"Planet B has been measured at about sixteen million miles, but that measurement is almost certainly the distance to our end of the wormhole not to the planet itself. We can't bounce radio waves directly off the planet, only off the mouth of the wormhole. But using the parallax method, we've determined that Planet B is about half an astronomical unit away from our end of the wormhole."

Preston whistled between his teeth. "Incredible. Are those measurements real?"

"What do you mean *real?*" Alice asked.

"I mean... is the wormhole somehow distorting things? Making Planet B seem closer than it really is?"

"Well, yes, in a manner of speaking. That's how they work. Wormholes are shortcuts from one point in space-time to another. They cut out some or all of the distance in-between, directly joining two points in space together. So, it's definitely making Planet B seem closer than it really is, but technically it actually *is* that close—as long as you fly down the throat of the wormhole to get there. Sixteen million miles plus half an astronomical unit, so approximately sixty-two million miles."

"And how far away is it really?"

"You mean the long way around? Who knows." Alice shrugged. "For all we know, Planet B could lie a hundred light years from here. Or a thousand. Or even millions. But thanks to the wormhole that magically appeared three days ago, we're able to get a much closer look."

"Do we need to worry about it sucking us in?" Preston asked.

"No, the black hole is at the other end," Alice replied. "This end is a white hole. Or, we think it is, anyway."

"We need more data to confirm," Julio added.

Preston's shoulders slumped. "Then we can't reach Planet B?"

"No. But it's still the most remarkable discovery of the century. I'd go so far as to say it's the most remarkable discovery of *any* century. Not only have we discovered a seemingly habitable exoplanet, but we've discovered a stable wormhole that leads straight to it."

Preston cradled his chin in one hand and stared hard at the data from the telescopes.

Alice watched him, sensing the man's disappointment. He was a space entrepreneur, just like his father, Alec Baylor. The holy grail for him would be a habitable planet close enough to Earth that he could actually send probes and colonists to it.

"Did you have any other questions, Mr. Baylor?" Alice asked. "We really should be getting back to work. If we don't share our findings soon, someone else will beat us to it. And then they'll get the research grants instead of us. So, unless you would like to fund our research yourself..." She couldn't help but throw it out there.

Preston's gaze swept back to her and the intensity of it actually made her flinch. "I'll fund you for life if you can figure out how to send a probe through that wormhole and have it survive the journey."

Alice's hopes died there. She frowned and slowly shook her head. "I thought I was clear... wormholes are not traversable."

"Clearly they are, or we wouldn't be seeing light from the other side."

"Maybe *light* can get through, but actual matter... the forces would rip it apart and probably destabilize the wormhole in the process. Sending a probe through is simply impossible, Mr. Baylor."

"Then why did they put it here?" he demanded.

"Excuse me?" Alice blinked. "Why did *who* put what where?"

"Aliens. The wormhole."

Alice's cheeks bulged with an exasperated sigh. She let it out slowly, her lungs collapsing like a leaky balloon. "You want to take this one, Julio?"

"Actually... Mr. Baylor makes a good point," Julio said slowly. "What are the odds of a wormhole appearing in our solar system, with the other end of it facing a habitable planet?"

"Wormholes don't really face anything," Alice said. "They're three dimensional objects that can be entered from any side. Light is pouring in from all sides on one end, and pouring out from all sides on the other. Or, it could be pouring in on both ends and colliding in the middle, but in that case we should be seeing Gamma Ray bursts and balls of plasma instead of Planet B."

"But that's not the case," Preston said.

"No, so it must be a white hole on this end, and a black hole on the other," Alice concluded. "And fundamentally, that makes it impossible for anything to enter from our side."

"Even light?" Preston asked.

"Even light."

"So if someone is looking up at the sky on Planet B and staring down their end of this wormhole, they won't see anything?"

"Bingo. To them it's just a big, black emptiness. Unless it's an active black hole... in which case matter is getting sucked in and lighting the event horizon on fire, which would mean that the planet definitely isn't habitable. There would be too much radiation."

"So their end is invisible. Kind of like our end was three days ago?" Preston asked.

Alice frowned. "That's not..."

"Possible?" Preston finished. "What's more likely? That the wormhole suddenly appeared, or that it was always there? What if someone flipped it around?" he insisted. "Maybe until now Planet B was looking at a white hole and wondering how to reach Earth."

"Wormholes don't just flip around like magnets," Alice said.

"Why not?" Preston asked. "One end could be positively charged, the other negative. And the polarities could reverse periodically."

PLANET B

"Hang on a second..." Julio muttered, wagging a finger at the data. "You said wormholes don't face anything, but we *do.*"

A quiet thrill shot through Alice's body, sparking down to her fingertips. "Holy crap!"

"What is it?" Preston prompted.

Julio illustrated with his fists, moving them around each other in circles. "As the angles between us and the wormhole change we'll get different views from the other end! Think of it like a spherical window. Depending where you're standing outside of it, you'll see different things. We might even see something that will tell us where Planet B really is."

"A spherical window... you mean like a fishbowl?" Preston asked.

"Yes! Well, no... not exactly. It's difficult to explain."

Julio yanked his chair out from the desk, almost knocking it over in his rush to sit back down. Attacking his mouse and keyboard, he pulled up magnified images of Planet B from the Galileo Space Telescope. And others from the Carl Sagan Space Telescope. "There!" Julio crowed, jabbing a finger at the virtual screens. "Look at that!"

Each of the telescopes was looking at Planet B from a slightly different angle. The images had also been taken from different points in time. All of them showed a hazy outline of stars and galaxies, blurring at the edges into a roughly circular formation around the mouth of the wormhole. Each telescope depicted Planet B in a different part of that sphere, and there was a clear progression to the images as time elapsed, showing that bright green orb marching across the warped, spherical patch of space.

In the latest images, taken just this morning, Planet B was drawing so close to the edge of the wormhole that it was about to disappear. And on the far end...

Was a bright blue speck.

Alice clapped a hand over her mouth. "How did we not spot this earlier?"

"We were too focused on the radio images!" Julio said.

"What is *that?*" Preston asked, leaning closer to the screens. "Can we get a closer look?"

Julio zoomed in to the maximum resolution, and that blue speck resolved into a blurry orb speckled with gray and brown spots and swirled with white streaks.

"Is that what I think it is?" Preston asked.

"It's another planet," Julio whispered.

Chapter 6

--:-- AM/PM, September --

"I THINK WE LOST it!" Tom called out. He took a break on the other side of the hill, hands on his knees, breathing hard. It was then that he realized the gash in his palm was gone. Fango had sliced it open with his shank right before that flash of light had knocked them out. Tom turned his hand over and frowned. Nothing but clean black skin. It was as though he'd never been cut at all. How long had he been knocked out? A few steps ahead of him, Fango collapsed in the grass, gasping for air.

"Did you see what it was?" he asked.

Tom sat down,shaking his head. "No."

Silence fell, and they listened to the whooping, trilling calls of the birds. The hill where they were sitting rolled down to another forest with a lake gleaming on the other side and snow-capped mountains above that.

Tom held a hand to his forehead to shade his eyes from the sun as he scanned the horizon. He was still trying to figure out where they were. The snow-capped mountains reminded him of the Rockies, but the grass and the plants were too green for this to be Colorado or Canada. It had to be somewhere with more rainfall. Odds were good that they weren't even in America anymore. The sun passed behind a cloud, dropping a shadow over them, and Tom shivered.

"*Eso que es?*" Fango asked.

"English," Tom barked at him.

Fango pointed up to the sky.

Tom followed the gesture, squinting at the dark blue expanse overhead. A bright ring of light shone down on them. He looked away sharply, blinking green, ring-shaped after images from his eyes. "Looks like an eclipse," he said.

"And that?" Fango asked, pointing in another direction.

Tom saw it. A blue marble in the sky, faded with daylight. Like seeing the moon in the early morning. But this wasn't the moon. It was too big—at least twice the size—and too blue, with no hint of familiar craters. "That's..." Tom trailed off, speechless. Glancing around suddenly, he took in the entire dome of the sky, studying it more carefully now. Hovering just above the mountains, across the lake was another mysterious sight—a second marble in the sky, this one the size of his fist, purple, green, and mauve, with flecks of blue and streaks of white. And those two weren't the only ones. There were at least a dozen more, all of them smaller or more distant than the first two, their features faded and indistinct.

"They're everywhere," Fango said.

The implications rocked Tom to his core. A shiver raced through him and he hugged his shoulders. "Where the hell are we?" he muttered, seeing their surroundings with fresh eyes. The grass was too green, the blades too thick and flat. The mountain ranges on the other side of the lake were too jagged, and the air felt wrong. The woody citrus smell of it was like nothing he'd ever experienced anywhere on Earth. The trees at the foot of the hill looked too tall, their shapes and colors also somehow *off*. Everything was both intensely familiar and alien at the same time, like someone had tried to copy Earth without actually copying it. The theory that they'd died and gone to heaven was looking more and more likely.

"*Mierda*," Fango muttered. He looked up again, his eyes searching. "*Dios? Está allí?*"

Tom understood that part, at least. Fango was asking if God was up there. That put a crooked smile on Tom's lips. It faded dramatically as he realized that Fango might actually get a reply.

But the only answer was a gust of wind rustling through the grass.

Something colorful crept about at Tom's feet, catching his eye. It stopped, staring at him with two massive, bulbous red eyes, and an elongated black body with blue spots.

Tom cursed and leaped to his feet. The creature skittered up the tall grass with a flurry of churning legs. Four massive, translucent wings fluttered, and it took flight. The sun emerged, seeming to melt out from behind whatever had eclipsed it, and the light caught the insect's massive wings, causing them to shimmer with rainbows as it buzzed away in the direction of the forest below.

Fango regarded Tom with wide, unseeing eyes. "What was that?"

"Dragonfly..." Tom said slowly. It definitely looked like one, but its wingspan had to be at least three feet. A distant recollection from his studies clicked into place. *Meganeura*. An extinct species of dragonfly. But that was absurd, wasn't it?

"You seen one that big before?" Fango asked.

"No," Tom replied. "Not a living one, anyway."

Fango nodded woodenly.

"We should keep moving," Tom suggested. "Find shelter, and figure out how to light a fire. If it's this cold with the sun shining, it'll be a lot colder tonight."

"Where do we go?" Fango asked, looking around quickly, as if expecting to find something creeping up behind him.

Tom jerked his head to the forest and the shimmering lake below. "The shore of that lake seems like a good place to start. We need to stay hydrated. Once we have a fire going and something to boil our water in, we can build a shelter. Maybe think about hunting for some food. You still have that shank?"

Fango blinked slowly at him, uncomprehending. "Oh." He patted himself down. "No. Something knocked it out of my hand before..."

"Something? Like *what?*" Tom pressed. "Did you see it?" He remembered seeing the blade fly out of

Fango's hand. He also remembered feeling something shove him back before that blade could open a second mouth beneath his chin.

Fango shrugged helplessly.

"Just as well you lost it, I guess. I wouldn't be here otherwise."

"What are you talking about?" Fango said. "I killed you. And then the guards shot me. Now we're in heaven."

"Maybe," Tom admitted. It sounded absurd, but at this point all explanations would sound equally crazy.

"What else could have happened? We're not in Sing Sing anymore!"

"I don't think we're even on Earth anymore," Tom replied.

"*Exactamente!*"

"That doesn't mean we're in heaven."

"You think..." Fango's eyes darted furtively. "This is Hell?"

Tom barked a laugh, but cut himself off sharply as he realized it could be a bad idea to draw attention to himself. "You hear about that planet they found?"

Fango's brow furrowed. "What about it?"

"A planet suddenly appeared where there wasn't one before. And then we disappeared. Maybe this is it? Somehow, something took us here."

"Something? Like aliens?" Fango asked.

Tom shrugged. "Maybe."

"But why *us?*"

"Now *that*, is a damn good question," Tom replied.

Chapter 7

2:05 PM

Bruce Gordon stood on the stage at the COP74 in New York, overlooking an auditorium that was much emptier than it should have been. Whole tables stood empty, the delegations from vast swaths of the world having simply upped and left before the conference even began. Others had summoned last-minute stand-ins.

Bruce had spent the better part of the past two months preparing for this speech, and these people didn't even have the basic decency to show up. The United Nations Climate Change Conference was arguably the most important meeting in the world, and they couldn't be bothered to attend.

Bruce took a deep breath, pushing down his growing frustration. "Your excellencies, delegates, ladies and gentlemen... as we spend the next several weeks here negotiating and debating what's to be done about our growing climate crisis, I beg you to consider one thing: this is the seventy-*fourth* climate change conference.

"We should be here today, celebrating seventy-four years of progress against a global enemy.

"Our parents' generation sat in a conference center like this one, lobbying for stricter measures and policies to roll back, or even just to halt, the growing tide of carbon dioxide that has been suffocating our world since the industrial revolution began.

"In May 2013, carbon levels rose above four hundred parts per million for the first time in several million years. Fast forward to 2069, and we have more than doubled that number to eight hundred and seventeen parts per million. Our parents broke their promises to us, to their children and to their grandchildren. As a result, global mean temperatures have increased since 2013 by more than two degrees.

"In that time sea levels have risen by almost two feet. Countries around the world are building walls to hold back the ocean and prevent the floods, as if the rising tide is somehow inevitable! Droughts, hurricanes, unprecedented firestorms and toxic algae blooms are ravaging every country and continent.

"At the turn of the century, a loaf of bread cost ten times less than it does today, and only forty percent of that rise is attributable to regular inflation. The rest is due to arable farmland turning into deserts at an alarming rate. The average household spends twice as much on food as they do on housing, a figure that amounts to *half* of their total income. Adding to it all, our population has exploded from seven billion in 2013 to over ten billion, and we're *still* growing, as if we have room for more!

"Our world is bursting at the seams. It's dying because we're killing it, and now we're caught in the death throes. Today, we stand on the threshold between two very different futures. In one, we continue to kill our planet until everything falls apart in a dramatic unraveling of Biblical proportions. Or, we make a real and lasting commitment to roll back emissions. It won't be instant. It won't be easy, and it won't be cheap. But if we can do it, I guarantee you that Mother Nature will do the rest.

"Let this be the turning point where all of humanity stood together and said with one voice, enough! Then one day we'll be able to tell our children and our grandchildren that we saved the planet; we kept the promises that our forefathers broke, and as a result, we ushered in a golden age of unity and progress.

"I don't know about you, but I know which future I want to live in. No one nation or person can accomplish this on their own, and that is why you are here, ladies and gentlemen, delegates, and excellencies. You are here to save the planet. Thank you."

Bruce Gordon walked off the stage to the lackluster applause of the half-empty auditorium. He went to take his seat with the American delegation, whose president, Adam Wallace, was conspicuously missing.

Of course, Bruce knew *why* so many people were absent. The world had bigger news than their dying planet, and attention spans were notoriously short.

News feeds were running day and night with speculation about Planet B. Its origins and purpose. Who might be behind its appearance, and why. And just this morning, they had a new head-spinner to discuss—the discovery of Planet C! It wasn't enough that they'd discovered one apparently habitable exoplanet seemingly within a stone's throw of Earth. Now they were multiplying.

And somehow, the revelation that these planets were fundamentally unreachable had done nothing to dull public expectations. Bruce watched as the Prime Minister of Canada, Marie Thubois, took the stage. Her short black hair contrasted sharply with her pale skin and blue eyes. She was relatively young for a world leader, at just forty-one years of age. But then, female leaders were typically elected at a younger age than men.

"Sobering words from Doctor Bruce Gordon," Mrs. Thubois said. "Thank you, Mr. Gordon."

He nodded to her, though he doubted she could see through the bright lights shining on the stage. His mind wandered, toying briefly with the fantasy that everyone else had clearly given into. What if this wormhole had appeared now for a reason? What if some incomprehensibly powerful species had been watching them from afar and had decided to intervene by providing them with a lifeboat?

Planet B... and now C. Two habitable worlds within easy reach of Earth. Except that so far, scientists were all in agreement that no one could safely cross the wormhole to reach them. So what was the point? Just to dangle the carrot? To taunt humanity in our final hour with the promise of virgin worlds?

It was an unwelcome distraction at a time when humanity needed all hands on deck to save the planet they had. The ones up in space may as well be heat mirages on the horizon of a burning Earth.

Even if we could reach them, we'd never be able to get any meaningful percentage of Earth's population into space. We could pick a few thousand colonists to jump ship. And then what? Leave everyone else here to go down with the S.S . Earth? As far as Bruce was concerned, nothing had changed. *Either we save the planet now, or we die with it.*

But as he glanced around the room, at the empty chairs and tables, a deepening scowl furrowed his brow. People were taking the bait. And not just any people. World leaders. Presidents, ministers, and monarchs. People who should have known better.

A stifled cry built inside his chest. *Idiots, all of them.* This was why he hated people. Give him a cabin in the woods a thousand miles from the nearest town, and he'd be happy. Unfortunately, his job as a climatologist demanded that he at least occasionally interact with others—to waste his breath, as he'd done today, reminding people of their agency and importance in a fight that he knew they would ultimately shrink from.

Bruce set his eyes back on Canada's prime minister, and listened as she droned on about her country's illusion of progress toward curbing emissions and reaching net zero. They'd increased their reliance on hydro-electric and fusion energy to the tune of ten percent, while over the same period expanding their total energy consumption by forty-five percent.

There was no sugar-coating it: clean energy was simply more expensive than the dirtier alternatives. And in order to disguise the problem, they kept moving the targets around like numbers on a very crooked balance sheet. Decades ago, the switch to EVs and eVTOLs took emissions off the roads and airways by putting them in the smokestacks of power plants. It didn't change anything.

These were age old problems with uncomfortable solutions. Who was going to foot the bill for clean energy production? The government, or the consumer? And what was the point of one country making that sacrifice if all the others didn't do so as well?

China didn't give a shit. They blamed the consumers in the rest of the world for making their factories churn. The US and Europe only pretended to care, while in effect, they were more concerned about keeping their proverbial pockets full. And the developing world? They couldn't afford to care.

Nothing had changed. Not since the onus of fixing things had fallen to his parents, or even to their parents. And he was quite certain that nothing ever would change. Fixing the problem was more expensive than pursuing short-term solutions to fight the consequences, so everyone would keep shifting blame and making empty promises at conferences like this one until eventually it was too late and there was nothing left to be done but watch the world burn.

Arguably, they might have already reached that point.

Bruce crossed his arms over his chest and watched as Canada gave the floor to Germany. Another elected leader spewing hot air about how the world needed to stop spewing hot air.

Bruce swallowed a sigh. He wanted nothing more than to get to the nearest bar and get drunk. If nobody cared to save the world, then why should he?

8:49 PM

"C HEERS," SAID... *WHAT WAS her name again?* Bruce couldn't remember the name of the beautiful blonde sitting next to him at the rooftop bar. *Blondie*, he decided. That would do for now. He'd remember later. At the moment, he needed to get drunk. Or drunk-*er*, anyway.

"To the end of the world," he replied, raising his tequila shot. A warm fall breeze blew, bringing with it the smells of beer and spirits intermingling with a dozen different perfumes. Blondie's included.

The bar was packed, and robotic servers whirred between the tables, delivering cocktails and pints along with greasy food. Flowers in pots and miniature trees decorated the perimeter of the rooftop, with strings of vintage lights hanging crosswise above the tables.

"Or, to the beginning of a new one...?" Blondie suggested with one eyebrow raised. She clinked her glass with his, and they both downed their shots at the same time.

Bruce grimaced and shook his head. "Not funny."

"What isn't?" Blondie asked while smiling wryly at him.

"I just finished telling you why that god-forsaken planet isn't going to save us."

"Maybe it will? Scientists are always changing their minds about stuff. They might figure out how to get us there."

"Let's say they do. You think they'll give *you* a ticket?"

What's-her-name scowled and crossed her arms over a prodigious bosom. The effect was to augment her already plunging cleavage, drawing his attention there for a second longer than was appropriate.

"My face is up here," she demurred.

"Sorry," Bruce said, smiling innocently. He grabbed a second shot, and raised it for another toast. "I was just admiring the scenery," he said, looking Blondie straight in the eye this time.

What was her name? he wondered again. *Sara... Sandra? Celine!* That was it.

Celine smiled again, uncrossing her arms to grab her second shot. "I was just messing with you. And I know not everyone will get to go there, but can you imagine? At least some of us will! A new colony, somewhere far away from Earth and all of its problems. It's some kind of hope, don't you think?"

"Yeah. Maybe. But we sure as hell don't deserve it."

Celine frowned. "Well, aren't you cynical."

Bruce shrugged. "Comes with the territory."

She raised her next drink. "To hope."

"To hope," he grudgingly agreed.

An hour later they went crashing drunkenly through his hotel room in Times Square. She shoved him back onto the bed, and ripped his belt off, then proceeded to kick off her heels and put on a show. Bruce propped his head up to watch. There were some perks, he supposed, to forcing himself out of his self-imposed isolation to attend these climate conferences. For a brief moment of time, environmentalists and climatologists turned into super heroes on a quest to save the world.

Celine's striptease went too long, prompting him to sit up. "Get over here," he growled.

"Grrr." A crooked grin touched Celine's lips. She took a step toward him, stumbled, then caught herself with a frown. She looked like she was about to pass out.

Bruce grimaced. She'd had too much to drink. How much was too much for consent? "You know what, maybe we should call it a night," he said.

"Whaaat? The party's just getting started! We should go to a club!"

Oh, hell no. This night was getting away from him. "Actually, I'm beat, and I have to get up early for the conference. It was great to meet you, Celine."

"Oh no you don't. We're not done yet, Bruce Wayne."

"Gordon."

"What?" Celine blinked in confusion.

"You just called me Batman."

"No, I didn't. I called you Bruce..." Celine's hand flew to her lips and a little giggle escaped. "Oh, I did, didn't I? Well, isn't that sexier, anyway?"

"No."

"You're no fun." Celine gave him another shove, pushing him back down. She unbuttoned his jeans and crawled on top of him, bringing her lips down to his for a sloppy french kiss.

"You want to know a secret?" she whispered as she straddled him.

"If this is the part where you tell me you used to be a man, I'm going to kick you in the balls."

Celine laughed prettily. "Why don't you check for yourself?"

He ran a hand up her thigh, past the hem of her cocktail dress. She grabbed his hand and shoved it higher.

"The secret is... I'm not wearing any panties," she whispered beside his ear.

It was fast, drunken sex, and she finished long before he did, leaving him unsatisfied.

Bruce sighed at the irony and rolled her off of him. Celine was already falling asleep.

"You're good..." she trailed off sleepily.

"Thanks," he said, and climbed from the bed, zipped up his jeans, and checked his watch.

9:57 PM

Still early. His buzz was wearing off quickly now. He could take his laptop down to the business center and get some work done while Celine slept off the booze.

But maybe a shower was in order first. Bruce stopped by his suitcase and picked out a fresh set of clothes.

He went straight to the bathroom, stripped, and showered quickly. The hot water and soap washed away the grime and sweat of a long day at the convention center, and eased some of the tension from his body. He still couldn't believe that people—no, *world leaders*—were more focused on what was happening in some far off galaxy than what was occurring right here on Earth.

Bruce turned off the shower and dried himself quickly in front of the mirror. He took a moment to regard himself. A hint of a six pack still shadowed his stomach. Not the chiseled physique of his youth, but not half bad for thirty-seven years old. He stroked his thick black beard, wondering if he should trim it.

Another look at his watch convinced him otherwise.

10:14 PM

Bruce dressed quickly and spritzed on some cologne before he left the bathroom.

"Where are you going?" Celine asked as he grabbed his laptop and started for the door.

He turned to regard her. She'd propped herself up on her elbows, looking suddenly wide awake. "You want to go again?" she asked.

"Uhhh..."

Before he could come up with a better answer, a bright flash of light erupted between them.

And the next thing he knew, he was lying in a bed of tall grass in the middle of the day, being hammered by a pounding rainstorm. He was soaked through and shivering before he even had a chance to sit up.

"What the hell!" he cried.

Icy rain ran in rivers down his back, dripping from his chin, clinging to his eyelashes and beard. Chilling him to the core.

Celine must have drugged him. *Shit.* She was a hooker. Of course, she was. Her pimp must have dragged him out of the hotel and dumped him in this field while they stole all of his money. But why drag him out of the hotel just to rob him blind? Surely drugging him was enough.

Logic eluded his fuzzy brain. Thankfully, so did the hangover he should have had by now. But that was little comfort in his present situation. If he didn't find shelter and get warm soon, he'd die of hypothermia.

Where the hell had they taken him? he wondered, glancing around at his surroundings with growing concern. Visibility was poor from the rain, so it was hard to tell, but nothing looked familiar. One clue was the cold. The temperature wasn't below freezing, that much was clear from the rain, but it was still a damn sight colder than New York in September. That meant they must have either driven him somewhere very far north or very high up. Was he in northern Canada right now? If so, how did they get him past the border, and why go to that much trouble for petty theft?

Maybe they'd dumped him here in lieu of actually killing him. After all, he could ID Celine to the cops. Spluttering in the rain, Bruce reached for his watch, expecting to find it stolen. But it was still on his wrist. He had his laptop and AR glasses, too.

If the goal was robbing him, why not take all of that? In his watch were the credentials for his debit and credit accounts. He supposed they could have hacked it and cloned the data, but how much could they steal before someone realized he was missing? Ten, maybe twenty thousand credits? No, they'd probably max everything out at fifty and change. As if he'd needed another reason to hate people.

"Damn it!" Bruce hammered the ground with his fists and let out an unintelligible roar.

Something roared back—a deep, groaning bellow, followed by the ground-shaking thunder of a very large creature crashing through trees.

Instinct took over. Bruce sprang off the ground, leaving his laptop behind, and ran in the opposite direction, stumbling and tripping up a hill.

Chapter 8

--:-- AM/PM, September --

B RUCE SHOT A LOOK over his shoulder as he sprinted up the hill. He caught a glimpse through the shifting veils of mist of something big loping after him on two massive legs. It had flashing yellow eyes and snapping teeth as long as his arm. A bellowing roar erupted, and the thundering footfalls came faster as the creature picked up its pace. Massive jaws dropped low, getting ready to scoop him up.

Bruce gasped and spurred himself to run faster.

This was impossible.

He must have passed out in his hotel room. This was nothing but a booze-addled nightmare.

Bruce's foot caught on something, and he went sprawling. His chin hit the ground, and his teeth clacked together painfully, drawing blood as he bit his tongue.

The monster thundered by, narrowly missing him as it was carried on by its considerable momentum. A fresh spurt of adrenaline shot through Bruce's system as he caught another glimpse of it. If this was a nightmare, it was the most vivid one he'd ever had.

He jumped back to his feet just as the creature skidded and turned at the top of the hill, kicking up clods of dirt and grass. A flicker of lightning silhouetted it against the dark, stormy sky. It had a thick tail to match the legs, and a massive head as long as he was tall. Two comically small and skinny arms were curled up against its chest. There was no mistaking the identity of this beast.

It was a Tyrannosaurus Rex.

Bruce barked a laugh at the absurdity of his dream.

T-Rex responded with a deafening roar that shook the air, and Bruce realized how big it really was. It must have stood at least twelve feet high at the shoulder.

He cast about wildly and spotted a jutting pile of rocks with a darkened hollow that might be a cave. The opening looked small enough that it might prevent that monster from crawling in after him.

Bruce ran for it. Rex bore down on him, roaring again as it closed the gap.

"Come on!" he screamed at himself. A sharp pain erupted in his leg. A cramp. His lungs burned fiercely for air.

Booming footfalls shook the ground...

Another roar reverberated. Bruce caught a whiff of its fetid breath and dove for the mouth of the cave.

Jaws snapped loudly behind him, and he landed hard on the rocky ground inside. Shocked to find that he was still alive, he picked himself up and spun around to look back the way he'd come. The rain was still pounding, cutting visibility to zero. Nothing but a wall of mist painted with shadows from the storm clouds beyond. Raindrops scurried against the sky, dripping like beaded curtains from the opening.

Rex must have given up and left.

Just as he decided that, a giant yellow eye appeared in the opening. It blinked, and a translucent membrane nictated over the eye. It almost looked like its head could fit through the mouth of the cave...

Bruce began backing away.

A sudden, violent snort sounded from the monster, and snapping jaws lunged through the opening.

Bruce moved faster than he ever had in his life, scurrying to the back of the cave and falling over as he tripped on something. Rex tried again and again, provoking a miniature avalanche from the opening.

"Wake up, wake up..." Bruce muttered to himself.

Those jaws kept getting closer with each attempt. He pulled his knees up to his chest, pinning them there with one arm. His back and legs ached sharply as he struggled to make himself a smaller target.

Claws scratched furiously as the T-rex used its stubby arms to pull itself deeper. Massive nostrils flared and snorted, and the beast paused, catching its breath. It was just a few feet away. If he stretched his legs out, he'd lose his feet. It was close enough that he could smell its musky odor.

Desperate, Bruce fumbled around blindly for a rock that he could throw at the creature. His hand seized a stick beside him, and he jammed it into one of those flaring nostrils.

Rex let out a deep, resonant cry and withdrew sharply from the opening, reaching with one arm to remove the foreign object from its nose.

"It's just a dream..." Bruce muttered.

The stick clattered to the ground, and an indignant roar echoed through the cave. Then the ground shook to the thunder of steady footfalls diminishing as the monster lumbered off.

Feeling something cold clinging to his frozen arm, Bruce glanced in that direction—

And jumped back with a shout.

It was a human skeleton—or what was left of it. Bruce leaned in for a closer look. Scraps of clothing still clung to the bones. Some of them were broken, others had been gnawed clean by sets of tiny teeth. Cold realization rocked Bruce's body as he noticed that one of the legs was missing. That hadn't been a stick he'd jammed up Rex's nose. It had been a human femur.

Bruce sat back down with a painful jolt, staring numbly at the remains. A gaping skull stared back. He pinched his arm—*hard*—and pain erupted from the spot, but he didn't wake up.

He wasn't dreaming. This was real.

Chapter 9

10:32 PM, September 25th

Layla Bester pushed through the door of the *Tap and Whistle*, stepping into a roar of music, laughter, and clinking glasses. She went straight to an empty spot along the bar, and held up a finger to catch the bartender bot's eye. It was an STA-9, but everyone just called those models *Stan*. He had two kind blue eyes and a rubbery white face, designed to mimic human expressions. Right now he was wearing a welcoming smile.

"What would you like, Miss Bester?" Stan asked brightly. This was one of her regular haunts, so she and Stan knew each other about as well as a bot and human could.

"Jack on the rocks, Stan."

"Coming right up!" he replied before whirring off to prepare the drink.

Layla sighed as she settled onto the barstool. She'd had a frustrating day at Sing Sing. The warden still hadn't gotten her the surveillance footage from the yard, his excuse being that it was a lot of data, and he needed at least a day to compile and send it. As a result, most of her day had revolved around taking witness statements from the guards and prisoners. But they all said the same thing. A flash of light, and then they were gone. To all appearances, Tom Smith and Fango Morales had vanished into thin air. But that was impossible, wasn't it?

Then again, as the warden had so gleefully pointed out, so was the fact that a new planet had appeared in the sky just three days ago. Layla had a sneaking suspicion that maybe he was covering his ass. But if so, was it incompetence or collusion? Had someone bribed him to get one or both of those prisoners out of Sing Sing?

Or was the warden covering up something else? Maybe he'd wanted to get rid of Smith and Morales for his own reasons, and he'd used Planet B's appearance as a convenient way to make his problems disappear.

An incoming call vibrated against Layla's wrist, interrupting her thoughts. The screen ID showed Captain Seth Fields. She tapped the watch to answer, and raised it so the mic could pick out her words from the background noise.

"I'm off the clock. What is it, Fields?"

"That's *Captain* Fields to you, Detective."

"Sorry, sir. Long day."

"Someone just reported another unusual disappearance, this time from a hotel in Times Square. The witness, Celine Walsh, called in the same particulars as your case from Sing Sing. Thought you might like to take the call?"

Layla's drink arrived, sliding across the bar into her waiting hand. She snatched it up with a frown and took a big sip. The bourbon went down hard, burning her throat and making her eyes water.

"Did you hear me, Bester? You want to take this, or should I get someone else?"

A second call began vibrating against her wrist before she could reply. This time the screen read: Neil. Her ex-fiancé.

"Is there anybody on the scene?"

"Nelson."

"Shit." Richard Nelson was a beat cop, and about as incompetent as they came. "Get him to take the witness statement, and tell him to stay the hell away from my crime scene. I'll be right over."

"Will do. I'll send the coordinates to your glasses now. You're a good cop, Bester."

"Yeah, sure." Layla hung up on the captain with a swipe of her thumb. Neil's call continued to vibrate against her wrist, and she almost considered sending it to her messaging service.

A pretty woman with short blonde hair and a familiar-looking oval face caught her eye from the adjacent stool. "Hard day?" the woman asked with a bland smile.

"Never ends," Layla replied and took another gulp from her glass. When she didn't immediately get up, the other woman's brow furrowed above the salted rim of a margarita.

"Aren't you supposed to be headed to the scene?"

"They can wait," Layla said, still sipping her whiskey. Her watch began vibrating once more. Neil again. A muttered curse escaped her lips. This night just kept getting better. She tapped the screen to answer.

"What?" she snapped at him.

Neil hesitated. "Are you at your apartment?"

"Why?"

"I'm in the neighborhood. Thought I'd pop by and pick up the ring."

"You're a real class act, you know that, Neil?"

"Look, I gave you a chance to reconsider. What else do you want from me? Keeping the ring would be theft."

"You want to know what's theft?" Layla asked. "You stealing the last seven years of my life!"

"You're the one who doesn't want to work it out."

"Because you decided to sleep with my maid of honor, you flaccid dick!" Layla screamed.

She realized she was catching looks from other people around the bar. Suddenly everyone was listening to her personal business, but Layla was way past caring about appearances.

"Let's just get it over with and move on," Neil said. "You'll never have to see me again after this, I promise."

Layla screamed unintelligibly into her watch.

"Hello?" Neil asked. "Are you still there? I caught a burst of static on my end."

"I'll see you in fifteen. Don't be late." She ended the call and snatched her drink off the bar, draining it in one gulp.

"Men are idiots, aren't they?" the woman beside her said.

Layla smiled tightly as she hopped down from the stool. Again, the woman's appearance struck her. As a cop, seeing a familiar face wasn't always a good thing. "Do I know you from somewhere?"

The woman stuck out a hand. "Alice Rice. I've been on the news a few times over the past couple of days."

"Detective Layla Bester, NYPD," Layla said, accepting the handshake. "I'm sorry, that doesn't ring a bell. I'm good with faces. Bad with names."

Alice's eyebrows shot up. "You're a detective."

Layla shrugged. "Life's full of bitchy little ironies."

Alice smiled. "Well, maybe this will help you. I discovered Planet B."

"Oh. Wow. That's..." Layla stood rooted to the spot, suddenly wishing she hadn't just made two commitments that required her to be elsewhere. "Well, cheers to that," she said, raising her empty glass and tipping it toward the other woman's cocktail.

Alice frowned. "Toasting with an empty glass is bad luck," she said, but clinked glasses anyway.

"Well, my luck can't get any worse," Layla replied. "Enjoy your celebrity, Miss Rice. Maybe you'll discover a way to get us to that planet of yours. Save me a ticket if you do."

"No promises," Alice said through another smile.

Layla rushed out of the bar onto a busy sidewalk. A camera flash caught her eye through the windows, followed by the sounds of muffled commotion coming from inside. Some kind of fight? Layla glanced at the window to see people shooting up from their tables, knocking over drinks and chairs. Whatever it was, she wasn't in the mood.

Layla raised her watch. "Call an AutoCar for the Acropolis, Brooklyn Heights."

"Calling the nearest available vehicle..." her watch replied. "Your AutoCar is a black Tesla Model Six, ETA one minute thirty-two seconds. The fare is five and a half credits. You will be sharing the vehicle with two other passengers. Is this acceptable?"

"Fine," Layla said.

"AutoCar confirmed. Routing to your location n ow..."

Layla had a moment to consider how pissed Captain Fields would be if he learned that she was handling a personal errand before heading to the scene in Times Square. She pushed the thought aside, pulling her AR glasses from her suit jacket and slipping them on. Moments later, a shiny black sedan pulled up and the back door slid open. She used her glasses to check the license plate. Plenty of black Tesla AutoCars roaming the city. Better to double-check than hop into the wrong one.

As she climbed in, Layla saw the other passengers, a middle-aged man in a trim black suit with dark hair that was probably dyed to hide the gray, and his date, a woman half his age in a bright red cocktail dress. Both of them were holding drinks in re-usable cups and making out in the row of seats ahead of hers. They'd probably come from a night club.

Layla grimaced at the awkwardness and said, "Excuse me," as she entered the vehicle. But the two drunken love birds appeared not to notice her arrival.

Layla scowled. AutoCars still beat the piss-smelling subways, but not by much.

About ten minutes later, her watch buzzed again. It was Fields. She swiped to answer it.

"Yes, Captain?"

"Where the hell are you going! This is urgent, Detective. I have your locator crossing the Brooklyn Bridge."

"I'm on my way, sir. The AutoCar already had two passengers inside. It has another stop to make first. ETA is fifteen minutes, max."

"Better be. Call me when you get there, Bester."

"Yes, sir."

Fields ended the call from his end, and she let her head thump against the headrest. If dealing with Neil didn't finish pushing her over the edge, her boss would.

Breathe, Layla. Just breathe...

Chapter 10

--:-- AM/PM, September --

TOM AND FANGO RAN for the trees, dashing into cover with seconds to spare. The gathering clouds rumbled ominously, and heavy raindrops hammered down, freckling the orange fabric of their prison uniforms. The trees only did so much to protect them from the icy rain, but they pushed deeper into the forest looking for better shelter. They paused beside a massive tree trunk to catch their breath. Tom shivered. If he had to guess, it couldn't have been more than fifty-two degrees. Definitely colder than the yard had been in Sing Sing.

Tom noticed the segmented vertical ribbing of the tree trunk. It looked like bamboo, but much thicker. Tom ran his hands along the trunk and looked up to see broad branches with long green needles and pine cones. He stepped back from the tree, slowly shaking his head in disbelief.

"Something wrong?" Fango asked.

"It's a calamite."

"A cala-what?"

"These trees have been extinct for more than three hundred million years."

Fango looked up, his eyes darting among the maze of branches as rain pelted the canopy high above their heads. "How do you know that?"

Shocked into silence by the discovery, Tom joined Fango in studying the quality of their natural shelter. Only a scattering of raindrops were making it through. The trees towered above them. Tom estimated that some had to be at least fifty meters high. The low-lying shrubs and ferns with their giant, colorful leaves seemed almost tropical despite the cool weather.

Tom couldn't remember ever seeing anything like this forest before. The gaps between the trees and underbrush were also a lot larger than he was used to seeing, with heavily trampled paths winding through the forest.

He remembered the sound of something large chasing them from the forest on the other side of the hill, and he wondered if the paths might have been created by a bear.

"We'd better keep moving," Fango said, stepping away from the tree and aiming for the nearest of the snaking paths. Tom followed along behind him, keeping his thoughts to himself. That woody-citrus smell was much stronger in here, but the rain was quickly dulling it.

A muted flash of lightning and another crack of thunder made Fango jump. Tom laughed quietly at his reaction. But then a distant moaning sound followed, and they both froze.

"What was that?" Fango whispered.

Tom glanced about quickly, wondering if that beast might actually be closer than it sounded. As he did so, he noticed the large, circular footprints in the muddy path that they were following. He dropped to his haunches to examine one of them. "What does that look like to you?"

Fango crouched beside him. "I don't know... a bear?"

Tom placed his hand with fingers splayed in one of the depressions. At six-foot three, his hands were not small, but they were dwarfed by these footprints. "Does that look like a bear to you?"

Fango shrugged.

Tom put his foot in the depression, and found that it fit comfortably with a little room to spare. And he wore size thirteens. But these prints were round, making him think of a hippo or an elephant.

A sharp trilling sound echoed through the trees, and Fango's head snapped up. "We should go," he said, sounding nervous.

"Yeah," Tom agreed.

They must have spent the better part of an hour getting down to the edge of the lake. The trip through the forest was otherworldly. About halfway through their hike, the rain stopped dripping through the trees, but the sky grew progressively darker until they were tripping over exposed roots and rocks.

Finally, they emerged along the pebbled shore of the lake to find that it was now fully dark. The sky was still overcast from the storm, making it impossible to see the stars, or those moons they'd noticed when they arrived.

"We should get a fire going," Tom suggested.

Fango nodded, and they walked along the beach, picking up sticks that were still wet from the rain.

"This isn't going to work," Tom muttered, discarding a soggy piece of driftwood.

"Let's just try it," Fango snapped. "I'm freezing my ass off!"

Ten minutes later, Tom was sitting on the shore of the lake, watching as Fango worked up a sweat rubbing two sticks together on a bed of relatively dry leaves and needles.

A cold wind blew across the lake, bringing with it strange floral and loamy smells. Tom hugged his shoulders and rubbed his arms vigorously to warm himself. "Give it up, man."

"Shut up," Fango said.

"You can't light wet wood."

"Shut *up*," Fango insisted.

Tom snorted and looked up to the impossible sight now appearing in the sky. The clouds were parting, revealing twelve moons scattered around like colored marbles. Each was a slightly smaller crescent than the one beside it, and the smaller ones were less colorful, faded as though from a greater distance.

Tom was still trying to wrap his brain around it all. Where *were* they? Was this really Planet B? If so, how had they gotten here? And why?

Tom spent a moment watching the variegated light of the moons glistening on the misty lake, and listening to the gentle swish of waves against the pebbled shore. His gaze roved on while Fango continued cursing and muttering to himself in Spanish.

About a kilometer farther down the shore, something was just now emerging from the mist. Tom picked out the blocky, rigid outlines of artificial structures. A city? No, too small, and there weren't any lights.

It was a facility of some kind.

Tom traced a series of gleaming spires along the far edge of the lake and listened to the distant rumbling sound coming from that direction. He'd first assumed it to be a waterfall, but now he had a different idea. Given the position of that facility, he guessed that this lake was actually a reservoir and that facility might be a dam.

"We should go check that out," Tom said, pointing to the distant specter of civilization.

Fango looked up and briefly stared at the sight. "Wearing prison uniforms?" He snorted and went back to rubbing his sticks together. "We go there, we get arrested. *Mala idea, hermano.*"

"Yeah, well building a fire in plain sight isn't any better," Tom said.

"You want to freeze to death?" Fango growled. "Building a fire was your idea!"

"It's not working, so we need to keep rolling. I'm going to check that place out. You can stay here if you want." Tom pushed off the pebbled shore.

Fango gave up and threw his smoking sticks down with an irritated sigh. "Fine. *Idiota,*" he muttered.

Tom glared at him. "Hey, I understood that."

"Good," Fango replied.

They walked briskly along the shore, keeping a gap of about six feet between them, and making sure to keep each other in sight at all times. Out here, under these impossible circumstances, it was easy to forget that Fango had tried to kill him just this morning. Or maybe, he'd gotten it right. It was still possible that he was dead or on life support right now. But somehow, that theory kept falling flat. If this was heaven, wouldn't there be more people? Streets of gold and all that?

"So you think this is an alien planet?" Fango asked while studying the moons once more.

"Where else could we be? It's either that, or I'm dreaming. Maybe I'm in a coma thanks to you and the other Fammies."

"That explains you. But what about me?"

"Figment of my imagination. Question is, why the hell would my subconscious give me you for company instead of an ebony goddess?"

"Maybe you secretly like me better."

Tom snorted. "You're a funny man, Fango."

He flashed his golden tooth. "*Gracias*."

Silence fell, leaving nothing but the steady crunching of their shoes on pebbles, and the chirping and trilling of nocturnal creatures. Moments later a deep, moaning sound erupted from the trees.

Both of them froze.

It was the same sound they'd heard periodically on their way down to the lake.

"Is it following us?" Fango whispered.

The sound came again, and this time Tom pinpointed its location. Somewhere up ahead, maybe a hundred feet away.

When it didn't repeat for a third time, Tom started forward again, but more quietly now. He held a finger to his lips. Fango looked at him like he'd lost his mind for walking *toward* whatever was making that sound, but he didn't stay where he was. Maybe he didn't like the thought of being alone out here with so many strange creatures skulking around.

But Tom hadn't lost his mind. Far from it. He knew that their best bet for shelter was that facility. And it was close now. The rolling thunder of what Tom had assumed to be a waterfall grew steadily louder, smothering the chirping, hooting, and trilling sounds from the forest.

The multicolored moonlight illuminated fast-moving ripples on the water. They were moving toward the facility, almost like a river.

A few minutes later, they came to the end of the lake and to the beginning of a long, stained metal walkway. Just as Tom had assumed, it was a dam. He started across it, following the railing and gazing down over a thundering torrent of water from a spillway beneath their feet that plunged into a broad river and a shadowy valley several hundred meters below. Beyond the lumpy green canopy of that jungle lay a vast, shining sea.

"*Increíble...*" Fango whispered.

"Yeah, in-cray-eeblay is right, *amigo*."

"Don't do that," Fango growled.

"Do what?"

"Butcher my language like that."

"I was trying to make you feel more at home," Tom said.

"Well, don't. Home for me was Sing Sing. I spent twenty-two years there. That's more than half my life. The last thing I want is to feel more at *home.*"

"Fair enough," Tom replied.

"Did you do it?" Fango asked.

"Do what?"

"Kill your wife and the guy she was screwing."

"Does it matter?" Tom asked.

Fango gave a lopsided grin. "Yes. I want to know if I'm hanging out with a murderer."

"Okay, then the answer's no."

"You *really* didn't kill them?" Fango pressed.

Tom slowly shook his head.

"But you were covered in their blood, and you ran from the police..."

"Wouldn't you? I'm a black guy in New York with all kinds of motive and no alibi."

Fango snorted. "Guess I would."

"What about you? You robbed a convenience store and shot a security guard. That true?"

Fango's eyes slid away, out to the shadowy valley and the shining sea.

"Well?" Tom pressed.

"Sí, lo hice."

"English, you mother—"

"Yes. I did it." Fango's eyes drifted back, looking suddenly darker than they had a moment ago. "He was going to shoot me. I had no choice."

"Sure you did. You didn't have to rob that place."

Fango sneered and shook his head. "It's old news. It was twenty-two years ago. I'm a different man now."

"Hope so," Tom replied, holding back a shiver as a cold wind blew. "Come on. Let's find a way inside."

Together they hurried across the walkway atop the dam until they came to a gleaming metal door with a black orb above it.

"That a camera?" Fango asked, pointing to it.

"Maybe." Tom tried the door handle.

Locked.

Fango began shifting his weight nervously from one foot to the other. "I don't like this. We're gonna get arrested."

Tom turned to him with a frown, then gestured to the dozen moons hovering in the sky. "Wherever we are, whoever runs this place, I don't think they care about what we did or didn't do, or who we were before. This is a clean slate."

"You don't know that," Fango said, and glanced back the way they'd come, as if he was thinking about making a run for it. "God is supposed to judge us for our sins. If this is heaven, then we're in big trouble."

"Speak for yourself. I'm innocent," Tom replied. "Besides, I don't see any prisons around here, do you?" He turned back to the door, eased up on tiptoes and rapped his knuckles on the black orb above the door. "Hello? Anybody in there?" Tom asked.

No answer.

"This is a dead end. We should go," Fango said.

"Hang on..." Tom ran his hands around the door, looking for a hidden control panel. There had to be a way to open it. He didn't see a keypad, touch pad, or a lock, so what other mechanism was there?

He looked back up into the gleaming black orb of the camera.

A chittering sound came from behind them.

"Tom..." Fango whispered. "What is that?"

He turned around. And saw something large creeping tentatively along the walkway. It was about waist-high, with a long, lashing tail, and feathers all over its body. Small, wing-like arms were curled against its chest. Its feet clacked softly on the metal as it walked toward them, with hooked six-inch talons on the inner digits of its feet.

Fango backed right up against the door, looking terrified, his eyes darting rapidly. "*Es un maldito dinosaurio!*" he cried.

"A dinosaur?" Tom whispered.

The creature straightened and froze, sniffing the air, as if trying to decide whether they were more difficult prey than they seemed to be. Tom realized from the fact that the railings came only halfway up its body that it was about as tall as him when it straightened like that. Probably ten feet long with the tail. *What kind of dinosaur?* he wondered with a growing sense of detachment from reality. He was definitely dreaming. *Unless dinosaurs go to heaven, too?*

The creature's head ducked back down, and it began creeping forward once more. In no particular hurry, content to make them squirm. Those wicked, curving claws scraped the metal walkway with each step, setting Tom's teeth on edge.

"It's a raptor," Fango whispered before Tom could make the connection.

"Yeah... no," Tom shook his head. "Not a raptor. It's too big. Velociraptors were the size of dogs. This is... it's a... Deinonychus," he supplied, pulling the name from his prior life. When he was a kid, he'd been obsessed with dinosaurs, so it had come as no surprise to his friends and family that he'd later become a paleontologist.

"Who the fuck cares?" Fango cried. "It's going to eat us!"

The growing volume of their argument drew a shriek from the creature. It ducked its head and burst into a sprint.

Fango grabbed him roughly by the shoulders and held him in front of the charging beast. Tom struggled in his grip. "What the hell, man!"

He wrenched himself free, and gave Fango a shove toward the approaching predator. Fango careened into the railing. Massive jaws snapped over his arm, and blood spurted out. Fango screamed and stared in horror at the dinosaur, as it chomped again and again on his arm.

Tom used the distraction, backing away quickly until he ran into the opposite railing.

Fango slammed the dino's snout with his fist, over and over again, screaming at the top of his lungs.

The Deinonychus let go of his arm, and Fango kicked it in the chest.

The dino gave an indignant squawk and took a quick, hopping step back.

Fango clutched his wounded biceps, blood running in rivers between his fingers. White membranes nictated over the dino's eyes. It cocked its head at Fango, first one way, then the other, as if sizing him up, or maybe trying to find the best angle for a second strike.

"*Meirda!* Do something, *pendejo!*" Fango screamed.

Tom spun around, contemplating the drop to the lake and the speed of the current. Could he stop himself before he tumbled over the spillway? He doubted it. The water was flowing too fast.

The dino shrieked, bringing Tom's head back around. He saw that it had reared up to its full height again. With the crown of feathers on its head, that made it even taller than Tom. Maybe seven feet. With teeth like switchblades, and those wicked, curving claws, Tom estimated their chances of overpowering it together were exactly zero.

"Get out of here!" Fango screamed as he backed up against the sealed door of the facility.

This time something happened. A metallic *clunk* sounded, and the gleaming metal slab slid aside with an echoing *boom.* Fango fell inside, and Tom ran for it.

The dinosaur chirped in alarm, backing up swiftly. It looked frightened, just about to run for it.

The door swished shut, and Tom caught a glimpse of the creature turning tail and running back the way it had come.

Tom thrust out a hand to help Fango up. He shrugged it off and sat up, leaning against the wall.

"*Ya valgo madres.*"

"What?" Tom asked.

"I'm fucked. My arm..." Fango's eyes narrowed swiftly in the weak golden light of the facility. "You did this."

Tom blinked in surprise. "What?"

"You pushed me into it!"

"Because you tried to use me a shield!" Tom roared, balling his fists.

Fango glanced around quickly, searching for something. His gaze sharpened on a rack right near the door. Four identical rifles were hanging there. He lunged for the weapons.

Tom's eyes widened as he realized what Fango was doing. Tom lurched after him, and they both grabbed the weapon at the same time, wrestling for control of it. Fango gritted his teeth and cursed at him in Spanish while they went stumbling through the facility. A wall of glass parted as they drew near, bringing in a gust of cool air and the woody-citrus smells of the jungle. Tom forced Fango steadily back, pushing him onto a balcony overlooking the spillway.

"I'm gonna kill you," Fango ground out, and brought a knee up into Tom's groin.

He grunted and some of the fight left him. Fango took full advantage, sweeping the rifle into line with his chest.

Realizing it was over, Tom held up his hands. "We can work this out. We stand a better chance together than apart."

"*Vete a la mierda*," Fango replied.

Click.

Tom frowned in confusion. A split second later, he realized what had happened. The gun must have a smart lock or a safety. Fango twisted the rifle around, regarding it with a look of sheer betrayal.

Realizing this could only end one way, Tom took a deep breath—

And charged.

Fango looked up just as Tom crashed into him. Picking him up like a linebacker, Tom threw him over the balcony. Fango screamed all the way down, his body vanishing into the spray of the falls.

Tom stumbled back on wooden legs, hands on his knees, feeling suddenly sick to his stomach. His whole body was shaking from spent adrenaline. He sank to the ground, his back to the glass and metal railings that he'd just thrown Fango over.

His brain struggled to catch up. Dinosaurs. Soaring jungles. And now this facility... He recalled the camera above the door, and how it had mysteriously opened just before the Deinonychus could kill Fango. Looking back to the view, Tom noticed those bright, colorful moons once more. The biggest one was nearly full, and predominantly blue with flecks of gray and brown. It lay low and shimmering above the sea on the horizon. Just then, a giant bird glided across that orb, a familiar form silhouetted darkly by the azure light. That was no bird. It was some type of pterosaur.

"Where the hell am I?" Tom muttered.

Chapter 11

10:57 PM

THE AUTOCAR SLOWED, AND Layla saw via her AR glasses that it was pulling up outside her building. She experienced a pang of guilt at coming here to deal with a personal errand before heading to the scene in Times Square, but she *needed* to put the final nail in the coffin of her relationship with Neil. Until she gave him his ring back, she would never really have closure.

"Destination reached, The Acropolis," her Auto-Car announced.

Layla's door slid open, and she hurried out with a brief glance at the lovebirds in the front row of seats—still going at it. She made a face and ran to the ballistic glass entrance of the Acropolis. She stopped briefly to look into the security scanner. It chimed pleasantly as it recognized her face, and the heavy slab of glass slid aside.

"Welcome home, Miss Bester," a purring female voice said as she stepped into a small foyer. A second glass door sealed the space at the other end. The one behind her slid shut, and the second set opened after a moment's hesitation. As a cop, she appreciated the touch of added security at the Acropolis. No one could sneak in behind someone else to get inside the building.

A robot doorman stood discretely off to one side of the lobby, equipped with integrated stun darts and a direct line to the nearest precinct—just in case any unwelcome guests made it past the doors. New York had never been the safest place, and if anything, it was only getting worse. Layla automatically felt for her sidearm, still hidden in a concealed body holster beneath her suit jacket.

She wasn't sure what was making her so edgy tonight. Maybe it was the booze. Drinking too fast on an empty stomach. Or maybe it was the thought of seeing her pig-faced ex-fiancé again.

Layla hurried across the gleaming black marble floors of the lobby to the cylindrical column of elevators that extended through the center of the building. She activated them with a verbal command before she arrived: "Thirty-seventh floor."

The nearest one dinged open, and she stepped in. The lift accelerated swiftly, plunging her stomach into her boots.

Her watch began vibrating with another call from Neil before she even reached her floor. She rejected the call as she crossed the threshold of her apartment and went straight to her coat closet. Crouching down, she rifled briefly through an old shoe box of sentimental things before finding the two and a half carat rock Neil had proposed to her with. On her way back out, she had a brief, intense urge to toss the ring down the garbage chute instead of giving it back to him.

What could he do about it? Legally, nothing. But then he'd probably never leave her alone. At least after this she'd never have to see his face again.

Layla swallowed thickly as she strode back across the lobby to the street. Both sets of doors parted in quick succession, and she spotted Neil's car waiting outside. Sleek and black with windows so dark that you couldn't even see a glimmer of the occupants. It was a luxury cross between a sports car and an SUV. A *Specter*. One of the few cars you could still drive manually if the mood struck. AI drivers were notoriously safer than humans. As such, Neil had been forced to take a road test and pay a fortune in insurance just to buy the vehicle.

The driver's side window rolled down as Layla approached. Neil flashed a grin. He was just as handsome as ever. Her palms began to sweat, and her stomach churned. She felt like she was going to be sick.

"Hello, Layla," he said.

"Hello, ass—" She cut herself off as someone else leaned into view from the passenger's seat. Layla froze at the sight of her. With long, straight blonde hair, bright blue eyes, a tiny waist, long legs, and a surgically enhanced cup size, Jessica Brady was easy to dislike. Layla couldn't believe she used to feel flattered that someone like Jess wanted to be her friend. As the daughter of a wealthy family with a trust fund bigger than her breasts, Jess could be a lot of fun when she decided to take her girls out for a night on the town. Somehow, Layla had seen that there was more to her than met the eye, and they'd become good friends. She'd believed that Jess wasn't a shallow, air-headed blonde who thought she was better than everyone else.

But then, nine days before their wedding, Neil had confessed to sleeping with Jess, and Layla realized that Jess's so-called friendship was all an act, inspired by guilt and not a genuine connection. Jess really *was* a shallow, cold-hearted bitch.

It was all Layla could do to keep from reaching for her weapon and shooting them both.

"It's not what it looks like," Jess said slowly. "I came to apologize."

"Save it." Layla threw the ring into Neil's car.

"Seriously?" he cried, catching it just before it could fall beneath his seat.

Layla bit back angry tears and began to spin away. She wouldn't give them the satisfaction of seeing her cry.

A flash of light erupted, dazzling her eyes before she could take another step—

Layla blinked rapidly to clear her vision...

And found that she was lying on her side in a dark green field of tall wet grass.

"What the hell?" Neil cried.

Jessica screamed in bewilderment and latched onto him like the urchin she was. "Where are we?"

"This is impossible..." another woman said. Her voice was familiar.

Layla sat up and saw a bright dome of stars, as well as a series of twelve different-colored orbs in the sky. Each of them was some version of a crescent or a half-moon.

"I must be dreaming," the woman with the familiar voice decided. Layla was inclined to agree.

Then the woman gave herself a roundhouse slap. Chirping and trilling animals took a breath, startled into silence. "Ow!" the woman cried, rubbing her cheek. And then the creatures of the night resumed their songs. "Okay, maybe not dreaming," the woman decided.

The light from the moons was enough for Layla to identify the woman. Oval face, button nose, short blonde hair...

It was that woman from the *Tap and Whistle*... Alice Rice. The astronomer who'd discovered Planet B.

"Where are we?" Neil shrieked, jumping up and spinning in a dizzy circle.

"Definitely not Earth," Alice replied. "Look—" She pointed to the series of moons hanging in the sky. Each of them was about half as big as the one beside it, and together they formed a bright, vanishing arc across the night. Layla counted a dozen moons in all. The nearest one was blue with flecks of gray and brown.

Layla shivered despite her suit jacket and hugged herself. "We need to find shelter. Make a fire if we can. It must be near freezing."

"Looks like someone beat us to it," Alice pointed up a shadowy hill to the steady flickering of flames dancing behind the waist-high grass.

Layla reached into her jacket and drew her sidearm from its holster. Holding it in a two-handed grip, she crept slowly up the hill toward the firelight. "Let's go check it out."

PART TWO: PLANET B

Chapter 12

--:-- AM/PM, September --

BRUCE SAT IN HIS underwear, warming his body and hands over the warm glow of the fire. His clothes were laid out and drying against the rocky wall of the cave beside him.

Just a few minutes ago, he'd found sticks for fuel scattered around the inside of the cave and had ignited them with the plasma lighter in his jeans pocket. Unlike most people, he didn't carry a fancy lighter to look cool or because he smoked—well, maybe partly to look cool. But mostly he kept one handy out of habit. Where he lived, deep in the woods of Maine, a dependable lighter was essential for survival. And unlike most plasma lighters, his was waterproof.

Thank God for that, he thought. Having woken up in the pouring rain, with the temperature maybe only five or ten degrees above freezing, he'd have been in big trouble if his lighter hadn't worked.

Of course, all signs pointed to him being trapped in a coma in some stupidly expensive hospital in Manhattan, so his lighter was technically only useful in his imagination. But the fire still *felt* warm, and without it he'd been shivering violently a moment ago.

Bruce glanced at the skeleton propped up against the wall beside him. "Thanks for gathering the wood, buddy." The dead *man*—identifiable as such by a large jaw, broad shoulders, and narrow pelvic cavity—had almost certainly gathered the wood to light this fire before he'd succumbed to whatever injuries had killed him. Maybe he'd frozen to death before he could find a way to ignite the wood. Bruce gave himself mental points for figuring out it was a man. Not many people would be able to pick out the differences between male and female skeletons. Especially not while in a coma.

That fact turned Bruce's grin to a frown. His brain was supplying all of the riddles, as well as the clues and the answers, which meant he was essentially making a fool of himself.

"Here's another riddle..." Bruce raised his Garmin smartwatch. The seconds' hands ticked steadily around an old-fashioned, bright green clock face. He took a moment to read the time.

7:07 PM.

That put a deeper frown on his face. Bruce remembered checking the time just before he'd seen that flash of light and woken up here. Somehow, it had been almost twenty-four hours since then? Bruce checked the date. Sure enough, it was September 26th.

He massaged his eyeballs with his thumb and index finger in an attempt to ward off an encroaching headache. None of this was making sense. What kind of sedative would knock him out for almost an entire day? Unless Celine had been dosing him steadily with repeated injections.

Then he remembered his working theory. *I'm in a coma.* Bruce nodded along with that. Dream logic didn't have to make sense. Before his watch screen flicked off to save power, Bruce noticed the icons that indicated it had lost its connections with both GPS and Starlink satellites. *Guess it can't find a signal from inside my subconscious.*

Bruce sighed and absently studied the skeleton. He noticed something lying half-buried in the dust behind it. Reaching for the item, he swept the dust off with his other hand and blew on it for good measure. It was a black leather bifold. A wallet.

Bruce frowned at the anachronism. People hadn't carried wallets for... he tried to think back to the last time he'd carried one. He couldn't have been more than fifteen years old. Not long after that, the widespread adoption of digital currencies had made wallets obsolete. These days smart watches, AR glasses, bio-implants, and wristbands were the only accepted forms of payment.

Bruce opened the pocket in the wallet and blinked in shock at the sight of actual *paper* currency. He carefully withdrew the bills and fanned them out in the firelight. The paper was crackly and old, but still intact. The denominations of the bills were even more shocking than the presence of the physical currency. There was a *two-dollar* bill. The last time he'd seen one of those was in his father's private collection. Two-dollar bills had been discontinued over a hundred years ago—sometime in the 1960s if his memory served.

Bruce slowly shook his head at how elaborate this dream was getting. He flipped through the photos in the wallet, and found two old pictures. One was black and white—a wedding photo of a handsome man with a dark mustache, wearing a tuxedo, his arm wrapped around his bride's waist. Curly hair cascaded beneath her veil. Her wedding dress was unusually modest, with long sleeves and a high neck line. Both of them were smiling in front of their wedding cake, hands together over the knife, just about to cut the first slice.

The second photo was a family portrait. It was the same couple, many years older now, with two kids, a girl and a boy. The boy was the oldest at maybe eleven years old. The girl, probably about nine.

Given those clues, this skeleton, AKA, *the man from the photos*, must have died here some time during the Cold War era.

Bruce frowned. Maybe his subconscious wasn't as smart as he thought it was. Would these remains still be intact after a hundred years? Hell, forget the remains—what about the paper currency and the photos in the wallet? And even if conditions in the cave were dry enough to preserve it all, the wallet should have been buried too deep to find.

A loud *pop* sounded from the fire, and a shower of sparks danced into the air, drawing Bruce's gaze up. The fire. That was another riddle. The sticks that Bruce had found scattered around the cave couldn't have been gathered by the dead man. After a hundred years, the wood would have rotted away completely.

The sharp *crack* of a twig and a rustling in the grass outside pricked Bruce's hearing. His attention snapped to the opening of the cave, and his heart began to pound. Seeing shadows moving against the black sky, he snatched the dead man's remaining femur and raised it high like a club.

Something was coming.

Realizing that it could be T-Rex coming back for round two, Bruce let out a feral roar. "Go away!" he screamed for good measure.

7:12 PM, September 26th

LAYLA CREPT TOWARD THE mouth of the cave with the others just a few steps behind. She saw the fire more clearly now, casting flickering shadows inside the cave. She stepped on a twig, and it snapped loudly. She froze.

A terrifying roar erupted from the cave, followed by a ragged human voice: "Go away!"

"Hello?" Layla tried. "We're friendly. I'm a cop."

"A cop?" the voice asked, sounding less defensive now.

Layla decided to risk stepping into view. She ducked through the opening of the cave, holding her hands up, her gun aimed at the ceiling.

The man crouching by the fire looked every bit the part of the quintessential caveman: half-naked with a scraggly beard. Mid-length hair clinging to his scalp in thick, greasy locks. Big and hairy, and holding a giant bone for a club. His mouth dropped open and he stood up inside the cave. The ceiling was higher farther from the opening, following the slope of the hill.

"Who are you?" the man asked.

"Detective Bester, NYPD."

"A detective..." he said slowly.

Layla nodded and took another step.

The man hoisted his club a littler higher, then appeared to relax.

The grass rustled behind Layla.

"Can we come in?" It was Neil's voice. "It's freezing out here!"

"Who's that?" the caveman asked.

"My ex-fiancé. Neil Forester. And you are?"

"Bruce."

"Okay, Bruce. Can we come in? That fire looks pretty inviting."

Bruce gestured to the space on the other side of the fire, then sat on a rock beside a human skeleton.

Suddenly Layla was on high alert, realizing that they could be sharing this cave with a murderer. Layla's eyes narrowed on the remains, trying to judge how old they were. No signs of flesh, so either animals had picked them clean, or the body had decomposed. Either way, it had been here a long time.

The others crowded in behind her, and Jess yelped at the sight of the bones.

"Who's that?" Layla asked before anyone else could, nodding to the skeleton.

Bruce reached for something on the ground. A wallet? The mystery deepened. He fished out a square piece of deteriorated paper.

"Hard to read..." Bruce said, studying the paper. "His driver's license says he was Edward Murphy."

"Who has a driver's license anymore?" Alice asked.

"I do," Neil supplied. "But it's digital. Paper hasn't been used for licenses for at least a century. My dad's used to be plastic."

"Well, that explains the expiration date," Bruce added. "1967."

"Incredible," Alice breathed while creeping steadily toward the remains. "That means the body has been here for more than a hundred years..."

Layla stayed rooted to the spot while the others edged closer to the fire and sat down.

A deep, moaning sound erupted in the distance, making her jump with fright and cast a sharp look over her shoulder.

"I'd come inside if I were you," Bruce whispered. "Something big chased me in here when I arrived."

Layla took his advice and sat down beside Alice, who'd taken a seat on the other side of the bones from Bruce.

Neil and Jess sat together with their backs to the mouth of the cave. Bad idea, Layla thought. But she was torn between watching Bruce and keeping an eye on the entrance.

"How did you get here? And when?" Layla asked. Just like with Alice, something about this man struck her as familiar. Hard to tell much through the beard, but his eyes were what stuck out in her memory. A warm light green, almond-shaped.

Bruce shrugged and set down his bone-club with a hollow sound. "No clue. One minute I was in my hotel, leaving my date to sleep off one too many shots at the bar, and the next I saw this blinding burst of light, and—"

"You're my missing person from Times Square," Layla interrupted, gaping at him.

Bruce's brow became deeply furrowed. "You were investigating my disappearance?"

"I was headed to the scene just before I woke up here. You saw a flash of light, what happened next?"

"I woke up out there—" Bruce gestured to the opening of the cave. "—in the pouring rain, and what looked like the middle of the day. It was supposed to be eleven PM, but somehow now it's—" He checked his watch. "—seven fifteen, on the 26th."

"That's a gap of almost twenty-four hours," Layla said.

Bruce nodded. "A total blank."

"I can tell you what happened," Alice said slowly, still studying the bones.

"Please do," Bruce replied.

She looked up from scrutinizing the remains. "We're not on Earth anymore. We've been abducted."

"Not on Earth?" Bruce echoed laughingly, revealing straight white teeth and a mischievous glint in his eyes. Again, his familiarity struck Layla. Was this someone she knew, or had known at some point? She prided herself on being good with faces, if not names. But this man... he was proving harder to recognize. Maybe it was the beard. He could have grown it since she'd last seen him.

"What's so funny?" Alice asked.

"It's just amazing how elaborate this dream is getting."

"Dream?" Alice shook her head. "I *hope* it's a dream."

Bruce gave her a skeptical look. "What other explanation is there?"

"If you're dreaming, then everything you're experiencing begins and ends inside your brain. That means you should know our names. Who am I?"

Bruce frowned. "You look familiar."

"I've been getting that a lot lately," Alice replied. "What's my name?"

"Something with an A? I don't know."

"Exactly. You don't know, because this isn't a dream. I'm Alice Rice."

"Aha! Told you it started with an A."

Alice regarded him with a look of strained patience. "So do a lot of names. "Try again." She pointed to Jess.

"Mary," Bruce said.

Jess's brow furrowed. "Do I look like a *Mary* to you?"

"What is a Mary supposed to look like?" he countered.

"My name is Jessica Brady."

Bruce shrugged and stoked the fire with his bone-club. Layla recognized it as a human femur from the skeleton.

"You don't have all the answers, which means you're not the one coming up with them," Alice said. "If this is a dream, you're not the dreamer."

"That doesn't prove anything," Bruce countered. "I don't always know what's going to happen next in my dreams, do you?"

"Have you seen the planets in the sky?" Alice asked.

"Planets?" Neil asked. "I thought they were moons."

"What planets?" Bruce added.

"Come see." Alice clambered to her feet, heading for the mouth of the cave. When Bruce didn't immediately follow, she glanced back. "Well? Are you coming or not?"

He pushed to his feet with a weary groan. Layla decided to follow them.

They waded a few steps into wet, waist-high grass, with Alice pointing up at the colorful, fading arc of crescents in the sky. "See?" she said.

"What the hell?" Bruce muttered. "They're too close together to be planets, aren't they? I mean, shouldn't they crash into each other or their orbits deteriorate from each other's gravity?"

"No," Alice shook her head. "Not if they're orbiting a black hole. Its gravity is so strong that it can sustain many more planets in stable orbits than a star can. In fact, if I had to guess, we're orbiting in close proximity to..." Alice trailed off, studying the celestial bodies. "More than a hundred other planets."

"A *hundred?*" Layla echoed. "Are you sure?"

"Give or take a dozen, yes. The section of the sky those ones are covering is only about a thirty degree arc. I count twelve visible worlds, and thirty degrees goes into 360 twelve times. Twelve times twelve equals one hundred and forty-four. Assuming the planets are evenly spaced, of course."

"Why can't we see the other ones, then?" Layla asked.

"For one thing, the ones on the other side of the black hole are so far away that they'd look like stars to us. And for another, look how small and faded that one is—" Alice pointed to the most distant of the series.

It was roughly the size of a pea. Half of a pea, actually, because the other half was facing away from the sun. Or was it shaded from the black hole? Layla's brow furrowed in confusion.

"Wait a minute," Layla said. "If we're orbiting a black hole, then how are those planets being illuminated?"

"I don't know..." Alice said, turning in a quick circle and scanning the sky. "I don't see an accretion disk, so it's not active. Good thing, I guess, or the radiation would bake us alive."

Bruce shivered and rubbed his arms, dragging his eyes away from the stars with a visible effort. "Let's go back inside," he said in a gruff whisper.

Alice and Layla followed him in. Bruce walked woodenly, staring straight ahead as he returned to the fire.

Alice stopped suddenly in the entrance.

"What is it?" Layla whispered, her hand tightening on the grip of her sidearm.

"That skeleton... I was trying to figure out why it hasn't turned to dust in a hundred years."

"And?" Layla frowned.

Alice looked to Layla, her brown eyes wide and gleaming with dancing firelight. "It's the black hole."

Chapter 13

7:15 PM

TOM WENT BACK INSIDE the facility, more cautiously now that he realized someone must have opened the outer door for him and Fango to keep them from being eaten by that dinosaur.

Tom's eyes darted among the shadows inside the dam. This was some type of entry corridor. It seemed to run the length of the structure, with a long wall of windows extending to his right, on the same side as the balcony, overlooking the spillway and the valley below. A chainlink fence ran the width of the corridor, barring the way. Beyond that, doors lined the wall on the side of the reservoir.

"Hello?" Tom tried, calling down to the other end of the echoing corridor. He waited fully ten seconds before deciding that he wasn't going to get a reply.

Tom went back to the guns by the outer door. Two racks, one to either side of the entrance, each held four rifles, though one was missing after Fango had taken it with him over the falls. Tom wondered if that number was significant. Eight. Was that the number of people who staffed the facility? Or the number of guards?

Tom studied the rifles more carefully. They were made of a glossy black material that reflected multicolored swirls like an oil slick. The empty spot where Fango had removed one glowed with blue lights and golden contacts that looked like they might be for charging. Tom grabbed another weapon off the rack, and it came to life in his hands with a subtle vibration. A glowing number on the back—*45*—made him think that's how much ammo it held per charge or clip.

Tom hefted the rifle, surprised at how lightweight it was. About the length of his forearm. He aimed experimentally down the light green square that served as the weapon's sights. That small display added a pale green tint to everything, somehow peeling away the shadows inside the dam. *Night-vision?* he wondered. Seemed like familiar tech so far.

A slider switch above the trigger could move through four different positions. One was the default, and the symbol looked like an X. That had to be the safety. Tom slid it to the next position, denoted by a circle.

He walked over to the chainlink fence, searching for a lock. It was a simple bolt lock, with a touchscreen beside it. He tried tapping the screen. It flashed red and gave a warning beep. Tom placed a thumb against it and got the same result.

Frowning, he raised the rifle and aimed it at the locking mechanism. Tom gently squeezed the trigger. A bright red beam flashed out with a sharp zapping sound, and the lock exploded in a shower of sparks and molten metal. Flecks stung his arm, and he recoiled, cursing.

Stepping back to the fence, he tried the gate again. It swung freely on the hinges, admitting him to the rest of the facility. Tom crept swiftly through with the rifle raised to his shoulder and sweeping for signs of trouble. If someone was still watching via hidden security cameras, then they knew that he'd just broken in, and that he was armed. That might provoke a reciprocal response from whoever staffed this place.

Walking quickly to the first door on his left, Tom tried the handle. It was unlocked. The heavy metal barrier swung wide, and lights flicked on automatically, revealing a bare concrete stairwell with grated metal steps. He started down and stopped on the first landing. *S1* was emblazoned on the wall beside the door. He continued to the next landing—*S2*, and tested the door. Also unlocked. Peeking out with the rifle, he checked both ways to make sure it was clear before stepping out.

A pair of elevators gleamed opposite the stairwell. Somehow he'd missed seeing those at the top of the stairs. Another door barred access at the end of the vestibule where he stood. This one slid open at his approach, and he found himself standing in some type of lounge. The finishings here were less utilitarian, with dark tile floors rather than bare concrete, painted walls with artwork hanging on them, and several sets of couches and chairs arrayed around the echoing space. The ceilings were at least twenty feet, and a wall of windows looked out through the billowing veils of mist that thundered down from the spillway above. The air in here was a lot warmer, too. Along the back wall where he stood was a bar or counter of some kind. To his right and left, more doors, these ones dark and wooden.

Choosing a direction at random, Tom decided to go right. He came to the dark cherry-wood door and reached for the recessed handle. The door slid away into the wall before he could even touch it, and he emerged in a hallway lined with more doors on both sides. At the end of the hall was yet another door. Tom stood in the opening from the lounge with his heart hammering in his chest. He felt like he was breaking and entering in someone else's home.

"Hello?" he tried again. "I'm not looking for any trouble..." No reply. None of the doors flew open. "I wanted to thank you for saving me up there."

Still nothing.

Tom decided the rooms must be empty. He noticed that the ones on his left had numbers on the golden plaques, going from *one* all the way up to *eight*. The ones to his right had names... *Electrical. Storage 1. Storage 2. Storage 3. Mechanical. Aux Armory. Printing.*

Strange. Tom tried the recessed handle of the first door on his left. Locked. Another blank black panel beside it flashed red. He tried the next door, and that one opened before he could touch it, revealing a small, but well-appointed bedroom with a clean white armchair beside the bed, and a picture window behind it that overlooked the valley and the misty spray of the falls. A door lay open to what looked like an en-suite bathroom. Tom stepped away, and the door slid shut. His mind spun with confusion. Who had built this place? Everything was made to human specifications, and yet this clearly wasn't Earth.

Or was it? Those dinosaurs he'd seen... maybe he'd somehow been teleported back to a time when they had roamed the Earth? But even if that were true, Humans and dinosaurs had never co-existed, and certainly not at a time when humans had technology like he was seeing.

Then Tom remembered the planets in the sky, and he shook his head. The solar system had never been that crowded. Not in any epoch.

Whoever had built this place was either human or knew humans very well. Not only that, but it took a lot of manpower and an advanced civilization to build a dam like this. So where were they? And where were their cities? He hadn't seen any sign of lights glowing in the valley below, or interrupting the jungles around the grassy hill where he and Fango had woken up. Maybe there weren't any cities.

But if not a city, then what was this dam powering?

Tom continued to the end of the corridor. He opened that door, too, and passed into a combined kitchen and dining area. A long, live edge wooden table with eight chairs and a hovering ball of light for a chandelier ran alongside more picture windows. The kitchen was open with six bar stools tucked into a gleaming stone island. Familiar-looking appliances were all the same resinous black as the rifle he held.

An open hallway led past the fridge to some other rooms. At the far end of the dining room was yet another door. So far, this level was laid out like someone's house. And it seemed to have been designed for at least eight people.

Tom checked the opening beside the fridge. He came to another door, which slid away with his approach, leaving him standing in a large antechamber with grated metal floors and an oversized elevator to his left. Across from it was a big metal door, the same size as the elevator. Tom wondered what was inside, and the heavy barrier slid into the wall, almost as if it had read his mind. Icy air billowed out in clouds of condensing vapor. Lights snapped on, revealing giant slabs of glistening red meat hanging on hooks above the grated floors.

It was a meat locker.

Tom stepped back, and the door rumbled shut.

This place was definitely occupied. The residents might simply be on another level. Or else they'd been watching their outer door camera remotely when Fango and Tom had arrived, and they'd opened the facility to prevent them from being eaten alive. Now they were probably on their way back to deal with him.

Tom's stomach fluttered with growing concern. How would the people who lived here react to his presence in their home? He'd shot through that fence to get in. They'd saved his life and probably assumed he'd behave himself and wait patiently in the entry hall. Then Fango went postal, and Tom had... He tried not to think about what he'd been forced to do. Fango was going to kill him. He'd acted in self-defense.

Hurrying back into the dining area, Tom went to check the door at the far end.

This one led to a shop of some kind, with all manner of tools and machinery for wood and metal-working. There were also a few advanced pieces of equipment that he didn't recognize, and others that he did: a 3D printer, and a synthesizer. More doors in here with labels on them: Lab. Infirmary.

And yet another oversized elevator. This time Tom headed for it. He tried a swiping gesture at the doors, as he might do back on Earth. To his surprise, the elevator dinged and the door rumbled open.

He stepped in and looked for the controls. A bright touchscreen panel caught his eye. The different levels were labeled and named.

M - Main Gantry
S1 - Spillway
S2 - Living Quarters
S3 - Hangar Bay
S4 - Generators
S5 - Tunnel Access
S6 - Tramway
S7 - River Access
S8 - Bunker
S9 - Gateway

Gateway? Tom wondered. He tapped that button. It flashed red and beeped. Frowning he tapped *S3 - Hangar Bay* instead, and the elevator rumbled shut. It shot down for several seconds longer than Tom thought it should, then opened into a vast chamber with glossy black floors and bare concrete walls. The sound of roaring water drew his gaze briefly to the outer wall, which was completely open to the falls. Tom stepped out, his attention sliding back over to the contents of the hangar.

Sitting on illuminated pads were three gleaming black vehicles that looked like some type of military aircraft. Except he'd never seen anything like them before. One was flat-bodied and relatively small, about the size and shape of a modern F-42 fighter jet. The next was big and boxy, easily fifty meters long, and maybe twenty high.

That gave a sense of scale to the massive hangar.

In the foreground, closest to the elevator, a big landing pad stood empty. The illuminated rectangular border glowed red rather than white like the others. Walking past the empty landing pad and the first two vehicles, Tom came to a third. It was also sleek and aerodynamic like a fighter jet, but much larger than the first.

Tom walked woodenly around the hangar, taking a closer look at the vehicles and searching for a way to enter them. The first and the third vessels definitely looked like they meant business, while the second craft seemed like it could be for transporting cargo.

Looking away, Tom spied an illuminated rack with matching black suits of armor along the wall beside the elevator. He counted eight spots on the rack, but only seven suits. Tom hurried over to get a closer look.

The armor had been built to human specifications as well. Two arms and legs. A head. A glossy black visor.

A whistling roar rumbled through the droning thunder of water pouring from the dam above. Tom spun around to see a large, boxy black vehicle flying in through the waterfall and dropping down over the empty landing pad. Four brightly-glowing engine nacelles swiveled down from each corner of the vehicle, blasting the landing pad with orange fire as it settled on the pad with a resonant *boom*.

Tom blinked in shock, belatedly reacting to the arrival of the aircraft. They were back. Terror clawed inside of him, spurring him to life. He ran for cover behind the largest vessel. Sheltering behind a big, cylindrical landing strut, he clutched the laser rifle close to his chest. A trickle of sweat from his scalp stung his right eye. He blinked rapidly to clear it, and worked to slow and quiet his breathing as the sound of thrusters cut off sharply, leaving nothing but the steady roar of the waterfall to hide his presence.

Machinery groaned to life, and Tom risked peeking around the landing strut and beneath the hull of the massive ship beside him. He caught a glimpse of a landing ramp telescoping down, and of a dark figure striding along it.

Tom lined up the target in his sights, blinking more stinging drops of sweat from his eyes.

The figure stopped at the bottom of the ramp, turned, and drew a sleek black sidearm.

"I know you're there!" a booming voice said as the figure looked directly at him. It slowly raised its gun.

Tom pulled sharply back into cover. "So you also know that I'm armed! I'm not looking for trouble!" he cried.

"Then drop your weapon, kick it away, and come out with your hands raised."

Tom grimaced, his chest heaving with indecision. If he did that, then he was at this person's mercy.

"How do I know I can trust you?" Tom asked.

"Because you know me. And I know you, Thomas Smith. That, and I saved your life by letting you in here. Now it's your turn for a show of good faith."

Chapter 14

7:25 PM

ALICE POKED THE FIRE with a stick, and a shower of sparks shot into the air. She stared into the mesmerizing swirl of the fire, her eyes drifting out of focus as shock set in.

"Explain it to me one more time," Bruce said, massaging his temples.

Alice drew in a deep breath to steady her nerves and collect her thoughts. She used a stick to draw a circle in the dirt between her and Bruce. And then another circle beside it. She pointed to the second one. "I think we're on Planet B, and we're orbiting a black hole. Because of their extreme mass, Black holes warp the space around them, causing relativistic effects."

"Relativistic? What does that mean?" Jess interrupted.

"The theory of relativity? Albert Einstein?" Alice said.

"Oh, right." Jess nodded along, as though she suddenly remembered what it was about.

Alice decided to explain anyway. "Essentially, because of the immense gravity of the black hole and our proximity to it, time is passing slower here than it is for everyone back on Earth."

"Oh, shit..." Neil muttered.

Bruce grimaced.

And Jess began waving her hands around in front of her face.

Layla frowned. "What on Earth are you doing?"

Jess shook her head. "I'm not moving any slowe r..."

Laughter burst from Layla's lips, but she quickly covered it with her hand.

"What?" Jess snapped at her.

Alice sighed. "This is why people need to pay attention in science class. You don't move slower because of relativity. We perceive time as passing normally, and so does everyone on Earth. But *relative* to each other, time is passing at a completely different rate on each planet."

"That's not possible," Jess said. Then she looked to Neil. "Is it?"

He smiled tightly at her. "Let's just listen to what Miss Rice has to say."

"*Mrs.* Rice," she corrected. And then her mouth dropped open and horror exploded inside of her.

"What's wrong?" Layla asked.

"My family..."

"What about them?" Neil pressed, sounding impatient.

"I have a husband and a son back on Earth."

"Don't worry," Layla said. "If someone found a way to bring us here, then I'm sure we can find a way back."

"I hope you're right, but that's not even the problem," Alice said. "If they're not here with me, then every couple of seconds that passes while I'm here could be a lot more to them."

"That doesn't sound so bad," Jess said.

"*Really?*" Alice challenged. "If I spend even a month here. My son could age by several *years* while I'm gone. And if I'm stuck here for a year, then he could be my age by the time I get back."

"A *year?*" Jess echoed in a shrinking voice. "You think we're going to be stuck here for a *year?* How are we... I don't even have any clothes!" She plucked helplessly at her sleek black dress, and for the first time Alice noticed how poorly the woman was prepared to be cut off from civilization. Expensive stiletto heels. A dress that made it hard to sit, let alone walk. She was in for a hard time.

"This *has* to be a dream," Alice muttered, glancing back to the opening of the cave.

"You're liking my theory now, huh?" Bruce said.

One of the more distant planets was shining through the mouth of the cave, a ruddy brown world. For it to have dipped that low in such a short time, Planet B had to be spinning unusually fast. How long were the days and nights here? Alice wondered.

"Let's assume it's not a dream," Neil said.

"I can't assume that," Alice replied, dragging her attention back to the others. "It's the only logical answer so far."

"Maybe," Bruce replied, "But then which one of us is doing the dreaming?" He regarded each of them steadily, his green eyes black and dancing with reflected tongues of firelight.

"It's got to be me," Neil decided.

"What's the last thing you remember?" Alice asked him.

"I was sitting inside my car, outside of her apartment," he said, pointing to the detective that Alice had met in the bar. "Then there was this flash of light, and I woke up with all of you in that field outside. Well, everyone except for him," Neil added with a nod to Bruce.

"Same here," Layla said.

"I was sitting at a bar..." Alice murmured slowly.

"The Tap and Whistle," Layla supplied.

"And then something blinded me, and I woke up here," Alice finished.

"There's your explanation," Layla said. "I'm the one who's dreaming. I'm the only one who already subconsciously knew each of you in some way. Neil and Jess were taken with me. Alice vanished from the bar where I met her, and Bruce is my missing person from Times Square."

Alice frowned at that. "Okay. What do you know about relativity?"

"What?" Layla asked.

"The theory that I just explained. About how black holes warp time as well as space."

"Well, I know what you told me..." Layla replied, sounding defensive.

"Let's try something else. How many light years are in a parsec?"

"Ah..."

"Isn't that from Star Wars?" Neil asked.

Alice had to resist the urge to laugh. "Yes, but in Star Wars they famously made the mistake of referring to a parsec as a measure of *time*, not distance." She looked to Layla. "So?"

"Five?" Layla guessed.

"Wrong. It's 3.26156, so you're definitely not the one who's dreaming."

"Did you know about the cases I was investigating?" Layla countered.

"No," Alice replied.

"Where was the other one? Two people who disappeared on the morning of the 25th. Where were they when it happened?"

Alice decided to take a stab at the answer. "Manhattan."

Layla snorted. "Wrong."

"Where were they then?"

"Sing Sing Correction Facility. Up in Ossining."

"This is going in circles," Bruce said. "What if none of us is dreaming?"

"Then we really are on Planet B," Alice concluded.

"The planet that you discovered three days ago," Neil pointed out.

"Four days," Bruce added, tapping his watch.

Jess's eyes collapsed to slits. "That can't be a coincidence. Did *you* have something to do with this?"

Alice stared unblinkingly at her for a moment, waiting for the other woman to realize how dumb that accusation was.

"What?" Jess asked.

"The fact that I discovered this planet has nothing to do with how we got here."

"Why does it have to be Planet B?" Layla asked. "We could be somewhere else."

"Granted," Alice said with a shrug. "This could be one of the other planets orbiting the black hole."

"And the time thing?" Jess asked. "How do we know that's real?" She nodded to the skeleton while hugging herself for warmth. "Haven't we found skeletons that are *millions* of years old? What's the problem with finding one that's only a hundred?"

"We've found *fossilized* skeletons," Alice clarified. "There's a big difference."

"What difference?" Jess asked.

Alice swallowed an exasperated sigh, but Bruce answered before she could: "Fossils are formed when bones get buried. Ground water dissolves the organic material and gradually replaces it with minerals, leaving behind rocks in the shape of the original bones.

"But out here, above ground, there aren't any processes to replace the bones when they decay. So, like Alice said, this skeleton should have turned to dust after a hundred years."

A knot tightened painfully in Alice's throat as she thought about her son, Sean, and her husband, Liam again. Their lives would race on without her. Milestones would come and go. Liam would follow up with the police, but they'd never find anything. They would grieve and hold onto hope, and then eventually, they would give up. How long would it take before Liam decided to move on and re-marry? Two years? Five? And how long would that be to her?

Tears stung Alice's eyes at the thought of Sean growing up without her. Graduating school, then university. Getting married. Having kids! "I have to find a way home," she whispered.

Layla wrapped an arm around her shoulders to comfort her. "We will find a way home. I promise."

"Okay, so it's not a dream," Bruce said, stoking the fire with the dead man's femur and throwing a shower of sparks to the ceiling of the cave. He looked up and regarded Alice steadily. "Then how did we get here? And *why* are we here?"

"Whoever did it, they're also the ones who created this solar system," Alice said.

"Hang on a second," Neil said, holding up a hand like a stop sign. "What do you mean *created*?"

Alice stared blankly at him. "You don't think a hundred and forty-four planets just happened to form in stable orbits around a black hole?"

"Well..."

"It's impossible," Alice said.

"Isn't *building* a solar system also impossible?" Layla asked.

"That would depend on how advanced your civilization is," Alice replied. "But if there is a species that could do it, then abducting us and transporting us through a wormhole to get here would be child's play to them."

"That answers the how," Bruce said. "What about the why?"

"You'd have to ask them," Alice replied.

"There must be something that all of us have in common that would make them target us specifically," Layla suggested as she withdrew her arm from Alice's shoulders.

"I might have a theory," Bruce said.

"What's that?"

"Well, not why *us*, specifically, but a theory about why anyone was abducted at all. What was going on in the world when this guy was taken?" Bruce jerked a thumb to the skeleton.

"The Cold War," Alice said slowly.

"Exactly."

"I don't get it," Jess said.

"We were on the brink of an all-out nuclear war," Bruce explained. "And UFO sightings were commonly reported around that time as well. So maybe this guy was taken to spare him from the war. Or to guarantee the survival of our species."

"Then they'd need to have taken more than just one guy," Neil said.

"Who says they didn't?" Bruce countered. "Besides, that might explain what I saw when I got here."

"What did you see?" Neil asked.

"Something huge chased me into this cave, and it was the spitting image of a Tyrannosaurus Rex."

Jessica giggled and smiled at that.

"You think I'm joking?" Bruce demanded.

The smile fell off her face. "You're not?"

"Hell no. Why do you think I crawled into this cave? I had to run for my life!"

"If that's true..." Alice began. "Then this planet could be like Noah's Ark."

"Exactly," Bruce said. "They brought T-Rex here just before he went extinct. Probably brought a bunch of other species, too. And now they've brought humans over, because just like in the Cold War, we're in danger of going extinct again."

"Don't you think that's a bit dramatic?" Neil asked. "We have more than ten *billion* people on Earth."

Bruce scowled at him. "It's short-sighted idiots like you who destroyed the planet. Just because you have enough money to live a good life and shelter yourself from the effects of climate change doesn't mean that everyone else is in the same boat. If we keep going the way we are now, in a hundred years we'll be lucky to have five billion people left. The other half will have died of starvation, disease, flooding, hurricanes, firestorms, algae blooms and every other natural disaster you can think of. And if all that doesn't wipe us out, we might just do it early by fighting over whatever fresh water and arable land is left."

"They were wrong about the Cold War wiping us out," Neil said, looking at the skeleton. "Maybe you'll be wrong about climate change, too."

"And maybe we'll find a unicorn that also got abducted and saved from extinction!"

"Are you *sure* you saw a T-Rex?" Neil asked skeptically. "Maybe you were smoking some weed before you got here."

"Screw you," Bruce replied. "I know what I saw."

"Our abductors must be an *ancient* species if they were around when dinosaurs walked the Earth," Layla said. "Wasn't that like sixty million years ago?"

"They'd have to be a lot older than that," Alice said. "No matter how advanced they are, creating a solar system like this one would take *billions* of years."

"Who cares how old they are?" Jess demanded. "We need to find them and get them to take us back."

"They might not take kindly to your demands," Bruce said.

Neil scowled. "Then we find whatever ship or technology they used to abduct us, and we use it to send ourselves back."

Bruce snorted. "Yeah, sure. We're going to find alien tech and magically figure out how to use it. You *really* are an idiot."

Neil shot to his feet, looking furious. "I'm done sitting on my hands. We're not going to get home by talking about it. We need to *do* something. Jess?" She stood up beside him, her heels making her wobble briefly on the uneven ground. "Layla?" Neil pressed.

Layla's brow screwed up incredulously. "You're joking right? You're the *last* person I'm going to follow around like a puppy dog."

"Suit yourself."

Neil took Jess's arm and started for the mouth of the cave.

"I wouldn't do that if I were you," Bruce said. "You forget about T-Rex?"

Neil turned to him with a sneer. "I don't believe you."

"I guess I'm hiding out in here because I like his company," he said, indicating the skeleton once more. "Good luck out there."

Neil hesitated.

"If you wait until morning, we'll go with you," Alice said. "We stand a better chance together than we do apart. And Layla's got a gun."

Jess looked uncertain now. "Maybe we *should* wait?" She shivered and glanced over her shoulder. "And it's really cold out there... at least when the sun comes up it will be warmer."

Neil gave in with a sigh and walked back over to the fire. This time he and Jess sat farther away from the rest of them, both leaning back against the curving wall of the cave. Jess winced and took off her heels to massage her feet. Neil loosened his tie.

Alice regarded them with a deepening frown. Neil wasn't much better prepared for this than Jess, with his brown leather oxfords and pinstriped suit.

Maybe she should have let them go. Working together was one thing, but those two were only going to slow the rest of them down.

Chapter 15

8:55 PM, September 26th

THE HEAT AND LIGHT of the sun blazed orange through Bruce's eyelids. A sharp pain erupted in his side, followed by one in his neck, and then in his hands which he been using for a pillow. Someone was tickling his legs with cold hands.

"Cut it out," Bruce mumbled. He stirred sleepily and slapped at those hands. He encountered something cold, hard, and round. His brain caught up a moment later, reporting far too many hands to be a person.

He sat up suddenly to find a massive black centipede crawling over his legs. Bruce cried out and pulled sharply away from it. The centipede fell from his legs with a chittering sound, and Bruce scrambled into the farthest possible corner of the cave.

"What's going—" Layla began, then she screamed and fumbled for her gun. "What the hell is that?" she demanded, shaking the weapon at it.

Neil sat up and gave a startled cry as the centipede began snaking toward him and Jess.

It reared up at the sound of his voice, reaching nearly the same height as Neil. Its forelegs fluttered in the air, questing blindly for purchase. Then it laid back down and its broad, segmented black body formed a U-shape as it scuttled for the entrance of the cave.

"That's..." Alice trailed off with a frown as it exited the cave.

"Another extinct creature?" Layla suggested.

"I can't remember the name now," Alice whispered. "But giant centipedes went extinct at least 300 million years ago. Fossils were found in Europe and North America."

"It had to be at least nine feet long," Bruce said, suppressing a shiver. He prided himself on being unflappable when it came to critters, but waking up to see a centipede bigger than him crawling over his legs had definitely left him feeling shaken.

"I guess that contributes to your Noah's Ark theory," Layla said.

Alice nodded.

Jessica gave a full-body shiver. "What do they eat?"

"They're pure carnivores," Alice said. Looking to Bruce she added, "You're lucky it didn't take a bite out of you."

He grimaced and looked away. "From now on, we set up watches at night. We can't afford to have things sneaking up on us while we're all asleep."

Neil groaned. "How long were we out? I don't feel rested at all."

Bruce raised his wrist to check his watch. Alice did the same, but he beat her to it. "8:55?" He frowned. "Same date. The 26th."

"I've got the same," Alice said.

"That can't be right," Bruce replied. "When I arrived, the sun was still up. The nights here would have to be incredibly short."

"Is that because time passes slower here?" Jess asked.

"No," Alice replied. "It's because Planet B is spinning faster than Earth. When did the sun go down?" she asked Bruce. "Did you check?"

"Soon after I got here. I only checked my watch at 7:07, after it was already dark, but that couldn't have been more than half an hour after I woke up in the rain with T-Rex barreling down on me. The sun was up then. So, maybe it set around seven?"

"And it's almost nine now. That means it's about two hours from sunset to sunrise," Alice concluded. "Assuming we're close to the equator, or that the planet's axial tilt is negligible, we're looking at four-hour days."

"But we don't know how long ago the sun came up," Bruce pointed out. He walked around the dying coals of the fire to where he'd left his clothes drying against the wall of the cave. Shaking the dust from his shirt, he pulled it on, finding the fabric starched with sweat and dirt, but otherwise dry.

"We could probably guess how long ago it came up from how high the sun is now," Alice said. "Failing that, we can estimate by watching how fast it moves across the sky."

Bruce nodded as he pulled on his jeans.

Jess stood up, barefoot, and cast about with a disgusted look. "What are we going to do now?"

"Survival 101," Bruce said. "We need a source of fresh water. Then shelter, then food. And if the days are as short as we think they are, then we'd better get moving. We don't want to be caught outside at night."

"We already have shelter here," Neil said. "Maybe someone should stay and guard the cave?"

Bruce looked pointedly at him. "Last night you were ready to leave on your own."

"And you kindly pointed out what a mistake that would have been."

"We don't know how far away our water supply will be, and we already know of at least two major predators in the area. You can stay if you want, but you could end up on your own in this cave."

"Is that a threat?" Neil asked.

"It's a reality."

"Okay, settle down," Alice said. "Whatever we do, we should stick together. No one gets left behind."

"Fine," Neil said, shrugging it off and looking to the opening of the cave.

"Do you think we'll have to walk a long way?" Jess asked.

"Maybe," Bruce said.

"But I don't even have proper shoes," Jess said. "How am I supposed to go hiking in these?" she pointed to her heels.

Bruce grimaced, considering the matter briefly. Someone could loan her their shoes, but they wouldn't be the right size, and that would only shift the problem to someone else. "Socks," he said. "If you wear a couple pairs of them, they'll give you some degree of protection." He bent down to untie his laces, then glanced up as he was pulling off his left boot. "Well? I can't be the only one."

Layla sighed and sat down to untie her laces. "I'll give her mine, too."

Jess flashed a sheepish smile, but the detective appeared to miss it. Bruce recalled Layla introducing Neil as her ex-fiancé, and wondered if Jess was his new girlfriend. There was obviously some kind of bad blood between them.

A few minutes later, Bruce and Layla both had their boots back on, but without the socks. Jess pulled on both pairs, Layla's first, followed by Bruce's. She scrunched up her nose as she did so, as if the thought of wearing someone else's dirty socks had turned her stomach.

"All right, let's move," Bruce said, grabbing the femur he'd been using to stoke the fire, and heading for the mouth of the cave.

"Wait, shouldn't Layla go first?" Neil asked. "She has the gun."

Bruce arched an eyebrow and hefted his bone-club. "I'll be fine."

"No, he's right," Layla said. "I should lead."

"Do you know how to find fresh water?"

"By walking down hill?" Layla suggested.

Bruce smirked. "Close enough. We can both lead. How about that?" He stepped past Neil and Jess, who waited for Alice to leave before following them out. Little did they know, being at the tail of a group is much more dangerous than being at its head.

The biggest threats in nature are the ones you don't see coming. But out here with real, live dinosaurs running around, Bruce supposed that all bets were off.

As soon as he left the cave, the cold air came rushing back. This time he checked his watch. "Nine degrees Celsius," he said.

"Pretty chilly," Layla agreed, and buttoned her suit jacket up.

"Didn't you say you saw a dinosaur?" Neil asked. "Aren't they cold-blooded? How could they survive in these temperatures?"

"Actually, that's a myth," Alice said. "They were mesotherms."

"Meso-what?" Jess asked.

"It's somewhere between cold-blooded and warm," Alice explained.

"How can you possibly know that?" Neil asked.

"From the fossil records. Cold-blooded creatures can't grow as fast as warm-blooded ones, and yet we see signs that dinosaurs grew very rapidly."

Bruce added, "We also know that back when T-Rex roamed the Earth, temperatures were much cooler than they are today. Around 50 degrees Fahrenheit, which is more or less what we're experiencing here."

"Again, how do you—" Neil began.

"From ice cores, tree rings, and sediment deposits," Bruce supplied. "I'm a climatologist."

"Figures," Neil muttered.

"How's that?" Bruce demanded.

"Let's stay on track," Layla said. "Water." She put a hand to her brow to shade her eyes from the sun and began turning in a circle to scan their surroundings. Alice was busy scanning the sky instead, staring up into the sun.

"Amazing..." she whispered.

Bruce noticed that the cave where they'd spent the night was set into a grassy hill that led down to the forest T-Rex had crashed out of a few hours ago. Between them and the forest was the relatively flat grassy field where he'd woken up. And far beyond those trees, at the bottom of a long slope, was a sparkling blue lake with soaring, snow-capped mountains on the other side. The lake was long and skinny, snaking around in a way that made it look almost like a river.

"I think we've found our water source," Layla said.

"There's just one problem," Bruce added. "T-Rex came from there."

Neil made a face. "Just pick a direction already."

Bruce pointed to the trees on the other side of the field from the lake.

"That's in the opposite direction of water," Neil pointed out.

"Big bodies of water attract big animals," Bruce explained. "They need to drink even more badly than we do. If we go to the lake, we're almost guaranteed to run into them. So we go the other way."

"And die of thirst?"

Bruce pointed to the green, forested slopes of the mountains on this side of the lake. "See that?" he pointed to a wrinkle in the green cliffs.

"What? Trees?" Neil asked.

"No, a river," Bruce said. "They carve depressions in whatever they run through. You can see it from here. If we move quickly we can reach it before dark." Bruce started toward the spot he'd picked, flourishing his bone-club as he went.

"Aren't jungles teeming with snakes and bugs and all kinds of poisonous things?" Jess asked.

"Probably," Bruce conceded, and shot a grin over his shoulder at the rest of the group.

He led them down to the field and began crossing it to the tree line. The whole way there, Bruce heard the strange fluted cries of massive winged creatures that circled high above. Deep lowing sounds rumbled from the forest, no doubt from large herbivores that they had yet to encounter, and then there were the more distant roars of giant predators. Everyone watched the trees warily.

Bruce kept a good grip on his club, but his weapon felt wildly inadequate. Even Layla's sidearm wasn't nearly enough. No way that pistol was stopping anything bigger than a dog.

Bruce still couldn't believe that this was another planet. Or that they were sharing it with a bevy of extinct animals from Earth.

Right before they entered the forest, the sun passed behind a cloud, and Alice called their attention to it. Everyone looked up, and Bruce saw that the sun had turned to a brightly glowing ring. Something was shadowing it.

"It's a black hole eclipse," Alice said. They stood watching for a few minutes. After a while that circle deformed, seeming to ooze out from behind the black hole. "Incredible..." Alice whispered. "If any of you were doubting where we really are, there's more proof for you. Only a black hole can bend light like that."

No one argued with her. Bruce led them into the forest. The trees were strange, with thick, needle-shaped leaves and big brown spores hanging beneath them. A bed of long brown needles and leaves padded the forest floor. Bruce marveled at the sheer size of the trees and at the wide, trampled paths that snaked through the underbrush. They stuck to those trails for convenience sake and to avoid making too much noise, but their footfalls and occasional comments were more than enough to silence the chirping and chattering of small woodland creatures. Bruce felt like he was walking in on someone else's conversation at a party. They were the strangers here, and now all eyes were on them, watching, and waiting for them to explain their presence.

A branch cracked high above their heads, followed by the sudden whooshing of several large, winged creatures taking flight. Everyone stopped and looked up, catching glimpses of triangular shadows darting among the trees. The branch that had broken came crashing down through a maze of older limbs, denuded of their foliage by light deprivation.

One of the birds swooped down and landed on a branch about fifteen feet up. Massive wings folded against its sides, while short, taloned feet gripped the branch. It had a long, vicious beak that looked almost like a spear. It was lined with sharp teeth, which it snapped warningly at them a few times, while tossing its head.

"Get back!" Neil cried, and the rest of the group retreated a few steps.

Bruce stayed rooted to the spot. The creature lifted its head straight up and the muscles in its throat moved as it swallowed whatever small creature it had caught. "It's okay," he said slowly. "I think it's just curious."

"It's a Pterodactyl," Alice breathed.

"Looks about right," Bruce agreed.

Layla crept back to Bruce's side, and grabbed his arm to pull him back. But he resisted.

The creature's head came back down, and tilted from side to side while regarding them steadily.

Bruce cupped a hand to his mouth and let out a booming roar.

The creature flinched and took flight, soaring back into the canopy.

"It's more scared of us than we are of it," Bruce concluded.

"That's what they say about bears and sharks," Neil said. "But people still get eaten by them."

Bruce regarded him with a frown. "I've seen plenty of bears. Sharks, too. Never once been attacked by one."

"Well, there's a first for everything, isn't there?" Neil quipped.

"Ummm... guys? What is that?" Jess whispered.

Bruce spun around to see that she was pointing with a shaking hand to someone peeking around a thick, ribbed tree trunk with one dark eye. The person hesitated only a second before dashing behind the tree. Heavy, thumping footfalls trailed into the distance, and the sound multiplied a moment later, making Bruce think there was more than one of them out there. He'd been to plenty of museums, so he knew exactly what it was. Powerfully built and fairly hairy with a long, flattened skull, and a bony brow ridge. It had a broad, protruding face with an overly wide nose.

"Was that... a caveman?" Jess asked.

"A Neanderthal," Alice supplied. "But yes. It was. We'd better keep moving. They hunted in groups, and they were very good at it."

"How do you know?" Neil asked.

"Can you take down a mammoth with a stone spear?" she challenged.

It was a stupid question for a man wearing leather oxfords and a pinstriped suit.

Neil's silence was telling.

"I didn't think so," Alice said.

"Are they hunting us?" Jess asked.

"Not yet," Bruce said. "But let's not wait for them to change their minds. Come on." He broke into a jog, following the trampled path in the opposite direction from this new threat. *Were Neanderthals cannibals?* Bruce wondered anxiously.

Chapter 16

10:05 PM

THE PATH CONVENIENTLY LED down into a ravine with a deep, rushing river at the bottom. Unfortunately, none of them had canteens that they could fill, or a pot they could use to boil the water and avoid contamination with unknown microbes. Layla hesitated, warming herself in the sun at the edge of the river. She was standing on a flat, jutting rock along the pebbled shore of the river, while Bruce kneeled at the end, repeatedly cupping his hands in the water and lifting them to his mouth, drinking greedily.

"Don't fall in," Neil jeered.

Layla scowled, but he was right. The river looked dangerous. Frothing white rapids lay both above and below the relatively flat, rippled stretch where they stood.

"Tastes good," Bruce said, wiping his mouth.

Neil looked on with a frown. "How do you know there isn't some Neanderthal pissing in it upstream?"

"If there is, it's the sweetest piss I've ever tasted," Bruce said.

"You've drunk pee?" Jess asked.

"He wasn't being serious," Layla suggested.

But to her surprise, Bruce smiled and shook his head. "Got lost in a desert once. That, and I grew up with three older brothers."

Jess wrinkled her nose.

Layla glanced around to make sure nothing was creeping up on them. They'd been hiking for about an hour, and had seen all manner of oversized bugs, including another giant centipede and dragonflies the size of crows, but so far no sign of the dinosaurs that Bruce had mentioned.

Not seeing any signs of immediate danger, Layla looked back to Bruce. "We've found water. Now what?"

"Shelter. Then food. If we gather sticks and mix pine needles with mud, we could create a lean-to against one of the trees. Just up the ravine from this river would be the smart place to put it."

"Here, in the forest—with the centipedes, Neanderthals, and pterodactyls?" Neil asked.

"At least we haven't run into anything bigger yet. I'd call that a win, wouldn't you?"

Neil snorted. "You have an odd definition of winning."

Layla noticed Jess sitting on another rock by the stream, massaging her feet through her socks. She carefully peeled one of them off, revealing angry red patches on the bottoms of her feet. She was going to have some impressive blisters soon.

"Who's helping me?" Bruce asked, aiming his bone-club at them like an extension of his arm.

"We'd all better help if we want to finish before dark," Alice said.

Layla sighed. "Then let's get to work."

"No one else going to get a drink?" Bruce asked.

"We'll wait and see what happens to you first," Neil said.

"Fair enough," Bruce replied.

Everyone peeled off, searching the immediate area for fallen branches that could work to make a lean-to. They stacked the material in a pile beside a large tree that Bruce had chosen for their shelter. Layla found a few branches with thick, brown needle-shaped leaves still on them. She carried the material to Bruce, who was busy sorting the branches according to length. He planted the longest ones in the ground and leaned them against a massive, ribbed tree trunk that reminded Layla of bamboo. They were still within sight of the river, where Jess and Neil were slacking off and talking. Jess hadn't gathered more than two branches before complaining that she was tired and her feet hurt.

Layla couldn't say she was surprised. Maybe that wasn't fair. But a wealthy socialite from New York was definitely not suited to this environment.

Bruce looked up and wiped sweat from his brow on his arm before peering down to the riverbank. "If you don't mind my asking, what did you see in him?"

Layla smiled bitterly. "Not much in hindsight. They say love is blind. How else do you fall head over heels for someone?" Layla mimed someone tumbling down a hill.

Bruce chuckled. "Good point." He went on assembling the shelter, and Layla left to gather more sticks. When she came back with an armful of them, she saw that Bruce and Alice had the lean-to established, with a triangular space beneath the sticks that looked like it would fit at least three of them.

"We're only about halfway there," Alice remarked, breathing hard as she stepped back to admire their work.

Bruce grunted and shook his head. "If Neil and Jess don't get back to work soon, we might just call it a day."

"You think this will keep predators out?" Layla asked, regarding the wall of sticks skeptically.

"Some of them," Bruce said. "Only so much we can do in a couple of hours."

There came a sharp scream from the river. Jess and Neil were standing at the farthest possible end of that flat, jutting rock. Neil was holding a long stick and thrusting it at a trio of relatively small, two-legged creatures with long tails.

"Those look like velociraptors," Alice said.

"Shit," Bruce muttered and snatched up his club. "We'd better help chase them off. Come on!" He ran down the hill to the river, shouting and waving his arms in the air like a madman.

Layla and Alice ran after him.

All three creatures turned at the sound of Bruce's headlong charge.

Layla noticed that all three were covered in feathers, which struck her as odd. One of them opened a mouth full of sharp white teeth and let out an almost bird-like squawk. The other two echoed that cry. Two peeled off, stalking toward Bruce. The third began inching toward Neil and Jess, looking for an opening to attack. Neil held it at bay, yelling, "Scat! Go away!" and thrusting his stick at its chest. But the raptor kept hopping back out of reach, as if it were a game.

The two raptors advancing on Bruce split up to circle around him. "Clever little bastards. They're trying to outflank us."

Layla stopped beside Bruce and drew her pistol, raising it in shaking hands. She took aim at the nearest raptor. A gleaming yellow eye met hers, and a milky-white membrane nictated over it as the creature sauntered to the left. It stopped and chirped something.

"Look out!" Bruce cried. He swung his club just as the second one lunged into the air with its legs raised and wicked talons poised to tear into their flesh. Bone cracked on bone as the club connected with the raptor's skull. The creature went flying and landed on its side.

"It's getting back up!" Alice cried, pointing urgently to the first raptor.

Layla saw it. She took aim and squeezed the trigger.

BANG.

The creature fell back down, shrieking pitifully.

The sound of the gunshot was muted by the rushing water, but still loud enough to startle the other two. Both of them dashed away, spraying clods of mud and brown needles as they went.

Layla approached the fallen raptor. Its legs were thrashing and blood was streaming from a dark red hole in its stomach. Grimacing, she aimed at the side of its head and pulled the trigger once more to end its suffering.

Jess screamed again, more sharply than before. A pterodactyl had landed on her shoulders and was pecking at her chest with its beak. She lost her balance on the rock and teetered into the river. The dinosaur leaped clear and flew away, leaving Jess thrashing and screaming as the river carried her toward the lower set of rapids.

"Jessica!" Neil cried.

Chapter 17

9:34 AM, November 7th, 2069

PRESTON BAYLOR STRODE PURPOSEFULLY through the field of cubicles that crowded the converted aircraft hangar. This building housed the Space Development Group's astrophysics lab in Houston, Texas. More than a month ago, he had bought the building and hastily refitted and staffed it with forty-six of the brightest minds from around the world. Since then, they'd been hard at work studying the wormhole and the one hundred and twenty exoplanets that had been found orbiting on the other side.

His very first hire had been Julio Acosta. After Alice Rice had disappeared under suspicious circumstances, Preston had decided not to take any chances with her colleague, offering him the opportunity to relocate and head up the research group at SDG. Julio had jumped at the offer, and not a moment too soon.

Labs like this one had sprung up in countries around the world. Preston knew of at least ten missions to reach the wormhole that were being hastily assembled at this very moment. But *his* was currently leading the race. *Hermes* was nearly ready to launch.

Preston vaulted up a metal staircase to Julio's second-story office overlooking the cubicles below. He threw the door open, drawing the astronomer's eyes away from his virtual screens.

"You're positive the result is real?" Preston asked. Julio had just called him on the comms to announce that he'd made a breakthrough.

The scientist's head bobbed, making his curly black hair shiver. He pushed his augmented reality glasses higher on his nose. "I was up all night checking and re-checking my numbers. There's no doubt about it. The entrance of the wormhole is only point one seven five astronomical units from Earth, so the radio bounce didn't come from there."

"You think it's from the Gateway System's sun?"

Julio nodded. "It was a lucky accident. I was trying to bounce a signal off one of the planets when the star crossed in front of the Gateway and I got a bounce from it instead."

Preston tried to keep his excitement in check. "Then this means that the wormhole *is* traversable."

"Yes, sir. Well—at least for electromagnetic radiation it is. I doubt actual matter will be able to cross."

"E equals MC squared, Dr. Acosta. Mass and energy are interchangeable. If the one can get through, so can the other."

"But not without converting from mass to energy first," Julio replied. "And unless you know how to turn a spaceship into a beam of light and back again, I would caution against getting too excited by the data."

"How are we only learning about the wormhole's traversability now?" Preston asked, dragging his eyes back to Julio and the virtual screens that populated the walls of his office.

"Well, measuring the distance to Planet B with radio waves was one of the first things we tried when we realized how close it must be. When we double-checked with the parallax method, we got a much different number for the distance, which made us realize that the radio bounce was from the mouth of the wormhole, not the planet. We assumed that the wormhole must be impenetrable from our side."

"I already know that, Acosta. What changed this time?"

"We tried again. And again. And then about a hundred more times."

"If you were so sure it was impenetrable, why bother?" Preston asked.

"Because, one of the biggest mysteries we've faced since discovering the Gateway is why the planets and stars on the other side appear to flicker every three point six seconds. The effect is so fleeting that it's hard to even see it with the naked eye, but of course it shows up in the data. We assumed it could be a cloud of dust or a dark star orbiting rapidly around the black hole and occluding our view. Instead, it turned out to be the periodicity with which the wormhole oscillates."

Preston blinked in shock. "You're saying that every three and a half seconds our side becomes a black hole, and theirs becomes a white hole?"

"Yes, but only for two hundred and five milliseconds. We only managed to get a signal to bounce off the Gateway's star because we got lucky with the timing."

"Does anyone else know about this?"

"Just Samar Argawal and Jennifer Kelsey. Why?"

"Make sure they don't tell anyone, and if they have, find out who and stop the news from going any further. We need to keep a lid on this for as long as we can."

"They've already signed NDAs," Julio pointed out.

"Get them to sign another one," Preston said.

Julio blinked at him. "May I ask why all the secrecy?"

Preston gestured to the window and the cubicles below. "We're in the race of our lives. The country that figures out how to cross the wormhole will be the first to set foot on the worlds on the other side. Better yet, that nation may also be the one to make contact with a vastly powerful alien civilization. They could gain access to knowledge and technologies that we can only dream about. It could usher in a golden age of discovery and progress."

"Or imminent destruction," Julio suggested.

"Let's assume that the Gateway and Planet B are signs of the Watchers' goodwill, which so far, they appear to be. Assuming that extends to sharing technological progress with us, we're about to enter a new age of enlightenment. Nations and individuals will kill to control the flow of the advances and discoveries. For all we know, that might have already begun."

"You're talking about Alice," Julio said.

"Among others. Cases of missing persons have surged since Planet B was discovered, and the witnesses always say the same thing—a bright flash of light, and then someone disappears without a trace. We're talking about more than three hundred people from the US alone, and so far none of them have been found."

"You think it's the Watchers?" Julio asked.

Preston considered the question. That's what the media was calling the species that had built the Gateway and its planets. "Them, or a group of people here on Earth that is systematically silencing or abducting people with the help of alien technology. It's possible that someone on Earth found and reverse-engineered some of the Watchers' technology long before the Gateway appeared. Either way, we need to be very careful about how we proceed."

"At the risk of repeating myself, sir, matter can't cross to the other side."

"How do you know?"

Julio blinked at him. "Well... the math would suggest—"

"It suggests that not even light can cross. It also suggests that wormholes can't spontaneously oscillate between white and black holes, and certainly not every three and a half seconds."

"I suppose that's true," Julio conceded.

"It's a moot point. We're going to find out soon. The *Hermes* Mission is launching in ten days. We're sending a probe through with a live crew."

"A live... are you insane? You can't send a manned mission. You'll kill them!"

Preston regarded Julio with eyebrows patiently raised. "I said a *live* crew, not a human one. If we kill anything it will be a few lab rats."

"Ah. Okay, that's better."

"Lock this up, Acosta," Preston said, indicating the screens on the walls.

"Understood, sir."

10:10 PM, September 26th, 2069

Bruce sprinted downstream, jumping over rocks and fallen logs.

"Keep your head up!" he screamed to Jess as she broke the surface, spluttering. "Watch the rocks!" he added.

Moments later, Jess reached the tufted white crests of the rapids. She bounced off a jutting rock, and vanished below the surface again. Bruce winced, still running to keep up. He scanned the shore, looking for a stick or a log he could use to reach her, but there was nothing within easy reach.

Neil came racing up beside him, breathing hard. "We have to help her!" he screamed.

"What do you think I'm doing?"

They splashed through the shallows to get around a boulder that interrupted the riverbank. Jess's head came up again, bobbing and weaving between submerged rocks, getting sucked through plunging drops and spun in circles by the current. "Help!" she cried, just before vanishing once more.

Bruce heard the ominous roar of the falls before he saw them. Jagged boulders jutted above the river, marking the top of the falls, while the river rushed through the narrow gaps.

"Run!" Bruce cried to Neil. "We can't let her reach those falls!" Jess came bursting to the surface again coughing and splashing, struggling toward the shore.

Neil made a strangled sound and ran faster, kicking pebbles as he struggled to keep up.

Bruce reached the falls and clambered up onto wet, slippery black rocks to the first of two forks in the river. The water was gushing through each gap and plunging over a sheer, dizzying drop of at least a hundred meters. Two separate falls forked into the dark green pool below. Bruce glanced back, judging which of the two Jess was headed for. It was hard to tell, but it looked like the nearest one. Neil had a big rotten stick that he probably hoped to give to Jess for a lifeline. But he wasn't even keeping up with her anymore. The river was funneling deeper and faster as it approached the falls.

Bruce lay down on the rocks and extended his bone-club as far as he could. His reach barely made a difference. The river was too wide. Gripping the bone firmly in both hands, he waited, watching as Jess expended what was left of her energy by fighting the current to get closer to him.

"Grab it!" he yelled to her, hoping she would see what he had planned. He needed her to snag the other end of the bone, and somehow hold on against the incredible force of the river. It was a long shot, and he knew it, but it was the only one they had.

Jess came within a dozen feet, and her eyes fixed on him. She noticed the waterfall for the first time and screamed.

"Grab it!" Bruce shouted.

Jess came into reach, and he thrust the bone closer.

Her hands burst from the water, grabbing on firmly, but the momentum of the river carried her over anyway.

Bruce's arms wrenched suddenly with Jess's weight. Tendons pulled taut and his shoulder sockets popped as she dragged him down the slippery rocks to greet the rushing water.

"Hold on!" Bruce gritted out, but she was completely submerged by the falls and couldn't possibly hear him.

Bruce heaved with all of his strength, but only succeeded in sliding faster down the rocks. He realized he'd miscalculated, and badly. There was more force pulling him down than keeping him up. He dragged his thighs against the rocks, struggling to find footholds.

Bruce's forearms plunged into the icy current. His head was next. He cried out in alarm as he realized that there was no stopping it now. He was going over with Jess.

Someone grabbed his ankles and said, "I've got you!"

It was Neil. Thank God.

And then the weight dragging him down suddenly vanished as Jess lost her grip. He saw her appear briefly, arms and legs flailing, screaming soundlessly as she vanished into the thundering white spray.

"No!" Neil cried.

Bruce dragged himself back up and kneeled on the rocks, peering over the edge, hoping to see some sign that Jess had miraculously survived the fall.

But he didn't even see the splash as she hit the pool below.

"Is she..." a new voice asked. It was Layla. Alice arrived next, gasping for air and leaning with her hands on her knees. She gave up and sat down, shaking her head, as if the answer to Layla's half-formed question should have been obvious.

Neil jumped to his feet, shrugging out of his wrinkled suit jacket and yanking off his tie. He thrust the articles at Layla, who took them with a frown.

"What are you doing?" she asked.

"I'm going after her," he said, and then took a quick step toward the edge of the cliff.

Bruce caught him by the arm and pulled him back.

"Let me go!" Neil screamed.

"Don't be an idiot! No one could survive that drop, and you wouldn't either."

"You don't know that!"

"I do," Alice replied. "From this height, it's like hitting concrete. She's dead."

Chapter 18

10:16 PM

"SHE COULD HAVE SURVIVED," Neil insisted in a small voice that was almost completely lost to the roar of the falls.

Bruce pulled him away, and they retreated to the safety of the riverbank. Layla laid a hand on his shoulder and squeezed.

He regarded her blankly.

"I'm sorry," she said. "She was my friend, too."

He accepted that with a shallow nod.

After everything Neil had done to her, it took a lot to feel sorry for him, but seeing that he'd been willing to jump to his death to save Jess had shown her another side to him—a side she'd almost forgotten.

Alice shook her head. "Even if the pool at the bottom is deep enough to cushion the impact, she'll still hit with enough force to knock her unconscious and break bones. That cliff is at least the height of Niagara Falls. Assuming similar gravity to

Earth's, we're talking about her hitting the surface at a hundred kilometers per hour. Does that sound like something she could survive?"

"People have survived going over Niagara Falls," Neil insisted as he walked slowly back to the edge.

Bruce followed him there, as if worried he might still try to jump.

"Any sign of her?" Layla called out to be heard above the thunder of the falls.

"None," Bruce replied.

"I'm going to find a way down," Neil said, and strode away from the cliff.

"We'd better go with him." Bruce raised his bone-club, warily watching the shadowy forest around them.

Layla reached into her jacket for her gun, reassured to find it still secure in the holster. Exploring on Planet B was terrifying. To make matters worse, night was already falling. The sun hovered just above the forest canopy below the falls, lighting the sky ablaze with fiery reds and cobalt-blues.

Neil came over and took back his suit jacket, no doubt for warmth. Layla offered Neil the tie as well, but he shook his head, and she dropped it in the mud with a crooked smile. "I guess you won't be needing that anymore."

A defense attorney from Manhattan stranded on an alien world full of prehistoric monsters was about as far out of water as the proverbial fish could get.

Neil didn't return her smile.

"We don't have long before dark," Alice said, pointing to the darkening sky.

"We'd better hurry then," Bruce replied, following Neil down the more gradual slopes beside the falls.

They found a circuitous path around the waterfall, at times grabbing and uprooting the surrounding shrubbery as they slid down the spongy slopes. Giant bugs skittered away as they crashed through the underbrush, along with a few small reptiles, but thankfully nothing bigger than a rat.

Layla kept reaching for her gun, convinced that she'd seen eyes glinting among the trees, following them down.

Every now and then Bruce would let out a primal roar, and thump his chest or clap his hands.

"Stop that," Neil snapped at him after the second or third time. "You want to get us killed?"

"Most animals startle easily," Bruce explained. "Even the big ones. And with all the noise we're making, it's not exactly a secret that we're here, so attracting attention is a foregone conclusion."

"You think you yelling and clapping your hands is going to scare off a T-Rex?" Alice asked.

"T-Rex doesn't hunt here. The terrain is too steep. And look how thick the underbrush is."

Layla decided not to point out that it wouldn't take a T-Rex to kill them. A pack of raptors would be enough, and they certainly looked small enough to negotiate these slopes.

By the time they reached the bottom of the cliffs, the sunset had given way to twilight. The neighboring planets were up and glowing brightly in the sky, sending shafts of light shimmering between the scraggly branches of massive trees. Fireflies the size of Layla's thumb came out, periodically flashing bright yellow. The glow of the planets pooled on the forest floor. It was enough to see by, but only just, and it did nothing to part the deep wells of shadows where the canopy was too thick to penetrate.

"There it is!" Neil cried, pointing suddenly through the trees to the gleaming, rippled surface of the pool beneath the waterfall. He took off at a run. Bruce cursed under his breath and raced after him.

"Come on," Layla whispered urgently to Alice. It was a bad idea for them to split up, no matter how briefly. The last time that happened, a pack of raptors attacked Jess.

Layla imagined her erstwhile friend floating face down at the edge of the water, and she winced. Maybe she'd been too hard on her. After all, Jess hadn't known that Neil was dating *her* when they'd slept together. She and Jess hadn't even met yet. But she had known that Neil was dating **someone**. She should have known better. Layla pushed those thoughts from her head as she ran to keep up with the others.

Layla and Alice reached the edge of the pool to see Neil and Bruce crouched about fifty feet away, with Jess's still form cradled between them.

"Over there!" Layla cried, and ran to join them.

She heard Bruce and Neil arguing in hushed tones long before she arrived. And then she saw Jess's face—

Her eyes were *open* and blinking. Her lips moved slowly, mumbling something. Layla couldn't believe it. Jess was *alive*—and conscious! Her dress was torn across her breasts where that pterodactyl had raked its claws, but she wasn't even bleeding as far as Layla could tell. Falling on her knees beside Jess, she pulled the other woman into a hug.

Layla withdrew with tears streaming down her face. Jess regarded her with a weak smile. "How is this possible?" Layla asked, looking from Jess to Bruce and Neil.

"I have no idea," Bruce replied, shaking his head.

"It's a miracle," Neil added, and pulled Jess into his lap. He cradled her head gently and stroked her wet hair. Layla noticed that Jess was starting to shiver violently.

"You were extremely lucky to survive that fall," Alice said.

"You want my jacket?" Neil asked. "Here." He took it off and draped it over Jess like a blanket.

"That won't be even close to good enough," Bruce said. "It's getting colder now that the sun's down, and it wasn't exactly warm a minute ago. We need to get a fire going before hypothermia sets in. Layla? Alice? I need your help gathering wood."

Alice jumped up and followed Bruce to the trees, but Layla lingered, frozen and staring at Jess like she was a ghost. "I'm sorry," she finally said.

"For what?" Jess asked.

"For holding it against you. I know it happened before we met."

"No. *I'm* sorry. I sh-should have told you," Jess said. "I didn't want to m-m-mess things up for you. And I r-really wanted to be your friend."

"Shhh," Neil whispered. "You need to rest."

"I'm f-fine," Jess said, adding more volume to her words. "Just t-tired."

Layla nodded, and smiled tightly. "Well, if you and Neil want to be together, that's okay. He and I are done, anyway."

"We're not together," Jess insisted.

Layla studied her and Neil—Jess lying in his lap and wearing his coat for a blanket. "Are you sure about that?"

"We're just friends."

"Okay. But don't let me stop you."

"Layla!" Bruce called, sounding far away now.

"I'd better go help them," she said, and pushed off the rocky ground.

"Careful," Jess mumbled.

A muffled roar shivered through the trees, causing Layla to freeze in mid-stride.

"What was that?" Jess whispered sharply.

"Sounded big," Neil muttered, his eyes darting.

Another roar came, but softer, as if it were moving away. "Not *too* close," Layla decided.

"Tell Bruce to stop shouting," Neil added in a sharp whisper. "The terrain is a lot more open here."

"I think he's already figured it out," Layla said. "But I'll let him know."

It took them the next twenty minutes to gather wood and build a fire at the water's edge. Bruce lit dry leaves and needles with his ARC lighter, and now the flames were roaring and crackling as they devoured sticks and logs alike.

The bonfire blazed warm and bright against the cooler blue light of the planets shining into the clearing around the falls.

"How are you doing?" Layla asked, nodding to Jess. She was still lying in Neil's lap under his suit jacket, no longer shivering thanks to the fire. She looked sleepy, her eyes periodically sinking shut only to snap back open, as if she were fighting to stay awake. But that could also be a sign of a concussion.

"I'm okay," Jess replied.

"No injuries?" Alice asked.

"No."

Bruce blew out a breath. "You're *really* lucky then. I saw that pterodactyl going at you. It shredded your dress."

Jess nodded slowly. "The river was worse. Slamming me into rocks, submerged logs scraping my legs..."

"You're sure you're not hurt?" Alice pressed.

"I was as surprised as you," Jess nodded to her bare legs. Aside from a few bright red scratches, and fading bruises, there was no sign of any injury.

"Amazing," Alice said.

Layla let out a long breath and glanced back at the shadowy pool behind them, her mouth watering suddenly at the sight of it. After all the exertion, she couldn't resist any longer. Jumping up, she hurried to the water's edge, cupped her hands, and drank until she could hear her stomach sloshing.

Neil and Alice followed suit, but Jess refrained, smiling weakly and shaking her head, "I've swallowed enough water already."

Bruce barked a laugh at that.

Something big groaned in response.

Everyone froze.

Silence rang loud, but for the snapping and cracking of the fire. Even the crickets seemed to have taken a breath.

Layla peered into the heavy shadows of the trees, parting them with her gaze and searching for signs of movement. A dark wall shifted and rippled. "There," Layla whispered, pointing to it. "What's that?"

Giant eyes gleamed, peeking between broad leaves.

Layla drew her gun and took aim.

Bruce jumped to his feet and waved his bone club in the air. "Hey! Get lost!" He slapped his knee and then clapped his hands a few times. "Get out of here!"

The massive creature groaned and stirred to life. Dark, jagged plates rippled along its spine, and a spiky tail swept into view, shredding through the underbrush. Fallen logs splintered, while saplings and ferns rustled violently before flattening beneath the beast's massive bulk.

It had to be at least the size of an elephant, but the armored plates on its back and that spiked tail made it impossible to mistake for one.

"Was that... a stegosaurus?" Neil asked quietly.

"Don't worry, they're herbivores," Alice said to Bruce, who had yet to sit back down.

"So are bulls and rhinos," Bruce replied. "You ever seen one charge? For all we know fire sets them off."

"That's a myth," Alice said.

"A myth about dinosaurs?" Bruce asked with a furrowed brow as he eased back down, this time sitting sideways to keep an eye on the trees.

"No. About Rhinos. They don't stamp out fires."

Bruce stared hard at her. "I never said they did..."

"Oh. Never mind, then."

Silence fell, and Layla sat fiddling restlessly with her gun in her lap as she listened to the hooting and groaning calls of large animals. Insects buzzed, crickets chirped, and frogs croaked. The occasional firefly still flitted among the shadows, pulsing brightly. Somehow, the nights were so much louder than the days.

"What's the time?" Layla asked, suddenly curious.

Alice checked her smart watch. The screen glowed to life with bright blue numbers. "It's eleven fifteen now."

"Man," Bruce muttered. "It's hard to believe that I haven't even been here for a day yet and the sun has already set twice."

"Speak for yourself," Neil said. "It's only been once for us. We woke up when it was already dark."

"That was, what—about four hours ago?" Alice asked, looking to Bruce.

He nodded. "Yeah. About that."

"We should probably get some rest," Layla said. "We'll need our energy to hunt for food in the morning."

"Good luck," Alice replied. "It's already been half an hour since the sun went down. That only gives us an hour and a half to sleep before it comes up again."

"Better than nothing," Bruce grunted. "Who's taking watch?"

"I will," Alice said. She looked to Layla. "Give me the gun."

Layla hesitated. "You know how to use it?"

"I used to go hunting with my granddad every fall."

"Okay." Layla placed her thumb against the biometric scanner on the back of the grip to unlock the weapon. "Careful. I just turned the safety off."

"Don't worry. I won't touch the trigger unless I have a good reason to. I'll wake you if I see anything."

Layla nodded and lay down on a spongy bed of pine needles with her back to the fire so she could watch for signs of danger as she fell asleep. The droning sounds of the forest and the crackling warmth of the blaze quickly lulled her to sleep.

Darkness fell like a heavy shroud over her thoughts.

Shapeless monsters darted through her mind's eye.

Glinting pricks of light watched from the trees.

Hissing quietly, they crept toward her with wicked, curving claws and snouts full of razor teeth.

"Wake up!" she whispered to the others. But no one stirred. She reached for Alice's shoulder and shook her. She was lying on her side, asleep, and Layla's gun was mysteriously missing. "Alice!" Layla tried again.

No response.

The monsters stopped advancing and chittered quietly amongst themselves. Raptors. Six of them, each the size of a large dog.

Layla shot to her feet. "Wake up!" she screamed.

Impossibly, none of the others so much as twitched. But the raptors did. One of them shrieked and tossed its head, snapping its jaws at her.

Was everyone else dead?

The raptors began advancing again, stepping closer and encircling the dying fire.

Layla realized that she had to flee before they cornered her. But she couldn't outrun them. She glanced to the shimmering pool behind her. Maybe she could swim to get away. *Dinosaurs don't swim, do they?*

She dashed for the pool, but her body felt numb and slow, like it was stuck in molasses. The monsters shrieked. Rapid footfalls hammered the soft ground. One of them hissed right in her ear, and she felt sharp teeth sink hotly through her flesh.

Claws tore her back open. Layla cried out and fell with blood pouring down her spine.

A woman screamed, and Layla's eyes flew open.

She blinked, staring hard into the fuzzy darkness of the forest. Her heart pounded hard and slow, flooded with adrenaline from the fresh terror of the nightmare.

BANG!

"Wake up!" Alice screamed.

Chapter 19

12:06 AM, September 27th

LAYLA SAT UP QUICKLY, her gaze sweeping the forest for signs of trouble.

Bruce jumped to his feet.

"What's going on?" Neil asked, voicing the question on everyone's mind.

But no one needed to answer. It was more than apparent what the problem was. A ring of orange flames encircled them. Pinpricks of fire in the dark, held aloft by shadowy figures. They advanced slowly, emerging in the light of the planets.

It was a group of *people*, both men and women, at least thirty of them. They all wore leathers and furs, and feathered hats. Some held spears with glinting metal points, while others had bows with the arrows already drawn.

One of the taller men stepped forward. He was a big man with thickly muscled arms. At least six-foot. He had a thick blond beard, scraggly shoulder-length hair, and a distinctive, broad-rimmed, feathered hat with a crown of spikes. Massive teeth and claws dangled from the necklace around his neck. He held his torch high in one hand, and a long spear in the other, but Layla also spotted a sword and a dagger sheathed at his sides.

He spoke to them in a grunting, guttural language that Layla had never heard before. She edged over to Alice and quietly took back the gun before she could accidentally shoot one of these people and get them all killed. Alice relinquished the weapon, and Layla let it dangle innocuously by her side.

"We're friends!" Bruce tried. Then he thumped his chest with his fist like an ape, as if that were some type of universal gesture of goodwill.

The man who'd stepped forward to speak with them frowned and looked back at his people. He said something to them.

"Maybe he's telling them to stand down?" Neil suggested.

But the opposite happened. Four burly spearmen marched out of the trees to join the speaker. A woman joined them as a torch-bearer. The speaker grunted something else when they reached his side, and then he pointed to Bruce.

One of those four replied in kind, and then they lowered their spears and began advancing.

"They're coming closer!" Jess cried.

"What do we do?" Neil asked.

Bruce shot a grim look over his shoulder. His eyes met Layla's. "Run," he whispered. "I'll hold them off."

"No," Layla replied. "They have archers. If we run, we're dead."

"We can't just let them capture us!" Neil objected.

"Layla's right," Alice said. "They have us cornered and outnumbered."

"So we're just giving up without a fight?" Neil demanded. "Shoot them! Put the fear of God into these barbarians!"

"If we kill one of them, they'll retaliate," Alice said. "And I already tried to scare them off by firing in the air. Our best bet is to make them realize we don't mean them any harm."

"So long as they're not cannibals," Bruce added darkly. He slowly bent down to lay his club at his feet.

The barbarian who'd spoken earlier grunted something else, but the four spearmen advancing from the trees didn't miss a beat.

"Now what?" Neil asked.

Layla turned her back to them, as if she were thinking about running for it. Instead, she deftly tucked her sidearm into the body holster beneath her suit jacket, hoping these people wouldn't find it.

She turned back around just in time to see two of them taking Bruce roughly by his arms. They shoved him toward the others, while the remaining two circled around the glowing coals of the fire to herd the rest of them in the same direction. Neil and Jess rounded the fire before the gleaming points of spears could reach them.

"No sudden moves," Alice whispered. She thrust her hands up and started after Bruce. Layla did the same, and the torch-bearer drew a wicked-looking knife as they approached. She barked something at them, and pointed to where Bruce was now kneeling in front of the man who'd first spoken to them.

"No problem," Alice replied, smiling tightly at her.

The woman grinned wolfishly back, revealing crooked yellow teeth. She had mid-length brown hair, and a dirty face with a long, lumpy scar across one cheek.

Layla thought the woman's face might have been smeared intentionally with mud to avoid catching the light. These people were obviously primitive hunter-gatherers. *But not so primitive,* Layla realized as she took in the metal points of their spears and arrows.

Rough hands forced her to kneel beside Bruce. Alice cried out and winced as she went down hard and one of her knees struck a rock.

Layla looked around and noticed that ethnically speaking, these people were all Caucasian. She wondered if that was significant, or simply a reflection of a racist culture.

The speaker barked and grunted at them, spitting with the force of his words.

Bruce slowly shook his head. "We don't understand you," he said.

Neil and Jess arrived and were forced to kneel with them.

The speaker sneered and made a sharp, cutting gesture before turning and walking away.

Layla's whole body tensed, expecting a hail of arrows to rain over them. But the spearmen yanked them to their feet, pushing and shoving them after their retreating leader. Layla let out a shaky breath. At least they weren't about to be summarily executed.

"Where are they taking us?" Jess asked.

"Probably to their village," Bruce replied.

"What for? What do they want from us?" Neil asked.

"Hard to say," Alice said. "If we're lucky, they'll keep us as prisoners for a while."

"And if we're not lucky?" Neil asked.

"They might be taking us home for dinner," Bruce suggested.

"You mean they're going to feed us?" Jess asked, looking confused.

"No, I mean we might *be* the dinner," Bruce said.

Chapter 20

12:31 AM

BRUCE WAS SURPRISED BY how close the village turned out to be. Walls of wooden stakes surrounded the enclave, with more planted at angles to ward against larger creatures knocking the walls down. Their captors led them toward a gatehouse with archers and flaming torches lining either side. As they approached, the massive wooden doors parted with a groan from rudimentary hinges. Bruce caught a glimpse of wooden huts with rounded thatch and bark roofs.

They passed inside the walls along a trampled dirt path, and were met with barking dogs and jeering villagers. Women were outside, roasting meat over cooking fires in front of the huts. Kids followed the hunting party and their captives. A young boy of maybe nine had a handful of river rocks, and he was shouting as he pelted Bruce and the others with his ordnance. Bruce winced as one struck him on the wrist, sending pins and needles cascading up and down his arm.

Jess cried out as one struck her on the side of the head.

"Cut it out!" Neil snapped, his nostrils flaring and eyes flashing as he rounded on the rock-thrower.

The boy took off with a yelp of fright.

One of the spearmen grunted and struck Neil in the small of the back, causing him to stumble forward.

Other kids followed them, laughing and yelling in their language. Dogs barked steadily, snapping and snarling as they went.

"Where are they taking us?" Neil asked, his eyes scanning the village.

Now that they were inside, Bruce realized the village was a lot larger than he had first thought. At least a hundred dwellings were tightly packed within the walls, and from the size of them, he guessed they were multi-generational dwellings. He estimated that as much as a thousand people might live here.

"Over there," Alice answered Neil belatedly, pointing to another wooden wall up ahead. This one was shorter than the one they'd already passed through, and the doors were barred with a thick beam. Someone lifted it, and they were led through to what looked like a quarry. Stepped stone cliffs led down to a shallow pool of water and a series of walled wooden enclosures that reminded Bruce vaguely of a zoo. Inside each pen was a different kind of dinosaur. He spotted a paddock with a small herd of triceratops inside. Another held what might have been a pack of raptors. And a third, larger pen was filled with a far more terrifying kind of monster, lying on the ground, apparently asleep.

"Is that what I think it is?" Neil asked, pointing to the sleeping mountain.

It was the exact same species as the creature that had chased him into the cave when he'd arrived.

"It's a T-Rex," Bruce whispered. He received a sharp jab with the haft of a spear for his gawking and stumbled forward with the others, following a long, rocky path down to the bottom of the quarry. Bruce noticed that together the enclosures formed a wall, leaving the bottom of the quarry completely enclosed.

Jess cried out as she slipped and fell, skidding on the rocks in her sock-shoes. Neil caught her arm and helped her back up.

"Slow down!" he snapped at the spearmen escorting them.

The villagers grunted and yelled at him, thrusting their spears warningly. "Okay, okay! We're going!" Neil said.

Jess was limping now, but to her credit she didn't complain.

Bruce glanced around, noticing that most of the other villagers had stayed by the doors at the top of the quarry, with only eight spearmen escorting them down. He wondered if they could make a run for it with such a light guard.

But where would they go? The bottom of the pit was completely walled off by those dinosaur pens.

"What do you think this is?" Bruce whispered, bumping shoulders with Layla.

"I don't know. Looks like they're planning to lock us up with their animals," she replied.

"Or feed us to them," Alice suggested.

Jess shot her a horrified look.

Bruce frowned and pushed his fears aside to consider the possibility. "Would the five of us even be enough? How much does a T-Rex eat?"

"What about the triceratops?" Neil asked hopefully. "They're herbivores. They might put us in with them."

"Maybe," Alice conceded.

They reached the bottom of the quarry, and Bruce noticed that the spearmen were leading them to a particular set of gates. He struggled to remember which dinosaurs had been in which paddocks.

A cool breeze blew, and he caught a whiff of something foul as they approached the pens. A mixture of dinosaur dung and rotting meat, if he had to guess.

The spearmen reached the doors, then stopped and turned, as if waiting for something. One of them grunted and barked a command, pointing to a wooden table along the wall.

It was only about fifteen feet away. Bruce spotted the glint of metal, and his eyes traced familiar shapes. The surface was littered with weapons: spears, swords, bows and arrows, axes... even some kind of rope net.

Bruce frowned. Why would these people let their prisoners arm themselves? Deciding not to question the stroke of luck, he took a quick step toward the table.

But one of the spearmen stepped in front of him with an upraised hand and shook his head.

"You want me to get a weapon or not?" Bruce demanded.

"Uhh, guys..." Layla trailed off. "I think I know what's going on here."

"Oh, shit..." Neil muttered.

Bruce spun around to look—

And saw that the stepped cliffs of the quarry were filling up with people.

Suddenly Bruce got it. This was an arena.

A wooden beam thundered to the ground, and the doors beside them groaned open—

Bruce whirled around to look, his heart hammering with dread.

A massive sleeping monster snorted and grunted as it stood up on two legs. It shook itself like a dog, throwing off sparkling clouds of fine gray rock dust from the quarry. It slowly turned to face the opening, giant yellow eyes blinking sleepily at them.

Bruce noticed a second wall behind the first, this one made from a row of wooden spikes like the ones they'd seen outside the village.

The spearmen pulled on two ropes lying in the dust, and four of those stakes fell with a ringing *thud*, leaving a clear path for T-Rex to get out into the quarry.

"Don't. Move." Alice spoke in slow, measured tones. "If you run, you'll trigger its hunting instincts."

Jess stifled a terrified scream as T-Rex took a step toward the opening, smacking its jaws a few times and working a massive pink tongue around inside of its mouth.

One of the spearmen let out a shout of warning, and then all eight men fled in unison, running back the way they'd come.

T-Rex gave a deafening roar and came lumbering out, giving chase almost lazily. Bruce stayed rooted to the spot, willing it not to see him.

Layla and Alice stepped slowly out of the way and flattened themselves against the walls of the pen.

But Jess and Neil were terrified beyond reason, screaming as they ran and limped away, heading for the cover of a clump of bushes along the base of the cliffs.

Fortunately, T-Rex seemed more concerned with the fleeing villagers. It snapped at the heels of the slowest one, catching a leg.

The man screamed as T-Rex tossed its head, sending him flying at least twenty feet into the air. Arms and legs flailed as he came down with a heavy *thud*, drawing a sparkling cloud of rock dust from the ground.

Miraculously, the man raised his head a moment later and slowly pushed himself off the ground.

And then gaping jaws closed around his torso with a sickening crunch. Rivers of blood gushed down the monster's jaws as it chewed and swallowed. A severed arm hit the ground with a meaty *thwup*.

Stunned silence was the only response from the villagers watching along the cliffs.

The rest of the spearmen reached the bottom of the path, and Bruce noticed a dozen men waiting there to receive them. Someone gave a shout. Six ropes snapped taut, and a wall of spikes emerged from the dust.

T-Rex was trapped at the bottom of the quarry with them. It stared balefully after the retreating villagers and then let out a bellowing roar. The spearmen backed away from the spikes, but they didn't turn and run back up the path.

Bruce realized why. They were guarding the only exit. Making sure that none of them could escape the arena.

T-Rex took a few lumbering steps, as if considering whether or not it could follow them. Then it stopped and slowly turned to look at the open gate of its pen—where Bruce was still standing with Layla and Alice.

"Arm yourselves!" Bruce cried, and then he sprinted along the wall to the table of weapons.

T-Rex roared again, and the villagers watching from the cliffs went crazy, cheering and screaming, and throwing rocks from above.

Bruce's heart beat out an erratic rhythm in his chest. He was running so fast that he saw stars. His whole body felt electric. His legs felt like they didn't even belong to him.

Booming footsteps echoed in his ears, rising quickly in volume as the monster picked up its pace.

Chapter 21

1:02 AM

THE SUN CAME CRESTING above the trees and fell on the arena, revealing the T-Rex in all of its terrifying glory. Its hide was striped brown and green, colors that gave it natural camouflage in the forest.

Layla reached into her jacket and drew her gun, struggling to hold it straight. She couldn't believe this was happening.

Bruce cried out in terror as the monster roared and stooped low to sweep him into its jaws. It snapped at empty air, barely missing as he dove beneath the table of weapons. Rex turned hard to avoid colliding with the wooden wall of the other enclosures.

Bruce sprang up and snatched a spear from the table.

"Hey, over here!" Layla cried, but the T-Rex ignored her. It stopped and turned back to look for

Bruce. He had the spear planted in the ground in front of him, and was crouched and hiding beside the table.

T-Rex regarded the spot where he'd been a moment ago with giant yellow eyes. Milky membranes flicked over them. It lifted its snout, sniffing the air.

It can't see him, Layla realized. She raised the gun higher, her hands shaking now.

"Don't," Alice whispered with a slight shake of her head.

T-Rex stomped back to the table of weapons, still snorting and sniffing. As it drew near to Bruce's hiding spot, Layla drew in a deep breath and shouted for the beast's attention.

Rex stopped, and its massive head swept toward her. It growled ominously, then gave a bellowing cry and broke into a sprint.

Bruce sprang out of cover and stabbed his spear into its thigh.

Rex shrieked in pain and batted him with its tail, sending him flying into the wooden wall. Rex twisted around to find him, and Layla pulled the trigger, hitting it just above the left shoulder. Again, the monster cried out in pain.

It roared and looked back at her, then charged.

"Run!" Layla shouted at Alice. The other woman took off, and Layla pulled the trigger repeatedly as Rex barreled toward her.

All the while the villagers cheered and shouted from above.

Layla backed against the wall of Rex's pen, still shooting. Each bullet struck Rex in the chest, but those projectiles were doing nothing to slow it down.

Bruce screamed incoherently, charging with another spear.

But Rex refused to be dissuaded from its next meal. Its jaws dropped low. Layla had nowhere to run. With only seconds before it reached her, she stopped firing, searching desperately for an escape.

The opening of the pen was the closest option. She ran in and darted behind the wall. Rex turned and barreled through with its momentum. Layla darted back out, and Bruce appeared beside her. Throwing his spear aside, he bent down and grabbed one of the ropes that the spearmen had used to drop the spike wall.

"Help me!" he cried.

Rex turned around, and Layla dropped her gun to find the other rope.

"Heave!" Bruce said.

They both pulled as hard as they could. Bruce's side came up a few inches, but hers remained where it was.

Rex roared again and pawed at the ground like a bull. Alice came running in to help on Layla's end. Together, the three of them heaved, and the logs shivered off the ground, ratcheting up on some type of mechanism. Layla's shaking arms gave way after only getting the spikes up about a foot.

Rex charged, heedless of the danger. They dropped the ropes and scattered to hide along the fence. Rex stomped on the spike wall, and the logs splintered. Then came an ear-splitting shriek, and the creature went tumbling through the opening. It skidded to a stop in the dust, thrashing and bucking on its side as it struggled to get back up.

Bruce recovered his spear and Layla found her gun.

Alice ran for the table of weapons.

The crowd jeered, making it clear that Rex was the favorite to win.

It stumbled to its feet and turned around, favoring one leg. Layla noticed blood trickling from its ankle where one of the wooden spikes had caught it.

"Get back," Bruce warned, planting his spear in the ground in front of them. Layla raised her gun in both hands.

Rex whined and whistled like an injured dog as it came limping toward them.

Alice reached the table, and raised a bow and arrow. She pulled back the drawstring and let the arrow fly. It lodged into Rex's right cheek. The monster screamed and gnashed its jaws, snapping off the arrow inside its mouth. Then it tucked its head and pawed at the other side, trying to pull the arrow out with its stubby arms.

"This is our chance!" Bruce cried. He took up his spear and charged.

Alice let another arrow fly, striking Rex in the back, but this time the arrow bounced off its thick hide.

Layla ran after Bruce, but stopped short of getting too close. He ran right under its belly and thrust his spear into its chest. Rex screamed again and blood gushed from the wound. It stomped its feet and snapped its jaws at him, narrowly missing him as he darted back.

Layla fired her gun in the same instant. The bullet vanished into Rex's throat. The dino gave a hideous scream, throwing its head back and snapping at the air, as if trying to kill whatever had just stung the back of its throat.

A horn sounded repeatedly from the cliffs, and they all looked up. The crowd fell silent.

Dozens of spearmen were rushing down the path from above. Layla noticed they were carrying much longer spears than the ones who'd first escorted them down. Bruce and Layla ran over to where Alice stood by the table of weapons, leaving Rex to thrash and paw at its injuries. It finally caught the arrow in its cheek and tore it out. Blood trickled down its torso from multiple bullet wounds.

The spearmen encircled the dino, jabbing at it with their weapons. Rex roared and snapped at them, but backed away slowly.

They were herding it back to its pen. They got Rex inside, raised the spike wall, and then shut and barred the gates.

A man set his spear aside and stalked toward them. It was the same one with the blond beard and the feathered hat who had first spoken to them at the pool beneath the falls.

"Careful," Bruce warned, stepping in front of Layla and Alice. He lowered his spear in warning.

"I think that's their leader," Alice said.

The advancing villager stopped, his dark eyes narrowing swiftly at the sight of Bruce's weapon being turned on him. He shouted something, then held out both of his palms and slowly lowered them to the ground.

When that didn't get a reaction, he repeated the gesture.

"I think he wants us to put our weapons down," Alice said.

Bruce snorted. "Yeah, no thanks."

The man tried again.

"Bruce..." Alice trailed off.

The village leader gave up and produced something from his belt.

Layla saw what appeared to be three rope necklaces, each with a large, curving black claw for a pendant.

The man held the necklaces up and thrust them toward Bruce.

"I think we just passed some kind of test," Alice said. "They're honoring our victory." She set her bow and quiver of arrows down on the table.

Layla holstered her gun, and Bruce grudgingly leaned his spear against the wall of Rex's pen.

The village leader started toward them once more, and the others fanned out behind him with their spears held straight up. They hammered the ground with the hafts and began humming and chanting in deep voices that reminded Layla of something Monks used to do—only much, much creepier.

The man with the necklaces stopped in front of Layla and slipped one over her head. The claw was a heavy weight above her breasts. She ran her fingertips over its curving length. It looked like a raptor claw. The end was surprisingly sharp.

The villager moved on and distributed another two necklaces to Bruce and Alice. Then he drew a massive knife from his hip.

Bruce cried out in warning and fumbled for his spear.

The man grabbed the blade with his bare hand and slowly drew it across his palm. Blood pitter-pattered at his feet, then he turned the knife around and held it out to them, handle-first. Bruce accepted it with a frown.

The man said something and nodded encouragingly.

"I think he wants you to cut your hand, too," Alice said.

"Hell no," Bruce replied.

The villager repeated what he'd said, more emphatically now.

Bruce shook his head.

The man sneered and reached for a sword on the other side of his hip.

"Okay, okay!" Bruce agreed. He grimaced as he grabbed the blade and slowly drew it across his own hand. Blood pooled in his palm. "Are you happy now?"

The village leader released the handle of his sword. He stepped forward and grabbed Bruce's bloody hand in his, holding it up and clasping it firmly as if they were about to arm wrestle. Blood flowed against blood, mixing and dripping from their grip. Finally, the village leader released Bruce's hand and stepped sideways to stand before Alice.

"Your turn," Bruce said, holding out the dagger to her.

Alice and Layla both repeated the ritual, and then the villager turned around and grabbed Bruce's and Layla's wrists, thrusting their bloody hands into the air. Alice quickly put her hand up, too.

The village leader shouted something in his language, and the crowd repeated that cry in one voice with a thunderous roar. The assembled spearmen stopped hammering the ground with their spears and raised their voices in a matching cry.

Silence rang clearly in the wake of the ritual.

"I think they just made us honorary members of the tribe," Alice whispered.

"What about them?" Bruce asked, jabbing a finger at Neil and Jess. They were only now crawling out from their hiding place in the bushes along the base of the cliffs.

The village leader barked a sharp command, and pointed emphatically to them. The spearmen gave a collective grunt of acknowledgment, then turned and marched toward Jess and Neil.

Layla watched with growing alarm as they lowered their weapons and encircled them.

"Hey!" she cried, grabbing the village leader's massive arm. "Those are our friends."

The leader smirked and muttered something in reply. Then he jerked his arm away from her and ran to join the others.

"This is not good," Alice whispered.

Chapter 22

1:35 AM

Bruce watched as Jess and Neil were herded into an empty pen at spearpoint. At least, Bruce assumed it was empty from the fact that no hungry dinos ran out when the gate was opened. Jess and Neil both objected vigorously, right up until the moment the gates were shut. At which point, their objections continued—banging on the walls and yelling to be released.

The villagers turned from their task as their tall, bearded leader gave his attention to Bruce and the others once more.

"Let them go," Layla intoned.

The leader growled something back and shook his head. Then he grabbed the raptor claw on his own necklace—which was festooned with all manner of teeth and claws besides that one. He held the curving black talon out and shook it at Layla, saying something else.

"I think he's saying that they didn't earn their place in the tribe," Alice explained.

The leader pointed up to the open doors at the top of the cliffs where the last of the villagers were still filing out. Mighty trees shivered above those walls. The bearded man began stalking in that direction, and the spearmen gestured and pointed with their weapons, making it clear that they had no choice but to follow him.

It took a few minutes to climb back up the sloping path to the doors. Their arrival wasn't greeted by any type of fanfare, but at least kids were no longer pelting them with rocks. The sharp, acrid smell of wood fires burning mingled with the appetizing smells of roasting meat, making Bruce's stomach grumble. How long had it been since he'd eaten? A burger at the bar. That had been around seven o'clock on the 25th. He checked his watch. It was going on two AM on September 27th. So about thirty hours had passed since his last meal. But he'd only woken up about seven hours ago. About a day was missing from when he'd vanished to when he'd woken up in that field.

His mind turned once again to wondering who had brought him here.

And why.

He wondered if Alice's Noah's Ark theory was correct. Finding all manner of extinct creatures here certainly lent credence to it. But these natives had obviously been here for a long time already. And then there was the Cold War era corpse in that cave. Humanity hadn't gone extinct on Earth. Not yet, anyway. So why had humans been brought—in multiple groups, from multiple time periods—if not to save them from extinction?

But the Cold War did bring us to the edge of self-annihilation, Bruce realized. And now, with Earth overpopulated and overburdened, falling apart at the seams from an ever-worsening climate crisis, it wasn't hard to imagine that they were on the brink of extinction yet again. Maybe not a rapid extinction, but an extinction nonetheless.

Feeling a sharp pang from his hand, Bruce looked down at his throbbing palm. It was crusted with blood, and still bleeding slowly. He grimaced at the sight. At least he'd been careful not to slice too deep during that ritual. By contrast, Alice had to clutch her fist up against her chest to staunch the flow of blood. Even like that, it was still seeping into her sweater, and she looked pale from blood loss.

"You okay?" he asked her.

"Such a primitive people," she muttered, shaking her head. "Don't they know we could get an infection and die?"

"They probably don't care," Layla said.

"What about their leader? He cut his hand, too."

"I guess they're used to it," Bruce said. "Probably have better immune systems than us."

"At least give us a chance to clean the wounds!" Alice exploded. "My hand was filthy when they made me cut it. I could get tetanus. Or necrosis from some flesh-eating bacteria!"

Bruce smirked. "Don't worry. A dinosaur will probably eat you long before bacteria does."

"You think this is funny?" Alice snapped. "We almost died in there."

"I know," Bruce replied more soberly now.

"And God knows what they're going to do with Jess and Neil!"

"Shhh," Layla whispered. "You're drawing too much attention."

Bruce saw that she was right. Their escort glared at them, and the villagers returning to the cooking fires in front of their homes watched them warily.

Their leader stopped in the center of the settlement, in front of what looked like a well. A circular wall of stones rose to just below waist height, and a tripod made of sticks held a wooden bucket attached to a rope.

The spearmen stopped and waited while their leader grabbed the rope and lowered the bucket, heedless of his injured hand. A moment later the bucket returned to the top of the well, filled to the brim with water.

Bruce's mouth watered at the sight of it. The exertion from the fight in the arena had left him parched. But rather than drink from the bucket, the village leader dunked his wounded hand into it. Bruce frowned curiously at that and nodded to Alice.

"Seems like they heard you."

Before Alice could reply, the man withdrew his hand from the bucket—

And Bruce blinked in astonishment.

"That's impossible," Alice whispered.

The bearded leader gestured for them to join him by the well.

When none of them moved, the spearmen shoved them forward, and their leader held the bucket out.

Bruce went first, carefully dunking his hand in the water. It was cold, and his hand tingled around the wound. He peered into the bucket, trying to see what was happening. When that didn't work, he pulled his hand out.

The ragged edges of the cut had turned silver and were rapidly growing together, leaving fresh pink skin behind.

Alice leaned in, gaping in shock at the sight.

"What *is* that?" Layla whispered.

"Some kind of nanotech," Alice said. "It has to be. Nothing else could do this."

"Magic," Bruce decided, and caught a flinty look from Alice.

"*Any sufficiently advanced technology is indistinguishable from magic,*" she replied.

"Arthur C. Clarke," Bruce added, causing her eyebrows to shoot up. "Like I said. Magic."

The bearded man said something, smiling broadly at their reactions as he nodded and pointed to the water.

Alice and Layla went next, each of them marveling at how their hands came out of the bucket with fresh skin in place of bloody cuts.

As soon as they were done, the bearded man emptied the bucket on the ground and then departed the well.

The warriors tried to shove them along again, but Bruce refused to be pushed around this time.

"We need to drink," he explained, gesturing insistently to the well.

The leader grunted something and the spearmen stepped back while Bruce lowered the bucket and filled it once more. The three of them drank their fill and then allowed the villagers to guide them back along the trampled dirt paths to the entrance of the village.

"They're not going to kick us out, are they?" Alice whispered as they approached the front gates.

"I don't know..." Bruce replied. His brow knitted into a knot. After being made honorary tribe members, it didn't seem reasonable to exile them. Maybe they'd assumed more goodwill than what was actually being extended to them.

Just before they could reach the gates, the blond-bearded leader veered off and tromped up the steps of a particular wooden cabin. He pushed the door open, and gestured for Bruce to follow. The man continued up the steps into an inviting room with a hole in the center for a fire pit. Six sets of furs and pillows ringed the pit. Sleeping pallets. It wasn't exactly a five-star resort, but it sure as hell beat sleeping on the rocky ground.

"There's more than enough space for Jess and Neil to join us here," Layla said as she and Alice crowded into the entrance behind Bruce.

She spun around and tried again. "Our friends," she insisted to the bearded man.

He growled something at her.

She pointed to Bruce, then Alice, then herself, and pointed twice more into empty air. Then Layla gave an elaborate shrug.

The leader grunted and shook his necklace at her again, causing the various teeth and claws to clatter together. Then he pulled the door shut. It banged against the frame.

"I think you'd better drop it," Bruce whispered.

"What are we supposed to do now?" Alice asked. "Are we prisoners in here?"

Layla yanked the door open to see two armed guards standing outside. They glanced her way and crossed their spears to stop her from leaving. One of them barked a warning.

Layla shut the door.

"Fantastic," Layla muttered.

Bruce shook his head and crossed the room to the table. He pulled out a tree stump stool and sat down. Exhaustion quickly took hold, but he didn't feel like he could sleep—at least, not yet. The others took their places around the table.

Layla eyed the pile of wood in the center of the cabin. "Maybe we should light a fire?"

Bruce shook his head. "Save it for the night. Firewood is probably rationed. Or else they'll make us go out and cut some more ourselves."

"Good point," Layla said.

Time passed in fits and starts. Bruce crossed his arms and made a pillow to rest his head on the table. His eyes drifted shut and his mind quickly drifted off in a daydream.

He woke with a start when the door banged open.

A pair of women came in carrying wooden platters. One was piled with roasted meat and some type of root vegetables. The other held a steaming clay pitcher, and three empty cups.

They set the platters down on the table.

"Thank you," Bruce said with a smile.

Without a word the two women turned and scurried out, slamming the door behind them.

"Are we that scary?" Layla asked with a frown.

"You still have your gun, right?" Alice asked.

"Yeah." Layla withdrew the weapon and ejected the magazine to count the rounds. "Only six shots left."

"I'm surprised they let you keep it," Bruce said.

"They've probably never seen one before," Alice said. "I bet they're afraid of what might happen if they tried to take it away."

Layla smiled at the thought.

"Think it's any good?" Alice asked, jerking her chin to the platter.

"Doesn't matter," Bruce said. "Either way, we need to eat."

Bruce picked up a roasted leg of something and took a tentative bite. Salty, tough, and gamy, but not bad. His mouth watered for more, and he smacked his lips appreciatively. "It's not bad."

The women fell upon the food, grabbing roasted legs and arms of whatever dinosaur this was, and stuffing their mouths with the tough meat. They poured the tea and sipped greedily to wash it down. Bruce burned his tongue, but refused to slow down.

It was almost more work to chew the meat than it was worth, and both Alice and Layla quickly switched to the roasted vegetables instead.

"Much better," Alice said. "This might just be the kick I needed to become a vegetarian."

Bruce grunted and shook his head. "Doubt you'll have the luxury, but good luck with that." He picked up an orange vegetable and took a bite. It was mushy and sweet like a yam. Delicious. He also began devouring the vegetables instead of the meat. A suspicious type of stew filled a recessed portion of the platter. Some type of fruit and nuts swam in the sauce, mixed with squishy bits of meat that were probably innards. Whatever it was, it was much easier to chew than the meat, and more flavorful, too.

"You should try some," he said, holding out a handful and dripping grease and sauce from his fingers.

Layla and Alice both declined.

Minutes later, the platter was empty but for a few half-eaten pieces of meat.

"I can't eat another bite," Alice said.

Bruce groaned and belched thunderously, drawing disgusted looks from the two women. He ignored them and began picking bits of gristle from his teeth with his finger nails.

"Really?" Alice asked.

Layla smiled and slowly shook her head. "You fit right in around here."

Bruce leaned back on his stool and stroked his greasy beard. "You think so?"

"Definitely," Alice replied.

He retired to the nearest sleeping pallet to lie down and take some of the pressure off his aching stomach.

Alice and Layla belatedly joined him, picking two of the other beds for themselves. A few minutes later, the two women who'd brought the food came back in and retrieved the platters with the scraps.

"Thanks," Bruce sat up to say as they retreated.

Again, they practically flew from the room.

Bruce lay back down and sighed, staring up at the dark ceiling. It was more rustic than what he was used to in his cabin, but not too far removed. Maybe the women were right. Life here might be all right. *Can't get much farther off the grid than this,* he thought, smirking to himself.

Layla and Alice were speaking amongst themselves in low tones. Bruce almost didn't want to know what it was about, but he knew he had to ask. Like it or not, their fates were tied to each other's.

Bruce rolled onto his side to face the women. "What are you two whispering about?"

They both stopped and looked at him. "We're trying to figure out how to rescue Jess and Neil," Layla explained.

"Are you crazy?" Bruce hissed.

"Who knows what they're going to do to them!" Layla replied.

"Probably feed them to some other dinosaur," Bruce said. "Unless..." His gaze drifted meaningfully to the table where they'd just eaten their dinner.

They caught his meaning, both looking horrified. Alice looked like she was about to be sick.

"Don't listen to him," Layla said. I saw scales on the meat, not skin."

"True," Bruce conceded.

"I don't know how you can be so nonchalant about it," Layla said. "Two people's lives are at stake."

"Better than five," Bruce replied.

"Don't worry. We'll leave you out of it," Layla said. "You can go back to sleep."

Bruce felt a flash of annoyance at her judgmental tone. "Hard to sleep with the two of you nattering in my ear. And anyway, didn't that jackass cheat on you with her? And then they ran and hid while we fought for our lives in that arena. Maybe they deserve what's coming to them."

"You don't mean that," Alice said.

Bruce blew out a breath. "Either way, it doesn't matter. They have us under guard. I don't see another exit, do you?"

Both women sat up and looked around pointedly.

"What's that?" Alice leveled a finger at a cubicle in the far corner of the cabin.

"Good question," Layla said. She got up and went to look. Bruce sighed and pushed off the floor to follow her. He almost laughed when he saw what was behind the wall. It was a slightly raised stool with a wooden cover over it.

Bruce lifted the cover by its rough metal handle, and a gut-sucking stench wafted out.

"It's a toilet," Layla said, burying her nose in her sleeve.

"You mean a hole in the ground," Alice added, having walked up behind them to see.

Noticing something, Bruce dropped to his haunches for a better look.

"What is it?" Layla asked.

"Light pooling around the hole," he explained. "These cabins are raised off the ground. There's a gap between the floor and the hole that they dug for the toilet. He bent even closer to the foul-smelling opening of the wooden stool. Grabbing the sides of the structure, he tried moving it. The simple wooden box shuffled over a few inches.

Encouraged by that, he gripped it harder and heaved, lifting with his back. The whole toilet came away, and he stumbled backward with the weight, setting it aside.

That left them staring through a square hole in the floor boards that was about one and a half feet wide.

"I won't fit through that," he said, then turned to look pointedly at Alice. She had the narrowest shoulders of the three.

"What?" she took a quick step back. "You can't be serious."

Bruce shrugged. "You want to rescue Jess and Neil?" He looked to Layla. "That's your only way out."

"I might also fit," Layla said. "We can both go."

Bruce shook his head. "If someone comes in and both of you are missing, we'll have a hard time pretending it's because one of you is on the toilet."

"I'll do it," Alice breathed. "Give me the gun."

"It was my idea," Layla replied. "Help me down.

She crouched down and lowered herself into the small opening. Her hips made it through, but barely, and then she got stuck under her armpits. She tried angling one shoulder down to squeeze through diagonally. After about a minute of that, she gave up, gasping from the exertion of repeatedly lowering her weight into the toilet.

"Pull me up," she said, holding a hand out to Bruce. He yanked her out, and she grimaced at the sight of suspicious stains on her jeans.

"I'll fit," Alice insisted.

Layla sighed and reached into her jacket to draw her gun. Then she appeared to think better of it, and removed the body holster, too. "Be careful," Layla whispered while securing the holster around Alice's torso.

The other woman nodded, looking scared.

"Hang on," Bruce said. "You can't just sneak out of here without a plan."

"What do you suggest?" Alice asked.

"At least wait until dark. Can't be more than thirty minutes from now at this point. Then sneak back down to the arena and let Jess and Neil out of that pen. When you're done, find some way to distract the guards so that we can escape. We're close to the gates, so we can probably make a run for it if Poky and Stabby aren't standing there anymore."

Alice nodded shakily.

Layla rubbed the other woman's arm reassuringly. "You'll be fine. Just take your time and stay out of sight."

"I'll do my best..." Alice replied in a shrinking voice.

Chapter 23

2:39 AM

ALICE SAT ON THE floor beside the fire pit, her feet resting in a fine dusting of ash. She watched the sky grow progressively darker through the hole in the roof. The tightness in her chest grew with every passing second, until she felt like she couldn't breathe.

Layla walked over and took a seat beside her. "You can do this." When Alice didn't immediately reply, Layla took one of her hands and squeezed. "Hey."

Alice dragged her gaze from the sky to regard the other woman with a blank stare.

"You don't have to do it. We'll find some other way," Layla added.

Alice shook her head. "There isn't another way."

"It's time to go," Bruce whispered, walking over to them. "You ready?"

Alice drew in a deep breath to steady her nerves and patted the holster against her ribs, reassuring herself that the gun was still there. "Ready as I'm going to be," Alice decided. She stuck out a hand and Bruce yanked her to her feet. Hurrying to the cubicle in the back of the cabin, Bruce moved the toilet again, and Alice lowered herself into the hole with his help. The smell was shocking, making her head spin and her guts churn.

It took some tricky maneuvering between her and Bruce to get her feet up on the edges of the hole beneath the floor, and then to lower herself to the crawl space without falling backward into the putrefied contents of the primitive septic system.

"You good?" Bruce asked as she crawled away from the toilet. The space was just high enough to shimmy on her elbows and knees to the back edge of the cabin. Peeking out, she found that the cabin backed onto an abandoned alley with more animal enclosures. These held sheep and several chicken coops.

Alice wondered why the villagers had given them dino meat if they had better options. But maybe these animals were kept for milk and eggs, not their meat.

Alice crawled out with her palms sweating and her heart hammering. She spied bushes and saplings growing along the perimeter walls that could provide some cover. She dashed over to the walls and crouched behind the bushes. A sheep bleated at her while munching on some hay.

Alice glanced in the direction of the arena, looking for a way to get there without being noticed.

The perimeter walls seemed like they would get her close. And the vegetation was a good bet for camouflage. To her relief, it was cloudy tonight, blocking the ambient light of the stars and the neighboring planets.

Whispering a silent thanks to whatever gods were listening, Alice began creeping along the wall. Thankfully the walls didn't have ramparts, so she didn't have to worry about guards spotting her. Leaving the animal pens behind, the distant sounds of children playing mingled with adult voices and the sounds of cooking. Then came the rhythmic clanging of a hammer on metal and the whooshing of flames. Alice spotted the source by a wooden cabin about thirty feet away: a big, sweaty, shirtless man hammering swords on an anvil with a clay forge glowing brightly beside him.

Alice noticed a point up ahead where the foliage was interrupted by a well-worn path that led to a set of wooden doors. There were also guard posts with stairs leading to them, and glowing orange torches blazing above the gates. Two archers stood watch, but they weren't looking her way. They were chatting in their grunting, guttural language.

Alice timed her movements to coincide with their booming voices. She reached the stairs to the first post and dashed into the shadows beneath it. She paused, eyes scanning the gaps in the floorboards, waiting for a reaction from the guard above her.

Nothing. He was oblivious. She breathed a slow, silent sigh, and steeled herself to dart across the path to cover on the other side of the doors.

Glancing down the length of the road, she checked to make sure no one was looking her way from the opposing rows of cabins and structures. The blacksmith was closest, but he was still hammering away. She waited for him to turn and plunge the sword he was working on into a barrel of water.

The sword hissed loudly as it cooled—

And Alice shot across the path.

Her foot skidded on gravel just before she reached the bushes.

The guards' conversation abruptly stopped.

Alice froze in the cover of the underbrush, cursing her carelessness and holding her breath.

The guard above her turned and peered over the edge of his post, scanning the road that led to the gate.

The other one said something, and pointed to the bushes where she was hiding. He was looking straight at her, but there was no sign of alarm. He said something else, then looked away.

A dog came trotting over, sniffing around. Then suddenly its tail shot straight up and its hackles rose. It began barking insistently at her.

The guards both went on high alert, drawing arrows from their quivers and peering into the bushes. The foliage was thick, and the angles weren't good, so Alice didn't think they'd seen her. Not yet.

The guard above grunted something and drew a sword with a shriek of steel against its scabbard. Heavy footsteps thunked on the boards as he headed for the stairs.

Alice reached for Layla's gun. Her heart was beating so hard she thought she might faint.

And then a boy came running over. He whistled at the dog. It looked to him. The boy waved a stick and then threw it. The dog raced away to fetch it.

A small lizard shot out of the bushes, running on two legs. The dog was busy with his stick, so he didn't notice. But the guards did. The one across from her drew his bowstring and let his arrow fly, striking the critter in the side and sending it skidding through the dust. The lizard's legs gave a few spasmodic kicks before it lay still. Alice blinked in shock—both at the accuracy of the shot and at her good fortune.

The guard with the sword stalked to the kill and stepped on the dead creature to yank the arrow out. He muttered something and shook his head, as if in appreciation of his colleague's marksmanship.

The dog came back, barking excitedly, and the guard tossed the creature to it. The mutt snapped the dead lizard from the air and ran off, shaking its prize vigorously to make extra sure that it was dead. Within seconds, another half a dozen dogs descended on the first, barking and snarling as they chased it through the streets, hoping to steal its treat.

The guards went back to their posts, watching the forests and chatting idly. Alice slowly released the air from her lungs, taking a moment to recover and steady her fraying nerves. That had been far too close.

She took extra care with her steps for the remainder of the journey along the walls. Eventually she reached a point where the wooden posts ended and a rocky bluff began. She crept along the vegetation below the rocks, finally coming to the doors at the top of the arena. She bided her time, noting that this area was at the end of the main street, and thereby far more exposed. But only a handful of people were out of their cabins, and none of them appeared to be looking her way.

Alice jumped out of cover and heaved against the wooden beam that barred the doors. It was heavier than she'd expected, taking precious seconds to carry it away and set it down gently. Not bothering to waste time checking behind her, she pulled the nearest door open and eased it shut. She stood listening to the silence that followed, expecting to hear shouts of alarm and rushing footsteps.

But so far, there were no signs that she'd been discovered.

Turning from the doors, she ran down the path to the bottom of the quarry. There she found the spike wall the villagers had used to deter the T-Rex was still raised. Squeezing between the sharpened logs, she sprinted for the dino pens.

Alice stopped when she reached them, and struggled to recall where Jess and Neil had been standing when those spearmen had herded them into an open pen.

The far left, she decided. Close to the cliffs where they'd been hiding. Alice ran over there and found another heavy wooden beam cradled in rusty metal brackets.

She hurried to remove the beam and set it aside. This time she didn't bother setting it down gently and let it clatter to the ground. She pulled the doors open—

To see Neil and Jess huddled together beneath a large wooden roof supported by four posts. It wasn't much of a shelter—certainly nothing to keep out the encroaching cold of the night. But at least the nights here weren't very long.

Alice ran over to them. Their eyes were shut, both of them asleep. Alice dropped to her haunches beside Neil and shook his shoulder.

He shouted and flinched awake, his fists flying up to defend himself.

"Shhh," Alice hissed. "It's me."

"How did you—"

"Doesn't matter. We're getting you out of here. Come on."

Jess stirred and blinked her eyes open. "Alice?"

"Let's go," she said.

"Where are Layla and Bruce?" Neil asked.

Alice jerked her chin to the stepped cliffs of the quarry. "Waiting in the village for us."

Neil stood up and helped Jess to her feet.

"Is there another way out of this pen?" Alice asked as she studied the fence.

Neil shook his head. "The walls are too high, and there's nothing in here to climb them."

"What about this shelter?" Alice asked, nodding to the roof above their heads. "Could we disassemble it and use the pieces to climb out? Make a ramp?"

"I already thought of that," Neil replied, "but the posts are too thick and they're in too deep. We tried shaking the structure, but it won't budge."

Alice's mind raced for a solution. Even if they could find a way out, they still needed a distraction to lure the guards away from the cabin where Bruce and Layla were. They also needed to escape the village somehow, and all of the gates were guarded by archers with terrifyingly good aim.

"Maybe we could try from one of the other pens?" Neil asked.

Jess looked horrified. "There are dinosaurs in them!"

"But not all of them are carnivores," Neil argued. "What about the triceratops? They can't climb, so maybe the villagers weren't as careful when they built that enclosure."

"They could still charge and impale us with their horns," Jess pointed out.

"Do you have a better idea?" Neil snapped.

"I might," Alice said, looking back up to the gates at the top of the quarry. A plan was coming together in her mind.

"Well?" Neil prompted.

"We release T-Rex," she replied.

Neil blinked in shock. "Are you insane?"

"We injured it, so it won't be very fast. We can lead it up to the village and let it through the gates. Then we use the ensuring chaos to escape."

Neil looked skeptical, and Jess was quietly shaking her head.

"It's the only way," Alice insisted. "And we'd better hurry. We might not have much time before they discover that I left the doors open."

"I can't run," Jess said. "I don't even have shoes."

Alice grimaced and looked to Neil. "Take her to the top of the cliffs, and wait for me by the doors. I'll lead the rex up."

Neil nodded and grabbed Jess by the arm. They went limping toward the spike wall at the bottom of the path. Seeing it, Alice grimaced and ran to catch up with them. "We need to drop those spikes first," she whispered to Neil.

He nodded, and the two of them skidded to a stop on the other side. Finding two dusty ropes they grabbed them and threw their weight against the lines, but it was no use. They weren't strong enough.

"I need you to get under the stakes and lift while we pull," Alice said.

Neil handed his rope to Jess, then crouched under the middle spike of the three sharpened wooden poles. He bent his back beneath the beam, getting ready to lift.

"On three," Alice said. "One, two..."

"Three!" Neil cried as he heaved and they pulled.

The logs came up a few inches, releasing the mechanism, and Neil groaned beneath the weight. He stumbled out and the spike wall fell with reverberating thunder.

"Shit," Alice muttered, scanning the gates above. "Someone might have heard that. Get to the top! I'll get the rex."

"Don't get eaten," Neil said.

"I'll try."

Alice sprinted for the T-Rex's pen. She arrived, breathless, within just a few seconds. Throwing the wooden beam aside, she pulled the doors open—

And saw what was left of the spike wall on the inside of the fence. It was still shattered. Rex lay on the ground like a dog, with his snout facing the door.

His eyes were shut. A rhythmic shuddering issued from deep inside the beast as it breathed.

Alice's heart climbed into her throat, and her legs began to shake. She resisted the urge to run. Instead, she hooked two fingers in her mouth and whistled sharply.

Yellow eyes snapped open. Rex snorted and clambered to its feet. Alice froze. It lifted its snout, sniffing at the air. Then it drew itself up and its head turned sideways, regarding her with one eye.

"You want me, don't you?" Alice whispered. "Let's go!" she cried.

T-Rex roared thunderously.

Alice's blood turned to fire in her veins. She spun around and ran for her life.

Thudding footsteps plodded after her. She cast a quick look over her shoulder to make sure she was staying ahead of it.

Rex roared again, its footsteps coming faster now. There was no sign of a limp. No sign of any injuries whatsoever. It was gaining on her rapidly.

A sharp spurt of fear lanced through her, and Alice's heart thumped painfully. She ran faster than she'd ever run in her life, but it wasn't enough. She gasped and whimpered in terror as the monster's deep, grunting breaths grew louder and closer with every thudding step.

She'd miscalculated. The villagers must have used the water from the well to heal Rex's injuries, too.

Chapter 24

3:37 AM

LAYLA'S BLOOD RAN COLD with the distant roar of a T-Rex. It was followed closely by sounds of commotion in the village and the muttered exclamations of the guards outside.

"Sounds like a distraction to me," Bruce said. "You ready?"

Layla hesitated. "Maybe we should wait a little longer."

"Let's find out," Bruce said. He jumped up from the table and strode to the door, then placed his ears against it, listening.

Layla crept over and waited, watching for his reaction.

Another roar sounded, and Bruce pulled away just as Layla heard the guards' footsteps retreating from the cabin.

"This is it," Bruce said.

He grabbed the door handle and pushed.

The door rattled on its hinges, but didn't budge. Layla's heart sank.

Bruce scowled angrily. "It's locked."

"Now what?" Layla snapped.

"Hang on." Bruce threw his weight against the door. It rattled more loudly than before, but still didn't give way. He pulled back and drew in a deep breath as he backed up.

Layla watched, biting her lip and anxiously flexing her hands into fists.

Bruce charged the door like a linebacker.

He slammed into it with a heavy thud—

Something cracked, and the door flew open. He went stumbling out with his momentum.

Layla burst into motion, running after him. She helped him to his feet and they ducked between the perimeter wall and the side of the cabin. But she needn't have bothered. Even the main gates were abandoned.

All of the villagers had their backs turned and were racing toward the far end of the street where the doors of the quarry lay.

Another roar split the air, sounding much closer this time. Then came the softer *pop, pop, pop* of a handgun being fired, followed by an agonized shriek from the T-Rex.

Bruce and Layla looked to each other, then back at the doors of the quarry. Alice was in trouble. They couldn't run away now. Bruce glanced longingly at the gates beside them, hesitating.

"Come on!" Layla cried. And with that, she sprinted after the villagers, not waiting to see if Bruce would follow.

3:42 AM

Alice was out of time. Rex was snapping at her heels. She would never beat it up the path. Spotting a massive boulder to her right, she dove behind it and drew Layla's gun. Rex tore past her, kicking up clouds of dust and careening into a shallow pool of water in the middle of the arena. It spun around and roared. Its head swept back and forth, appearing not to notice her, but it was snorting and sniffing, trying to catch her scent.

Alice willed it not to find her, sweaty palms flexing restlessly on the grip of the gun. A cool wind blew, taking Alice's scent and her hopes with it.

Rex snuffled loudly and its head swept directly into line with her chest. A low growl shuddered out and it came sauntering toward her, taking its time for the kill.

Alice brought the gun up and aimed shakily for the gaping jaws. She screamed and pulled the trigger three times fast. Two bullets vanished into its mouth, and a third shattered one of its teeth. Rex screamed and veered away, shaking its head and whistling in pain.

Realizing this might be the only chance she got, Alice ran for the foot of the pathway. She raced by the flattened spike wall and pounded up the dusty slope. Thudding footsteps echoed after her. She shot a look over her shoulder just in time to see the rex giving chase. She'd bought herself a few precious seconds. The top of the cliffs loomed ahead. Neil and Jess waved frantically.

Just before she reached them, Neil pushed one of the doors open and pulled Jess through into the village. Alice burst through behind them with the thunder of rex's pursuit loud in her ears.

Villagers swarmed to the gates with weapons raised. They spotted Neil and Jess and shouted at them.

"Over here!" Alice cried, turning sharply to the right and diving into the cover of the bushes along the base of the quarry wall. Neil and Jess came dashing through after her—

Thwip. Thwip, thiwp! Arrows sliced through the underbrush and shattered on the rocks behind them.

And then the rex crashed through the wall, splintering it.

The villagers screamed and shouted at each other. A volley of arrows filled the air. Rex bucked and thrashed under the assault.

Spearmen rushed out in a tight formation, making a wall. But the rex was in too much pain for reason to enter its tiny brain. It charged and trampled the spear wall. Men and women screamed as they died. More arrows whistled out even as the rex stormed their line, snapping up archers two and three at a time. The cries of wounded and dying villagers filled the air.

Alice watched one man trying to crawl away with both his legs missing, leaving a bloody trail in the dirt. Rex stomped on him and ended the struggle before storming another line of spearmen and crashing through a cabin, collapsing the walls and roof.

Scattered archers rained arrows on the massive beast from afar, but most bounced harmlessly off its thick hide.

A group of children emerged from the front door of the collapsed cabin and ran away screaming. Dogs ran in, barking and snapping at rex's ankles.

The beast flicked one away with its tail. The dog yelped sharply and landed hard in the grass before limping away.

Alice felt sick. She couldn't believe the carnage she'd unleashed.

"We need to get out of here," Neil whispered. "Where's the nearest gate?"

Alice was too shocked to reply.

Rushing footsteps heralded someone's approach.

"Look out!" Jess cried, just as they crashed through the bushes.

Alice swung her gun into line with the nearest one—

And almost pulled the trigger.

"It's me!" Layla hissed, pushing the barrel away, and then taking the weapon from her.

Bruce was crouching behind her, looking grim. "Hell of a distraction. Nice work."

But Alice couldn't bring herself to accept his praise.

"The gates!" Neil hissed as the T-Rex came stomping back to the main street and roared once more. "Where do we go?"

Alice recalled the side entrance where she'd almost been captured. "This way," she said, squeezing past Layla and Bruce to follow the foliage back the way she'd come.

The screams of the villagers chased her the whole way, echoing sickeningly in her ears. By the time they reached the gates and Bruce unlocked them, Alice was numb with shock. She followed the others out and up a steep slope into the suffocating shadows of the forest.

An agonized roar split the night, followed by an ominous *thud,* and then ringing silence.

"I think our distraction just ended," Bruce whispered from the front of the group.

"We'd better pick up the pace," Layla added.

But Alice no longer cared what happened to her. Tears slipped quietly down her cheeks. It had seemed like a good idea at the time. Release the monster and let it distract the villagers while they escaped. Somehow, she hadn't considered the consequences of that distraction. The image of those terrified children fleeing their shattered home flashed through her mind. She gritted her teeth and squeezed her eyes shut to make it go away. But the scene only snapped into sharper focus as she remembered that she was a mother with a child of her own. How *could* she?

She was a murderer.

A sharp whistling sound interrupted her self-recriminations. An arrow lodged in a tree just in front of her.

"Take cover!" Bruce yelled.

Something sharp sliced through her shoulder. Alice stared dumbly at the gleaming point of the arrow sticking out above her left breast. "They got me...?" She mumbled stupidly.

And then Layla slammed into her and flattened her to the spongy ground.

Her gun went off—

Pop, pop, pop—

Clack. The slide locked back.

"I'm out!" Layla cried.

"Here they come!" Bruce added.

Layla yanked her back up and shoved her up the hill. "Run!" she screamed.

Alice's mind spun dizzily as she scrambled up the slope. Pain was breaking through the shock, and her shoulder was throbbing painfully. Layla pulled ahead of her, weaving between the trees to avoid getting hit by whistling arrows.

Alice realized she was falling behind. She could hear the pursuing villagers now. Grunting and barking commands at each other as they came rushing up the hill.

"You have to push yourself!" Layla shouted.

Alice tried, but a wave of nausea broke through the pain, and her legs grew weak.

"She's not going to make it!" Layla screamed.

Bruce came crashing back down the hill, caught her by the arm, and dragged her the rest of the way up. They burst into a clearing to see light from the neighboring planets shining brightly on the rippling grass.

"It's too open here!" Bruce cried. "They'll cut us down before we can reach the other side!"

As if to confirm it, an ominous whistling sound split the night.

"Get down!" Bruce said.

Neil and Jess were still stumbling on up ahead.

They ducked into the tall grass, and Alice twisted around in time to see warriors bursting into the light of the clearing—

Only to be cut down by bright crimson beams that buzzed and zapped through the air.

The villagers scattered and fled back into the forest.

"What the hell...?" Bruce muttered. He slowly rose to his feet, gaping at the sight of something big and dark hovering above the field.

Four cylindrical engines were pointing straight down and glowing bright orange as the craft descended. The grass rippled, then blackened as it landed.

Chapter 25

4:11 AM

LAYLA STOOD IN A line with the others, waiting and watching as a landing ramp extended from the boxy black hull of the mysterious craft. Bruce had an arm wrapped around Alice's waist to help her stay on her feet despite the arrow stuck in her shoulder.

"Ready to meet your maker?" Bruce asked, glancing around at the others.

"Maker?" Alice mumbled. "Maker of what?"

That's a good question, Layla thought.

A door opened somewhere above the ramp, and rapid footfalls rang with metallic thunder, approaching quickly.

Layla held her breath and raised her sidearm, releasing the slide catch. She took aim on the ramp. Her gun might be empty, but whoever was coming out didn't know that.

Two humanoid figures in full suits of glossy black armor came rushing down the ramp, each of them holding matching black rifles across their chests. Before they even reached the waist-high grass at the bottom of the ramp, the leader stopped and made a beckoning gesture.

"Hurry!" he said in an amplified voice. "They'll be back soon, and with greater numbers."

It was a human voice, which put Layla's mind at ease. She dropped her aim and slowly let out her breath.

Bruce was the first to snap out of it, leading the way toward the craft. He struggled along with Alice, and Neil likewise with Jess.

Layla noticed that the second armored figure stood watch at the top of the ramp, the rifle casually aimed at the forest where the locals had disappeared.

"Thanks for saving our lives," Bruce said as they reached the armored figure at the bottom of the ramp.

"No problem," the man replied.

That voice tickled her memory. She stopped in front of the man with a frown while the others struggled up the ramp.

"Do I know you?" she asked, while staring into an inscrutable black visor.

"Let's go inside," he replied. "We're too exposed out here."

The voice was even more familiar now, as if each word were another piece of a puzzle that was rapidly coming together in her mind. She didn't need him to answer the question. She *definitely* knew this man.

4:16 AM

THE INSIDE OF THE ship was less alien than the outside, with grated floors, smooth gray walls, and a shadowy black ceiling with recessed lighting. A door slammed shut behind them as soon as they reached the top of the ramp, trapping them in a small antechamber.

Neither of the two armored strangers spoke. Bruce and Neil both looked nervous, waiting to see what would happen next. Jess and Alice were too preoccupied with their respective injuries to wonder much about what was happening. But Layla was highly suspicious. Angry. And bursting with curiosity.

"Who are you?" she demanded of the one who'd spoken to them outside. Her hand flexed restlessly on the grip of her gun.

Another set of doors opened, and the man led them wordlessly inside. Right behind those doors was another vehicle—much smaller and less aerodynamic than the one that contained it. From the windows and the seats she saw inside, Layla assumed it was some type of land vehicle, but it had no wheels, so maybe it was a boat?

To either side of the smaller craft, the walls were gunmetal gray and lined with three padded black seats.

"You should sit," the one with the familiar voice said, pointing to the seats.

Neil, Jess, and Alice did as they were told, but Layla and Bruce followed the two faceless strangers to a windowless cockpit.

There were far fewer displays and controls than what she'd expected to see, and four seats in two rows. The armored men sat in the front row and the one on the left touched a silver button. Buttons and control panels glowed to life. A panel in the minimalist dash slid open and familiar-looking flight controls slid out. The walls and sloping ceiling swirled, becoming transparent. Layla's head spun as the floor appeared to vanish, leaving her with the disconcerting impression of standing on thin air several feet above the dark, grassy field below.

A pleasant chime sounded, and the pilot grabbed the joystick and throttle, then touched a few more buttons.

The craft shivered slightly and engines roared, propelling them swiftly off the ground. But Layla barely felt the movement. The pilot turned them on the spot, and a swath of brightly glowing planets swept into view, illuminating the clouds in strange, shifting patterns of colored light and shadow. Seeing the ground spin away through the transparent floor, both Bruce and Layla fell into the second row of seats. There was plenty of leg room, and the seats were comfortable. Layla fumbled around for a seat belt, but didn't find anything. In the process, her fingers grazed a button on the side of her headrest. A pair of black snakes shot across her chest, crossing each other to form an X across her torso.

Layla blinked in shock and probed at the spongy cords of a safety harness.

Bruce was watching her with a heavy frown. He tore his eyes away to glare at the back of the pilot's seat. "Is someone going to explain what the hell is going on?" Bruce asked. "Who are you two? Did you abduct us?"

The pilot touched another button and then released the flight controls before reaching for something beneath his seat. Mechanisms whirred noisily, and the seat pulled back from the controls before spinning around to face them. The pilot leaned back with his hands folded in his lap. Layla casually aimed her gun at him.

"No, we didn't abduct you," the one with the familiar voice said.

The other man was leaning forward and probing below his own seat as if hunting for the button the pilot had used to turn around. He found it, and his chair spun around, too.

Layla glanced at him.

"My name is Tom Smith," he said.

That name rang a bell...

Layla sucked in a sharp breath as she remembered why, and who this must be. "From Sing Sing?"

The man appeared to hesitate. He tilted his head to one side, regarding her quietly. Then he looked to the pilot. "How does she know about that?"

Bruce looked shocked. "You *know* him?"

"I know *of* him," Layla replied. "I was investigating the disappearance of two convicted felons from a prison in upstate New York. Thomas Smith and Fango Morales."

Tom grew suddenly very still. "You're a cop?" he asked a moment later.

"Detective," Layla clarified. "And you're a convicted murderer."

"Allegedly..." Tom said, but somehow not even he sounded convinced.

"You killed your wife and her lover with a baseball bat. Your fingerprints were all over the murder weapon."

A ragged sigh escaped the man's suit. He reached for his helmet, twisted, and pulled it off, revealing the face of a handsome black man. His eyes were dark and angry. His head shaved.

"My fingerprints were on the bat because it was *my* bat, and I'd played a game with it the night before. And I only found out my wife was cheating on me when police arrested me for her murder. The husband's always the last to know, right?" He scowled. "If you'd even bothered to check the body cam recordings from when I was arrested, you'd see how shocked I was. Either I'm a hell of a good actor, or I'm innocent."

Layla frowned. She hadn't familiarized herself with more than the basic particulars of the case before rushing off to Sing Sing to take witness statements.

"And where is Fango?" she asked.

Tom appeared to freeze, and his expression flickered.

"He disappeared from the prison with you," Layla prompted. "Was he there when you woke up?"

Tom nodded. "But a deinonychus got him a few hours later."

"A *die-non-ikus?*" Bruce asked. "What is that?"

"A giant velociraptor," Tom explained.

"You know about dinosaurs?"

"I'm a paleontologist," Tom explained. "Or I was, before I wound up in prison for a crime I didn't commit."

Silence followed Tom's insistence, as if no one really believed he was innocent.

"If it helps, I can vouch for him," the pilot said.

"No, it doesn't fucking help!" Bruce exploded. "Because I don't know you. And I sure as hell don't trust you."

"Actually you *do* know me. And I saved your life," the pilot pointed out. "Doesn't that get me some credit?"

"You probably also brought me here, so no, it doesn't."

"That's a big assumption."

"You see anyone else around here piloting an alien spaceship?" Bruce challenged. "That gives you the means."

"All that's missing is the motive and the opportunity," Layla added.

"Then who abducted *me?*" the pilot challenged.

"Alice needs help," Neil said suddenly.

Layla turned to see him standing in the open doorway of the cockpit, leaning hard on the jamb.

He looked like a shadow of himself. His wrinkled suit jacket was unbuttoned. The expensive white cotton shirt underneath was filthy with dirt and blood. And Neil's typically orderly black hair was thoroughly mussed with more of the same.

The pilot stood and hurried down the aisle. "Excuse me," he said as he walked by Layla.

Bruce watched him go with a scowl. "Hey! Shouldn't you be flying the ship?"

Layla glanced briefly at the escaped convict and the racing carpet of trees below. The gleaming ribbon of a river appeared, and the ship banked slightly to follow it before leveling out.

Seeing that they weren't about to crash, Layla touched the button beside her headrest, and the harness retracted. She jumped up and tucked her gun into her belt before hurrying after the pilot.

Alice was slumped sideways in the seat next to Jess, who was holding her up by her good arm, keeping her from falling over.

"She's drifting in and out," Jess said as they arrived.

The pilot dropped to his knees and reached into a compartment beneath the seats to withdraw a big black case. He opened it on the floor beside Alice, revealing four fat black cylinders. The pilot flexed one armored hand into a fist, and a sharp blade shot out above his wrist, extending eight or nine inches from his knuckles. It began glowing bright orange, and he used it to slice off the metal head of the wooden arrow.

That done, he opened his fist and the blade retracted. He grabbed the back of the arrow in one hand, and Alice's shoulder with his other. Hesitating, he said, "This is going to hurt."

Alice's eyes fluttered beneath heavy lids, and she mumbled something.

Then the pilot ripped the arrow out, and she roused with a ragged scream. But that burst of energy didn't last more than a second. She sagged toward the floor, and Layla helped Jess catch her. The pilot ripped Alice's shirt to expose the wound on both sides, then removed one of the cylinders from the case and pressed a hidden plunger at the back. Clear fluid sprayed against Alice's wound. Instead of running down along her skin and soaking into her clothes like it should have, the liquid clung to the wound in a shimmering pool. It sank in and the ragged, bloody edges turned silver. The puncture closed before their eyes, leaving a patch of fresh pink skin in its wake.

The pilot repeated the process with the entry wound at the back, and then leaned Alice against the padded seat.

"She needs to rest," the pilot said.

Jess pulled Alice's head into her lap, stroking her sweaty hair. The woman's eyes fluttered open. " Where..." Her gaze flicked around to take in their surroundings. "Where am I?"

"You're safe," the pilot said, returning the cylinder to the case before shutting it and sliding it back into a compartment under the seats.

"What *was* that?" Tom asked.

"Water," the pilot replied.

"I've never seen water do *that.*"

"Because you've never seen *living* water."

Tom swallowed visibly, and nodded. Layla could have sworn he looked scared, but maybe that was just shock.

"Why do I recognize your voice?" Layla asked. She'd already seen the water from that well heal her hand, so Alice's miraculous healing was less mysterious than the identity of the man who'd healed her.

"You do?" the pilot asked, sounding strangely flattered. "After all these years, I didn't think you would. At least, not without seeing my face." He reached up for his helmet, then twisted and removed it as Tom had done.

Layla gasped at the sight of him. Besides the thin white scar snaking down from his forehead to his right eye and the patchy brown beard growing in on his cheeks and upper lip, he was exactly as she remembered him: high, jutting cheek bones. A narrow face with warm hazel eyes. Straight, short brown hair, raggedly cut and matted with sweat.

"Axel?" Bruce managed, finding his voice a split second before Layla did.

"This is impossible," she added.

He smiled crookedly, and Layla's heart gave a familiar flutter. Axel slowly shook his head. "You have no idea how much I've missed you, Lulu."

Chapter 26

4:27 AM

NEIL CALLED AXEL'S ATTENTION to Jess's feet. They were dirty and bleeding after their hasty escape from the village. Axel tended to those injuries with another cannister of the so-called *living water*.

After Axel had revealed his face, Layla's mind was spinning with questions. Nothing was making sense. She had to sit down.

"How did that happen?" Tom asked quietly, nodding to Jess's feet.

"She's been hiking around in socks this whole time," Neil explained. "That, and she fell over a waterfall."

Tom's eyes widened noticeably. "She fell?" he asked. "Was it a long drop?"

"Very," Jess said with a shiver. "I thought for sure I was going to die, but somehow..."

"The water," Axel said. "If you did suffer any injuries, it would have healed them."

"Even a broken neck?" Tom asked.

"You'd be surprised what it can do," Axel replied.

Tom nodded again, wordlessly, and they all watched as Jess's feet were miraculously healed.

"If the water healed her, then how did she hurt her feet?" Tom asked.

"It was after the river," Jess explained. "Running from the natives."

Layla's attention was on Axel. She couldn't tear her eyes away from him.

Tom caught that look and nodded slowly. "Yeah, that's about how I felt. Hasn't aged a day since high school, has he?"

"No," Layla replied. He still looked exactly the same as he had when they'd been dating—except for the patchy beard and the ragged haircut. A young man, barely seventeen years old. Now, twenty-one years later, he could have been her son.

"Relativity," Alice said, as if reading her mind.

Layla nodded.

Bruce looked sharply at Tom. "Wait a second. I thought I recognized you! You went to Middleton High."

Tom frowned. "Yeah, so?"

"So did I! You don't remember me? Bruce Gordon."

Tom slowly shook his head.

"Picture me without the beard. Forty pounds lighter, and twenty-one years younger. I used to go by my middle name. Vic. Short for Victor."

"Damn," Tom muttered. "Yeah, I know you."

That was why Bruce had looked so familiar. Layla hadn't known him personally, but she'd seen him around school. He and Axel used to be friends, but they had a falling out over something before she and Axel had started dating.

As for Thomas... Layla frowned, remembering him vaguely from their school. He'd been a lot skinnier back then and with an afro instead of a shaved head, but his face was still the same. He'd been in grade 10 when she'd graduated. She sifted through twenty-year-old memories, trying to place his name and face in some other context.

One memory snapped into focus: hanging out in Axel's basement one night with some friends from his neighborhood. Bruce hadn't been there, but Thomas had been sitting on the couch with his girlfriend—a petite young girl with short blond hair and light brown eyes.

Layla's gaze drifted over to where Alice lay with her head still cradled in Jess's lap. Alice had been Tom's girlfriend.

Tom smirked. "A real blast from the past, right?"

Layla rounded on Axel who was quietly watching them, waiting for everyone to catch up. "You knew all of us!" she cried.

"Yes," Axel said.

She drew the empty gun from her belt and shook it at him, rattling the slide. "You brought us here!" she accused.

He stepped back, slowly shaking his head. "I swear it wasn't me, Lulu."

"Stop calling me that!" Only Axel had called her Lulu, and it was pissing her off.

"What else should I call you?"

"Detective Bester," she replied. Her chest was rising and falling in quick, shallow breaths. Her nostrils flared. She couldn't see straight.

The corners of Axel's mouth drooped in a frown. "Okay, Detective."

"She's right," Bruce said. "The circumstantial evidence is hard to argue with. Why us? We all knew you before you disappeared."

"It's the only connection," Layla added darkly.

"If you give me a chance, I'll explain," Axel said.

"Speak," Layla growled.

"Are you going to lower your gun?"

She dropped it to her side.

"The Architects brought us here," Axel said.

"Architects?" Bruce asked.

Alice sat up woozily. "Have you seen them?"

Layla regarded her steadily, wondering how much of their conversation she'd overheard. She seemed to be taking Axel's appearance in her stride, as if she'd expected something like this. Maybe Layla should have, too. He'd disappeared without a trace; then twenty-one years later so had his friends. The facts had been staring her in the face.

"Not exactly," Axel replied.

"Is it really you?" Alice added wonderingly.

He smiled crookedly. "It's good to see you, too, Ally."

"You were saying?" Layla prompted. "How did we get here?"

"I told the Architects that I needed help to do my job. That I needed some type of human interaction. Put yourself in my shoes. I've spent seven hundred and fifty-two days alone in this place. They took me away from my friends, my family... my *girlfriend!* Everyone I'd ever known. Poof."

"You *asked* them to bring us here?" Bruce asked, his eyes narrowing sharply.

"No." Axel tapped the side of his head. "They're in my head, so they know everything that I do. They must have taken me too literally when I mentioned my friends and my girlfriend. I was actually asking them to let me interact more with the natives, maybe recruit a few to help me, or maybe even to date one of them, but apparently that's against the rules for a *minder.*"

"A minder?" Neil asked. "What is that?"

"A caretaker," Axel said.

Bruce looked skeptical. "What do you mean they're *inside* your head?"

Axel shrugged. "Man, I don't know. They must have put some kind of implant in my brain when they abducted me. That's also how we communicate. You probably have the same thing. If you haven't heard them speak to you yet, you will."

Layla reached for her scalp, feeling around the back of her head, running her fingers through her hair...

"You won't find anything," Axel said. "Even if they did make an incision, you've seen what the water can do. It'll be long gone."

"Then how did you get that scar?" Layla demanded, pointing to the one on Axel's forehead.

"I got stuck out in the desert, and I had to ration my water."

"What do they want from us?" Alice asked. "You said you're a caretaker? A *minder?*"

"A minder's job is to keep the different species in harmony with each other and the environment."

"Fantastic!" Neil said. "I'd be terrible at that, so you can tell them to send me back. I'm a lawyer, not some fascist environmentalist. And I never knew you."

"Neither did I," Jess added.

"I have to go, too," Alice said. "You have to tell them to send us back. My son and husband are still on Earth, and time is passing much more rapidly for them than it is for me. You said it's been seven hundred days for you?"

"Seven hundred and fifty-two."

"Local days?" Alice pressed.

"Yes."

"And they're four hours each. Six local days to an Earth day... so you've been here... about a hundred and twenty-five regular days. Roughly four months, or a third of a year. I was fifteen when you disappeared. I'm thirty-six now. Twenty-one years to your four months. That means..." Alice trailed off with a furrowed brow, her lips moving silently and her gaze drifting out of focus. Suddenly, her eyes flew wide and snapped into focus. "Time is passing sixty-three times faster on Earth!"

Layla's stomach dropped. Neil swallowed thickly, and Jess looked horrified.

Bruce took a long step toward Axel and grabbed him by the shoulders. "Give your alien buddies a call and tell them that we need to go home. Right.

Now." He added, rapping Axel's skull audibly with his fist.

Axel ducked out of Bruce's grip. "If I could get them to do that, don't you think I would have had them send *me* home a long time ago? No one is allowed to leave the Menagerie System. They bring species here to save them." He blew out a ragged sigh and shook his head. "They never take them back."

"But we don't need saving!" Neil roared.

Axel just looked at him. "The Architects obviously think we do."

A subtle jolt rang through the deck, and Layla noticed that the aircraft had stopped moving.

"Sounds like we've arrived," Axel said. "Come on. I'll show you around your new home."

9:41 PM, November 24th, 2069

"THIS IS IT. THE moment of truth," Preston said. Everyone in the control center sucked in a collective breath as they watched live footage of the Hermes probe shooting out from the nuclear-powered Eagle II Rocket that had carried it to the mouth of the wormhole.

"Timing is good," Julio Acosta said, checking the telemetry from his control station. "We should hit the throat in the middle of the Gateway's oscillation. ETA ninety-eight seconds."

"Real-time?" Preston asked.

"No, sir. ETA is eleven seconds real-time. The rest is the delay to reach us." Even as he said that, an audible countdown began echoing through the control center.

"Ten, nine, eight..."

Preston listened and focused on taking deep, calming breaths. He watched footage from the Eagle rocket. Cameras zoomed in, automatically tracking a vanishing silver speck against the glassy black marble that was the Gateway. Another screen beside the Eagle Rocket's feed showed the footage from Hermes' cameras as it accelerated toward the wormhole. Alien stars shone brightly within an ordinary-looking patch of space, but the shining green planet in the center was a glaring clue that it was far from ordinary. The blue dot that was Planet B's nearest neighbor lay just off to the right. It appeared to be an ocean world with an archipelago of rocky islands.

The countdown continued. "Two, one—*Hermes* has crossed over!"

Nobody dared to applaud or cheer. Silence rang like a bell inside the control center. Everyone's eyes were glued to the curving black wall where they'd pegged their virtual screens.

Preston clasped his hands in front of his mouth, waiting anxiously for the result, which would come 87 seconds later thanks to the time delay.

He could only imagine what secrets they would learn if they could get to the other side of the wormhole. Would they meet the species who had opened the Gateway and built the system of one hundred and twenty planets on the other side? So much was riding on the outcome of this mission.

He heard someone begin speaking in low tones on the far side of the control center. Glancing over there, he spotted a reporter and her camera crew from Global News. This mission was being broadcast live to the entire world via Starlink.

All of that anticipation was about to fall utterly flat if Julio turned out to be right and matter couldn't cross the wormhole.

"Real-time telemetry catching up in five, four, three, two—"

The stars and planets on the other side of the wormhole appeared to flicker ever-so-slightly.

"We have a signal!" Kelsey Hunter, the mission coordinator, cried.

Everyone cheered and burst out of their seats, gawking at the screens in front of them. The footage from the probe's cameras expanded to fill the entire wall. They were looking at the exact same view as they'd seen moments ago. But for them to still be seeing anything at all meant that the probe had survived crossing the throat of the wormhole.

"Are we on the other side?" Preston asked. "What's the status of the passengers?"

Julio tore his eyes away from the screens to check his terminal. He tapped a few keys and scrolled down a list of numbers and data points. "Alice and Rice are... alive and well!" Julio crowed as he pulled up a view from the probe's internal camera. Those were the names Julio had given to the rats on board.

In honor of his missing colleague. The global tally of mysterious disappearances was creeping up on two thousand now. Conspiracy theories abounded, and rightly or wrongly, most of them centered around alien abductions. For once, those ideas didn't seem so far-fetched.

Thanks to the probe's acceleration, the two rats were enjoying simulated gravity that kept them rooted to the floors of their cages. They weren't moving, but they looked fine. Probably just frozen in terror.

Preston grinned and clapped a hand on Julio's shoulder. "What did I tell you? Why else would they put a wormhole here if not to use it? Or to allow *us* to use it."

"They?" Julio turned to regard him with a furrowed brow. "You mean the Watchers?"

"Who else?" Preston asked.

The room was alive with chatter as technicians and engineers remarked loudly on the data. Kelsey Hunter was busy explaining the results in front of the camera crew for the rest of the world to digest.

Preston glanced over there, wondering when they would ask him for a statement. He hated being in the public eye, but it went along with the territory. Especially these days.

Julio began nodding to himself. "Hermes is accelerating to exit the wormhole... wait... that can't be right."

Preston leaned closer to Julio's virtual screens. "What is it?"

"I've got packets dropping!" someone said. "The signal is cutting in and out."

Preston looked up at the camera feeds from the probe. He didn't see anything wrong. The forward screens weren't showing any change, since Hermes was holding course. Then he noticed the footage from inside the probe: both of the rats were still frozen.

"Is the crew okay?" Preston asked.

"Vitals are good. Just not updating. All of the data coming through to our end is getting out of sync."

"Because of the Gateway's oscillation?" Preston suggested. "Every three point six seconds, we lose contact, right?"

"We accounted for that and built in a delay to buffer the data, so that's not it," Julio said. "The only possible explanation..." He trailed off, his jaw slackening and eyes widening. Julio burst out of his chair to check someone else's screens. Preston strode over there, wondering what it was about.

"There!" Julio pointed to his colleague's screen. "See that?"

"The mission clock?" Preston asked. There were two. One was here on Earth. The other on Hermes.

Julio nodded. "To be fair, we expected some time dilation due to gravity."

"Just not *this* much," his colleague added. Preston recognized him by his olive skin and Indian accent, but he still had to scan the man's name with his glasses to remember it—Samar Argawal flashed up above his head.

"How much are we talking?" Preston asked as he studied the mission timers. The seconds were ticking normally on Earth's clock. But Hermes' was frozen. Only the milliseconds were changing, and much slower than they should have been. "Oh, wow..." Preston muttered, realizing just how pronounced the time dilation must be.

"It explains everything," Julio said. "We're not dropping packets. The signal is just arriving later than expected. In fact—" He looked up at the feeds from Hermes, then pointed to the one with the rats on it. "It's not even frozen. Look. They're still moving."

Someone zoomed in on one of the rat's faces, and Preston studied the imagery. He saw Alice's whiskers twitch ever so slightly. Then the rat began turning on the spot. It took a full minute for her to turn around, and another three minutes to reach the water dispenser on the other side of its cage.

"Hermes is clear!" someone announced.

Cheering and excited exclamations rolled through the mission control center.

"What's the time dilation factor?" Julio asked.

"Uhh..." Samar tapped a line of code into his keyboard, then looked up from his screens. "Rounded to the fourth decimal, it's point zero one one seven. Or, about eighty-five times faster here on Earth."

"That's..." Preston trailed off. "What does that mean for *Hermes* and her crew?"

Julio shrugged. "Nothing, really. Time is passing normally to the rats. But to us, they're moving agonizingly slow."

"The rate is dropping, though," Samar said. "The farther we get from the Gateway, the more the time dilation should abate."

"How long before *Hermes* reaches Planet B for its flyby?" Preston asked.

"I don't know. I'd have to calculate how quickly the time dilation factor is dropping, but it could easily be several months for us," Julio said.

"Months," Preston muttered. "We don't have months."

"What do you mean we *don't have* months?" Julio demanded, turning to face Preston with his eyes narrowed to suspicious slits.

"The *Hermes* mission was a success, and that means the follow-up should be, too. There's no need to wait for the probe to reach Planet B."

"We shouldn't get ahead of ourselves," Julio insisted. "There's a lot of work still to be done to ensure that we can duplicate the results with a manned mission."

"We can't just sit on our hands," Preston growled. He gestured to the Global News camera crew. "What do you think the rest of the world is going to do about this?"

Julio frowned and pushed his AR glasses up higher on his nose. "What do you mean?"

"Russia and China have their own missions launching soon. Now that they know the wormhole can be crossed, they'll probably skip straight to preparing manned missions. We're in a new space race, and we can't afford to lose."

Julio ran his hands through his curly hair, scratching furiously at his scalp. The stress was clearly getting to him. "I-I... I guess I just thought that we were all in this together. As a species."

Preston smirked. "What if Planet B is as habitable as it looks? Who gets to colonize it first? Who picks the best spot and stakes their claim to its resources?

This is now a matter of national security. No one was expecting *Hermes* to make it. But now that it has, government agents and Space Force will be swarming this place within the hour."

"But..." Julio trailed off. "There are a hundred and twenty planets! There's more than enough for everyone to explore."

"Why have a piece when you can have the whole pie?" Preston countered.

The clip-clopping of stiletto heels on the polished concrete floors interrupted their conversation.

"Mr. Baylor! How does it feel to prove everyone wrong about the *Hermes* mission?"

Preston pasted a smile on his face and turned to greet a pretty anchorwoman with long legs and bright blue eyes. "It feels like history in the making."

PART THREE: DEADLY ENCOUNTERS

Chapter 27

4:47 AM, September 27

As Axel showed them around the inside of the dam, Bruce couldn't help wondering why the so-called Architects hadn't dropped them off directly here instead of in the middle of that field. It would have saved them a lot of trouble.

The living quarters of the facility seemed familiar and comfortable enough. The temperature was much warmer, too.

Now they sat in the living room, watching through a curtain of spray as the rising sun bathed the valley in a warm orange glow. Bruce nearly drained his third cup of water while quietly contemplating the view.

Axel sat in an armchair beside him, sipping something that looked and smelled exactly like rum. But rum was made from molasses, which required sugar cane. Could sugar cane even grow in this climate?

"Any questions?" Axel asked, speaking into the silence that had fallen over their group.

"About a million," Layla said, frowning at him from the couch where she sat with Alice, Jess, and Neil.

Tom sat by himself, his arms spanning the back of another couch. Both he and Axel were still wearing their armor, but they'd left their helmets and weapons inside the ship—with the exception of a sidearm that Axel had holstered to his hip.

"Go ahead," Axel encouraged between sips of his drink.

"The natives," Alice said, speaking before Layla could. "Who were they?"

"The Jakar," Axel explained.

"But where did they come from?"

Axel blinked at her. "Where else? Earth."

"Do you know when they arrived?"

"No clue, but they must have been here for a long time already to have built their villages."

"Not to mention capturing that T-Rex they made us fight," Bruce said.

"Hold on—" Axel put up a hand. "—they made you fight a T-Rex? And you killed it?"

"We wounded it badly, and then they stopped the fight. How do you think we got these?" Bruce asked, holding out his raptor-claw necklace.

"I don't know, I guess I thought the Jakar were in a good mood when you met them, or that you managed to impress them in some other way. But beating a T-Rex... that really is impressive."

"We almost died," Layla said through a scowl.

"But you didn't," Axel replied.

"If they've been here longer than you, why did the Architects bring you here to make you a minder instead of appointing one of the locals?" Alice asked.

"I don't know."

"You might not be the first," Layla pointed out.

An uneasy look crossed Axel's face. "What do you mean?"

"Maybe there were others before you, but something happened to the previous minder, and they had to find a replacement."

"The skeleton we found," Bruce suggested, and Layla nodded.

"What skeleton?" Axel asked.

"Some bones we found in a cave. The ID in his wallet puts him as being from the nineteen sixties."

"I guess there could have been others," Axel decided. "Does it matter?"

"Maybe," Bruce said. "It means we're replaceable. It might also mean the job is dangerous."

"That ship we flew in on," Alice said. "Can it get into orbit?"

Axel drained his glass and grimaced. "No."

"You're lying," Layla said.

Axel's eyebrows shot up. "What?"

"You don't think I remember your tells? We used to play poker. Every time you were bluffing, you'd take a big sip of your drink."

"Look, I've tried it. The autopilot kicks in and takes it back down. We're not allowed to leave Novus."

"Novus?" Bruce asked.

"That's what the natives called this place. For a good month or two, I was convinced that I'd died and gone to heaven."

Tom smirked and nodded. "Yeah, I thought the same thing."

"I guess anywhere that isn't a nine by five cell would be heaven, wouldn't it?" Layla said.

Tom scowled at her.

"What was your first clue that you hadn't actually died?" Bruce asked.

"Hearing the Architects speak and getting answers from them," Axel replied.

Neil's eyes narrowed. "Are you sure you've been hearing *them?* Maybe you lost your mind after all those months on your own, and now you're hearing voices."

"What did they tell you?" Alice asked.

"Not a lot at first. They told me where to find this place. They also told me to use the water to heal my injuries, and it worked. Then they taught me the native languages, and how to use the spaceships and these suits," Axel patted his armored chest.

"You can speak to the Jakar?" Alice asked.

Axel nodded and uttered a series of grunting, guttural words to prove it.

"What does that mean?" Bruce asked.

"I said, *Hello, I am a friend, and I would like to trade.*"

"You trade with them?" Layla asked.

Axel tipped his glass toward her. "I can't make everything on my own. Agriculture requires land and people to work it, and I need to eat more than just meat."

"What do you give them in exchange?"

"All kinds of things." Axel reached for his waist and opened a rectangular compartment on his belt. He withdrew a curving black raptor claw, like the one that Bruce wore at the end of his necklace. "3D Printed. Looks just like the real thing."

Bruce snorted. "And here I thought they cut them off raptors that they'd actually killed."

Axel shrugged. "The Jakar are superstitious. They think wearing dino claws and teeth gives them a portion of the spirit of whatever creature they came from."

"So they don't just wear them as trophies," Alice said. "They wear them as a talisman."

"Exactly," Axel replied.

Layla held out her necklace, studying it. "I wonder if this one is real."

"Probably. I haven't traded much with that particular village. They're too hostile. The agricultural villages in the valley are a lot more welcoming."

"They're also Jakar?" Alice asked.

Axel nodded. "But the Jakar are not a unified group. They fight amongst themselves all the time. There are only two distinct human groups in Novus—well, besides us—and the Jakar is the oldest one."

"What's the other one?" Bruce asked, his mind flashing back to the skeleton in the cave.

"The Novians," Axel said. "They speak English. They have a relatively small settlement on an island a few hours' flight from here. They all seem to be from the 1960s—like the skeleton you found. That's how I figured out that time was passing slower here.

I mean... that's about a hundred years ago, and they seem to think they've only been here for a year and a half."

"Sounds right," Alice said. "We have to visit them and find out what they know."

"I wouldn't recommend that," Axel said, shaking his head. "The last time I went, they ambushed me and tried to steal my ship."

"There's more of us now," Tom said. "I'm sure we could fend them off."

"What's the point?" Neil asked. "They're obviously stranded here the same as we are. Worse! They're stuck on an island."

"Neil is right," Axel said. "They can't help us. And they're barely getting by themselves. It's sad to visit and see how much they're struggling."

"Why don't you help them?" Alice asked, glancing around. "This place..."

"Isn't nearly big enough to house them all," Axel explained, shaking his head. "There are about five hundred Novians."

"How long has it been since you last saw them?" Layla asked.

"Maybe..." Axel appeared to think about it. "A few hundred local days."

"A month or two of Earth days," Alice decided. "In our frame of reference, anyway. Based on what you're saying, we should at least go see if they're still alive. And if so, maybe we can help. Isn't that what a minder is supposed to do?"

Axel frowned. "No. We're not meant to interfere unless a species is in danger of going extinct."

"But they might be!" Alice insisted.

"Even if *they* are, the Jakar are doing just fine. And we're all human. One group lives, the other dies, but the human race goes on."

"How can you be so cold?" Layla demanded.

Axel shot to his feet and placed his palm against the center of his chest. A panel glowed to life, and the suit clicked and whirred as it splayed open. He stepped out wearing a skintight black jumpsuit. The armor remained standing behind him like some kind of mechanical statue. Axel held up his right hand, revealing a missing pinky finger.

"When I told them I couldn't fly them home, they thought I was lying, and they cut it off. And that was after burning my face with hot coals. If it weren't for the water, you might not have even recognized me when I removed my helmet."

Layla gaped at him and slowly shook her head. "They tortured you."

Axel nodded gravely and a muscle jerked in his cheek.

"Is there anything to eat around here?" Jess asked. "I'm starving."

"Me, too," Neil added.

"The Jakar didn't feed you?" Bruce asked.

"No," Neil replied, and Jess shook her head.

"I'll show you to the kitchen," Axel said.

Neil and Jess stood up. She was still barefoot, but at least her feet were no longer swollen and bloody.

"What about us?" Layla called after Axel.

He spun around, walking backwards toward the kitchen. "Make yourselves at home. Pick a room. The doors are all open except for mine."

Bruce sighed and eased out of his chair, following Axel. The bedrooms were in that direction, between the living room and the combined kitchen and dining area. Bruce wasn't hungry thanks to the Jakar's hospitality, but now seemed like a good time to finally get some rest. Up until now—with the ridiculously short days, and the prehistoric monsters lurking in the forests—getting a good night's sleep had been a fantasy.

Rapid footfalls indicated someone following him. Bruce stopped and turned to see Layla running to catch up. "Wait for me," she said, smiling briefly.

He smiled wanly back and then continued on his way.

"We need to watch our backs around Tom," Layla whispered.

"And if he's innocent?" Bruce whispered back.

"He's not. Murder wasn't even his first conviction. Assault before that. He beat some guy in a bar for hitting on his wife. Does that sound like a pattern to you?"

Bruce glanced back with a frown to see Tom and Alice leaning toward each other, already deep in conversation.

"A smoking gun, maybe," Bruce admitted.

"You think?" Layla said. "Axel used to tell me stories about him. He had one hell of a temper."

"Then why isn't Alice afraid of him?" Bruce asked. "Didn't they used to date?"

"You knew them?" Layla asked.

Bruce shook his head. "Not really. Axel and I had stopped hanging out by then. But I saw them around school."

"Just be careful until we know more."

"I'll sleep with one eye open," Bruce agreed as he passed through the sliding door to the bedrooms.

Chapter 28

1:04 PM

ALICE AWOKE TO THE sound of someone screaming. A moment later she realized it was her. She'd been dreaming of that T-Rex massacring the village again.

Guilt and sorrow tore through her as she lay awake and blinking at the hazy ceiling, hoping she hadn't woken anyone else. She rolled over to face the window beside her bed. A chair sat beneath the window. An inviting space to read a book, if only she had one.

It was utterly dark in the room, but recessed lights were busy swelling around the edges of the ceiling, and the window was gradually going from opaque and black to clear. She remembered wishing there were curtains just before she'd laid down to sleep, and the window had promptly tinted itself in response, as if this facility were somehow able to sense her needs. The same thing had happened when she'd tried to lock her door—just in case Tom wasn't as innocent as he claimed, or Axel turned out to be an alien in disguise.

Alice sat up and swung her feet over the edge of the bed, her attention on the view. Water was no longer pouring from above, leaving the window clear and bright with an unobstructed view of the verdant forests, grassy clearings, and the snaking river to the ocean beyond. A bright blue sky stretched above it all.

It was day. But what time of day? She checked her watch. Glowing blue numbers flicked on.

1:04 PM.

Still the 27th. After showering and changing it had been almost six in the morning, so she'd slept for about seven hours. Checking the *sleep* app in her watch, she saw that it had recorded six hours and fifty-two minutes.

She got up and stretched, then walked to the bathroom in the formfitting two-piece black jumpsuit that she'd found in the room's tiny closet. There'd been underwear and socks, too, all made of the same black, resinous material. The clothes were all somehow exactly the right size for her—or maybe the material was just that stretchy.

Alice sat on a familiar-looking toilet—black, of course. It was metal, not ceramic, but the seat was surprisingly warm to the touch. Heated like the floors? she wondered.

There wasn't any toilet paper, but when she was done, a warm spray shot up from the bowl and scared her to her feet. The spray stopped the instant she stood up, and a heated blast of air followed. She sat back down, allowing it to dry her.

The Architects must be Europeans, she thought with a crooked smile.

The toilet flushed itself, and Alice pulled her pants back up. She found herself staring at her haggard reflection in the mirror. At least her face was relatively clean after the shower she'd taken, but she had dark circles under her eyes. No make-up. And her teeth felt furry beneath her tongue.

She hunted around for a toothbrush, but didn't find one.

The extent of the toiletries were an off-white bar of soap like the one she'd used in the shower before climbing into bed, an empty glass beside the sink, and a black paste in a square glass container that looked like it might have charcoal as an active ingredient.

Alice wondered if she was supposed to use that paste to clean her teeth. She was tempted to try, but decided it wasn't worth the risk of poisoning herself.

Seeing how greasy her hair still was, she decided to strip down and take another shower. A rough rock wall divided it from the toilet and kept the water from spraying out.

The floor was bumpy and made of smooth, colorful river rocks. Alice looked up at the big silver grate in the ceiling, and thought about turning on the water. A dense spray gushed out, warm but not hot. She luxuriated in the shower for a moment, letting it ease away the lingering aches and pains from the day before. It was just the right pressure and temperature. Water trickled away into a matching grate at her feet.

A full length window looked directly out over the river valley. Alice stood admiring the view while she scrubbed herself with a lumpy yellow-white bar of soap. She managed to work up a lather and clean her hair with it, too. When she was done, she stood for a few extra minutes, tracing the winding river through the forested valley to a delta and what looked like an ocean.

She realized how little of Planet B they'd actually explored so far. Now that they'd met Axel and learned that he had access to those aircraft, maybe they could get him to take them on a tour. And maybe, she could also get Axel to demonstrate the autopilot that supposedly kicks in if they try to leave the atmosphere. Maybe she could find a way to disable it so they could get home.

A painful knot formed in Alice's throat as she thought about her husband and son. What did they think had happened to her?

Alice squeezed her eyes shut to ward off the tears. It didn't work, but the shower washed them away. Feeling suddenly numb and hollow, Alice shut off the water with a thought.

The two big grates to either side roared to life, blasting her dry with hot air. She stood over the spot and slowly turned, letting the gusting air dry her whole body and mostly dry her hair before stepping out of the shower.

As familiar as the accommodations in this place might be, it was more advanced than any home Alice had ever lived in on Earth. But not to the point that it felt *alien.* Except for the way that everything seemed to respond directly to her thoughts and needs.

Alice shivered as she stepped out of the shower, but not from the cold. Something Axel had said echoed through her mind. The Architects must have implanted something in their brains. How else could this place be responding to her every whim?

She hurried to get dressed and leave her room. The door unlocked itself with a *thunk* and slid open as she approached. Feeling even more nervous now, she strode quickly to Axel's room at the end of the hall and knocked on the door, the one with a glowing number 1 on it. Hers was room 3.

"Axel is in the dining area," a pleasant female voice said.

Alice flinched at the sound of it and hurried for the door to the kitchen at the opposite end of the corridor. It slid open as she approached, revealing everyone already seated around the dining table, eating breakfast.

"You're up!" Axel said rising from the head of the table to greet her with a smile. "Come, have some breakfast. I made steak and eggs."

"Dino steak," Bruce clarified, and he exaggerated his chewing before swallowing thickly. "Stick to the eggs if I were you."

Alice sat beside Layla at the foot of the table. She poured herself a glass of water from a pitcher while Tom stood up beside Axel to serve her a plate of eggs. He hesitated with his eyebrows raised and a big fork poised above a platter of rare-looking meat.

Alice shook her head. "No, thanks." He slid the plate over, and she dug in with a black fork. When she took a sip of the water, it began fizzing inside her mouth, and she almost spat it out.

Bruce laughed. "I had the same reaction."

"It's cleaning your teeth," Axel explained.

Alice swished the water around for a few seconds before swallowing. "I guess that explains why there wasn't a toothbrush in my room."

Axel smiled and sipped his own water.

Everyone went back to eating. Bruce finished first and propped his elbows up on the table, watching Axel. "I guess it's our first official day on the job. What's on the agenda?"

Axel stood up and began collecting dirty dishes. "Mind helping me out, Lulu?"

Layla scowled. "I told you—"

"Layla," Axel said, correcting himself.

"Okay," she agreed.

"You didn't answer my question," Bruce pointed out, twisting around to watch as they rinsed dishes in the sink and stacked them in a familiar-looking dishwasher.

"No agenda," Axel replied. "Species aren't exactly threatening to go extinct every day."

"Then what do you do around here?" Alice asked.

Axel gave her a knowing look. "Now you know why I told the Architects that I needed some company."

Bruce grunted and crossed his arms over his chest. "Thanks a lot."

"There has to be some way to leave," Neil muttered.

"The ships..." Alice said slowly, while pushing the rest of her eggs around with her fork. "If we can figure out how the autopilot works, maybe we can find a way disable it."

Axel fixed them with a scowl. "I told you. We're not allowed to leave. Even if we could disable the autopilot, the Architects would find another way to stop us. Besides, do *you* know how to manually fly us back to Earth from here?"

Alice frowned. "I'm sure I could figure it out."

Layla came to take her dirty dishes. "I didn't see a lot of controls in the cockpit," she said. "The ships must be automated."

"They are," Axel confirmed.

"So if we disable the autopilot, we might crash," Bruce concluded.

"We can't just give up!" Jess exploded. She was sitting between Layla's empty seat and Neil, facing the view.

"We don't have a choice," Axel replied. He finished stacking the dishwasher and sat back down at the head of the table. Everyone stared expectantly at him, as if he were secretly holding out on them.

"Don't look at me," Axel said. "I didn't bring you here."

"Actually, you kinda did," Bruce replied. "By telling the people that run this place how sad and lonely you were."

Axel scowled at him. "It wasn't like that, Vic. They're in my head. I didn't tell them anything! They were responding to my thoughts."

"It's Bruce. Not Vic."

"Whatever!" Axel exploded. "You know what, go ahead. Go down to the hangar. Tinker around with the ships. See what you can figure out. And if you *do* find a way home, sign me up."

Uncertainty creeped in at the edges of Alice's thoughts, and no one spoke for several seconds.

"The elevator," Tom said quietly.

"What?" Axel asked.

Tom looked down to Alice's end of the table, and she felt an old, familiar flutter as his eyes bored into hers.

"Ally, do you remember the options on the panel inside?"

She thought back, closing her eyes and struggling to remember. She'd been so distracted when they'd arrived that she'd barely glanced at the touchscreen inside the elevator. "No," she decided.

"There are ten levels. Nine sub levels. The bottom one was labeled *Gateway*."

Suddenly all eyes were back on Axel. He was shaking his head. "I know what you're thinking, but I've never been there. The elevators won't go to that floor, and the bottom of the stairwell is locked.

"And you haven't even tried to get in?"

"Are you kidding?" Axel snapped. "I spent weeks trying to cut through that door!"

"Show us," Bruce said.

"All right." Axel shot to his feet, looking frustrated and offended by their mistrust. "Let's go."

Chapter 29

1:37 PM

"It's no use," Bruce said, stepping back from the oily black door and shaking his head. Everyone else was watching from the flight of stairs above. The barrel of the rifle in Bruce's hands was glowing red-hot, and the blue number on the back now read 0. He'd shot the door forty-five times, trying to blow a hole in it so that they'd have something to hold onto or at least to stick a lever through and pry it open. On its lowermost level, the door and the stairwell was made entirely of that strange black alloy, and apparently, it was impenetrable—at least to lasers anyway.

"There has to be another way in," Neil insisted.

"Yeah, like what?" Axel asked.

"Like... we cut a hole through the floor of an elevator and climb down."

"Tried it," Axel said.

"Did it work?" Jess asked.

"Sure. Then I got to the bottom and found another door like this one blocking the way."

"What about the floor above us?" Tom asked from where he stood on the landing behind Bruce.

"The bunker," Axel said. "The whole floor is made of the same material. As far as I can tell it's impenetrable."

"Nothing's impenetrable," Bruce said. "What about that shop we saw on our way in? Do you have cutting tools? Anything that allows you to work with this stuff?" He pointed to the door.

"Just regular drills, saws, and welding torches. They work on ordinary metal, but not whatever this is."

"Great..." Bruce muttered. "Mind if I take a look, anyway?"

"Be my guest," Axel replied, stepping aside so Bruce could head up the stairs.

"Can you give us a tour?" Alice asked as the others followed him up.

"We already did that," Axel replied.

"No, an aerial tour. In one of the ships."

"Oh, sure, I can do that."

"Good idea," Layla added. "If we're going to be here a while, we should at least get some idea of what's around us."

Nothing but trees and dinosaurs, Bruce thought bitterly.

Somehow, these *Architects* had managed to take all the fun out of living off the grid. Choosing to live away from people and being *forced* to do so were two very different things.

2:16 PM

Alice sat in the co-pilot's seat watching the forests scroll by through the transparent walls and floor. She wondered what kind of meta materials the ship must be made from to accomplish that feat. When she ran her hands over them, she felt that the walls were cold and slippery. Her fingertips left greasy smudges, but even those quickly vanished. Besides their seats and the narrow section of the dash with the controls Axel was using to fly, there was no hint of the vehicle that carried them.

"Not for the weak of stomach," Tom muttered. He was standing in the aisle with Layla and Bruce, leaving Jess and Neil to sit in the other two chairs.

"You get used to it," Axel said.

A break in the trees appeared up ahead, and Axel hauled back on the throttle, leaving them to hover above a familiar-looking village with wooden walls and cabins. The chaos wrought by the T-Rex was still evident. Cabins were shattered. Rex lay dead in the middle of the street, the dirt stained dark red around him. Not far from there, a charred pile of human bodies lay smoking on the main road. A group of villagers was assembled beside the smoking funeral pyre with someone standing before them, giving a speech. They thrust their weapons into the air, responding to something that their leader was saying.

Alice's guts churned with guilt and horror as Axel flew them in closer. She gripped the armrests of her chair in white-knuckled fists.

"They can't see us?" Bruce asked.

"No, the ship is invisible right now," Axel explained. "Helps me to do my job without drawing too much attention."

Axel glanced at Alice. He was wearing his suit again, but not the helmet. His narrow face pinched into a frown, and his hazel eyes hardened with concern. "Are you okay?"

Alice shook her head. "Why did you bring us back here?" she asked in a small, cracking voice.

"I needed to see what the Jakar are up to. They know me and where I live. As I suspected, they're getting ready for war."

"Can they get into the dam?" Tom asked. "It seemed to be locked up tight, and the entrance from the gantry is made of the same black metal as that door we tried to blast through in the stairwell."

"They've never made a determined effort to get in before," Axel said. "But you're right. It's probably not an issue. And we have the advantage of air support and our armor and weapons."

"Speak for yourself," Bruce muttered.

He and Layla had wanted to put the suits on before they left, but Axel had said it would take too long, and they needed to take advantage of the daylight if they wanted to see anything from the air.

Alice's gaze settled on the char-blackened pile of bodies again, and she found herself counting the pairs of arms and legs. She stopped when she reached ten, and looked away. "Let's go. Please."

"Okay." Axel pushed the throttle up and sped away.

"It's not your fault," Layla said quietly, stepping forward and laying a hand on Alice's shoulder. "Who knows what they would have done to Jess and Neil if you hadn't done what you did. Besides, they subjected us to the T-Rex first. Do unto others, right? They broke the golden rule."

Alice grimaced. "So you're saying they got what they deserved?"

"No, I'm saying Karma's a bitch."

"Can we change the topic?" she asked, scanning the scenery. If it weren't for their history with this particular village, and the destruction they had caused, Alice would have enjoyed the view. The Jakar had built their settlement on a plateau above the quarry and the reservoir, and it looked idyllic from the air.

"What about the other villages you mentioned?" Bruce asked.

"Similar to the one you saw, but the people are friendlier." Axel flew back down from the forested mountain. The lake swept beneath them, sparkling in the fading light of the sun. It slipped behind the black hole, dimming and turning to a glowing ring before oozing back out on the other side.

Alice studied the sheer, snow-capped mountains on the other side of the lake. Axel was flying straight for them. He pulled up hard to climb over the top. Dark clouds enveloped them as they crossed the jagged peaks. Pristine white glaciers rolled by below, peeking through misty cracks in the clouds. Rain pitter-pattered against the hull, smearing the transparent walls with racing rivulets of water.

Axel dove sharply on the other side of the mountains. Glaciers gave way to forests and bright green fields. A herd of familiar, elephantine creatures with massive tusks was grazing in one of those fields.

"Are those woolly mammoths?" Tom asked, sounding shocked.

"What else would they be?" Axel replied.

Layla pointed over Alice's shoulder, into the distance. "And those?"

"Sauropods," Tom breathed.

The lowlands on the other side of the mountains were more open, with the forests broken by vast, grassy plains, gleaming lakes, and broad, snaking rivers.

The long-necked dinosaurs slowly lumbering through the lakes and the fields around those forests were the largest creatures Alice had ever seen.

Axel flew in close to a herd of two adults and one calf. The adults were at least three times as tall as any giraffe. They were busy grazing on the broad leaves at the top of deciduous forests this side of the mountains.

Alice watched them walk, massive muscles rippling beneath their thick tan and brown hides.

"Brontosauruses?" Neil suggested.

"Looks like it," Tom replied.

Axel slowly turned them on the spot, aiming the nose of the craft at a snaking river and the gleaming shore of a lake. Dozens of different species gathered in groups along the edges of the water: stegosauruses, ankylosauruses, triceratops, and a few others that Alice didn't recognize.

A muffled roar sounded, and Axel glanced at a screen with colored blips on it. Some type of radar. He turned them back the other way, just in time to see a pair of T-Rexes burst out of the forest where the brontosaurs were grazing. They vectored in on the calf from two different sides. It had wandered too far from its parents and had its back turned to them while feeding on a clump of smaller saplings.

The two adults reacted instantly, charging after the predators and sweeping their tails. One rex stumbled and almost tripped as the tail caught its feet.

The brontosaurs bellowed a warning to their calf. It reacted belatedly by turning to face them and the two advancing predators.

"We have to do something!" Layla cried.

"We can't interfere," Axel whispered. "T-Rex has a right to live, too."

The Rexes reached their target at almost the same time. One of them snapped its neck, while the other grabbed a thigh. The adult brontosaurs screamed and ran faster while the rexes fled with their kill. The brontos slowed to a trot and turned away.

"Hell of a nature show," Bruce muttered.

"Why did you show us this?" Layla asked, wiping tears from her cheeks.

Alice felt sick.

Axel shook his head. "Sorry. Obviously, I didn't plan it."

"But you stopped to watch," Layla accused.

"I wasn't thinking. I guess I'm desensitized." He pushed the throttle up and went racing past the Rexes, who had stopped running so that they could eat. A flock of pterodactyls had formed overhead, circling like vultures above them. The gory details blurred against the green fields as they flew by. Then came the lake, with more brontos and other herbivores strolling peacefully along the pebbled shore.

Silence reigned inside the cockpit.

"So that's it?" Jess asked, breaking the quiet. "A whole planet full of nothing but dinosaurs?"

"Them, and any other species that's already extinct on Earth," Tom suggested. "The mammoths we saw in the mountains, for example."

"We also saw Neanderthals," Bruce pointed out.

"Did you?" Axel asked. "I'm surprised. They're quite shy. I've only seen them a handful of times myself."

"Shy, or scared?" Neil asked. "Imagine if you were a caveman living in this place. At least you have a proper shelter, guns, and armor. But what about them?"

"Good point," Axel said.

"You never answered my question," Jess added. "Isn't there anything else to see around here?"

"Like what?"

"I don't know! A city. Some kind of civilization. What about the Architects? Don't they live here, too?"

Alice's curiosity was pricked by that question. She looked to Axel for his response.

"No," he replied, dashing her hopes of finding and appealing to the real caretakers of Planet B. "But there is something that you might be interested in seeing."

"And that is?" Jess asked.

"It would be better if I showed you."

Chapter 30

1:36 PM, December 21th, 2069

PRESTON STOOD AT THE bottom of the launch tower beside the *Emissary* with the afternoon sun beaming down on his white pressure suit. In front of him was a Global News camera crew and Amanda Hayes, the blue-eyed, blonde-haired anchorwoman who'd covered the story of the *Hermes* mission. Now she was back for the *Emissary's* launch. Preston might have invited her out to dinner again if he weren't already planning to eat it in space. He smiled broadly for the camera with his helmet tucked under one arm.

"What do you have to say to the shareholders of SDG?" Amanda asked. "People are worried that you won't survive this trip. You've been called reckless. A maverick. Why risk your own life?"

"I'll tell my detractors the same thing that I told my crew and General Ryker when they signed on:

you don't get to where I have without taking risks. Big risks equal big rewards."

"And what kind of reward do you expect to find on Planet B?"

Preston smiled winningly. "Think about that name for a minute—Planet *B*. That says it all. Earth is in trouble, and it's only getting worse. What do I expect to find? I don't know. But I *hope* to find that Planet B really is as habitable as it appears, and that we can start sending colonists over ASAP."

"What about the Russian and Chinese missions? Are you aware that they're waiting for you to cross the Gateway before they schedule their own launches?"

"I am aware, and all I can say is that history remembers who was first, not who was second and third, and America is going to make history again. We were the first to put boots on the moon, and we'll be the first to set foot on Planet B, too. But make no mistake, this is a triumph for *all* of humanity. And everyone is going to reap the benefits."

"Is there anything you'd like to say to Apokalypsis?"

"No, because I deal in facts, not fear-mongering and ancient prophecies. This is not the end. It's a new beginning."

"What about the abductions? Where do you think all of those people went? Is this the rapture as some people are saying?"

Preston frowned. This interview was going off the rails. "If it's the rapture, then why are only a few thousand people missing?" He raised his watch to check the mission clock. They were coming up on

T minus thirty minutes. "I'm afraid that's all the time I have. No further comments."

"Mr. Baylor!" Amanda called after him as he turned and strode for the elevator in the base of the launch tower. "Just one more question!"

Preston heard her chasing him. The two Space Force corporals standing by the elevator bristled, their postures shifting and weapon barrels rising by a couple of inches.

"What happens if the *Emissary* does make first contact?" Amanda asked.

"Then General Ryker and Ambassador Jansen take over. I'm not authorized to say anything to an actual ETI. But if I could, then I'd say *thank you.*"

"Thank you?" Amanda asked.

"Earth is dying, so they threw us a life preserver. A hundred and twenty of them, to be precise. I'd say that warrants our gratitude, wouldn't you?"

Preston waved the elevator open and stepped through sideways while the gate was still rattling open. He shut the door right after that, silencing whatever follow-up questions Amanda Hayes might have asked.

He rode the elevator up past the gleaming hull of the Extra Heavy Booster to the cockpit of the Voyager Starship. The rest of the crew was already on board, including Ambassador Jansen from Brussels and General Ryker of Space Force with a fire team of crack operatives.

Their mission had been thoroughly vetted and endorsed by both the EU and the North American Union, as well as in passing by a handful of other space-faring countries who wanted their names attached to the *Emissary*. As far as Preston understood it, the general and his men were not authorized to open fire on ETI, not even in self-defense. But they were still bringing multiple cases of weapons and ammo to deal with any non-intelligent lifeforms that the mission might encounter.

Russia and China, of course, had not been consulted during any of the planning or crew assignments. Despite an initial attempt to include them, they'd both decided to put together their own missions with their own protocols for first contact and colonization.

Preston grimaced as he remembered sitting in on that conference call with presidents of the EU, NAU, Russia, and China. The former two unions had been attempting to browbeat the latter two nations into signing off on a set of 'global' interests that almost entirely favored the West.

Preston could have predicted that they would ultimately decide to go it alone—and that they would choose to ride the SDG's coattails through the Gateway.

The elevator stopped and Preston stepped out, walking down the gantry to the Voyager Starship at the end. The outer hatch swiveled open with his approach and Commander Anderson popped his head out.

"Good to have you on board, sir," the commander said as Preston ducked through the opening.

"It's good to be here," Preston replied. "What's our status?"

"We were just running through the final checks now," Anderson said as he shut and locked the outer door. "All systems green. You'd better get settled in your jumpseat, sir."

"I know the way," Preston said, pushing down the lever to open the inner airlock door. It swung wide into a large cargo and maintenance area. Preston walked halfway around the circular deck to reach the access ladder. From there he climbed up to the hatch to the crew deck.

The crew was already seated in a ring of deployable jumpseats around the circumference of the deck. Each of them faced the outer wall, with their seat backs reclined all the way to the floor so that they could lie down to better endure the G-forces. Preston went straight to the nearest empty seat and folded it out, being careful to make sure that the locking bolts clicked into place before sitting down. Moments later he was fully reclined and lying down beside the ambassador.

Jansen nodded and offered a tight smile. Preston smiled back as he slipped on his helmet. He dropped the visor and activated a series of virtual screens via his heads-up-display. He set most of those screens to views from the ship's various external cameras. Steam billowed from vents along the length of the booster. The sky was clear and blue above, with the sun at its zenith.

Preston set his helmet comms to the mission control channel and listened in as Commander Jake Anderson and his co-pilot, Lieutenant Sara Young, went through their final systems checks from the cockpit. Every now and then Dr. Julio Acosta chimed in to update them on the status of the Gateway. The wormhole was still oscillating every three point six seconds.

The time to launch ticked down rapidly. Preston listened past the comms to the ambient chatter from General Ryker and his soldiers.

"T-minus thirty seconds," mission control announced.

"All systems nominal," Commander Anderson replied. "Booster is pressurized. Closing vents now. Flight, we are go for launch. Repeat, we are go for launch."

"T-minus twenty seconds," control added.

"Copy that, *Emissary.*" Preston recognized the voice of Chief Flight Director, Eileen Voss. "Begin ignition sequence now."

"Copy, starting ignition," Anderson replied.

Preston felt a rumbling roar building through his seat, starting from deep within the massive rocket. The Voyager Starship began shivering and shaking violently as the roaring of the thrusters reached a crescendo.

Mission control continued its audible countdown: "Five, four, three, two—and liftoff!"

The thrusters blasted at full force, and Preston felt himself pinned by an invisible elephant sitting on his chest. His guts pressed flat against his spine, triggering spasms as his diaphragm struggled to keep him breathing. His vision grew dim and hazy. The *Emissary* rattled and shook violently, threatening to tear itself apart. Chatter went back and forth between mission control and the crew, making Preston wonder if he was the only one suffering from the intense acceleration.

And then, what seemed like just a few moments later, he was blinking up at his screens, watching as blue sky turned to black. A sharp jolt kicked through the deck, and then the roaring vibrations from the thrusters vanished with a sudden, ringing silence, followed by the stomach-churning sensation of weightlessness.

Preston sucked in a deep breath and his vision rapidly cleared. He worked hard to hold onto his lunch. He'd deliberately eaten a light meal in preparation for this. It wasn't his first time in space, so he knew how disorienting and nauseating the transition to zero-G could be.

A cheer went up from the soldiers. "Hooah!"

"Hoo-ah," General Ryker agreed, and glanced around with a growing smile.

Ambassador Jansen appeared to be conducting an invisible orchestra, his arms floating weightlessly in front of him. He looked a shade paler than before, but steady enough. He had gone through a brief, but intense training program back on Earth, which included zero-G practice, so they already knew that he wouldn't throw up the minute they reached orbit.

And as it happened, that was an important thing to know. Space vomit had an annoying habit of floating around in spinning globules that would splash and ricochet across absolutely everything and everyone.

A subtle vibration rumbled through the deck, and some semblance of gravity returned as the maneuvering thrusters kicked in. "Control, we have reached orbit," Commander Anderson said. "Beginning docking operation now."

Preston watched via his screens as they drifted toward the giant, reusable Eagle II nuclear rocket that SDG kept in a permanent orbit for their missions to Mars and the belt. A pair of conventional, Max Heavy Boosters were also waiting nearby. They had already been fueled up and sent over from the depot on the Moon. In order to reach Planet B, land, and then still take off again for the return trip, they needed a booster just like the one they'd used to lift off from Earth. Fortunately, thanks to the colony on Mars, they already had a system in place for manned surface missions to other planets.

This landing was a lot more challenging, however, due to the much higher surface gravity expected on Planet B versus Mars. According to Dr. Acosta and his research team, Planet B had anywhere from 0.83 to 1.18 times of Earth's gravity. Hence *two* boosters. They'd need to stack them both if surface gravity turned out to be stronger than Earth's.

Preston let out a shaky breath and settled in for the long, tedious docking operations with the Eagle Rocket and boosters.

An hour and twelve minutes later, everyone was cheering again, and mission control was ecstatic. They'd done it.

"Course set, we are on our way, Control!" Commander Anderson reported.

"Copy that, *Emissary*. Good luck and Godspeed."

Preston smiled. Next stop Planet B! But his good mood was dulled by the look on Ambassador Jansen's lined, age-spotted face. His visor was up, making it easy to see his knitted brow and blue eyes cradled deep within their crow's feet. He was watching their progress on the physical viewscreen in the ceiling of the crew compartment, which conveyed the view from the forward cameras.

"Is something wrong, Ambassador?" Preston asked.

He nodded slowly. "I can't help feeling like this is a mistake."

"Don't worry. We double and triple checked our data. We can definitely make it to the other side. *Hermes* did it, and so can we."

"Oh, I believe you," Ambassador Jansen replied. "That's not the problem."

"Then what is?"

The Ambassador looked straight at him. "The Watchers. They're baiting us, and we're chasing the proverbial carrot right down the rabbit hole."

Preston frowned. "That's a decidedly negative way to look at things."

"Is it? Then where are they? Why not introduce themselves and explain their motives? If they can open wormholes and build solar systems, communicating with us should be child's play. So why are they keeping us in the dark? And why are they abducting people from Earth? Where are they taking them?"

"Maybe it's not them," Preston said.

"Then that is even more troubling, because it means we're dealing with more than one advanced alien civilization."

"I'm with the ambassador," General Ryker grumbled. "I've stopped counting the ways this could all go to hell."

Preston smiled tightly. "Well, it's nice to hear how positive everyone is."

"Got to manage those expectations, Mr. Baylor," Ryker said. "We all know what we signed on for. We said our goodbyes already."

Preston worked hard to control his growing irritation. This mission might have been funded by the nations who had endorsed it and contributed to its crew, but all the hardware belonged to SDG, and if the *Emissary* didn't return, stock prices would tank, paving the way for their competitors to surpass them in the increasingly competitive field of space exploration and development.

Not to mention that I'll be dead, and I won't have to worry about stock prices or competition, Preston thought.

He'd bet a lot more than just his company's future on this venture. Maybe people were right. Maybe he was being reckless. But it wouldn't be the first time he'd proved the naysayers wrong. Confidence trickled back in, and excitement overtook apprehension. He would return to Earth, and he would return triumphant, having planted flags in the dirt of a new world. Reams of colonists would follow, and SDG would be the company to take them there.

Chapter 31

2:59 PM

THE SUN WAS SETTING over the water as Axel flew above the ruins of a coastal city that looked like it had come straight out of Medieval times.

"What is this?" Bruce asked, scanning the crumbling stone walls atop the cliffs.

"Just what it looks like—an abandoned city," Axel explained.

Alice shifted nervously in the co-pilot's seat. "Jakar?"

"No," Axel replied, then appeared to hesitate. "At least, I don't think so. Seems like their tech levels were slightly more advanced, or at least their architecture was."

"Could be a divergent group," Tom said. "Assuming the Jakar have been here for..." Tom trailed off. "A *long* time, as you say, it's possible that some of their settlements progressed at different rates and developed their own socioeconomic groups."

"So why is it abandoned?" Layla asked from where she stood beside Bruce.

"See that?" Axel pointed to one of the walls facing the overgrown fields on the inland side of the city.

Bruce saw that one section of the wall had collapsed in a pile of rubble, leaving a broad gap. What was curious was that only that part of the wall had fallen, and there were no obvious natural causes like ground water.

"Looks like a battle was fought here," Layla said.

"My thoughts exactly," Axel added.

"But how did they knock down stone walls?" Tom asked. "Do the Jakar have siege weapons?"

"Not that I've seen," Axel replied. "But with metal-working, and domesticated dinos, I wouldn't put it past them."

"Maybe they used some of those dinos to batter down the wall?" Tom suggested.

Axel hovered their ship above the shattered section of wall, giving them a moment to search for clues.

"What's that?" Alice asked suddenly, pointing out the right side of the cockpit, toward the center of the city.

Bruce followed the gesture to a huddled group of figures standing around an overgrown city square.

"I don't know..." Axel trailed off uncertainly. He touched a button on the dash, and Bruce glimpsed a screen flash with a shaded blue model of the boxy vessel they were riding in. The opaque blue shading turned translucent and a line of text appeared below the image: *Cloaking Shield Engaged*.

Bruce frowned at the display, wondering why an alien ship would be programmed in *English*. "I thought you said this city was abandoned?" he said, tearing his gaze away.

"It *was,*" Axel replied, leaving them to draw their own conclusions as he flew above the growing knot of people in the crumbling stone square. The remains of a bronze statue stood there, a warrior holding a spear and shield, but the arm holding the shield lay in the grassy cobblestones at its feet. And the head was missing entirely.

"Are they Jakar?" Neil asked from the back, leaning out of his seat, then standing up for a better look.

"Definitely not," Bruce said.

"They look like they stepped right out of the twenty-first century," Alice added. "Look at their clothes."

"Shit," Axel muttered. He made a pinching gesture at the transparent floor, and the imagery zoomed in.

People's features emerged, looking tense and confused. They were wearing smart watches and AR glasses of various makes and models.

"Definitely from our time," Bruce decided.

"They look like they've just arrived," Layla said.

A bright flash of light erupted from the square, dazzling their eyes, and three more people appeared, lying flat on the cobblestones.

"They're still arriving!" Alice cried.

Another flash, and four more people materialized. People were reacting now, with some scattering and others running to greet the newcomers.

"There must be hundreds of people down there..." Neil muttered. Even as he said that, another seven appeared. Then six more. Then two.

Bruce gaped in shock at the scene, realizing that there was no visible sign of any vehicle delivering the abducted here. The flashes continued, sporadically even as dusk fell, cloaking the square in the dark blue and mauve light of nearest planets.

"There are kids down there!" Alice said, pointing through the floor. "What if my husband and son are here?"

"I doubt it," Axel replied. "The Architects select people at random. What are the odds that they would pick you and then also your family?"

Bruce arched an eyebrow at that. "Probably about the same as the odds of them picking all of us because we were connected to you twenty years ago."

"That's different," Axel said. "They read my thoughts and decided that I would be more effective as a minder if they brought my friends here."

"Maybe they're doing the same thing with Alice," Bruce suggested. "I can't imagine she'll be able to focus on anything besides getting home if they don't bring her family here."

"Even then," Alice said. "But it would be a good start."

"You would want them to come here?" Jess asked suddenly. "Even with all of the dangers?"

"This is a pointless conversation. It doesn't matter whether I want them to come or not. If they're here, I need to find them."

"It might matter," Axel admitted quietly.

"Land," Alice intoned. "I have to check."

"That might be a bad idea," Axel replied, holding up one hand to wiggle his pinky finger and remind them of the missing digit. "Those people won't be thinking rationally."

"We're cloaked, right?" Bruce asked.

"Yes," Axel said.

"Is that why they're not reacting to us?" Layla asked.

Axel nodded.

"So those flashes of light," Bruce began, pointing to a fresh one as it erupted on the far end of the square. "There could be ships like this one bringing the abductees here?"

"I suppose there could be, yes," Axel said.

"You never thought to check?" Bruce demanded.

"And how would I do that?" Axel asked.

"I don't know—shoot one of them!" Bruce gestured vaguely to the ship's controls. "Maybe you'll damage its cloaking shield and then we can follow it and find out where these Architects of yours are coming from. Then maybe we can speak with them for ourselves."

"That's actually a good idea," Layla said.

"No, it isn't," Axel said. "Even if we managed to do that, you don't want to meet them."

Alice glowered at Axel. "Land," she said.

"I'd do as the lady says if I were you," Bruce added.

Axel gave in with a sigh, veering away from the square and finding a grassy clearing to set the ship down. The thrusters roared briefly louder as they landed with a subtle jolt.

"We'll have to use the mech suits to avoid being seen," Axel said as he unbuckled and rose from his seat. "But I only have two on board besides the ones Tom and I are wearing. Alice, I assume you'll be taking one?"

She nodded.

"Okay," Axel said. "Who else is coming?"

"Me," Bruce said before anyone could beat him to it.

Layla regarded him with a frown.

He smiled apologetically at her. "Sorry."

"I guess we'll wait around here, then," Layla said.

Axel led the way down the aisle between the seats. "Come on, I'll give you a crash course in using the suits," Axel said.

3:15 PM

THE ARMOR WAS EASIER to use than Alice had expected. Like the dam, everything responded to their thoughts and unspoken needs. Engaging their cloaking shields was as simple as picturing the armor turning transparent. The displays inside the helmet overlaid the armor with green virtual shading so she could still see what her arms and legs were doing.

The helmets also enhanced the available light, making the night much brighter than it should have been, a fact which she appreciated greatly while searching the milling crowds for her family.

"Be careful you don't bump into anyone," Axel whispered. "They're panicked enough without adding fears of invisible wraiths stalking among them."

"I'll be careful," Alice said.

"Before I went to prison, I used to like watching these reality TV shows about paranormal encounters," Tom said. "People's reactions were hilarious. But now I'm the ghost, and it's not so funny anymore."

"Let's cut the chatter," Axel whispered. "It's hard for sound to make it past the aural dampeners, but not impossible. Watch your footsteps, too."

Alice nodded, but said nothing to that as she walked around the square, scanning people's faces, looking for one that might be familiar.

Some were shouting hysterically. Others were collapsed and crying. Still more stood with their hands raised to the sky, calling for their gods to have mercy. And the rest stumbled around with dazed expressions on their faces.

Realizing there were far more people gathered *inside* the square than clustered around its edges, Alice ducked into the crowd. Someone bumped into her and bounced off. He stood blinking in confusion. She moved on, still searching. Her heart hammered erratically in her chest, making it hard to breathe. Time seemed to slow right down. Everyone around her moved at a crawl, while she flitted and raced. Her movements, aided by the armor, were much quicker and easier than she was used to.

Alice slammed into a woman and knocked her over. She screamed and flailed against an invisible enemy. Alice hurried on, running now. She bumped into a young couple, locked in each other's arms and making out in the middle of the square. The two lovebirds flew apart, with exclamations of alarm rising between them.

A spreading wave of concern rumbled through the group.

"Alice, what did I say about revealing yourself?" Axel said.

She ignored him and made a bee line for a young boy of about Sean's age. She stopped short as he turned his face into the light. Too round. Hair black, not blond.

It wasn't him.

Her heart sank.

Alice continued searching, more frantically now. The crowd was also growing more agitated.

A gunshot rang out, and Alice froze. A spreading wave of panic rippled through the group, sending people bumping and jostling by her as they fled the scene.

A middle-aged man wearing a fancy suit stood in the center of the square, near the bronze statue. He was waving a hunting rifle around, the shoulder strap dangling. His victim lay in a spreading pool of blood at his feet—a young black man, holding a zippo lighter in one hand, and a flashlight in the other. He looked like he was dressed for cold weather, and his camo-pattern pants and jackets suggested he might have vanished in the middle of a hunting trip. Which would also explain where the rifle had come from. The victim had a heavy-looking pack on his back and a flashlight had rolled out of one hand.

The man in the suit had a handsome face and thick black hair, his blue tie had been loosened and his collar unbuttoned. Between the man's coiffed appearance and attire, Alice thought he might be a lawyer or a stock broker.

"If anyone comes close, I'll shoot!" the man in the suit cried.

"We should take him down before he hurts someone else," Bruce said.

"We can't," Axel replied. "No interference, remember? Minders observe. We don't intervene."

"Fuck that," Bruce said, and Alice saw a green-shaded figure moving swiftly around the square, angling to get behind the gunman.

"Bruce!" Axel hissed. "It's not worth it. They punish rule breakers."

The gunman's aim wavered as he bent down to retrieve the victim's flashlight, and then the pack. A stunned silence rang across the square, and Alice stood frozen, watching as the gunman switched to a one-handed grip on the rifle, diverting his attention briefly from the crowd to zip open the pack and study its contents. He set the flashlight inside and pulled out a candy bar, grinning triumphantly.

"That's not yours," someone intoned.

The man shouldered the pack and looked up sharply, bringing the rifle into line with the speaker's chest.

Alice watched a powerfully built Latino man wearing an orange jumpsuit step out of the crowd.

He held a glossy black rifle against his shoulder, aiming down the glowing green sights. That weapon looked exactly like the ones Axel and Tom had brought with them.

"I don't believe it," Tom muttered over the comms. "It's Solo."

"Who?" Axel asked.

"Fango Morales. The guy who disappeared with me from Sing Sing," Tom explained.

Chapter 32

3:36 PM

Layla checked her smart watch. It was already half past three in the afternoon, on Earth. And that wasn't even the actual time anymore thanks to the effect of the black hole that they were orbiting. All signs pointed to the fact that time was passing much faster on Earth than it was here on Planet B—or Novus, as Axel called it. Yet the relationship between the local days and her watch gave Layla the impression that exactly the opposite was happening: time seemed to be flying by faster than her old Earth-bound watch would indicate. Case in point, just a couple hours ago they'd left the dam at sunrise, and now it was already the dead of night.

Periodic flashes of light erupted above the moldering roofs of old stone buildings.

"What do you think they're doing?" Jess asked quietly.

Layla twisted around to look at the other woman. "They're searching for Alice's family."

"No, I mean the aliens," Jess said. "Those flashes of light." She pointed to the forward screen. "That's them bringing more people here, right? But what for? There were plenty of people in that native village. Even if we were about to go extinct on Earth, it's not like they need to bring more people here to save the species. What was that Axel said? There's no need to help the Novians because the Jakar are doing fine?"

Layla nodded along with Jess's logic. "So you're wondering if they have some other motivation for bringing people here."

"They'd have to, wouldn't they?"

"Maybe it's not just about preserving species," Neil said.

Both women looked at him.

"They could be trying to preserve cultures, too."

"Then there should be a whole lot more people here," Layla said. "Babylonians. Romans. Aztecs. Mayans..."

"Good point," Neil said. "Well, what the hell, I don't know. Maybe they just like plucking fish out of water and watching them squirm? Or maybe they have some kind of quotas to fill."

"Maybe," Layla said. "Whatever they're up to, I'm not sure Axel is going to give us the answers."

"If he even knows the answers," Jess said.

"He knows more than he's letting on," Layla added.

Neil perked up with that. "You think he's lying about why we're here?"

"Maybe. Or lying about whether we can leave? I don't know, but the Axel I knew in school was a rebel. He didn't live by anyone's rules, and now here, all of a sudden he's following them to the letter? No interference. Can't help the Novians. Not allowed to escape."

"Maybe he's already tried pushing those limits, and now he knows better?" Jess suggested. "They might have broken him," she said, her eyes darting around the transparent ceiling, as if she thought alien eyes might be watching from above.

A familiar *crack* ended the brief lull in the conversation. Layla's head snapped toward the sound. She found herself peering over the roofs of the short stone buildings between them and the town square.

"What was that?" Jess whispered.

"A gunshot—rifle from the sound of it," Layla replied.

"You think they're in trouble?" Neil asked.

"I don't know," Layla admitted. "But if they are, they might need our help." She jumped from the co-pilot's seat and hurried by Neil and Jess.

"Where are you going?" Neil called after her.

"To look for guns!" Layla said.

She walked all the way around the rover in the back, not really sure what she was looking for. A weapons rack, or a door to a storage compartment ... something. Coming back to the open entrance of the cockpit, she found both Neil and Jess standing there, looking uncertainly between them.

"Maybe we should stay here," Jess said. "We don't have armor. If someone shoots one of us, we won't live through it."

Layla stopped at the bottom of the access ladder on the rear bulkhead of the cockpit. Axel had led the others up there, and they'd left via an upper egress hatch rather than going out the ramp at the back. They'd found the spare mech suits up there in some type of airlock. Layla wondered if there might also be extra weapons up there. She tried waving her hand to open the octagonal barrier as she'd seen Axel do.

It slid aside, revealing a small, gleaming white room that made Layla think of a hospital, or some type of clean room. Layla was just about to climb up when Neil pointed to the floor beneath her feet.

"What's down there?" he asked.

Layla stared at the spot. There was a matching octagonal access recessed into the floor. She shook her head. "I don't know..."

Another *crack* of gunfire sounded in the distance.

"If we're going to do something, we'd better hurry," Neil said.

Layla stepped off the lower hatch and waved to open it as she had with the upper one.

A soft *thunk* sounded and a square black panel in the middle of the recessed octagonal section of the floor glowed red. Layla bent down and tried touching that panel. It flashed red this time and beeped at her.

"I think it's locked," Jess said.

"Let's see if we can find a way to get it open," Layla added.

"Do we have time for that?" Neil asked as she spun away, heading for the bench seats along the walls. Axel had pulled a medkit out of a compartment beneath the seats after rescuing them from the Jakar. Maybe there would be something else in those compartments that she could use. A plasma torch, if she was lucky.

Neil followed her there and stood off to one side, watching as she kneeled on the floor and opened the storage compartments one after another. The first one held the medkit. The next two held matching black cases. Layla pulled one out and pressed a button to open it, revealing all kinds of handheld scanners and devices, none of which she recognized. They didn't look like they'd be helpful, and she didn't have time to figure out what they did, so she slid that case back. Pulling the final case out, she repeated the process.

She pulled out a black cylinder with a curving dish at one end. It looked vaguely like a flashlight, but it was ribbed for added grip. There was a button where her thumb naturally rested. She angled it toward the shadowy back end of the ship and flicked the button forward. A gleaming black blade snapped out to a length of about a meter. It began glowing red hot and humming as it threw off searing waves of heat. It was somewhat uncomfortable to hold the blade as a result, but the dish-shaped projector around the base seemed to have been designed to deflect the heat away from her hand.

"Is that... a *lightsaber?*" Neil asked.

Layla frowned. "It kind of looks like one, doesn't it?"

Except that it was made with a solid, physical blade that had somehow extended to more than four times the length of its handle before sizzling to life.

"Let's go with *plasma sword*," Layla decided. She recalled seeing Axel deploy a similar blade from his suit gauntlet to cut the head off the Jakar arrow that had pierced Alice's shoulder.

Layla stood up and carefully tested the weapon on the deck, letting the tip graze the metal floor. It sank in like butter, drawing a molten orange line. She angled the blade away to examine the cut. The edges were still glowing, but cooling rapidly, leaving a smooth black gash in the floor.

"Think it will work?" Neil asked.

"Only one way to find out." Layla carried it over to the locked access hatch. Jess was still standing there, watching with wide eyes as they approached. She backed up a few hasty steps, and Layla set to work, drawing the blade around the inside of the hatch.

As soon as she'd finished, the cut section fell away with a resounding *boom*. The rungs of the ladder continued below into a shadowy space.

"What's down there?" Jess asked, peering through the hole.

"Let's find out." Layla flicked off the sword and the blade retracted. She grabbed the rungs. Realizing she needed both hands free to climb down, she handed the plasma sword to Neil.

"Mind the switch," Layla warned. "You don't want to cut your foot off."

He nodded stiffly.

As soon as Layla's waist crossed the threshold to the lower deck, lights flicked on automatically, and she descended the rest of the way into a wide open space. It was also clean and white, the walls gleaming like they did in the compartment above. A resinous octagonal pedestal stood in the center of the deck, rimmed with glowing red lights. Some type of projector dish was aiming down from a matching octagon in the ceiling. Six concentric rings of light bathed the area below in a bloody crimson glow. The whole thing looked ominous, like some type of weapon. But it was pointed at the deck, not mounted outside on the hull.

Layla crept in for a closer look, noticing as she did so glowing racks of rifles flanking the black pedestal on three sides, and there were illuminated alcoves with four more mech suits standing in them.

"So much for only having two spares on board," Layla muttered.

"What do you see down there?" Jess called out.

Layla opened her mouth for a reply, but stopped herself. She hadn't decided what she was looking at yet.

A gleaming speck caught her eye, shining bright against the raised black platform. Layla edged closer to see what it was—

And gasped sharply as the shape of it became clear.

It was a two and a half carat diamond engagement ring.

Chapter 33

3:38 PM

"WHERE DID YOU GET that?" the gun-wielding man asked, his eyes narrowing suspiciously on Fango's alien rifle.

"Does it matter?" Fango asked, smirking. "If you don't put that rifle down, I'll vaporize you."

"I'll shoot, too," the man countered.

"Yes, but I'll live. I can't say the same for you."

Alice watched as Bruce snuck in behind the gun-wielding thief. He grabbed the rifle, and the man reacted by jerking it away and pulling the trigger reflexively. The shot went into the air, and the gunman wrestled briefly with Bruce, cursing and screaming something about demons and hell.

As soon as Bruce had control of the gun, the crowd gasped and backed up a few more steps. Alice tried to imagine what they were seeing. Thanks to the sensors in her suit, she saw Tom as a shaded green figure. But anyone not wearing a helmet like hers would see that hunting rifle floating impossibly in the air.

"This is bad," Axel muttered. "You need to drop that gun right now."

"So that psycho can pick it up again?" Bruce countered. "Not happening."

Instead, he carried the weapon to the edge of the square and laid it down in front of a man with thinning gray hair. He wore army fatigues, and Alice noticed he was wearing a sergeant's stripes on his collar. The soldier hesitated briefly before lurching forward to pick up the weapon. He held it high and said, "If anyone else attacks another abductee, they'll answer to me!"

Fango Morales nodded and glanced about warily before shouldering his weapon. The crowd devolved into chaos as arguments erupted over who should be in charge, and why.

"Alice, is there any sign of your family here?" Axel asked.

"No!" Alice cried, turning in a quick circle to study the milling crowds.

Bruce was checking on the gunshot victim from a distance while two abductees attempted to administer first aid. One of them stepped back, shaking her head. "He's dead!"

Loud voices rose as a group of people grabbed the man in the suit who'd shot him and began shoving him toward the sergeant with the rifle.

"We should get back to the ship before things get ugly here," Axel suggested.

"I'm not done searching!" Alice said. "I need more time."

"How much more?" Axel demanded.

"I don't know!"

"How can we help?" Bruce asked. "What do they look like?"

"My son is nine. He has short blond hair with bangs."

"Tall, short?" Tom asked.

"Regular nine-year-old size!" Alice said, casting about frantically as she ducked and spun through the crowds.

"Can you be more specific?" Bruce asked.

"About four feet tall," Alice said, breathing hard. She focused her search on the children, of which there were only a handful. She pushed and shoved her way through the sea of people, checking each child. Her disappointment and frustration rose each time she glimpsed their faces.

Another flash of light tore across the square and three more people appeared out of nowhere, lying on the cobblestones. One woman and two men. They sat up quickly, blinking and looking around. The woman screamed.

The others reacted to their arrival, some gesturing frantically to the spot where the newcomers had appeared. Others searching the sky for signs of whatever invisible entity or craft had deposited them there.

Alice checked the last child—even though he was too tall and his hair too dark for him to be her son. She stifled a frustrated scream when she saw his face. He had to be fifteen, at least, and his features were nothing like Sean's.

"Are you okay?" Tom asked.

"They're not here!" Alice gasped between shallow breaths.

The people around her were losing their minds, too. Screaming theories and rebuttals at each other and railing at whatever had brought them to this place. All that negative energy was contagious. Alice began hyperventilating. Her anxiety was spiking. Vision dimming. She felt like she was going to die. Or go crazy. She recognized the sensation. She was having a panic attack. "I can't... breathe," she managed.

"Where are you," Tom said sharply.

"I don't..." Alice distracted herself by wondering where he was and searching for him. A flat circular display appeared in the top left of her HUD. It was crowded with a sea of yellow blips, as well as four green ones. One of the four green dots began flashing, and Alice realized that it must represent Tom. She turned in a circle, searching for him, and the contents of the circular display rotated, too. She caught a glimpse of a shaded-green overlay flashing and flickering through the crowds. She began stumbling toward it on wobbling legs. Now Tom's blip was dead center at the top of the display. He parted the crowds and rushed in just as Alice's legs gave way. He caught her.

"Are you okay?"

Alice shook her head and collapsed, sobbing.

"Be thankful you didn't find him," Tom said. "This is no place for a child."

"But that means—" Alice broke off to draw in an aching breath.

"I know," Tom said quietly. "But he has his father. And they have each other."

Alice's throat felt cut. Her chest tight. If Sean wasn't here, he was going to grow up without her. From Earth's perspective, at least two or three months had passed already. What did Sean think had happened to his mother? And Liam. How long would he wait before he moved on and found someone new? Maybe he'd wait two or three years, holding onto hope, but that would only be a couple of weeks to her.

If she didn't find a way home before then, it would be too late, and the life she'd left would be long gone.

"Are you good?" Tom asked. "Can you stand?"

Alice nodded and he helped her up.

Another gunshot split the night. Followed by buzzing reports of crimson lasers strobing the sky. Fango and that Sergeant were both standing on a pile of rocks from the crumbling wall of a nearby building, each of them holding their weapons high and shouting for attention. The suit-wearing murderer had been forced to kneel before them, as if he were awaiting judgment.

"We need to go," Axel said again.

Tom led her to the edge of the square where he was standing with Bruce. Halfway there, another flash of light erupted right in front of them, dazzling Alice's eyes. She stumbled sideways and brushed against an invisible wall.

Realizing what it must be, she felt around frantically, searching for something to grab onto. Her hand curled around an invisible surface, catching hold of something round and hard. She felt it pulling sharply away, lifting off.

"Alice!" Tom cried, and lunged for her ankles as she shot into the sky with the invisible craft. He missed and landed hard before springing up to watch her soaring into the night.

"Where are you going!" Tom called to her over their comms, as if she were flying away under her own power.

"Alice, let go!" Axel cried.

But she was already too high off the ground for that. The people in the square had turned into ants. Rather than release the ship, she brought her other hand up to strengthen her hold.

The rippling fields and shining sea around the city spun away as the invisible ship carried her down the coast, picking up speed. The scenery became a blur.

"How did she do that?" Bruce asked.

"She didn't!" Axel cried. "She grabbed a harvester!"

"A what?" he asked.

Axel's reply devolved into an unintelligible roar of static. She must have passed beyond the range of their comms. Alice clung to the invisible ship with all of her strength. The mech suit made it easier by enhancing her grip strength.

Where was this thing taking her? A *Harvester.* That was what Axel had called it. So he knew about them. Had he already tried this? Alice wondered if the vehicle were manned, and if so, how the Architects would react when they discovered her clinging to their ship. Maybe they were going to scrape her off on one of those dark patches of trees flashing by to her right.

But the ship wasn't changing course or shedding altitude. It kept to an even height above the shore, racing along the coast to parts unknown.

Alice felt hope stir inside her chest. She hadn't planned this, but discovering the harvester had been a fantastic stroke of luck. If she wanted to find a way home, then hitching a ride on one of the vehicles that was responsible for bringing people here was a good bet.

A trickle of doubt wormed through her thoughts. If this ship was headed back to Earth to pick up more people, then why wasn't it blasting into orbit? And if it did, what would happen to her once they reached space? Was her suit pressurized? And if so, how long would her air last?

Fear shattered Alice's rising hopes. Even if the harvester did go back to Earth, she wouldn't survive the trip.

4:19 PM

THE RUNGS OF A ladder slid out of the green-shaded hull of their ship, making a way for them to climb back up to the top hatch. Bruce clambered after Axel and Tom. He was the last one to jump down through the hatch.

Axel waved it shut and his shaded armor turned opaque and black once more.

"De-activate the cloaking. Save your power cells," Axel suggested.

Bruce thought about it, and raised his arms to watch as his suit went from a shaded, translucent green to solid black once more.

The lower hatch slid open and Axel hurried down the ladder to the cockpit.

"Do you know where it's taking her?" Tom asked.

"Yes, but we need to catch her before it arrives," Axel replied.

"Why?" Tom demanded as he followed Axel down. "What happens then?"

But Axel never had a chance to reply. A bright flash of light erupted from below, and he fell off the ladder with a noisy clatter of his armor striking the deck.

Tom cried out in alarm and jumped down after him.

Bruce kneeled beside the open hatch and ducked his head through to see Layla and Neil dragging Axel's lifeless form across the deck while Jess watched uneasily to one side.

Tom aimed his rifle at them. "What the hell?" he demanded. "Why did you shoot him?"

"Because he's been lying to us!" Layla released Axel's legs and fished into her pocket, producing a ring with a big, gleaming diamond.

"What is that?"

"My engagement ring," Layla said. "I'd just given it back to Neil when we disappeared."

"So?" Tom asked, his aim wavering now.

Bruce hurried down the ladder, being careful to mind the ragged, gaping hole beneath it. He twisted his helmet and pulled it off, freeing his sweaty hair and scratching furiously at his scalp. "Where did you find it?" Bruce asked.

"Down there." Layla said, and nodded to the hole in the deck.

"So Axel did bring us here?" Bruce asked, scratching his beard and frowning into the darkened space.

"He had to have," Layla said. "Neil didn't plant the ring down there, and he didn't have it with him when he arrived."

"Is Axel dead?" Tom asked, nudging him with his boot.

"Stunned—I think," Layla said, reaching for the alien rifle dangling from a strap around her neck. She turned the weapon on its side and checked a slider above the trigger.

"So we can get back to Earth with this ship," Bruce concluded.

Layla nodded grimly, looking from him to Tom and back again. A frown creased her lips. "Where's Alice?"

"Shit!" Tom cried. His helmet snapped up. "They took her."

"They?" Neil asked.

Tom gestured frantically for lack of words. "Some kind of invisible spaceship. Axel called it a harvester. It was delivering people here. Alice grabbed it before it could fly away. We were going to follow her."

"Follow her where?" Layla demanded.

Bruce shook his head. "Nowhere good. Axel was worried about what might happen if we didn't catch her before it arrived."

"Do you know how to fly this ship?" Layla asked, looking at Tom.

He shook his head. "I'm a paleontologist, not a pilot."

"Then we'll have to wait for Axel to wake up," Neil said.

"Maybe we can speed that along somehow?" Bruce suggested, dropping to his haunches and setting his helmet down to see if he could get Axel's off. He twisted and pulled. The helmet came away with a hiss and Bruce leaned in close to put his ear beside the boy's mouth and nose.

"What are you doing?" Jess asked, taking a step toward them.

"Checking to see if he's still breathing," Bruce explained.

"And?" Neil prompted.

"Shut up and let me focus," Bruce snapped. He waited a beat—

Then felt and heard the air whisper out of Axel's lungs.

Bruce withdrew with a sigh. "He's alive."

"Then let's wake the bastard up," Tom suggested. Before anyone could stop him, he gave Axel a swift kick in the head.

"Are you insane?" Layla cried, and her rifle snapped up to aim at his chest.

"Alice could die!" Tom raged at her, his fists balled.

"Killing Axel won't improve her chances!"

"If I wanted him dead, he would be," Tom growled. He jerked his chin to Bruce. "You wanted to know if we could wake him. Now we know."

"Let's hope you didn't put him in a coma," Neil muttered.

Bruce glared at Tom and checked Axel's life signs again. He was relieved to find the boy still breathing steadily. "We'll have to wait for him to wake up," Bruce said as he eased off the deck. "In the meantime, why don't you show me what you found below?"

Layla hesitated, looking pointedly at Axel. "Someone needs to watch him in case he comes to."

"Don't worry, he's not going anywhere," Tom said, and raised his rifle. Axel's own weapon was trapped under him.

"Better disarm him first," Bruce suggested.

Neil and Layla rolled him over and Neil took the rifle for himself. Bruce realized that he and Jess were the only ones who weren't armed.

"Come on," Layla said, stepping toward the open hole in the deck.

When they reached the bottom of the ladder, Bruce saw the raised black platform and the suspicious-looking ray gun in the ceiling.

"You think it's some type of teleportation device?" he asked.

Layla blinked a few times, as if only now considering the idea. "Is that even possible? De-materialize something and re-materialize it in a different place? Wouldn't that kill us?"

"Maybe that's not how it works," Bruce said, walking slowly around the platform. "If the Architects figured out how to create and manipulate wormholes like Alice said, then maybe they can do that on a smaller scale? They might have some kind of portable generator that opens a portal between the device and this chamber. That would explain how you found your ring here."

"And dinosaurs?" Layla challenged. "No way a T-Rex would fit in here."

"No, but there was a much larger version of this ship in that hangar back at the dam. Pretty much anything would fit inside of that one."

"I guess," Layla admitted.

"The better question is why did Axel lie? If he could use this ship to go back home, why not simply do that? Why would he abduct us instead?"

"Because he's a psychopath," Layla said.

"Maybe," Bruce said.

"You can ask him about it when he wakes up. Just don't expect to get a straight answer."

Chapter 34

4:19 PM

ALICE PASSED THE NIGHT watching the neighboring planets rise and fall, studying each and trying to imagine what alien wonders they held. None of them looked anything like Planet B with its predominantly blue and green surface. The largest and closest world appeared to be covered in water, with tiny islands like freckles on its surface. The next nearest was some mixture of purple, green, and blue. Both were close enough that she could see signs of what might be clouds, which meant they had atmospheres and might be habitable—to some kind of life, at least. Probably not to humans.

The sun rose swiftly above the ocean, shining bright on the water and washing the clouds with crimson fire. Daylight erased all but the largest of the neighboring planets, turning them to faded blue crescents.

The invisible craft carrying Alice veered inland and thick carpets of trees undulated below. Grassy clearings and winding rivers sporadically broke through, revealing grazing herds of giant herbivores. Alice mentally cataloged the ones she recognized, and studied the ones she didn't.

Boredom crept in. With every minute that passed she became more and more convinced that the ship carrying her was some type of drone. If it had a living crew, surely they would have reacted to her presence by now?

Then again, her suit's cloaking shield was still engaged. Maybe that was why they hadn't noticed her? After all, she couldn't see them, so maybe they couldn't see her.

Regardless of who or what might be piloting the vessel, Alice was no longer afraid that it might carry her up into space and kill her in the process. It had been flying at the same relatively low altitude for the past hour or so, which told her that it was headed somewhere on the surface.

A shadow passed over the land, and Alice craned her neck to see the sun dimming and turning to a shining ring as it passed behind the black hole. She idly wondered about the period of the sun's orbit and tried to recall how many times she'd seen that eclipse happen since she'd arrived. Maybe three or four? Whatever the sun's actual orbital period, it was obviously measured in hours, not days or years, and that meant that the sun had to be locked in an incredibly close orbit around the black hole.

She wondered how long Planet B took to complete a lap around them both. Maybe a day or two?

This solar system was spinning incredibly fast, a fact which was no doubt contributing to the time dilation caused by the black hole's massive gravity.

Pins and needles shot up and down Alice's arms, bringing her back to the moment. The mech suit must have detected the weakening signals from her nerves. Her grip began to slip. Alice grimaced and stared hard at her hands, willing herself to hold on.

The invisible harvester flew on for long minutes, racing across fields and forests. Alice gritted her teeth and tried flexing her hands one at a time to return the feeling to them. It didn't work. Panic fluttered inside her chest.

And then the craft began to slow. The trees fell away and it shot out over a shining black structure. It was cylindrical, the top of it vaguely sloped. It reminded Alice somewhat of a grain silo. The harvester dropped steadily toward the roof. But it wasn't landing fast enough. Alice's grip was still slipping, and she was at least a hundred meters up. She bit her tongue and pulled herself up, hooking her arms over the pole-shaped surface she was clinging to. That worked.

Machinery groaned to life, drawing her eyes down to the structure. The roof was irising open, revealing an indeterminately long, dark tunnel that plunged straight down into the bowels of the planet. The harvester accelerated through the opening, and Alice's stomach lurched into her throat as she became suddenly weightless. She stifled a scream. At least the feeling was returning to her aching arms.

The hull of the ship she clung to shimmered and turned opaque and black as it finally dropped its cloaking shield. She gasped as she realized how similar this so-called *harvester* looked to Axel's ship. The cylindrical projection she was clinging to turned out to be one of two weapon barrels attached to a turret beneath the hull.

Running lights snapped on, revealing the smooth black walls of the tunnel, and providing a pale source of illumination to replace that of the sun as the roof of the silo rotated shut overhead.

Alice marveled at the endless depths of the pit, wondering where it could possibly lead. The walls didn't seem to be made of dirt, which meant that she was descending into some type of vast alien facility. She gazed down into the vanishing depths, waiting to see some sign of the bottom.

After a few more seconds of accelerating weightlessly, a blazing light appeared. Alice thought the harvester might begin to slow as it approached the source of that light, but instead, it actually sped up.

Apprehension swirled and panic gripped her once more. She managed to control herself until just a moment before that terrible light consumed her.

And then she screamed freely, no longer caring who or what might hear.

Chapter 35

6:08 PM

"Is anyone else wondering why we woke up in that field, instead of in this city?" Neil asked, gesturing to the transparent walls of the cockpit. The sun was at its midpoint in the sky, the overgrown rubble and moldering stone buildings shining brightly on all sides of their ship. "They're obviously bringing everyone else here, so why not us?"

Layla considered the question from her vantage point in the pilot's seat. Axel lay in the aisle between her and Bruce, who had retrieved a weapon for himself from the lower deck. He and Tom were both aiming their rifles at Axel while they waited for him to wake up.

"Axel said we're supposed to be minders like him, so maybe that's why he left us close to the dam?" Jess said.

"A T-Rex almost ate me within seconds of my arrival," Bruce pointed out. "Each and every one of us has almost died at least once since we arrived. Axel would have been better off taking us directly to his place—if our lives actually mattered to him, that is."

"But then he wouldn't have been able to pretend that he didn't bring us here," Layla said.

Bruce grunted. "Good point."

Layla pulled out the ring, studying it once more. Neil watched her with a frown. She wondered if maybe he was feeling some sense of remorse. Maybe she'd overreacted. After all, he'd slept with Jess while they'd been dating, not while they'd been engaged, and years had passed since then. As far as she knew, he'd been faithful since that one drunken mistake with Jess. Here, so far from Earth, with much bigger problems facing them, it almost felt like she could begin to forgive him and put the past behind her. She peered into the depths of the ring, testing it out on her right hand—not the left. If it was going back on that hand, Neil was going to have to put it there himself.

"Don't lose it," Neil said, breaking the spell.

Layla yanked the ring off and pocketed it with a scowl. "Seriously? After everything we've been through, you're still worried about getting your ring back?"

"What? I'm just saying! It's not like I'll be able to buy you another one around here. Maybe we can still use it?" He stood up from the seat behind Bruce's and stepped over Axel's unconscious form to reach her.

Layla's umbrage faded as she realized he had been thinking along similar lines to her.

Axel stirred and groaned, sending Neil scurrying back into his seat. Axel's eyelids fluttered and he reached for the side of his head, which was swollen and purple where Tom had kicked him.

"Ow..." he mumbled, then began to sit up.

"Good morning, sunshine," Bruce said in a dulcet voice. "You have a nice rest?"

Axel looked around, appearing to notice all the weapons pointed at him. "What's going on?"

Layla smiled thinly, "Hi, baby." The old endearment took on a whole new meaning now that Axel was twenty years younger than she.

"Lulu?" he asked with a furrowed brow. "What did... did you shoot me?"

"I told you not to call me Lulu."

"Why?" Axel demanded. "And where's Alice?"

Bruce just shook his head. "We don't know."

"Shit," Axel muttered. "This is bad."

"You know what else is bad?" Layla asked. "Lying." She produced the ring from her pocket. "I found this on the lower deck. Do you know what it is?"

A sly grin snuck onto Axel's face. "Are you proposing to me?"

Bruce cuffed him in the back of the head.

"Ow!"

"Don't be an idiot," Bruce added.

"It's my engagement ring. From Neil. I was giving it back to him when I disappeared. So why was it on your ship?"

"I..." Axel trailed off, shaking his head. "Where did you say you found it?"

"Below deck," Bruce repeated. "You can drop the act. We know you brought us here."

"But I didn't! It wasn't me!" Axel erupted.

Bruce cuffed him again.

"Stop that!" he snapped.

Bruce pasted an innocent look on his face. "But it wasn't me..." His expression collapsed in a scowl a split second later. "See how annoying that is?"

"Fuck you!" Axel shot to his feet.

"Watch it," Tom growled, jerking his rifle up to aim through the glowing green sights.

"Layla. You *know* me," Axel tried.

"I thought I did."

He gritted his teeth. "You think after everything I've been through here, I would intentionally subject seven other people to the same hell?"

"If you didn't bring us here, then how did the ring get on your ship?" Bruce challenged. "You're saying that the Architects planted it to incriminate you?"

"No. At least... I don't think they did. They gave me this ship just before you arrived. Right after a stampede of Brontosaurs damaged my old one."

"A stampede of Brontosaurs?" Tom asked.

"Big ones," Axel confirmed.

"That's a hell of a convenient story," Bruce said. "Right up there with the dog ate my homework."

"That actually happened to me," Axel said. "Remember Ignacious?"

Bruce's brow furrowed. "The Rottweiler?"

Axel nodded and smiled.

"He used to play fetch with rocks," Layla recalled.

"You remember that?" Axel asked. He snorted and shook his head. "It didn't matter how far you threw them, he'd always come back with the exact same one. Hell of a nose on that mutt."

Bruce frowned.

"He hated my guts," Tom said. "Every time I came through the door, he'd come running, barking and snarling like he was going to rip my face off."

"Dogs have a sixth sense about people," Layla pointed out, and Tom's eyes cinched down to angry slits.

"I'm not a killer."

"Jury's still out on that," Layla said.

"And who's the jury?" Tom growled. "The six of you?"

Layla smiled thinly. "Neil's a lawyer. We could have a trial."

"Or, I could shoot you in the head," Tom said, switching his aim to her.

Layla's eyes glittered. "The prosecution rests."

Tom heaved a sigh and dropped his aim. "You ever hear of a self-fulfilling prophecy? Happens with kids and their parents. Negative expectations lead to kids' fulfillment of them."

"Sounds like a good excuse for misconduct. Besides, you're not a kid and I'm not your Mommy."

Tom ground his teeth for a moment before saying. "I'm going to take a beat. You five better figure out how to squeeze the truth out of Axel, or I will." With that, he turned and stalked out of the cockpit.

"See?" Layla said, looking to Bruce.

"Let's try *not* to anger the escaped convict, shall we?" Neil suggested.

Layla threw up her hands in surrender.

"Maybe someone should take his gun away?" Jess asked.

"Good luck with that," Bruce said.

"Are we good?" Axel asked, turning in a slow circle.

Neil shook his rifle at Axel. "No, we're not *good.* You're lying. You brought us here, and that means you can take us back."

Axel looked disappointed. "Look, man, we don't know each other, but you need to trust me."

"Trust," Bruce snorted. "Like I trusted you with my girlfriend?"

Axel appeared to hesitate.

Layla stared hard at him. "What's he talking about?"

"He slept with Kaitlyn and then ditched her. That's what."

"We were kids!" Axel objected. "And I must have apologized a thousand times."

"You're *still* a kid!" Bruce thundered. "It might have been twenty years ago for us, but you said it yourself, you've only been gone for four months. Screw it. Don't believe a word Axel says. Let's get this ship in the air." He grabbed Axel by the neck and jabbed the barrel of his rifle into the small of his back. "We're leaving."

"What about Alice?" Layla asked as she vacated the pilot's seat.

"We don't even know where they took her," Bruce pointed out. "Nothing we can do."

"That's not true," Axel said. "If she held on until the end..."

"Then what? You know where they took her?" Bruce demanded.

"I might," Axel said.

"He's lying again," Neil hissed through his teeth.

"Fly," Bruce intoned as he eased back into the co-pilot's seat, keeping his rifle trained on Axel the whole time.

"Where?" Axel asked.

"Into orbit! Back to Earth!" Bruce roared. "You really *are* an idiot."

Axel sighed and grabbed the flight controls. "This is a bad idea."

Layla sat down behind him and across from Jess, while Neil remained standing in the aisle behind Axel. Tom was still taking a breather in the back.

"A bad idea?" Neil echoed. "Why, because we'll get in trouble? Or because you actually like it here and you don't want to leave?"

Axel cast a pleading look over his shoulder, trying to leverage their old relationship for whatever it was still worth. But she'd just learned that he'd slept with his best friend's girlfriend, and that had struck a raw nerve.

Layla set her jaw. "You heard Bruce. Let's go."

Chapter 36

6:18 PM

THE GLARE FADED AND Alice emerged from the light, blinking and gaping at the most incredible sight she'd ever seen. And that was saying something considering she'd seen at least a dozen different dinosaurs in the past twenty-four hours.

The light she'd seen at the bottom of the tunnel was still far below her. Almost impossibly far if she could trust what she was seeing. The harvester was falling down a tunnel, but now there were giant, diamond-shaped gaps in the walls between massive trusses and beams, revealing a gargantuan hollow space beyond the tunnel and what had to be hundreds of other tunnels just like it, radiating from the outer shell of the planet to its glowing blue core. Tiny black specks flitted around those spokes.

Alice gasped as one of them drew near and flew alongside the harvester from the outside of the tunnel.

Was it looking at *her?*

It was a much smaller ship than the harvester. Sleek and aerodynamic with two sweptback wings that jutted forward at the ends in the rough shape of a flattened W. Two thruster nacelles glowed bright blue at the back. It looked a lot like one of the other ships she'd seen in Axel's hangar at the dam.

Alice swallowed thickly and tightened her grip on the barrel of the gun emplacement she was clinging to.

The harvester shuddered, picking up speed and pinning her to the belly of the craft, making hanging on a foregone conclusion.

The fighter craft flying alongside them flitted away, but the harvester continued on for the core, still accelerating. Alice's mind spun. Planet B was hollow. And artificial. It wasn't a natural world that had somehow been created or moved into orbit around a black hole. It had been deliberately *constructed* around one. Axel's name for the alien civilization responsible for all of this suddenly took on a whole new meaning—*Architects*.

These beings had *built* artificial, planet-sized megastructures. With the intention of... saving extinct or soon-to-be extinct species from around the galaxy?

She stared hard at the swelling blue orb at the center of the planet, wondering if she was about to be fried or crushed by it. Something had to be generating the planet's gravity, and it wasn't a solid planet full of regular mass.

How many kilometers was it to the core? Alice wondered. Earth's radius was 6371. Assuming Planet B was a similar size to Earth, how long would it take for her to reach the core?

But that assumption didn't necessarily hold. She and Julio had never had a chance to measure the size or mass of Planet B. Since arriving on the surface she'd merely assumed its size was similar to Earth's due to the familiar sensation of gravity. But clearly that gravity was being generated artificially, which meant that the planet's actual size and mass were unknown.

Alice tried to guess how far it was to the core. She couldn't see her watch, but she estimated that she'd been traveling for about ten minutes already. Based on the fact that she'd been weightless for much of that trip, she could assume that the harvester's acceleration was roughly the same as the acceleration due to gravity on Earth, so $9.8 m/s^2$. Round up to ten to make calculations easier, and because she was currently pinned to the bottom of the ship, meaning the harvester's acceleration was greater than the planet's gravity. Ten minutes was 600 seconds. Given an initial velocity of 0 when the ship had entered the top of the silo...

The number Alice came up with for the distance traveled over that time was much larger than she'd expected. Almost two thousand six hundred kilometers. But of course she wasn't factoring wind resistance.

Alice concentrated on the vibrations carrying through the hull of the ship. They were weak. Far too subtle for a ship with so many flat surfaces. If there were any air inside the planet's hollow interior, then by now the harvester should have been shivering like a leaf.

She couldn't recall if the solid top section of the tunnel had been filled with air or not. Probably, otherwise that silo opening would have created a tornado as the planet's atmosphere got sucked into it. Even so, it had taken her, what—a minute?—to emerge from the outer shell. Her estimate of the distance traveled so far had to be close. Glancing out the sides of the trussed cylinder she was traveling down, Alice estimated that she couldn't be more than halfway to the core. So the planet's radius was comparable to Earth's.

Alice blinked in shock at the sheer magnitude of the structure around her. The idea of an artificial shell the size of Earth with trillions of tons of air, dirt, rock, water, and vegetation layered on top of it was unbelievable. Alice would have sworn up and down that such a feat was impossible if she wasn't already seeing it for herself.

The minutes slipped by with the harvester racing toward the core with no signs of stopping. The acceleration wasn't so much that it was uncomfortable, freeing Alice's thoughts of more immediate physical threats and allowing her to focus on the sight ahead of her. As she drew near to the core, it resolved into three distinct points of light—the largest was at the very center of the planet. All the hundreds of trussed cylindrical spokes were connected to it like pillars holding up the world above. The other two points of light were much smaller than the core, and they orbited slowly, passing through the spokes.

What were those orbs, and what forces were guiding them? Alice wondered. Then they stopped, and apprehension trickled through her. One of them was now lined up directly below her. In a matter of seconds she was going to collide with it at an incredible speed. If either that glowing blue orb or the core behind it were solid she was about to be pulverized by the impact.

Alice screamed as blinding light consumed her for the second time.

And then she shot out the other side, racing up a matching hollow spoke to the dark, hazy shell of the planet above. Now her perspective had flipped. Down was up, and up was down. Rather than being pinned to the harvester *above* her, it seemed to be below, with gravity pulling her firmly against the craft's hull. It felt weaker than it should have been, which meant that the ship was slowing down.

Alice held on and listened to the echoes of her own shallow breathing.

The harvester had flown her straight through the core and out the other side. What was the point of that?

Better than colliding at relativistic speed with a deadly ball of light, she decided.

Maybe the spokes radiating from the planet's surface provided shortcuts from one hemisphere to another? Traveling through the core was certainly quicker than flying all the way around the planet's circumference.

Alice risked kneeling and peered through the blurry, racing black mesh of beams and trusses. The incredible scale of the planet's interior struck her once again. More black specks were flitting around on this side of the core, but thankfully, this time none of them flew in to investigate what she was doing clinging to the hull of this harvester.

Maybe they were all drones.

Hopefully.

After seeing this, Alice wasn't sure she wanted to meet the Architects anymore.

What can mortals do but cower in the presence of gods? she wondered.

Chapter 37

6:22 PM

Axel's ship rocketed toward outer space, angling almost straight up. Layla sat next to him with her rifle casually aimed, and her flight harness secured. Fluffy clouds raced by on either side of them. Stars pricked through the blue sky. Neighboring planets snapped into focus. And then the atmosphere fell away entirely, leaving nothing but the black of space and the diamond eyes of the stars.

A vanishing ring of planets curved ahead of them—all variations of slivered crescents, halves and quarters. Combinations of light and shadow formed by the angle of the sun.

"Seems like we can get into orbit after all," Bruce muttered from the seat behind Layla's. Neil was in the back with Tom.

"I told you, the autopilot will take us back down," Axel said.

"Not if you don't touch it," Bruce growled. "Hands off the controls."

"What?" Axel asked.

"Now!" Bruce jammed his weapon into Axel's ribs. He was still wearing the mech suit, so Layla doubted he felt anything, but the threat was clear.

"Okay, okay," Axel raised his hands. He glanced over at Layla, and she was surprised to see fear in his eyes.

"Something else you need to tell us?" she asked.

Axel's gaze darted to the ship's displays. One of them, the radar screen, had some activity on it. A group of blue blips were racing from one end to the other.

"If we don't turn around, they'll make us," Axel said. "We can't get too far from the planet."

"*They*—you mean the architects, right?" Layla asked. "So we'll get to see them?"

"Just their ships."

"How will they force us down?" Bruce asked.

Axel slowly shook his head.

A bright flash of crimson light flickered through the cockpit, and a siren screamed to life.

"What was that?" Jess asked.

"That was a warning shot!" Axel replied, reaching for the controls. He slammed the flight stick forward, pushing the nose down until Planet B swept into view beneath them, tufted clouds shone like a wavy golden carpet in the sun. It hovered just above the horizon, revealing the day-side of the planet.

"We're just going to give up?" Bruce demanded.

"If they're shooting at us, what choice do we have?" Jess asked.

"How about we shoot back?" Bruce suggested.

"Are you insane?" Jess asked.

Layla frowned, unsure which side to take.

"What's going on?" Neil called from the back.

"Set a course for the wormhole," Bruce said. "And gun it. Try to outrun them."

Axel looked to him with widening eyes. "No."

"Then get out of the seat. I'll do it myself." Not waiting for Axel to move, Bruce touched the button on the headrest and Axel's flight harness retracted. Layla heard mechanisms whirr to life in Bruce's mech suit as his left arm shot out and he yanked Axel from the pilot's seat, sending him tumbling down the aisle. It shouldn't have been possible to throw him around like that, not even in the lighter than standard gravity they were currently experiencing. Layla realized that those suits must convey a ridiculous amount of strength to the wearers.

Axel sprang off the deck, looking furious.

"Don't even think about it," Bruce warned, aiming his rifle at the young man. "Go sit in the back with Tom. You were such good buddies, I'm sure you two still have lots to catch up on."

Axel hesitated, his eyes on Layla. "Don't let him do this. He doesn't even know how to fly!"

"Wrong. I took lessons in an old Cirrus SR22."

"Because that's the same as an alien spaceship!" Axel said.

"You figured it out. I'm sure I'll be fine. Layla, keep that rifle trained on him."

She adjusted the angle of her weapon.

Axel threw up his hands in exasperation. "Fine! Let's all die together. That's a fantastic plan!"

He turned and stalked back into the vehicle hangar. Layla watched him go, then glanced at Bruce, who was busy sitting down behind the controls. He laid his rifle on the deck and tucked it behind his feet.

Layla took a moment to collect her thoughts. In the process, she noticed that the direction and force of gravity seemed to be wrong. If Alice were here, she might be able to explain it, but Layla's understanding was that anything in orbit above a planet should be weightless, so why did her body still feel normal? Maybe it was because the floor of the ship was facing the planet below.

Bruce grabbed the flight stick and pulled up sharply, changing those angles completely. Layla still felt forces pulling her *down* to the deck of the ship. She could have stood up and walked into the hangar if she wanted to, and that was definitely wrong. Was this craft generating some type of artificial gravity?

Bruce pushed the throttle control all the way forward. He glanced at the radar display, and Layla followed his gaze to see those blue blips again. Two were flanking them on either side, trailing just out of sight of the cockpit.

Another flash of red light tore across space, again accompanied by an alarm. A few seconds later, a third flash came. This time Layla noticed that the light was being produced by tiny, pea-sized fixtures that were flaring to life inside the cockpit. She stared fixedly into one of them until it blazed to life once more, dazzling her eyes. "Bruce!" Layla said, patting his arm urgently.

"I know!" He began rocking and rolling the flight stick. Stars pinwheeled around them. The flashes came more rapidly now, as if struggling to keep up with his maneuvers.

"No, Bruce. Stop it. Look!" she pointed straight at a flickering light at the edge of his peripheral vision. Bruce glanced at it in time to see another burst of crimson fire.

Bruce abruptly stopped the maneuvers. "Son of a... it's not real?"

Layla slowly shook her head. Flickering pulses continued stabbing through the cockpit. The shrieking alerts almost became a steady tone, and Layla picked out meaty, crunching and hissing sounds that were likely meant to convey impacts.

"It's simulated," Layla said.

Bruce gave her a baffled look. "Why? To scare us into flying back down?"

"Maybe they never expected us to call their bluff," Layla said.

Tom came running into the cockpit as the simulated attacks intensified. "What's going on?" he demanded.

The lights in the cockpit abruptly died, and the displays vanished. Utter darkness and silence filled the ship.

Axel broke it a split second later, calling out from the aft end of the ship, "I warned you this would happen!"

A dim, pulsing red light filled the cockpit. The walls turned transparent once more, and the control systems swelled back to life, along with a shrieking alarm. The volume of the alarm subsided suddenly, and Axel came running into the cockpit. "We have to land, right now!"

Bruce snatched his rifle up and aimed it at Axel's chest. He pointed to the pea-sized light fixtures, now pulsing steadily. "It wasn't real. We saw it with our own eyes. Each time the lasers fired, those lights flickered."

Axel scowled and pushed past Tom.

"Hey! Not another step!" Bruce warned.

Axel bristled, looking like he was about to explode. "Trust me. It's real. You think I haven't already tried this? Those lights are part of some kind of combat warning system."

"You said the autopilot would take us back down."

"I lied!" Axel screamed.

"So how do we know you're not lying about this?" Bruce insisted.

Neil appeared in the opening of the cockpit, looking terrified. "I think Axel is right."

"How do you know?" Bruce demanded.

"Because you can't hear sounds in space. Or see lasers. And because I think I just found a hole in the ship. We're losing pressure."

"Push the stick back down," Axel said. "You should still have control of the emergency thrusters."

Bruce frowned and did as Axel had indicated. The planet swept into view once more. A pair of sleek black ships raced by them, each with sloping, sweptback wings and recessed cockpits that made them look like inverted W's. Two sets of glowing orange thrusters blazed brightly from the back of each craft.

"There go the interceptors," Axel breathed.

Another two rocketed after the first, all four flying into the sun and leaving them drifting in their wake.

"Can we still land?" Jess asked in shrinking voice.

Bruce was pushing and pulling the throttle controls, and jerking the stick around. "It's barely responding."

"Because they took out our reactor!" Axel roared. "They were shooting to cripple us. Have you even been listening to me? I said they'd force us down, and now they have."

"Looks like we're still in space to me," Bruce muttered.

"In a decaying orbit!" Axel snapped.

"We didn't reach escape velocity?" Neil asked.

"If we did, they would have blown us up," Axel pointed out. "I took it easy with the thrusters for just that reason."

"Great, so now we're going to crash," Bruce said. He jabbed a finger at Axel's chest. "You deliberately sabotaged our escape."

"Because I knew what would happen! And it *did* happen. Exactly the way I said it would. Now, do you want to live, or should we just wait and see how big of a crater we can make?"

Bruce held Axel's gaze, glaring at his old high school friend.

"Bruce..." Layla said slowly.

He let out a frustrated roar and shot out of the pilot's seat. "You know, I forgot how annoying you used to be."

"And I forgot what a stubborn idiot *you* used to be," Axel said, squeezing past Bruce in the aisle. He settled into the pilot's seat with a shaky sigh and grabbed the flight controls gingerly. "I just hope we still have enough power in reserve to make a controlled descent. You three had better buckle up," Axel said, glancing back at Bruce, Tom, and Neil.

Bruce settled into the seat he'd vacated earlier and touched the headrest to deploy his safety harness, while Neil and Tom hurried into the rear compartment.

"What about the pressure leak?" Layla asked, her ears pricked to listen for the hiss of escaping air through the whooping siren. Axel killed the alarm, and that sound snapped into focus. Soft, but steady.

"It's a slow leak," Axel said after glancing at one of his screens. "A lack of air won't be what kills us."

"You mean something else will?" Jess asked.

"Auxiliary power is down to seventy percent already. I have to kill the artificial gravity. Nobody throw up."

Axel stabbed a button on one of his screens, and the comforting sensation pinning them to their seats vanished. Layla's stomach dropped, and she resisted the urge to scream. It was like going over a steep drop on a roller coaster—except that this one never ended. Layla's gorge rose and she tasted bile. She swallowed thickly and forced herself to take long, slow breaths.

Axel nosed down toward the planet, and a subtle kick of thrust shivered through the back of her seat. It wasn't much, but within a few minutes the planet had grown significantly larger and closer. A few minutes after that, and the atmosphere swelled darkly around them, with the sun slipping below the horizon off the starboard side.

"Where are you taking us?"

"Back to the ruins."

"The..."

"The city we took off from," Axel explained. "It's the closest refuge I can think of, and at least we know it has a big flat space where we can land."

"You mean the city square?" Jess asked.

"Exactly."

"What are we going to say to all of those people?" Layla wondered as clouds swept by the cockpit in a shadowy haze.

Axel grimaced and flexed his hand on the flight stick. Layla noticed that his pinky finger moved sluggishly. The stump of his missing digit wasn't enough to properly control the mechanized glove.

"You'd better start getting our story straight."

"Why me?"

"Because as you already know, I'm a bad liar, and because you're a detective, so you have practice picking holes in other people's stories. Hopefully you can reverse that process to plug the holes in ours."

"You think they might try to hurt us?" Jess asked.

"We're about to find out," Axel replied.

Chapter 38

7:05 PM

ALICE WATCHED AS A bright circle of sky opened at the top of the smooth-sided black tunnel. She counted down inside her head as she raced upward, waiting to breach the surface. She felt and heard the air whipping around her now, where before there'd only been the still silence of vacuum. Good thing she was wearing a mech suit or she would have died. Remembering that she was standing on the hull of a spaceship, Alice crouched down and grabbed the gun turrets she'd been clinging to earlier.

The harvester shot out of the planet's crust, and the ship abruptly changed its direction of thrust. Alice held fast to the gun turret, fighting the inertial forces threatening to tear her from the ship. She barely kept from falling, and risked a look at where they had emerged.

The sky was shades of lavender. Ocean stretched as far as the eye could see, with waves crashing and sloshing against the silo she'd just emerged from.

But none of that compared to the shock of what she saw directly overhead: a familiar bright green world, divided with a narrow blue ocean and swaddled in clouds.

She'd spent enough time looking at that planet through telescopes on Earth to know what it looked like from a distance, and as it happened, that distance wasn't much. Planet B was at least four times the size of a full moon on Earth.

The problem was, if Planet B was up there, then where in the galaxy was she? Alice took a moment to assess. Gravity felt heavier here. Maybe as much as double that of Planet B and Earth. She suspected the atmosphere would be much thicker to match the increase in gravity. Judging by what she'd seen in the sky of the two planets closest to Planet B, this one seemed like it might be Planet C. A water world with an archipelago of islands.

Speaking of islands, she saw something on the horizon. Sheer white cliffs. Some type of greenery...

The closer she got, the less familiar it looked. The beaches were the only familiar aspect of the island. As the harvester jetted over the forests, she noticed spiky green stalks with no leaves interspersed with giant, translucent pink and purple trees. They rose high above the green stalks, and terminated in upside down umbrellas. Water shimmered in shallow pools within the bowl-shaped tops of those trees. The harvester slowed and dropped steadily toward the surface. Alice saw schools of frog-like creatures with multiple limbs, and big, floating green lily pads.

Alice's heart began slamming in her chest as she realized how alien this place was. Could she even breathe the air? she wondered as she leaned over the edge of the ship for a better look.

She was so distracted by those thoughts, that she didn't even notice the harvester flipping around. Top became bottom, and she went sliding right off. Alice flailed briefly before landing in the pool, parting lily pads with a thunderous *splash.* Crystalline water enveloped her, and plum-colored frog creatures darted toward her. Each of them was at least as long as she was tall. One of them stopped in front of her. It had two big black eyes and a long, glossy body with six legs and webbed joints. A lumpy head with dark whiskers around a grinning mouth regarded her.

Alice sank to the bottom with the creature, and her feet touched the spongy floor of the treetop. The bottom was a waving forest of long pinkish hairs that waved in the currents of the pool. A swarm of wiggling black worms burst out of that forest, disturbed by her arrival.

The frog creature reacted by lashing out with its arms, scooping up the worms with fin-like hands and stuffing them by the hundreds into the sucking horror of its mouth.

Revolted and terrified that she might be next, Alice kicked and clawed to the surface. The suit turned out to be fairly buoyant, perhaps because of its internal air supply.

Alice breached the surface. The sun shone from a clear lavender sky, hovering almost directly overhead. Treading water, she began to feel the warmth of it bleeding through her suit. What was the external temperature here?

Wondering about that triggered a familiar number and symbol in the top right of her helmet: 32C. A lot hotter than Planet B.

Alice wondered about the air composition next. And more familiar numbers and symbols appeared:

O_2: 37%
N_2: 61%
H_2O: 1.1%
CO_2: 0.55%
Argon: 0.21%
Other: 0.14%
Pressure: 209 Pa

At 37% Oxygen, and an atmospheric pressure that was almost double that of Earth's, Alice realized that breathing the air here would be toxic.

"How long before I run out of air?" she asked aloud this time.

To her surprise an audible female voice replied: "At present rates of consumption, you will run out of air in approximately five hundred and ninety-seven Earth Standard Hours when your mech suit runs out of power."

Alice blinked in shock. "You can speak?"

"Yes."

"I..." Alice struggled to arrange her thoughts. Almost six hundred hours. The suit must have some type of air filtration system. Assuming that was true, she would die of dehydration long before she suffocated. Or maybe she would die of exhaustion first. Alice kicked over to the edge of the giant bowl she was swimming in.

Halfway there, she felt something brushing her legs. She yelped in alarm. Then it grabbed her ankle and yanked her down. It was one of the purple frogs. It opened its mouth in a giant O and swallowed her arm up to the shoulder.

Alice screamed and kicked it in the stomach. The creature reacted instantly, releasing her and darting away with a burst of bubbles. Alice breached the surface once more, and finished swimming to the edge of the tree. Dragging herself up the ridged, bony sides of the upside-down umbrella tree, Alice lay gasping from the exertion beneath the heat of the midday sun.

This was bad. She'd hitched a ride on that harvester assuming that it might be headed back to Earth. Instead it had plunged through the hollow center of Planet B to some kind of dimensional gateway that led to the equally hollow core of Planet C. Now she was stranded on the surface of that world, surrounded by giant alien frogs in a potentially deadly environment.

"Contact Axel Harper," Alice tried.

"I'm sorry, there are no contacts by that name within contact range."

"Contact Layla Bester."

"I'm sorry, there are no contacts by that—"

"Stop." Alice struggled to contain her rising panic. "Is anyone in contact range?"

"Minder 2972 is within range. Would you like to speak with it?"

"It?" Alice asked.

"The *Gesselt* do not possess a gender, as they reproduce by fragmentation. Would you like to contact Minder 2972?"

"Are they friendly?" Alice asked.

"They are an intelligent species of carnivorous cephalox with a low tolerance for alien lifeforms."

"Then that's a *no*," Alice decided.

"Odds are high that it would prefer to eat you than reason with you."

Alice laid her head back against the bony shell of the treetop. She couldn't believe that this was how she was going to die. Alone on an alien world, eaten by a six-legged frog.

Then again, what better way for an astronomer to meet her end? It was some twisted fulfillment of the old adage—*watch what you wish for.*

Alice shook her head to snap herself out of it, and sat up. She crawled the rest of the way up the slope of the bowl, slipping and sliding as she reached the rim. Grabbing the curling, bony ridge along the edge, she pulled herself to it and peered over, hoping to find some way that she could at least climb down.

The spiky green forest lay at least fifty feet below. Falling with this gravity and from this height would kill her, even with whatever protection the suit could afford.

Alice leaned back from the edge, breathing hard from the climb. A splash caught her eye from the lily-pad pool below. One of those six-armed frogs jumped out of the water and dove back down, snatching some kind of bug from the air.

A giant, balloon-like creature appeared across the pool, rising above the edge. Alice stayed frozen as it glided over the water, trailing dozens of tentacles. Its translucent skin inflated and deflated with steady breaths, seeming to swim through the thick air. Tentacles pierced the surface of the pool. The water stirred violently, and then the jellyfish creature floated away with one of the frogs twisted up and struggling in its clutches.

Alice remained as still as she could, watching the massive, flying jellyfish drift away.

She was lucky it hadn't targeted her instead of that amphibian.

Planet B was starting to look pretty good right now.

"Is there any way I can get back to Planet B?" she asked.

"I'm sorry, I have no record of a Planet B. Could you be more specific?"

"The planet next to this one."

"There are two planets located beside this one. Novus, and Arcos."

"Novus!" Alice cried, recognizing the name.

"The fastest way to reach Novus would be to take a harvester through the Planetary Gateway."

"I don't have a harvester!" Alice cried.

"Interplanetary travel requires a Class A starship, and the proper clearances for Gateway access."

"Can you send a distress signal?"

"Of course. Which Minder would you like to alert to your distress?"

"Any Minder on Novus!"

"Contacting..."

Alice's heart fluttered in her chest. Maybe this suit was good for something, after all.

"I'm sorry. There is no reply. It is possible that the minder you are trying to reach is currently outside of emergency beacon range. Please try again later."

Alice screamed in frustration—

Then cut herself off as she noticed a pair of amphibians crawling out of the water to stare at her with those big, glassy black eyes and their grinning, toothless mouths. Alice scuttled away from the advancing creatures, drawing herself up against the bony edge of the bowl-shaped treetop.

The amphibians continued approaching steadily, crouching low and chittering to each other.

"GO AWAY!" Alice screamed, and they froze, hesitating. Seeing how easily they spooked, she shot to her feet, screaming like a maniac, and charged down the sloping side of the treetop. The amphibians chirped in alarm and dove back into the water.

Alice stopped, breathing hard and blinking sweat from her eyes. She sat down with her knees drawn up to her chest. The blazing heat of the sun warmed her back, prickling it with sweat. Her suit was struggling to keep her cool in the sweltering heat of this place. How much longer could she hold out? Maybe Axel would get back into comms range soon, and she could call him for help. Surely he knew how to get here and find her?

If not, she was going to die from the heat and dehydration. Or maybe she'd crack her suit open and take a drink from that pool first. Then alien microbes and oxygen poisoning would kill her instead.

Chapter 39

7:21 PM

AXEL BROUGHT THEM IN hot, roaring toward the town square. Bruce caught a glimpse of a group of three T-Rexes outside the walls, two adults and a child, busy fighting over a kill that was too small to see.

The cobblestones of the square raced up beneath them.

"Hang on!" Axel warned.

"Slow down!" Layla cried.

A thinning group of people in the square scattered with the approach of Axel's harvester. The ship touched down with a deafening roar, skidding into the stone pedestal of the broken bronze statue, and flattening what was left of it.

Bruce recovered a few moments later, shaking his head and tasting blood. He'd bit his tongue.

"Nice landing," he spat, painting the deck crimson.

"You're lucky you're alive right now!" Axel snapped. "Layla, are you okay?" He reached for her arm.

"I'm fine," she replied, jerking away from his touch.

He regarded her with a frown. "This isn't my fault! I warned you!"

"One way or another, it's definitely your fault," Layla replied. "The only reason we're here is because of you." Axel's cheeks bulged with protest, but Layla cut him off with a venomous look. "Whether you brought us here or not," she added.

A crowd had gathered around their crash site. Bruce released his safety harness. "You have any idea what we're going to say to them, Detective?" he asked, standing up.

Layla shot him an angry look. "No!"

"Speaking from experience," Axel began, "we can't give them the impression that we know more than they do, or that we enjoy any type of privilege that they don't. But if we're lucky, we won't have to deal with any of that..." Axel tapped a series of buttons on one of the displays. An error beeped and flashed on the screen. "Damn it!" He slammed the dash with an open palm.

"What's wrong?" Bruce asked.

"The landing ramp is jammed. I thought we might be able to use the hovercraft to escape."

"So what are our options?" Bruce asked.

"Suit up and cloak ourselves so no one can see us, then hike back to the dam," Axel said.

"We don't have enough suits for that, do we?" Jess asked.

"The deck below this one has more," Layla explained.

Axel stood from the pilot's seat. "Let's go get them."

A minute later they were standing on the shattered deck below with Tom, Jess, and Neil peering down from above the access ladder.

"Well?" Neil pressed.

"Doesn't look good," Bruce said.

The transporter room had crumpled to the point that the ceiling was barely four feet high, and the spare suits were scattered in pieces around the deck.

"What's the backup plan?" Bruce asked.

"What makes you think I have one?" Axel demanded. "This was your idea, remember?"

"We have to go out and tell them everything we know," Layla said.

Axel snorted. "Assuming they believe us. Speaking *again* from *experience*, if we walk out wearing these suits, they're going to think we had something to do with bringing them here. Our best bet is to convince them we were abducted, too, but unlike them, we woke up early and hijacked the harvester, forcing it to crash here."

Bruce scowled. "Even under the armor, we're all wearing those black jumpsuits from the dam."

"We can explain that," Axel said. "We'll say it's some kind of uniform and we were abducted from the same place."

"What place?" Jess asked from the top of the ladder.

"They look a bit like wetsuits," Layla said. "Maybe we can say it was an aquarium. Or a diving school."

"Diving school," Bruce muttered. "Okay, that might work. Let's go." He climbed the ladder back to the main deck, then turned to help Layla out, but she batted his hand away.

"I'm not helpless," she snapped.

"And so died chivalry," Bruce replied.

"There's just one problem with your plan," Tom said as Axel emerged from the lower deck. "Fango is down there."

"The other inmate from Sing Sing? I thought he was dead?" Layla asked.

Tom frowned. "Yeah, so did I. Anyway, the point is, he'll recognize me if I walk out of here without a suit. And he'll remember that we were abducted together, which will shoot your alibi full of holes."

"So you keep your suit on," Axel suggested. "In fact, Bruce and I should, too. The three of us can sneak out of the city undetected and make our way back to the dam. Once we get there, I can grab another ship and come pick the rest of you up."

"Why don't we just wait in here while you do that?" Neil asked.

"Could be a long wait," Axel said.

"How long?" Neil asked.

"I don't know, but I'd guess it's at least a five or six-hour hike to the dam from here. You can wait in the ship, assuming no one finds a way in. But if they do..."

"They'll assume we're hiding something," Layla finished for him. "Otherwise we would have come out sooner."

"Exactly."

Neil blew out a ragged sigh. "Well, they're just like us, right? Confused and scared. I'm sure it will be fine. We'll go out and pretend to be as clueless as them, and wait for Axel and the others to return."

"Or, we could just tell them the truth," Layla pointed out.

Axel regarded her with a deepening frown. "Even if they believe you, we'd have to take them all back with us to the dam. How do you suppose we're going to feed and shelter that many people? There isn't enough space. The Architects brought them to this city for a reason. It's a lot bigger, and at least most of the shelters are already built."

A clanging sound drew their eyes down to the lower deck. Someone was banging on the hull.

"We're out of time," Axel said. "Stick to the plan. We'll be back soon." Looking to Tom and Bruce, he said, "Where are your helmets?"

Tom gestured vaguely, and Bruce ducked into the cockpit to fetch his.

"What about guns?" Neil asked, patting his rifle. "We need some protection while we wait. Bewildered humans aren't the only danger out there."

Axel hesitated. "Take them. I guess that's easy enough to explain. Whatever you do, remember, you're as clueless as they are."

Layla nodded slowly. "We'll be okay."

Axel held her gaze for a long second while the banging outside grew more violent and insistent. Muttered voices sounded from below, followed by a stuttering *zapping* sound. "Tom! It's time to go,"

Axel said. "Your friend is shooting his way in with that arc rifle he stole from the dam."

"Arc rifle?" Bruce asked.

Axel nodded to the weapon he was holding across his chest. "My name for them. Arc, as in Architect. Helmets on," Axel indicated. He lowered his and twisted it to engage the seals. A moment later his armor shimmered and he vanished, then reappeared as a translucent green silhouette.

Bruce and Tom each cloaked themselves next.

"Be careful," Axel whispered, his voice echoing tinnily through the ship.

Before anyone could reply, the sound of heavy boots and muttered voices came drifting up from below. Bruce waited for Axel to lead the way up the ladder to the top hatch.

Layla and Neil backed steadily away from the ragged hole beneath the ladder, each of them aiming their rifles at the spot.

Tom was the last one up the ladder to the upper airlock. Axel waved the lower hatch shut, and cycled the top one open.

"Let's go," he said, his voice coming to Bruce's ears through his helmet speakers this time.

He followed Axel warily up the ladder and out into the star-studded night, the three of them appearing as nothing more than imperceptible shivers in the air.

Chapter 40

7:42 PM

Layla spotted a big man in an orange jumpsuit before he noticed her. That had to be Fango. She hefted her rifle a little higher. "Freeze! Who are you?" He glanced up through the hole in the deck and casually raised his own weapon. "I said freeze!" Layla insisted.

"I heard you," he replied.

Someone else appeared behind him, holding a conventional hunting rifle. He was wearing combat fatigues. A sergeant, if his lapel insignia was anything to go by.

"Were you piloting this craft?" the sergeant asked, edging Fango out of the way.

Layla shook her head and lowered her arc rifle. "No. We... we woke up on board. And then we found the controls. I-I think we crashed it."

"Well, come on down," the sergeant waved to her. "Let's get you situated."

Layla shouldered her rifle and descended the ladder. Neil and Jess followed. Fango eyed them warily, crouched and hunching from the low ceiling of the collapsed deck. One side of the ship had been blasted open, leaving a hole just big enough for them to crawl out.

Once they were standing outside, a crowd gathered around, and the sergeant introduced himself.

"I'm Marine Gunnery Sergeant Gil Cameron, but you can call me Cam."

Layla nodded and shook his hand. "Detective Layla Bester, NYPD."

"A cop?" Fango sneered.

Layla ignored him, focusing on Cam. He was of medium height, relatively trim with thinning gray hair and a deeply-lined face. A career soldier, she guessed, given that he had to be about fifty. Hard to tell much else in the night, but the nights were never particularly dark here.

"What can you tell us about that?" the sergeant gestured to the planets in the sky.

Layla looked up and sucked in a sharp breath, hoping it was enough to fool them. "I... I don't... w-where are we?"

Neil and Jess did a good job of gaping at the sight and looking scared. Knowing what they did about this place, that wasn't hard.

"Not Earth," Fango said. "That's for damn sure. There's dinosaurs out there."

"So you've told us," Sergeant Cam said, glancing sideways at him. "Do you know anything about that?" he asked, jerking his chin to Layla.

She just shook her head, pretending to be shocked into silence.

Fango smirked again. "She's lying."

Sergeant Cam regarded him with a look of strained patience. "I thought we agreed that I would be asking the questions."

"Did it sound like a question to you?" Fango snapped. "It was an observation."

Layla summed up the interaction quickly. These two were jockeying for position, with each of them trying to be the leader, and it wasn't working. Especially not since the sergeant was armed with a simple hunting rifle and Fango had one of the architect's much more advanced energy weapons.

"Neil?" Layla asked.

"Y-yeah?" he stammered.

"Would you give your rifle to the sergeant, please?"

"What? Why?"

"Because he has experience with firearms, and you don't."

Neil grimaced and stepped forward, holding out the arc rifle.

"Thank you, sir," Cam said, switching the hunting rifle to a one-handed grip as he accepted the other weapon from Neil. He slipped the metallic strap over his head before checking it over. "Any idea what these fire modes are?" he asked, touching the slider above the trigger.

Layla explained that the X was the safety, followed by an open circle for lethal lasers, and the third setting, denoted by a wavy equals sign, was the stun mode. The fourth was a solid dot. "We haven't tried that one yet, so we don't know what it does."

"I have," Fango said, smiling and pointing to the hole in the side of the harvester.

Layla accepted that with a nod. Of course he hadn't blown the ship open with a simple laser bolt. She wondered absently if that would also work on the door of the dam's lowermost level.

"You've stunned someone?" Cam asked, his eyes narrowing fractionally.

"What?" Layla blinked at him.

"You said you tried all the settings except the last one."

"Oh, yeah. Her," Layla lied, indicating Jess. "She woke up a few moments before you came in."

"I see. Well, thanks for the weapon..." Cam trailed off, looking at Neil.

"Neil Forester," he supplied.

Cam repeated the name, as if committing it to memory, then said, "If Mr. Morales here is to be believed, we're going to need all the firepower we can get."

"How long have you been here?" Layla asked, thinking that might be something she would ask if she'd just arrived.

"Not long. Morales has been here the longest, but all he seems to know is that if we leave the city we'll get eaten by something scary with big teeth."

"Have you seen anything like that yet?" Layla asked.

"Not yet, but then, we haven't left the city. We're busy posting guards on the walls to see if we can—"

Someone shouted for their attention, and came running into the square, bursting through the wary line of onlookers.

"Sergeant! Sergeant!"

A young man with shaggy blond hair skidded to a stop with his hands on his knees, his head low to keep the blood flowing.

"Take a beat, son. Breathe. What's going on?"

"I saw—" The man sucked in a deep breath. "T-Rex. Three of them. Outside the wall."

"Show me," Cam replied.

Layla followed the sergeant from the square at a brisk pace with her heart hammering in her chest. Did these people know there was a hole in the wall? Probably. She hoped the rexes were far away from that breach.

The other abductees murmured and pointed to them as they walked by. Layla regarded them with wide, glassy eyes, as if she were still in shock.

Pretending to know less than she did was easier than she'd expected, but the longer Axel took to come back and get them, the harder it was going to be to keep their stories straight.

Layla went back over details in her head: she'd shot Jess by accident and stunned her; the three of them had woken up on board and crashed the ship.

So far not a lot to keep straight, as long as they didn't accidentally allude to the time they'd already spent here, they'd be fine.

"What's with the matching pajamas?" Fango quipped as they jogged down the cobblestone street.

"Wet suits," Neil explained before she could say anything.

"Diving classes," Layla added.

"Oh yeah? No oxygen? No masks?"

"We hadn't got that far yet," Layla said.

"Right. Tough break getting abducted by aliens, huh?" Fango smiled as if it were the best thing that had ever happened to him. Having come straight from prison, it probably was.

"What about you?" Layla asked, even though she already knew the answer. "Looks like a prison uniform."

"Nah. I was an extra in a prison break movie."

Layla smirked. So that was his story. "Sounds interesting. What was it called?"

"Uh. Yeah, it was uh. If I can remember. Shit, I don't always pay attention to my gigs, you know?"

"You don't remember?" Layla repeated.

Cam shot a glance over his shoulder.

"Give me a minute, okay?" Fango said. "Ah... *A Long Day in the Yard*, I think. Yeah that was it. Long Day in the Yard."

"Pretty clunky title for a movie," Layla said.

"What do you want from me? I didn't write it. It was just this low-budget action flick. I needed the money, so I took the part." Fango shrugged.

They reached the wall and Cam stopped, catching his breath. The young man who'd led them there looked like he was about to pass out. A shuddering roar split the air, and all of them shut right up, holding their breath.

Cam let his out slowly, and crept up the stone stairs to the ramparts. Layla followed with Neil and

Fango. They crouched low behind the crumbling battlements at the top.

The mauve and blue light of the nearest planets shivered along the mighty spine of a T-Rex as it ripped a glistening strip of flesh from its kill. A slightly smaller one growled at it and snapped at the trailing piece of flesh, trying to steal it away. They each roared and growled, snapping their jaws at each other as they tugged on it like a rope. A much smaller rex stood between them, head down and munching away.

"I don't believe it," Cam whispered.

"It's what I been telling you," Fango muttered. "Dinosaurs."

Layla stood up slowly.

"Are you crazy? Get down!" Fango hissed.

"Shhh," she replied, looking around in a quick circle. She found the gap in the walls on the far side of the city from the rexes, and let out a shaky sigh.

"You saw that, too?" Cam whispered as she ducked back down.

She nodded. "Briefly, just before we crashed."

"We have guards posted," Cam added. "So far nothing's come in, but now that we know exactly what's out there..." He trailed off, watching the rexes feed.

"Are they armed?" Layla asked.

"What?" Cam asked, sounding faraway now.

"The guards on the wall. Are they armed?"

"No," someone else said. Layla turned to see the boy who'd come running to get them. "We don't have any guns. We're just spotters."

Layla did the math. With her rifle, they had three arc weapons and one regular hunting rifle that was probably already half empty.

"We need to arm the guards around the breach," Layla suggested.

"No shit," Cam muttered. "Okay." He drew in a shuddering breath and motioned to the stairs they'd come up.

Layla led the way down this time. At the bottom, Cam said, "Fango, we're going to need that rifle."

"What?" He snorted. "No way."

"Detective Bester is right. There's no point posting guards if they're not ready and able to defend us."

"I'm not giving up my weapon, man."

Layla noticed the shining *14* on the little display at the back of his rifle. Hers had only been fired once, and a stun bolt at that. It was still set to stun, and reading 79. She flicked it over to the open circle of the lethal setting, and the number turned to a 44.

Cam stared hard at Fango, visibly clenching his jaw.

"You have two guns," Fango said. "You can give up one."

"We need at least two armed guards to defend the breach," Layla said. "There were more of these rifles on the ship we crashed."

"Show me," Cam replied.

Layla led the sergeant back to the square and through the hole in the side of the ship. They found the rifles scattered from their racks and lying in the twisted remains of the deck. Several of them were inoperable, but they managed to recover three working rifles.

"This is going to be a big help," Cam said, looping two of the arc weapons over his arm with the straps while holding the hunting rifle in his other hand and leaving Neil's weapon to dangle by its strap. "Let's get them to the walls."

Back outside, Neil and Jess were waiting for them, rubbing their arms and hopping up and down.

"Chilly, huh?" Fango said. "You'll get used to it."

"We should make a fire if we can," Cam said. Noticing some of the other abductees standing around idly, others sitting with their backs to the crumbling stone buildings, he raised his voice. "Search the city! Gather anything useful you can find and bring it to the square!"

"Like what?" a woman called back.

"Wood for a fire and anything we can use as a weapon. Food and water and containers for gathering it. But whatever you do, don't go outside the walls.

"Why?" the woman asked. "What's out there?"

"You don't want to know," Cam muttered. He nodded to Fango. "Go with them. If you see anything dangerous, shoot it."

Fango made a face, but gave in with a nod. Neil and Jess followed him across the square.

Cam nodded to Layla and added, "Let's go."

They ran to the broken section of the wall and found six people up on the ramparts, gawking at something on the other side—a big, brown and green creature. It stood low to the ground, with four stout legs, and had spikes all over its back. A clubbed tail waved idly as it meandered through the rubble and the fields of grass below the wall.

"Is that another..." Cam trailed off.

"Dinosaur," Layla whispered.

"An ankylosaurus," someone said haltingly.

Cam stood up and asked who had experience with weapons. A young woman raised her hand, and Cam approached her with one of the arc rifles. Layla explained how the weapon worked, and then they went to the ramparts on the other side and repeated the process, this time handing out the hunting rifle and the other arc weapons.

Cam gave the guards instructions to watch the breach and make sure no carnivorous dinosaurs made it through, and if they did, to send that young kid running to find him in the square.

"You mean there's more of them out there?" an elderly man asked, while anxiously flexing his hands on an arc rifle.

"Yes," was all Cam said before hurrying back down the stairs.

He and Layla left them, with Cam promising to be back soon.

When they returned to the square, they found a pile of lumber forming beside the crashed harvester. A short distance away, there was another pile, this one contained gleaming metal tools and implements.

Layla walked over there with Cam. The abductees had found rusty swords, axe heads, dented shields, broken arrows, and a collection of wooden spears with rusty metal tips.

"Looks about as old as this city," Cam muttered, picking up one of the swords and testing the edge with his finger. "Still sharp, though."

"Then it'll do," Layla decided. "We should distribute these and make a fire."

"What about food and water?" someone asked as they brought in another shield with a leather-bound bundle of daggers.

"We found water!" Neil said, struggling to carry a giant, dripping wooden bucket between him and Fango. They set it down and everyone gathered around. Cam fished a chipped clay bowl out of the bucket and drank deeply from it before passing it to Layla. She did the same, and then passed it to the next person in line.

Fifteen minutes later, and after refilling the bucket several times, they'd all drank their fill. There was no sign of anyone noticing the strange properties of the water, except for one person saying their toothache was suddenly better. And someone else complaining that the water was fizzy. No one made the connection, though.

Cam used a laser bolt from his arc rifle to light a roaring bonfire in the middle of the square, right beside the crashed harvester. The medieval weapons were distributed, and everyone kept a wary eye on the gap in the walls at the end of the street.

Layla sat off to one side with Neil and Jess, warming herself by the blaze, while Cam went to check in with the guards on the wall. Her gaze drifted out of focus on the mesmerizing swirls within the fire.

"When do you think they'll be back?" Jess whispered.

Layla shot her a warning look. "Five or six hours is what he said, remember?"

"And it's been about, what—half an hour?" Neil asked.

"More like an hour," Layla said, checking her watch and seeing the numbers glow to life—8:52 PM. The sun was already swelling on the horizon, peeling back the shadows of the night and washing the clouds in vibrant reds and oranges.

People were pointing to the sky and remarking on it. Layla blinked sleepily and shook her head. To them it was just a sunrise on an alien planet. To her it was the mark of yet another local day having passed. How many times had the sun risen and set since she'd arrived? Six? Layla had been here for almost a full Earth day, and the local version was six times shorter, so that tracked.

It was almost nine at night on September 27th back in New York, not counting whatever time dilation was doing between the two places. What was it Alice had said? Time was passing sixty times faster on Earth? So it had been a day for her, but several months had passed back home.

It didn't seem possible.

A rising commotion rolled through the group. The abductees began murmuring, then shouting and pointing to the sky. Several people shot to their feet.

Layla stood up with them, shading her eyes against the glare of the rising sun to see the long, billowing orange tail of a meteor streaking into the atmosphere.

Her thoughts flashed to the meteor that had wiped out the dinosaurs, and apprehension gripped her as she wondered if this was take two. Maybe Planet B wasn't an ark at all, but some type of re-enactment of history.

But that didn't make any sense, and this meteor wasn't nearly big enough to cause any damage. It was long and cylindrical, bright and reflecting the sun, with a tapered tip facing up.

It was a spaceship, and not one of the boxy or sleek black ones of the Architects. This was a much more familiar vessel. It looked just like a Mars lander from SDG.

"Is that..." Neil trailed off. "One of ours?"

There was no longer any doubt once it dropped to a hundred feet above the city, now slowing dramatically with a plume of orange fire jetting from the bottom of the rocket. Clouds of smoke and dust billowed out as it landed just outside the breach in the wall. The towering ship stood still with smoke curling around it, a monument to human endeavor.

An actual rocket had arrived from Earth. Layla's heart jumped in her chest. The rest of the abductees let out a collective roar, whooping and screaming as they sprinted toward the ship.

"Come on!" Neil cried as he and Jess ran after them.

Layla was the last to leave the bonfire, but she was no less eager than the others. This was it. Their ticket home. Axel hadn't been able to take them back on the harvester, but that rocket could take them home.

Couldn't it?

Layla remembered the quartet of interceptors that had shot them down from orbit just a few hours ago, and her stride faltered. Then she recalled something Axel had said the day before: *No one is allowed to leave the Menagerie System.*

8:55 PM

"Hey, hold up!" Bruce shouted while peering at the scudding orange tail of fire cutting across the sky.

Both Axel and Tom froze and slowly turned from the bank of the river that they were following back to the dam. Their suits shone with rainbow-colored reflections in the gilded light of the rising sun. None of them were cloaked now, since dinos couldn't smell them through the suits, and there weren't any hysterical abductees to hide from.

"What the hell is that?" Bruce pointed to the sight in the sky.

"I don't know..." Axel said.

"Looks like a comet," Tom added.

"Maybe," Bruce replied, tracking it for a moment. "No." He shook his head. "Looks too artificial."

"Architects?" Tom asked.

"More like one of ours," Bruce realized. "It's a rocket!"

"Impossible," Axel said.

"Is it?" Bruce countered. "We have to follow it. That could be our ticket out of here."

"Are you crazy?" Axel demanded. "We just got shot down in my ship, and now you think some rocket from Earth is going to get you home?"

"Why not? If it can get here, then it can leave."

"I already told you, the Architects won't let any of us leave."

"Yeah? Or maybe they just don't want people leaving in one of their ships. You know, grand theft spaceship? Seems like the kind of thing that an alien might object to more than, say, a few people disappearing from one of their game parks."

"You're wrong," Axel insisted.

"You've never had the chance to try, so you don't know that."

Bruce watched the rocket intently, noticing how slowly it was falling. "It's making a controlled descent. Looks like it's going to land somewhere along the coast."

"We can check it out from the air on our way to pick up Lulu and the others."

"Screw that," Bruce said. "I'm checking it out now."

Tom began stalking back along the pebbled shore of the river. "I'm coming with you."

"Don't be stupid," Axel said. "Even if you could get back, they'd take you straight to prison."

"Sounds like you're afraid we might make it," Bruce said.

"I'm not," Axel replied. "But of all of us, Tom has the least to gain by finding a way home."

"I'm just going to see who it is," Tom explained. "You can pick us up when you swing back around to get the others."

"How am I supposed to know where to find you?"

"Doesn't the radar screen in those ships show you where lifeforms are?" Tom asked.

"Well... yeah, kinda."

"Then it should be easy to find us, but failing that, we'll either meet you at the rocket or in the city with the others."

"Fine," Axel muttered, then sounding almost sincere, he added, "Good luck."

Bruce smirked and shook his head. He quietly followed Tom along the river, aiming for the coast before peeling off to track the landing rocket through the woods. "Looks like it's coming in for a landing around the city," Tom said.

"Could be," Bruce agreed. They were still a few miles out from the city, but it certainly seemed to be headed there. Bruce imagined all of those abducted people swarming the rocket ship, begging to be taken home. How many could it hold? he wondered. Would they select people on a first come first serve basis? If so, he and Tom might get there too late to reserve seats for themselves. "Let's pick up the pace," Bruce suggested, and broke into a light jog.

"Good idea," Tom replied.

They didn't make it more than a hundred feet before Bruce spotted something else—a marching line of Jakar, their spear points glinting in the beams of sunlight slanting through the trees.

Bruce grabbed Tom's arm to stop him from barreling ahead. The two of them engaged their cloaking shields and ducked behind the trunk of a fallen tree just in time to avoid being seen. They crouched in the shadows, peeking over the top of the log at the marching horde.

"Jakar," Bruce muttered. They were covered in furs and scaly plates of armor. Most had swords strapped to their hips and bows on their backs. "There must be at least a hundred of them," Bruce added. "Looks like an army."

Tom nodded. "Where do you think they're going?"

Crashing trees and splintering logs accompanied heavy, plodding footsteps. A scattered group of horned dinosaurs followed behind the marching villagers, with Jakar sitting in saddles on their backs.

"Triceratops for horses?" Tom remarked.

The beasts had giant lizard skin bags strapped to their backs. "They brought plenty of supplies," Bruce said, counting no less than seven triceratops lumbering along behind the army. There were other dinosaurs as well, being carried individually in long, rectangular wooden cages. They were small, two-legged creatures with a hint of feathers on the crowns of their heads.

"Velociraptors," Tom breathed.

"I think they're headed for the city," Bruce said, belatedly answering Tom's question.

"Or tracking that rocket?" Tom suggested.

"No, it looks like they've been marching for several hours already. Maybe ever since we buzzed their village in Axel's ship."

"They're the same ones?" Tom asked.

"Look like it to me. They're bringing the same dinos we saw in their pens."

"Then they're probably out for blood. We'd better get there first so we can warn the others," Tom said.

"Yeah... let's go," Bruce agreed.

Chapter 41

9:24 PM

LAYLA STOOD OUTSIDE THE walls with Sergeant Cameron, Neil, Jess, Fango, and about a hundred other people, all of them gazing up at the towering rocket. They were about fifty feet away, standing on a char-blackened patch of grass that was still burning weakly at the edges.

Everyone watched in silence, shading their eyes from the glare of the rising sun as the outer hatch popped open in the gleaming ship. Machinery clunked and whirred inside the rocket, and a large metal platform slid out of the side, right beneath the hatch. Men in white space suits emerged, peering over the sides and gesturing animatedly at the crowd below.

Layla couldn't help but notice that fully half of them were armed with compact-looking rifles.

"Soldiers?" Layla asked.

"Space Force," Cam clarified, as if they weren't really soldiers.

The platform came whirring down, and someone else reached out from inside the rocket to shut the hatch.

Before the platform even reached the bottom, an amplified voice bellowed down to them.

"I am Ambassador Jansen from Earth. Please do not be alarmed. We are here to help."

Another voice joined his almost as soon as the ambassador had finished talking, "This is General Ryker of Space Force. Drop your weapons and keep your hands where we can see them. I will not ask again."

Layla and Cam traded wary looks before ducking out of their rifles' straps and laying the weapons at their feet. Fango, however, chose to fall back into the crowds rather than relinquish his weapon.

The platform touched the ground and a group of five soldiers fanned out, with four unarmed crew behind them. Layla eyed the soldier with four black stars on his shoulders. The General. He led the landing party, with two civilians hurrying to keep pace on either side.

"Who are you, and how did you get here?" the general demanded.

Sergeant Cam stepped forward and saluted, identifying himself, and then offering a brief explanation.

"Abducted, huh?" the general glanced around. "Never thought I'd see the day where that didn't sound like BS."

Someone else stepped forward from the landing party. "I'm Preston Baylor of the Space Development Group."

Layla recognized both the name and the face behind the helmet. At his introduction, the crowd surged forward, screaming and shouting for Preston to take them back to Earth.

The soldiers snapped their rifles up to their shoulders and the general roared, "Everyone back it up!"

The crowd subsided.

"My kids!" a woman cried. "I have to get back to my children!"

Preston looked around slowly, his triumphant expression fading to a mixture of confusion and awe.

The ambassador reached up and touched a button to lift his visor. It opened with a hiss of escaping air, and he sucked in a deep breath. "What is that? Cinnamon? Lemons?"

"What are you doing?" one of the unarmed crewmen said.

"If it's not safe to breathe, don't you think they'd be keeling over by now?" the ambassador replied.

"We've only been here a few hours, sir," Cam said. "But so far, no negative effects."

"Good enough for me," Preston said, and raised his visor next.

The general and his men grudgingly followed suit. But the other civilians kept theirs lowered.

"Planet B," Preston whispered, looking around with wide eyes, his jaw agape. "I can't believe we made it."

"We need to get inside the walls," Layla said suddenly. She took two quick steps forward and added, "It's not safe out here."

General Ryker's lined face tightened and his eyes hardened. "What do you mean by that, ma'am?"

"There are dinosaurs," Neil said.

"The meat-eating kind," Jess added.

Preston's cheeks bulged, and a peal of laughter burst from deep inside his chest. But no one else laughed with him. "You can't be serious," he said.

"Dead serious," Cam replied.

Preston's jaw slackened. "That's impossible."

"Does any of this seem possible to you?" Cam countered. "Someone would be contradicting me right now if I was lying."

"I have to see them," Ambassador Jansen said.

"Definitely," Preston agreed.

"You could see the inside of their stomachs if you're not careful," Cam muttered, and bent down to pick up his rifle. When General Ryker didn't object, Layla did the same.

"General?" Preston said. "We'll need an escort. Would you and your men join us, please?"

"Very well," he said. "Alpha One and Two, you're with us. Three and Four, stay here and guard the LZ."

"Yes, sir," one of the soldiers said before rushing back to the elevator platform at the base of the rocket.

"This is a bad idea," Cam said. "You can't stop a T-Rex with those guns."

"Watch me," the general replied.

Preston hesitated. "You've seen a T-Rex?"

"A couple of hours ago," Cam said. "Family of three, fighting over a kill just outside the walls."

Another laugh bubbled from Preston's lips, but he cut himself off with a smile. "Sorry. I just don't think I'll be able to believe it until I see them with my own eyes."

"Take us," Fango said, stepping forward with another man. Both were armed with arc rifles.

"And who are you?" General Ryker demanded.

The smaller man beside Fango stood at attention. "Corporal Kent Morgan, Army reserves, sir!" He clicked his heels together and saluted. "But more to the point, we're extra sets of eyes, boots, and ears. Can't hurt to have that in hostile territory."

"What about Orange Julius?" General Ryker asked, jerking a thumb at Fango. "Some kinda escaped prisoner?"

"Movie extra," Fango said, grinning easily.

Layla had to bite her tongue not to reveal who he really was. But Fango couldn't possibly try anything while he was surrounded by soldiers, could he? And if he did, what did he have to gain by turning on them?

Then again, what could he gain by joining them? He had to be up to something. She was just about to insist that she go with them when General Ryker said, "All right, hustle up and fall in."

He started across the field. Glancing back at the other two soldiers, he added, "We'll do one lap around the city and scout the clearing to establish a perimeter. Keep your eyes on the trees!"

"Yes, sir!" one of his soldiers said.

Layla watched them go with a frown.

"Don't worry. Sounds like they're not going far," Cam said. "But let's get back up on those walls and keep a lookout just in case."

9:38 PM

Bruce reached the edge of the forest and saw the city walls soaring across a grassy clearing. The gleaming, missile-shaped tower of the lander stood beside those walls with the ocean behind it. They'd left the Jakar behind, but they couldn't be more than ten or fifteen minutes away.

"We'd better hurry," Bruce breathed.

"Look—" Tom pointed toward the ocean where the rocket was.

"I already saw it," Bruce said.

"No, look again!" Tom insisted.

A group of people was headed their way, moving quickly through the waist-high grass. Bruce picked out the gleaming white of space suits and the bright orange fabric of a prisoner's jumpsuit.

"Fango's with them," Tom muttered. "Why the hell would they trust him?"

"They probably don't. But you gotta have some dino bait, right?"

Tom snorted.

"Let's go introduce ourselves," Bruce suggested.

"Are you sure that's a good idea?"

Before Bruce could reply, he heard someone shout a warning, and a giant shadow swooped down, sending the landing party scattering.

"Pterodactyls!" Tom said.

Gunfire erupted from the clearing as the swooping shadows multiplied. Someone screamed as they were knocked down, and Bruce saw a clean white space suit splashed with blood. There was a brief struggle, and then someone riddled the creature with bullets, and it collapsed on top of its prey. A second man went down as another dino slammed into him. A stream of bullets chased it back into the air.

Two unarmed crewmen descended on the second injured man and began dragging him toward the trees where Bruce and Tom were hiding. The others fired steadily into the air.

"We have to help them," Bruce said.

"Wait!" Tom shouted.

Bruce burst out of cover, firing controlled bursts from his rifle. Lasers stitched the sky with crimson fire both from his weapon and the clearing as Fango and another man opened up on the flock of dinos with arc rifles. Three of the pterodactyls fell, tumbling, with their wings limp and folding around them.

The group reached the trees, and Bruce disengaged his cloaking shield.

The armed crewmen shouted in alarm and their rifles snapped up at his sudden appearance.

"Friendly!" Bruce cried, releasing the rifle and raising his hands.

"Who the hell are you?" an old man asked as he dashed into the cover of the trees.

"Human," Bruce said.

"Abducted?" the man asked.

"Yes," Bruce replied.

"Where'd you get the suit?"

"I found it in a facility close to here. A dam up on the river." He pointed behind him.

"Uh huh. Alien tech?"

Bruce nodded and left his rifle dangling while he reached up and twisted off his helmet. He tucked it under one arm and extended his other hand. "Bruce Gordon," he said, introducing himself.

The man relaxed visibly at the sight of him, as if he'd been expecting to see an alien instead.

"How long have you been here?" the man asked.

"Little over a day now," Bruce replied.

"General Ryker, we need to get Mr. Baylor back to the lander," one of the others said, stopping and standing at attention. "He's not going to make it if we don't stop the bleeding."

General? Bruce wondered. Then these armed crewmen were actually soldiers.

Another one propped the bleeding man against a tree, and began tearing his suit open to reveal his injuries.

"Not going to make it?" the wounded man asked, sounding confused. "I'm fine. I just..." His head sagged to his chest, and he spotted the ragged crimson gashes in his flesh. "Wow. Oh, that's a lot of blood..."

"Where's the ambassador?" the old man asked, looking around suddenly.

"Bled out instantly, sir. Those things slashed his throat open."

"Shit," the general muttered. "Keep Baylor alive. With those things flying around, we're cut off for the moment."

"Yes, sir."

That bald Latino prisoner and another man were still holding their ground in the field, firing a steady stream of lasers at the circling dinos. Two more fell from the sky, and then they fled for the cover of the trees as the rest of the flock swooped down on them in unison.

The dinos peeled off at the last possible second, squawking and shrieking in frustration.

"Well, I haven't hunted *those* before!" the smaller man exclaimed. Bruce eyed him. He had straight, thinning black hair, darting brown eyes and a patchy beard. Blue jeans and a red flannel shirt made him look like a wannabe lumberjack.

Looking away, Bruce searched the trees for Tom, and found a shaded green silhouette, still cloaked and crouching in the shadows. "Come on out, Tom."

"Someone else is here with you?" the general asked sharply.

Bruce nodded and pointed to him. Tom disengaged his cloaking shield, and straightened. The general's rifle snapped up to cover him.

"We're on your side, remember?" Bruce said.

General Ryker relaxed his stance and nodded. "Fine. More the merrier at this point."

"Looks like they're leaving," one of the unarmed crewmen said, watching as the rest of the giant reptiles flew away. "We should get back to the lander while we can."

"We're losing him!" one of the soldiers cried.

"You'd better not, corporal!" the general snapped, rounding on him. "You let Preston-fucking-Baylor die, and you'll never live it down."

Remembering the wounded man, Bruce looked to him and grimaced. *Preston Baylor?* He wondered. *The* Preston Baylor? His face did look vaguely familiar now that Bruce had a moment to study it.

Whoever he was, the soldiers were right. Their hands were soaked with his blood. One of them had a white case open, and was attempting to staunch the blood with a giant field dressing.

Bruce reached for his belt and withdrew a boxy black canteen that he'd filled from the river. "Pour this over the wounds," he said, holding it out to the soldiers. They looked at him like he'd lost his mind.

"What is it?" the general asked suspiciously.

"Alien tech," Bruce said.

The general nodded, and one of the soldiers unscrewed the cap of the canteen and poured the water over Preston's chest.

"It's just wa—"

He never got to finish that sentence. Ragged flesh turned silver at the edges, then pink as microscopic machines came to life, stitching Preston back together before their eyes.

"What in the Sam Hill is that?" the general muttered, stepping in for a closer look.

Everyone gathered around to watch as the soldier poured out the rest of the water.

"Impossible," one of the unarmed crewmen said.

"Evidently not, Commander Anderson," the general said.

"But... how?" a female member of the crew asked, crowding in and shaking her head.

"It's some kind of nano tech," Bruce said. "As far as we can tell, anyway."

None was more astonished than Preston Baylor himself, who sat up suddenly, blinking rapidly and patting himself down. "We have to get a sample of this home. Where did it come from?"

"The river." Bruce pointed through the trees. "About two miles that way."

"Show me!" Preston shot to his feet and swayed woozily.

"You're in no condition to go hiking through a jungle teeming with hostile alien lifeforms," the general said. "Alpha One, and you two—" He pointed to Fango and his buddy. "Take Mr. Baylor and the rest of the crew back to the rocket."

"Alpha Two and I will collect the samples."

"We'll go with you," Bruce suggested. "As guides."

Tom inclined his helmet, but didn't speak.

"Hmmm. Very well. Let's move out!"

"Wait," Bruce said, stopping him with an upraised hand. "There's a hostile group of natives headed this way."

"Natives?" General Ryker echoed. "You mean more dinos?"

"No, I mean native humans. Barbarians with spears and swords, and maybe a few tame dinos. They call themselves the Jakar."

"Hostile?" General Ryker asked.

"Very," Bruce replied.

"We can't leave without those samples," Preston said, leaning hard on the two unarmed crew. "Just think of the lives we could save."

"Then we'd better hurry," General Ryker said.

"I'll go with you," Fango put in suddenly.

"Sure, why not," his buddy added with a shrug.

"You two?" General Ryker regarded them warily. "What the hell for?"

Fango smiled blandly. "Backup. Extra guns and boots, right?" He slapped his rifle for emphasis.

"You don't want to take him with you," Tom said.

"It speaks!" General Ryker exclaimed. "And why not? You know him?"

"Damn straight I do," Tom replied.

"He's just sore that I stole a part in that movie from him," Fango explained. "Remember, the one they were shooting at Sing Sing?"

Tom said nothing.

Movie? Bruce wondered.

"You two came here together?" Ryker asked.

"We did, but then we got separated when I fell over the dam where he found that suit of armor."

"You fell?" Ryker asked.

Fango nodded. "A dino attacked me while we were exploring and knocked me right over the falls. Isn't that right, Tom?"

"Right," Tom replied.

Those specific details were new to Bruce, but from the way they were talking, it sounded like there was still more to the story.

"Whatever the hell, I don't care," General Ryker said. "Just stay close and show me to the river."

"Yes, sir," Bruce replied, putting his helmet back on and giving it a twist to engage the seals. He stepped past the general, heading deeper into the trees. Tom kept pace with him. "It's not true," he said, whispering over their shared comms.

"What isn't?" Bruce demanded.

"I threw him over the falls."

"You did what?" Bruce demanded, drawing looks from the two soldiers.

"Everything all right, boys?" General Ryker asked.

Bruce turned and gave him a thumbs-up. The General scowled and flicked the visor of his helmet down.

"Explain yourself," Bruce muttered.

"Fango tried to kill me. I was just defending myself."

"Why would he do that?"

"Because he's a psychopath, and unlike me, he wasn't wrongfully convicted. He was trying to kill me with a shiv in the yard just before we vanished and woke up here. He tried to finish the job at the dam, but I stopped him by throwing him over the falls."

"Except he lived."

"Thanks to the water," Tom replied.

"What will he say if I ask him for his side of the story?" Bruce countered.

"He'll lie and pretend that I'm the psycho."

"Hmmm. So it's your word against his."

"Have I done anything to make you think I'm actually a killer?"

"Up until now? Nothing. But throwing a former cellmate over a cliff is a good start."

"Then why would I admit to it?" Tom asked.

"Good question."

Tom blew out a noisy breath and surged ahead of him, shaking his head. "You're dumb as a rock."

Bruce watched him go with a frown. Like Layla said, the jury was out on Tom. Killer or not, he definitely had a temper, and finding out that his wife was cheating on him seemed like just the sort of thing to make him lose his head. As far as Bruce was concerned, the murder conviction fit like a glove, but Fango gave him an even chillier vibe than Tom. He didn't strike Bruce as the type to stick his neck out for others, so why was he coming along?

Bruce scowled as he realized that he might have to watch his back from a more imminent threat than blood-thirsty Jakar or dinos.

Chapter 42

9:39 PM

"THEY NEED OUR HELP!" Layla insisted.

"It's already over," Sergeant Cameron said. "Look."

Half of the group emerged from the trees. Two unarmed crew stumbled along with an injured person, guarded by one of the three soldiers.

"Where are the rest of them?" Layla asked.

"I don't know..." Cam said.

"Probably dead or wounded," Neil said. He and Jess were crouched along the ramparts with them.

Layla frowned. Having seen an armored figure helping the landing party from the trees, she wondered who it could be. Axel? Tom? Or maybe Bruce? Were they back already? It was far too soon, but maybe they'd turned around for some reason.

"They might still need our help," Layla decided. "Come on." She shot up from the ramparts and hurried for the stairs.

"We'll stay here and keep a lookout," Neil offered.

Layla smirked at his cowardice. Then again, after watching those flying monsters tear into the crew from the lander, she couldn't really blame him.

Cam followed her down. Together they crossed the pile of rubble in the broken section of the walls and ran out to meet the incoming landing party.

As she drew near, Layla realized that the wounded man was Preston Baylor. From the amount of blood staining his lacerated spacesuit, she worried that he might have sustained serious injuries. But he was alert and his expression didn't show any signs of distress.

"Is he okay?" Layla asked as the pair of crewmen helping Preston hurried by her, heading for the elevator platform in the side of the rocket. The two soldiers standing guard at the bottom saw them coming and ran out to greet them. The other soldier gave a hand signal, and those two fanned out to rearguard positions.

"I'm fine," Preston said. "Someone in a suit of armor came and poured water on me, and... I'm fine."

Fine? Layla wondered. He sounded delirious, but maybe that was to be expected after witnessing his own miraculous healing.

"Did you catch the man's name?" Layla asked, drawing a questioning look from Sergeant Cameron.

"Bruce," the male crewman answered.

Layla nodded absently.

"Do you know him?" Cameron asked.

"No," she lied.

Cameron frowned at that, but didn't say anything. Together they hurried after the landing party, following them onto the platform.

"You aren't authorized to enter the lander," one of the soldiers said.

"It's okay. I'm authorizing it," Preston said.

"Here," the male crewman said, folding a railing out from the platform and placing Preston's hands on it.

"Going up," the female crewman said.

"Where did the others go?" Layla asked as the elevator jerked into motion, swiftly rising up the side of the rocket.

"To get samples of that water from the river," Preston explained. "Do you know what it does?"

Layla hesitated, then shook her head, and pretended to be surprised when Preston told of its healing properties. Sergeant Cameron's surprise was genuine, however.

They reached the top of the rocket and one of the crew waved the outer hatch open. Layla ducked through with the rest of them into a cramped airlock. There was barely enough room for everyone to stand shoulder to shoulder. As soon as they shut the outer hatch, the inner one sprang open. They bustled out into a relatively roomy cargo area where the walls were stacked with plastic crates and giant canvas bags secured behind heavy-duty black straps. Layla followed the crew up a ladder to another deck.

Another crewman was waiting for them up there. Unlike the others, she wasn't wearing a helmet. She had short black hair and bright green eyes. She was anxious to know about the pre-historic creatures that had attacked them in the field.

Layla tuned out the crew's urgent conversations while she studied the inside of the lander. Her heart sank as she realized how little living space was on board. Doors to maybe half a dozen compartments ringed the circumference, and another access ladder led straight up into a cockpit with just two seats.

"This is *it?*" Layla asked. It didn't look like it could hold any more than the ten people it had arrived with.

"What were you expecting?" one of the two female crew asked.

Layla shook her head. "More room!"

"We can't take them all," the woman replied, as if reading Layla's mind.

"How many *can* you take?" Layla asked.

Preston glanced back from where he was following someone up a ladder to the cockpit. "If we ditch all of the cargo, we could carry twenty or thirty, but it would be standing room only."

"And what about the rest?" Cam asked.

The female crewman just shook her head.

"We'll send a colony ship back for them," said the woman with black hair who'd been left behind. "They can trade places with the colonists," she added. She stuck out a hand. "Lieutenant Sara Young. Space Force."

Layla nodded and introduced herself.

"Message sent!" someone called down from the cockpit. He emerged a moment later, hurrying down the ladder. It was the male crewman. "Earth has been informed of the situation. Now all we have to do is get home." Preston clambered down behind him, and Lieutenant Young made the rest of the introductions. The male crewman was a civilian pilot from SDG—Commander Jake Anderson. He had blue eyes, and acne-scarred skin that implied his family might have been poor growing up. Deep lines ran on either side of a permanent frown, making Layla think he was about middle-aged.

The female crewman who'd gone out with the landing party was Nubia Whitman, an olive-skinned woman who was the ship's flight engineer and a micro-biologist. She had helped carry Preston back with Commander Anderson.

The other three were loosely introduced as Alpha Team, Space Force operatives under General Ryker's command. A fourth was out with the general and Bruce and Tom, as well as Fango and that Reservist from the city. The five of them were going to get samples from the river so that they could leave. Getting that water home and preparing a more robust follow-up mission to rescue the abductees was apparently their top priority.

Layla noticed that no one had mentioned Ambassador Jansen. She asked about him, and Nubia grimaced, shaking her head. "He died almost instantly."

Sergeant Cameron sighed. "Okay, so how are we going to do this?"

"Do what?" Preston asked while guzzling water from a flask. One of the soldiers was busy hooking him up to a bag of blood to replace what he'd lost.

"How do we choose the people who get to leave with you," Cameron clarified.

Preston's brow furrowed as he considered the question.

"A lottery," Commander Anderson suggested. "We'll draw names randomly."

"There could be sore losers like that," Preston pointed out.

"There will be anyway," Anderson replied.

"But some of them might have guns," Preston insisted, and nodded to indicate the arc rifle dangling from a strap around Layla's neck.

She grimaced, realizing that they had no clue how dangerous leaving Novus could be. If Axel was right, and the Architects weren't going to let anyone leave, then there was a good chance that this ship would get shot down before it could return to Earth, and she doubted it would have enough fuel left to make a controlled descent after taking off.

They had to know the risks. As much as she hated the thought of admitting to Cam and the rest of the abductees that she had been lying about how and when she'd arrived, this ruse had gone on too long. The things she knew about Novus could save lives.

Layla drew in a deep breath to steady herself before she came clean with them.

And then a thunderous tumult began, muffled by the hull of the lander.

"What is that?" Commander Anderson asked, and twisted his helmet off to reveal buzz-cut black hair. The rest of the crew removed their helmets, bending their ears to listen.

"Sounds like... drums? Chanting?" Cam decided.

Layla recognized that thumping sound. Not drums. Spears hammering the ground. Her eyes flew wide and she dashed to the ladder to the cargo area below.

"What is it?" Cam demanded as he followed her down.

"The locals."

"What locals?"

"The Jakar."

"The... how do you know what they call themselves?"

"I'll explain in a minute," Layla said, and jumped the last few rungs to land with a *boom* on the cargo deck. She ran to the airlock with Cam and the others right behind her. She held the door open for them, and then waited for Commander Anderson to cycle the airlock.

As soon as the outer door swiveled open, Layla jumped onto the elevator platform and stood by the railing, gaping at the source of the commotion.

A massive group of Jakar had assembled along the treeline across from the breach in the walls. At least half a dozen triceratops stood amongst the warriors with Jakar riders.

A familiar horn blew, and one of the triceratops lumbered forward. It was draped with scaly plates of armor, not supplies, and the man sitting atop it wore a familiar, spiked and feathered hat.

"Are you going to explain how you know them?" Cam whispered darkly.

Layla glanced at him, and found that he was casually aiming his rifle at her. Commander Anderson, Nubia, Lieutenant Young and two of the soldiers from Alpha team were there, too, but they were regarding her with curiosity rather than suspicion.

None of them had seen her crash in an alien ship, so they hadn't heard her lie about it afterward.

It took a moment for Layla to gather her thoughts. "We don't have time for explanations. We have to warn the others."

"Make time," Cam growled. "Because right about now, I'm assuming that you're actually an alien in disguise and that all of this is somehow your doing."

Chapter 43

9:47 PM

Layla's explanations were met with plenty of skepticism.

"So you know those two armored men who went with General Ryker?" Commander Anderson asked.

"Yes," Layla said.

"And you've been here for a whole day already," Cam added.

She nodded.

Preston emerged from the ship, holding his blood bag high, and adding his scrutiny to the mix.

"If you've been lying all this time, then how do we know that we can trust you?" Cam demanded.

"You can't," Commander Anderson replied.

"Lying?" Preston asked, glancing around. "What did I miss?"

"I'm exactly who I told you that I am," Layla said. "The only thing I lied about was how long I've been here." She looked to Cam. "We didn't want an angry mob to think we could get them home in the ship we crashed, or to wonder if we had something to do with abducting them."

"Assuming we believe you," Anderson began, "you're saying we're stuck here, too, because these *Architects* won't let us leave?"

"They shot us down," Layla confirmed.

Another horn call drew their attention to the Jakar army on the fields below. They were advancing steadily on the walls, and more were pouring from the forest with every passing second.

"There must be hundreds of them," Preston muttered, squeezing in to grip the railing beside them.

"There are hundreds of us, too," Cam said. "And we have guns. They don't."

"But how many of us have guns?" Preston asked. "Ten?"

Cam made a show of counting them, starting with himself. "Five on this platform. Three more in the city. And the General's group."

"Another six," one of the soldiers supplied.

"But they're not here," Preston pointed out.

"They said it was only a few miles to the river. They shouldn't be long."

Layla noticed that the one with the spiked hat was still leading the army out on his triceratops mount, which she thought to be strange. Maybe he was going to attempt negotiating with the people in the city? "We have to go down and try to speak with them," Layla said.

"They don't speak English, do they?" Cam asked.

"We have to try," Layla insisted. "Maybe we can stall them until the general comes back."

"Why are they even here?" Cam asked, watching her with narrowed eyes. "We just arrived, but apparently you already know them. Should I assume they're here because of you? Maybe they followed you?"

Layla considered the answer. Axel's ship had been cloaked when they'd flown it here, but she supposed the Jakar could have seen it crashing. That implied they'd already been in the area. Maybe headed for the dam.

"It's possible," she admitted. "We were their prisoners until we released a T-Rex inside their village. It must have killed at least twenty of them."

"So they're here for revenge!" Cam said. "This just keeps getting better."

The Jakar's leader blew his horn again, and the soldiers went back to thumping the ground with their spears.

"We'd better go," Preston said. "Detective Bester is right. We need to stall them until the general arrives. Maybe if they see her, she can hash things out with them."

"Or we can give her up as a hostage to appease them," Cam suggested.

Layla scowled at him.

"Take us down," Commander Anderson said.

"Are you sure about that, sir?" Lieutenant Young asked.

"Yes."

Machinery whirred to life as the dark-haired co-pilot touched the controls, sending the elevator platform whirring down the side of the lander.

As soon as it touched the ground, Layla ran out with her hands raised and her rifle in the air. She was determined not to let anyone else answer for her mistakes.

"Hey, get back here!" Cam cried.

"Alpha Team, cover her!" Commander Anderson said.

Layla heard the soldiers' rapid footfalls thumping after her on the char-blackened field.

The Jakar reacted to her approach by sending a group of archers forward. They promptly drew their bowstrings. Layla froze on the spot, breathing hard. Rivers of icy sweat trickled down her spine.

The horn blew again, and their leader turned his mount to face her. He raised another kind of horn to his lips, and addressed her in a deep voice, amplified through the simple device.

"The witch approaches!" he said.

Layla blinked in shock with the realization that she could understand what he was saying. She recalled Axel mentioning that the Architects had taught him the Jakar language via an implant in his brain. At some point, they must have conveyed that knowledge to her, too.

The Jakar leader went on, *"Where is the rest of your entourage?"*

Layla cleared her throat and racked her brains for a reply. Could she also *speak* their language? *"They are not here,"* she tried, surprising herself with the guttural words that rumbled out of her. *"You will deal with me."*

"Bold words from a witch. Perhaps we should search for them ourselves."

"Turn back, or I will use my magic to kill you all."
"If you had such magic, then why do we yet live?" the Jakar leader countered.
"I am showing you mercy, by giving you a chance to turn back."

The assembled ranks of spearmen and archers wavered, their armor and weapons rustling.

"Hold your ground!" their leader snapped. *"She is but one, and we are many. We are Jakar!"*

His army took up that shout in unison, and began thumping their spears into the ground once more.

"Silence," their leader ordered. *"If you will pay us our blood price, then we will leave. If not, we will compel it from you by sword and spear."*

Blood price? Layla wondered. *"Name your price!"* she shouted back.

"Fifteen adult males. Nine females. And two children, both male. As well as the witch and her companions."

Layla's felt sick to her stomach as she realized what they were after. The Jakar were demanding that they offer up the same number of people as had been killed in their village, as some form of bloody restitution.

"Take me. The witch. I am worth twenty others."

The Jakar murmured amongst themselves. Their leader conferred briefly with someone wearing a hollow dinosaur skull on his head and a necklace replete with dino teeth and claws. He carried a wooden staff with a smaller skull mounted at the tip. *Some kind of shaman?* Layla wondered.

"Our Seer says you are but an apprentice to the witch. Agama demands that blood be paid with

blood. Until the price is paid in full, there can be no peace. You have until the setting of the sun to make payment."

The Jakar leader turned his mount and slowly lumbered behind the ranks of his army. As soon as he was gone, the archers lowered their bows and retreated with him. The spearmen arranged themselves in a solid wall, lowering their spears and raising wooden shields.

Apprentice to the witch? Layla wondered. Maybe they meant Alice? She was the one who'd released the rex, so that had to be it. And that meant that satisfying the Jakar's demands on any level would be impossible. Alice was long gone, and not even Axel knew where she was.

"How can you speak their language if you've only been here a couple of days?" someone whispered. Layla belatedly recognized Cam's voice. She turned to see him standing half a step behind her, looking more suspicious than ever. The soldiers were kneeling behind them with their rifles warily trained on the Jakar.

This was going to take a lot of explaining, and something told her that this time Cam wasn't going to believe a word of it.

"We need to organize a defense," Layla said.

"Did you even hear me?" Cam demanded.

"I'll explain on the way," Layla replied, already running back to the rocket where Preston and his crew were waiting.

She raised her watch to check the time. It was 10:07 PM. They had less than an hour before sunset.

She just hoped that would be enough time for Bruce and the general to return. Or better yet, for Axel to fly in with air support. Preston and his crew had only mentioned two armored figures, so the missing third one had to be Axel. He must still be hiking back to fetch another harvester, but if his estimate to reach the dam was correct, then they still had at least three or four hours to go before he returned.

And by then the city would be overrun.

Layla grimaced.

"Well?" Cam prompted, running effortlessly beside her. "Spill it. What's going on?"

"When we get there," she said, nodding to the lander. "There's no time for me to explain everything twice."

Cam set his jaw, but didn't object again.

Layla reached the elevator platform and leaned heavily on the railing to catch her breath before turning to address the landing party.

By the time she was done explaining, no one looked happy, but they seemed to realize that they had bigger problems than her.

"We'll help you defend the city," Commander Anderson decided. "We have plenty of guns in storage."

"You do?" Layla blinked in surprise, hope swelling in her chest.

"We do," he confirmed.

"What about the lander?" Lieutenant Young asked.

"They seem to be ignoring it for now."

"And what if that changes?" she asked.

"What are they going to do?" Anderson challenged. "It's too big to move, and arrows and spears aren't going to do anything but scratch the hull."

Lieutenant Young accepted that with a frown.

Anderson went on, "Stay here with Nubia and Preston—you three can guard the lander just in case. Take the platform up and shut the hatch. Should be impervious as a rock."

"And what are you going to do?" Lieutenant Young asked.

"I'm going to join the defenders on the walls."

"You could die," the lieutenant pointed out.

"If the city falls, and Detective Bester is to be believed about the Jakar's intentions, then a lot more people will die. We can't allow that to happen."

"I agree," Preston said. "I'll also join the defense."

"You're wounded," Commander Anderson objected.

"I *was*," Preston clarified.

The thunder of spears striking dirt started up once more, followed by a deep, ominous chanting that Layla recalled from the ceremony where the Jakar had conferred her, Bruce, and Alice with raptor-claw necklaces. She felt for hers through the fabric of her jumpsuit. The ranks of Jakar soldiers hammered the ground in unison as they hummed and chanted. The Shaman came out and began dancing in front of them and shaking his staff at the sky, probably calling on their god to smite their enemies. What had they called their deity? Agama?

Layla found herself rubbing the raptor claw necklace and hoping the Jakar were right about it imbuing the wearer with the spirit of the animal it came from.

"Let's get those weapons out," Preston muttered. "It sounds like the Jakar are growing impatient."

Chapter 44

10:52 PM

LONG BEFORE HE ACTUALLY saw them, Bruce knew the Jakar had arrived outside the city. The steady thumping of their spears and their ominous chanting assaulted his ears as he moved through the forest. "Quiet," he whispered to the others as they reached the edge of the clearing. The sun was busy setting over the ocean, a blazing orange eye hovering just above the city wall.

"I see them," General Ryker said, crouching beside him with Alpha Two. "Those the barbarians you mentioned?"

Bruce nodded and Tom crowded in on his other side.

"What are they doing here?" Fango asked from behind them.

"A good damn question," Ryker replied.

Tom glanced pointedly at Bruce, but said nothing.

Bruce sighed. He had an idea that the Jakar might be there for him and the others, but he wasn't about to go into all of that now. "Does it matter why they're here? We have to stop them. There are hundreds of unarmed civilians in that city."

"We don't have to do anything," General Ryker replied. "Our mission was recon, not war. We have our samples. It's time to leave."

"But you're a soldier," Bruce objected. "You can't let those people die."

General Ryker ground his teeth visibly, and looked through his rifle's sights. "Well... it looks like you win, Mr. Gordon. I see our guns and my people up on those walls."

Bruce blinked. "What?"

"Take a look for yourself. Assuming you can zoom with that scope..."

Bruce peered through the arc rifle's sights and scanned the walls. He found that he could zoom in the same way as he used the rest of the Architects' tech, just by thinking about it.

"He's right," Bruce muttered. "I count... about thirty people with guns up there."

"Thirty against that angry horde?" Tom asked. "There must be five hundred natives, at least, and I don't think bullets are going to stop a charging triceratops."

"Maybe not, but I don't see dinos getting up on those walls," General Ryker said. "We can hold them."

"We're cut off from the city," Alpha Two put in. "How do we get there without being seen?"

Ryker glanced pointedly at Bruce and Tom. "I imagine they could do it easy."

"We could," Bruce agreed.

"And leave us here?" Fango asked, glancing around nervously at the darkening forest. "We should stick together."

"Light's fading fast." General Ryker pointed out. "Soon we won't need active camo to sneak around."

"Night's aren't that dark here," Bruce said. "Too many planets in the sky."

"I bet. Must be a hell of a sight. But it's fairly overcast, so we should be fine."

Bruce spotted plenty of gaps in the clouds, but he decided to drop it. No one else objected, so they stayed right where they were until the sun had fully set. The neighboring planets cast bright pools in the clearing, making the cover of night a dubious prospect.

"Not as dark as you thought it'd be?" Bruce ventured.

"It'll do," Ryker said. "Stay low and stick to the shadows."

The Jakar stopped chanting and thumping, and promptly lit torches and arrows instead.

"Looks like we're out of time," General Ryker growled. "Let's push up!"

Before Bruce could say anything Ryker and Alpha Two burst into the clearing, running for the lander rather than the walls. Probably because it was the only cover between them and the city.

"Let's go," Tom whispered before running after them.

Fango and Kent, the reservist in the flannel shirt, hung back, as if they hadn't decided whether or not to join the fight.

"It's too far," Fango objected, shaking his head. "Someone will see us."

Bruce wasn't entirely convinced of this plan either—he wasn't a soldier, so charging into battle against an army seemed like a good way to get himself killed. But at least he had experience with guns. That was probably more than he could say for most of the people in the city. And he refused to be an accomplice to Fango's and Kent's cowardice.

Gritting his teeth, Bruce steeled himself for whatever fate awaited and sprinted after Tom and the general. As he went, the first volley of flaming arrows streaked high into the night.

The people on the walls opened fire before those arrows even reached the top of their arcs. Automatic rifles roared and stuttered wildly on full auto. Bruce frowned at the copious waste of ammo and their lack of training. Anyone who'd ever fired an automatic weapon knew that it was pointless to spray bullets continuously, especially at range. Short, controlled bursts were the only way to hit a target.

Tom was right. These people didn't stand a chance against the Jakar.

Screams erupted from the walls as arrows found their marks.

Bruce stopped running and dropped to one knee in the field, lining up the nearest enemy archer. He squeezed the trigger and a bright crimson beam leaped out, burning a hole in the man's chest. The archer fell, and the ones around him scattered, pointing furiously in Bruce's direction before redirecting their aim. Arrows whistled back, digging into the dirt in front of him—*fwip, fwip, crunch!*

He rocked back on his haunches as an arrow shattered on his armor. Bruce snapped off another two shots, dropping two more archers in the process.

Some twenty feet away, Tom joined in with stuttering flashes of light.

A group of about twenty spearmen broke off from the main army, charging after them with long, rectangular shields raised. Bruce redirected his aim and squeezed off a few more shots, but he couldn't find a gap, and those shields were absorbing the brunt of the energy from his rifle. Those spearmen weren't falling as the archers had.

They drew rapidly closer to Bruce's position, then the group forked in two, with half of them going after Tom. He was on his feet, firing and backpedaling steadily, but missing half his shots as arrows splintered on his armor, throwing off his aim.

"It's not working!" Tom cried, his desperation coming loud and clear over their shared comms. "I'm bugging out!" he added.

Bruce aimed beneath the spearmen's shields for the soldiers' shuffling feet. He missed, and the ground erupted with clods of dirt and grass.

Having reached point-blank range, the enemy soldiers dropped their spears and charged with a collective cry.

Bruce sprang up from his shooter's stance and activated his cloaking shield before dashing away.

The soldiers slowed and cast about furiously for their now-invisible target. He caught a glimpse of them pointing to the rippling grass that was parting like a wave around his churning legs.

With another roar, they ran after him.

Not so invisible after all. Bruce's heart hammered in his chest as he fled, angling for the stalky, char-blackened patch around the base of the lander. There wasn't enough grass left to give him away there. Rifle fire rattled through the night. No longer continuous roars, but sporadic bursts. Someone must have taught the defenders on the walls how to shoot.

Up ahead, the General and Alpha Two had already reached the lander, and now they were turning their weapons on the spearmen chasing Bruce. He noticed a few yellow blips wink off the circular map in the top left of his HUD as those bullets crunched and plinked into shields and armor, but somehow that only seemed to spur the others to run faster.

Bruce picked up the pace, bursting into the blackened clearing and catching up with Tom. They reached some type of elevator platform in the side of the rocket just as it was coming down, carrying two women in spacesuits armed with rifles. Bruce disengaged his cloak at the same time as Tom did—

And heard a furious cry erupt from the Jakar chasing them. A spear flew past his head, and he belatedly ducked.

"There you are!" General Ryker cried as he stepped onto the elevator. "Get on! Quick!"

Bruce and Tom both jumped on, and the elevator quickly sped back up the side of the rocket. The spearmen charged beneath it, shouting and shaking their weapons and shields in the air. Ryker and Alpha Two leaned over the sides, raining bullets and taking them all out in a matter of seconds.

"Nice work, Two," Ryker said.

The soldier nodded back—

And an arrow promptly buried itself in his neck. He stumbled backward over the edge, gurgling and clutching his throat.

"Get down!" Ryker screamed.

The five of them plastered themselves to the elevator platform as more arrows whistled by, plinking and crunching against the side of the lander.

Bruce caught a glimpse of the battle raging at the walls. Four triceratops were busy charging through the gap with several hundred spearmen storming in behind them.

The city's defenses were being overwhelmed.

Chapter 45

11:05 PM

AXEL CRASHED THROUGH THE underbrush. The dam was just ahead. He picked up the pace, jumping over logs and ducking branches.

He arrived a few minutes later at a lower level access and opened the door with a thought, rushing into the generator level. Machinery hummed and whirred to all sides, the entire facility singing with the torrents of water falling from the reservoir and driving the turbines here.

He hurried to the nearest elevator and rode it straight up to the hangar. Wasting no time, he clambered to the top hatch of the largest harvester. This second vessel was big enough to carry almost anything on its transporter level. It would be more than large enough to evacuate everyone from that city and bring them here, but he wasn't going to do that. Minders weren't supposed to interfere.

Having learned from bitter experience, Axel knew that the consequences for breaking those rules were not worth it.

He climbed down the ladder from the upper airlock and hurried into the bridge. This harvester had seats for all eight minders up front rather than the four in the cockpit of the model they'd crashed in the ruins.

Axel dropped into the captain's chair and activated his seat restraints from the headrest. Springy cords whipped out from the seat and fastened themselves around his chest. He powered the ship on and watched as the entire bridge turned transparent, giving him a perfect view of the hangar and the waterfall across the opening. He seized the controls, and powerful thrusters thrummed to life. He nudged the throttle up and roared through the shimmering curtain of water, then over the gleaming blue ribbon of the river below. The neighboring planets hung high above, several of them shadowed by clouds, others peeking through. A dozen colorful orbs and crescents lay in a row, curving around the sun, with over a hundred others reduced to gleaming specks from the distance.

Axel banked left over the forests to reach the city, then hesitated and hauled back on the throttle to hover in place.

Alice was still missing. The others should be safe for now, so she was the priority.

"Locate Minder Alice Rice," Axel said.

"I'm sorry, there are no minders by that name within range," his suit replied.

Axel frowned. If Alice was out of range, then she must have ridden that harvester all the way into the core. That was going to make finding her complicated to say the least. She could be on either of the two neighboring planets, but which one? And which conduit had that harvester carried her through? He couldn't very well search an entire planet for her at the other end.

It was impossible to be certain, but knowing how efficient the algorithms were that governed the Architects' ships, he had an inkling that the harvester must have taken the conduit closest to the ruins.

Layla and the others could wait. If Alice had traveled through the Gateway, then she was in much greater danger.

Axel banked his ship in the opposite direction from the ruins and rocketed down the coast. He followed the shore to a specific point, then flew over undulating forests and fields and snaking rivers. Long minutes passed like that until the trees parted to reveal the giant, shining black cap of the nearest conduit. He hovered directly above it and accessed the controls with a thought.

As soon as the conduit irised open, he killed the harvester's thrusters and dropped straight down. Axel felt a muted sensation of falling bleed through the ship's buffering system, and then darkness swallowed his ship as he dropped below the surface of the hollow world. He activated external running lights to part the shadows as he fell straight down the kilometers-deep bore hole. Just one of many. He'd found hundreds more scattered around the globe.

Axel passed a ribbed section of the tunnel where secondary seals had opened to transition him smoothly into the vacuum of the core. Long minutes passed as he fell, and the speed of his descent increased steadily as the air in the conduit grew progressively thinner.

Moments later he shot from the solid tunnel into the girdered section beneath the crust. The black specks of harvesters flitted about, some racing up or down the neighboring spokes. Axel accessed the Gateway through the ship's primary display. Two different destinations appeared: the mauve, freckled orb that was the archipelago ocean world of Cavos, and on the other side of Novus, the brown and tan desert world of Halus.

Alice could have been taken to either planet, but which one? It was also possible that she'd been taken through the core and back to Earth, but Axel doubted that. The harvesters' automated subroutines weren't exactly intelligent, but they were certainly smart enough to detect any lifeforms illegally hitching a ride back to their homeworlds.

Axel picked at random, deciding that if Alice had been taken to Cavos there was at least a chance that she'd survived. The same could not be said for the hellish environment of Halus.

Hoping he was right, Axel locked in the water world as his destination and waited his turn while the harvesters flying down the other conduits flitted in and out of the two shining portals below. The larger one in the center would lead straight to the throat of the wormhole and from there to Earth.

It was a good thing the others didn't know about that. But if he did find Alice, she might ask about it now that she'd seen the core. He needed to get his story straight in advance to avoid being pressured into taking them home.

After what had happened in orbit, he knew they couldn't be trusted to follow the rules just yet. They were still too desperate to return to their old lives. Especially Alice, who had a family back on Earth.

But maybe there was something that could be done about that. Axel collected his thoughts and put in a request.

There was no response, but he knew that they'd heard him. It remained to be seen if the Architects would make an exception for her, but he wouldn't know if he never asked.

The portal to Cavos swung into line beneath the harvester, and a bright flash of light dazzled his eyes. When it cleared, he was racing *up* from the core of the water world to the distant surface above. Several minutes later, a portal irised open in the crust, and the trussed cylinder became solid. Two more doors opened after that, and then he shot out over the rippled blue surface of Cavos.

"Locate Minder Alice Rice," he tried again.

"Locating..."

This time his request wasn't followed by an immediate denial. That was encouraging. Axel held his breath, waiting for the result.

"Minder Alice Rice located," his mech suit replied. A green arrow appeared on the ship's forward display, indicating her position. Axel banked in that direction, and a green target box swept into view on a nearby island with sheer white cliffs and bright green vegetation.

Axel throttled up, racing toward the island.

"What is her status?" Axel asked.

"Alice Rice is in moderate distress," his suit replied, and a string of vitals appeared on the HUD inside his helmet.

She was overheating dangerously and badly dehydrated. Her pulse and blood pressure were both spiking erratically. How long had she been here? At least four or five hours, he decided. It didn't sound like much, but the surface temperature was much higher here than on Planet B, and she probably hadn't known to activate her thermal shield.

He activated his comms. "Alice! It's Axel. Come in!"

But there was no reply.

Chapter 46

11:12 PM

"Focus fire on the spearmen!" Sergeant Cameron ordered.

Everyone was already doing that, firing steadily from either side of the gap in the walls. Layla noticed sporadic weapons fire joining theirs from the elevator at the top of the lander, both lasers and bullets, but they were still being overrun.

A collective shout went up from the handful of people guarding the harvester in the town square. They'd been armed with nothing but old, rusty swords and spears, and now four triceratops with Jakar riders were barreling toward them. Everyone who wasn't already defending the walls had been herded into Axel's crashed ship, but there wasn't nearly enough room for all of them. The remainder hid behind rickety wooden doors in the crumbling stone buildings around the square.

"Here they come!" Cam cried as spearmen began charging up the stairs on their side.

Layla spun away with the sergeant and the crew from the lander to defend the stairs. This time even they opened up on full auto, dropping Jakar soldiers in waves.

Layla popped off precision shots from her rifle, periodically blinding the enemy with the dazzling light of the lasers. She was trying to spare the charge, but even so, the weapon soon clicked and hissed with steam. The glowing number on the back read 0. She ducked out of the weapon's strap and tossed it aside. She patted herself down, feeling for her sidearm, only to remember that she hadn't brought it, and she'd expended the clip in her last encounter with the Jakar.

One after another, the defenders on the walls ran out of ammo and began retreating steadily as they struggled to reload with spare magazines. More spearmen charged up the stairs, taking full advantage of the weakening resistance.

"Fall back!" Cam cried as thrusting spears found unarmored flesh and people fell clutching gushing wounds.

Alpha Three took a spear through his hand. He stared in shock at the bloody point of it protruding mere inches from his face, and then an arrow struck him in the chest and he fell off the stairs. A group of swordsmen came roaring up, slashing wildly and lopping off limbs.

The defenders screamed, stumbling and tripping over each other in their haste to get away.

"Layla!" Neil yanked on her arm to pull her back from the top of the stairs. "We have to go!"

She snapped out of her shock and backed up with Neil and Jess. They were both still firing short bursts from their rifles, having saved their ammo. Sergeant Cam and Preston fell in around them, forming a unit. Cam handed her a spare rifle, and she joined their fire with hers, focusing on the swordsmen who were leading the charge.

Dozens fell, and then someone blew a horn twice, and the spearmen retreated. The Jakar stopped coming, leaving just nine defenders blinking sweat and choking on acrid peals of gunsmoke.

"Reload your rifles!" Cam ordered.

They took advantage of the lull to swap out their spent magazines.

Screaming voices drew Layla's attention to the ramparts on the other side of the breach. The last of the defenders there were being overrun. Commander Anderson and Alpha Four were backed right to the edge of the gap with Jakar forces charging them. Before anyone could react, both of them fell before a thrusting wall of spears. The two men landed on the rubble below with sickening thuds.

"Commander!" Preston screamed. His rifle snapped to his shoulder, and he sprayed the enemy soldiers on the other side, largely missing them.

"Save your bullets!" Cam ordered. "Precision bursts, remember?"

Then all of them opened fire on the flanking force, and the Jakar fired back with a whistling hail of arrows. Defenders on either side of Layla fell and tumbled from the ramparts. Cam cried out as an arrow pierced his leg. Neil and Jess turned and ran, following the length of the walls.

"Fall back!" Cam ordered. He cursed and yanked the arrow out of his leg before turning and hobbling away as fast as he could.

Layla lingered with Preston to pick off another handful of archers before racing after him. Arrows clattered around them, missing by inches and skipping along the walls. They reached a crumbling stone tower and ducked inside, taking a moment to catch their breath.

"It's over," Preston mumbled, staring out a narrow window in the tower.

Layla pressed in beside him to see what he was looking at.

Fully half of the Jakar army had been held in reserve and was camped out with flaming torches and gleaming spear points held high.

A group of about one hundred more had surrounded the base of the rocket where the general had retreated with Bruce and Tom. Flaming arrows rained on them from below while a pair of triceratops who'd been tied to the lander with ropes were being whipped in a crude attempt to topple the rocket.

To Layla's relief, it didn't appear to be working.

A burst of laser fire flickered down from above, sending one of the triceratops to its knees. The other one was promptly cut loose and ridden away before it could die, too.

Seeing those beasts reminded Layla of the ones that had charged through to the town square. She listened to the muffled screams coming from that direction and winced. "We have to help them," she said.

"Help them?" Jess echoed. "We can't even help ourselves!"

"She's right," Neil added. His face was shining with sweat and smeared with blood that wasn't his own. "We have to get out of the city while we still can. Maybe if we make our way around the walls, we can sneak out the back?"

Cam scowled at them. "Cowards," he sneered.

"What about Axel?" Jess asked.

"What about him?" Neil countered.

"When he comes back, he could help us, just like he did the last time."

"Who is Axel?" Cam demanded.

Before Layla could explain, a familiar shriek sounded, followed by the sound of claws skittering on stone.

One of the defenders Layla didn't know screamed and ran out the other side of the tower. A short, darting shadow with a plume of feathers on its head tore after her and leaped on her back, raking her open with its claws and chomping on the back of her neck before Cam shot it. It was a raptor.

Both the dino and the woman lay still with a dark pool of blood quickly spreading around them.

More skittering claws sounded, followed by the snorting of charging beasts. Layla's rifle snapped up to the entrance of the tower as two more raptors burst inside. She and Cam both shot the first one, while the second seized Jess's ankle and yanked her off her feet. She went down screaming, and Neil jammed his rifle against its body, riddling it with bullets.

Another lull came.

Jess was whimpering and clutching her bloody ankle.

"Find something to stop the bleeding!" Cam ordered.

"Like what?" Neil cried.

"Contact front!" Cam cried as a group of Jakar rushed in, thrusting spears in all directions.

Layla felt a searing heat pierce her side, and she fell down with everyone else. She lay there for a moment, feeling pleasantly warm and numb. That feeling quickly spread, taking her thoughts down into a dark, hazy well.

The last thing she saw was a bearded man in a familiar feathered hat with a crown of spikes bending over her with an angry sneer. He produced a water skin from his belt and poured it over her just before she blacked out.

Chapter 47

12:05 AM, September 28th

BRUCE PLASTERED HIMSELF TO the elevator platform to evade another hail of arrows. So far they hadn't been able to pierce his armor, but he wasn't taking any chances.

"The city's overrun, and we're pinned down," Ryker said.

The hatch behind them *thunked* open, and one of the two crew from the ship ducked out, crawling across the platform to join them. Her dark hair shone with purplish highlights in the light of the planets.

"What's our status, Lieutenant?" Ryker asked.

"We're bleeding fuel, sir."

"How is that possible?" he roared.

Another handful of arrows shattered against the bottom of the elevator platform, and one whistled by inches above her head. The woman flattened herself between Bruce and Ryker.

"I don't know. A lucky shot?"

"Can we still take off?"

"Yes, but maybe not for long, and we'll need refueling in Earth's orbit before we can land on that end."

General Ryker grimaced. "So you're saying that we're on a clock. Give me numbers, Lieutenant."

"At the current rate of bleed, maybe an hour? And that's assuming they don't punch a bigger hole in the tank."

"Call it half an hour to be safe," the general said.

"What happens if they hit the leak with one of those flaming arrows?" Bruce asked. "Or drop a torch in a puddle of rocket fuel?"

The lieutenant winced. "Then we might just make it into orbit anyway. The fact is, we need to patch the leak before we can even take off, or else there's a risk of our thrusters sparking a chain-reaction."

"Great, so we're sitting on a ticking time bomb!" Tom muttered. "We have to get down."

"I was just about to order you to do that anyway," General Ryker said.

"Order us?" Tom asked. "We're not your soldiers."

"Maybe not, but you have people down there, too. People that I assume you don't want to see killed or stranded here."

Tom didn't reply to that.

Ryker's gaze turned to Bruce and he jerked his chin. "You still able to use your active camouflage?"

Bruce tried it, and his armor turned translucent and green once more.

"Good," Ryker said. He sighted down his rifle's scope to the city. "Looks like they're rounding everyone up in the square around that debris."

"The harvester," Bruce supplied, and deactivated his cloaking shield, just in case it was depleting his suit's power levels.

"Whatever. The point is, they're not executing everyone on the spot."

"What does that mean?" Tom asked.

"It means they're taking prisoners," Ryker said.

"Or they're planning to make a show of the executions," Bruce suggested.

"Let's hope not. Either way, we have a window of opportunity."

"To do what?" Tom asked.

"For you to sneak into the city and rescue our people."

"We're out of charge on our rifles," Bruce pointed out. "And your guns won't cloak with our suits."

"There should be a few of those weapons still scattered around where the defenders died. Failing that, you recover conventional rifles and give them hell."

"With just the two of us?" Tom asked.

"Invisibility is practically a superpower," Ryker said. "And I bet these Jakar are superstitious bastards. If you can't figure out how to leverage that to your advantage, then maybe you should give me a go in one of those suits."

"If they were that scared of us, they wouldn't have chased us here," Bruce pointed out.

Ryker scowled. "Their arrows can't even pierce your armor. Find yourself a rifle with half a dozen spare mags, and a high vantage point, and you could take them all out single-handedly. At the risk of repeating myself—"

Bruce heard a clicking and whirring sound, and then Tom's suit splayed open on the platform. He eased out of it, being careful to stay low, and rolled over to lie on his stomach beside the general. "If you think you can pull that off, then give them hell."

Ryker smirked. "Can't take the heat, huh?"

"You'd be surprised, but I'm no soldier. You'll be more effective than me in this situation."

"How do I operate it?" Ryker asked.

"Easy. It responds directly to your thoughts."

"Does it now?"

"We don't know that," Bruce pointed out. "The Architects brought us here. You came on your own. We think they might have put implants in our heads that allow us to interact with their tech."

"Shit," Tom muttered, glancing back to his suit.

"Looks like you're back on the front line, son. Nice try, though."

"I'm not a coward," Tom insisted.

But Bruce wasn't so sure. Had Tom been trying to save his own skin, or was it just because, as he'd said, the general would be able to make better use of the suit?

"All right, how are we going to do this?" Bruce asked. He dragged himself to the edge of the platform and peered over the side at the horde of Jakar camped out below the rocket. They'd broken off their attacks, and now they appeared to have adopted a waiting game.

"Make yourselves invisible, then ride the elevator down and sneak into the city," General Ryker said. "We'll take cover inside the rocket and wait. Once you have them and you're safely away, let us know." He reached to his ear and removed a comm unit. Bruce accepted it and twisted off his helmet to fit the comms to his ear.

The general accepted a replacement ear piece from Lieutenant Young.

"Testing, testing," Bruce said.

"It's already set to the right channel. Just touch it to transmit." Ryker illustrated by pressing a hand to his ear. "Like this," he said, and this time his voice echoed through Bruce's comms.

"I'll have to take my helmet off to communicate," Bruce pointed out as he put it back on.

"Still better than having no means of contact," Ryker replied. "We'll try not to read too much into your comm silence."

Bruce nodded and sighted down the scope of his spent arc rifle to the city square, trying to get a rough count of how many Jakar were gathered there. He estimated at least a hundred, and four triceratops with their riders. "Even if we *can* kill all of the ones in the city, how do we get back to the lander with their reserves still out there?" Bruce asked.

A clicking and whirring sound interrupted as Tom sealed himself back inside his suit.

"Their leader went into the city," Ryker said. "When they see him come under attack, I fully expect the reserves to be deployed, and we'll do our best to prod them from behind."

"But that means we'll be overrun!" Tom objected.

"You'll have a bit of time before reinforcements arrive. I'd suggest that one of you do the shooting while the other leads the captives away. They'll be so focused on the shooter that they won't have time to deal with a few escapees."

"A few?" Tom asked. "There must be hundreds of people in the city."

"The lander will never fit all of them," the lieutenant said.

"Rescue your people and ours," General Ryker added. "Ours will be hard to miss, wearing spacesuits. And yours... how many?"

Bruce counted off in his head. "Assuming they survived? Just three."

Ryker nodded. "Good. We can't take much more than that anyway. Bring the sergeant if you find him."

"Sergeant?" Tom asked.

"His name's Gil Cameron. Wearing combat fatigues."

"Got it," Bruce said.

"Good luck, and be quick. I'll keep you apprised of the mission clock. If you're not back before our fuel reaches critical levels, we're taking off without you."

The black-haired lieutenant looked alarmed. "But sir, the thrusters could spark—"

"We'll have to risk it."

"One of their friends warned us that we could be intercepted if we try to go back to Earth," she added.

"Intercepted?" General Ryker demanded. "By what?"

"The same thing that intercepted us when we hijacked that ship," Bruce explained, pointing to the debris in the city square.

Ryker blew out an angry breath. "And you're just telling me this now?"

"It didn't come up until now," Bruce pointed out.

"Go. Stick to the plan. If there's any change on our end, we'll let you know."

Tom sighed, and the general sprang off the elevator platform and dove through the hatch into the lander's airlock. The lieutenant slapped the controls to send the elevator down just before she ducked inside.

Tom's suit shimmered and turned green as he cloaked himself. Bruce did the same and worked to control his breathing. They needed to concentrate on staying quiet if they wanted to avoid being detected. Last time they'd been tracked by the way the grass parted around them. At least here that grass had been burned down to ash and stalks from the rocket's landing, but they could still be found if they accidentally bumped shoulders with the Jakar waiting below.

As they drew near to the ground, Bruce and Tom both pushed off the platform and carefully stood with their backs to the rocket.

The Jakar were shouting and pointing excitedly to the descending elevator, their spears lowered and arrows drawn.

Bruce braced himself, looking for a gap in their ranks. Not seeing one, he began backing away from the edge. Tom joined him and together they pressed themselves closer to the gleaming hull, keeping as far from the barbarian horde as they could.

The elevator touched down, and a few Jakar leaped onto it, casting about warily with their spears and swords.

The horde shuffled and muttered something about bravery and the path to paradise. Bruce blinked in shock, realizing that he could *understand* what they were saying.

More Jakar stepped onto the elevator, and a gap in their ranks opened up. Bruce seized the opportunity, stepping swiftly off the elevator and twisting sideways to squeeze between two archers. Then he was clear and walking briskly toward the city and the hole in its walls.

Tom appeared striding beside him. "Did you hear what they were saying?" he asked over their suits' comms.

Bruce nodded. "I thought it was just me."

"When did *that* happen?"

"The hell if I know," Bruce admitted. "Maybe while we slept."

"Maybe," Tom agreed.

"Get your head in the game," Bruce said.

His ear piece crackled with the general's voice. "Twenty-seven minutes, boys."

Bruce couldn't reach the comm unit through his helmet to activate it for a reply, but he did pick up the pace, breaking into a jog.

They passed through the rubble-strewn gap in the walls. A pair of dead men in spacesuits lay in a twisted, bloody heap. Dozens of others in civilian clothes were scattered around them. Bruce hurried to gather their weapons, finding an arc rifle with fourteen shots left. As soon as he had it in his hands, it shimmered and cloaked itself with his armor. He ditched his depleted rifle, and slipped the strap of the new one over his head. Tom found a conventional rifle and began collecting spare magazines.

"They can see that gear," Bruce pointed out.

"There's no one around to see it," Tom replied. He found a black satchel bag with more magazines and stuffed it full of ammo before looping the rifle's strap over his head and ditching his arc weapon.

"I'll lay down covering fire while you lead them away," Tom said.

Bruce frowned at that, about to object that Tom was choosing the safer job for himself. But General Ryker was right, the Jakar would focus on the shooter, not a handful of escaping captives. There was a good chance that Tom would get pinned down and killed, invisible or not.

"You'd better find one hell of a good sniper's nest," Bruce said.

"I will," Tom replied. "You just make sure you're in position when I start shooting."

"I will be. See you on the other side, Tom."

Tom nodded and slunk away, aiming for a dark alley between buildings that he could use for cover while he made his way toward the square.

Bruce watched him go, wondering if he'd ever see Tom again. Maybe this was the escaped convict's shot at redemption. He'd tried to pass the torch to General Ryker, but it seemed like Fate had other plans for him.

Bruce snapped out of it and hurried for the knot of Jakar gathered around the city center. He ran straight down the main street, since he was perfectly invisible to them.

As Bruce drew near, he slowed his pace to avoid being heard, but it almost wasn't necessary. The Jakar were chanting again, and their leader was pacing back and forth, shouting insults at a crowd of people on their knees with their hands bound behind their backs.

"May these feeble souls please Agama with their service to the mighty Jakar! We accept your surrender and your bondage as payment for the blood of our courageous brothers and sisters."

To one side, a man wearing thick furs and a dino skull hat was dancing about, chanting and babbling incoherently.

"*For the fallen!*" their leader cried. And his warriors repeated that cry, raising their voices in unison.

Bruce crept around behind them, peering through their ranks to look for familiar faces. There was only one person in a spacesuit, and it was shredded and bloodied, making it easy to identify him. Preston Baylor. To Bruce's relief, he spotted Layla, Neil, and Jess all kneeling in a row beside him. Their clothes were drenched with blood, but it was hard to tell if it belonged to them or someone else. They didn't appear to be in any distress.

Noting the rearguard positions of the four triceratops and their riders, a wicked idea occurred to Bruce. Slinking into the shadows of an alley, he whispered over his comms. "Tom? Are you in position?"

"Almost," the other man replied, breathing hard. "I just had a pretty thought."

"Do tell," Tom replied.

Halfway through Bruce's explanation, General Ryker interrupted, saying, "T-minus twenty minutes and counting!"

Bruce grimaced and related that news to Tom. "We're running out of time."

"I'm set," Tom replied. "Let's do this."

Chapter 48

12:27 AM

LAYLA KNEELED ON THE cobblestones with pebbles digging painfully into her kneecaps. She couldn't understand how she'd blacked out and woken up in the square with everyone else, all of their hands already bound behind their backs. If she didn't know better, she'd have said that the Jakar had injected her with some type of sedative.

She remembered that spear slicing through her side, and wondered if those weapons had been dipped in some type of natural tranquilizer? Maybe venom from one of the many creatures roaming Planet B.

Whatever the case, she was in trouble. The Jakar's leader and their Shaman were busy designating them as slaves to make restitution for the Jakar who'd died. Now, it seemed, their blood price had swelled to include everyone who had survived.

Maybe that was to include the Jakar warriors who'd fallen in the battle.

"Are they going to kill us?" Sergeant Cameron asked from Layla's left.

"No." She shook her head without looking up. As soon as they'd awoken, the captives had been ordered to kneel and bow their heads in penance to *Agama*. Layla had relayed that command, but one of them had vocally refused, saying that he only kneeled for one God. The Jakar had turned him into a pin cushion with their arrows, and since then no one had dared to disobey.

"Then what?" Cam whispered.

"Slaves."

"That's not much better," Preston said.

"Quiet!" The Jakar's leader slammed the butt of his spear into Preston's back, and he gave a stifled cry before crashing into the cobblestones with his chin.

Their leader paced on, ranting about their disgusting heathen ways.

To her right, Neil glanced pointedly at Layla and gestured with his eyes to a bulge in his pants pocket.

Layla frowned.

"Lightsaber," he whispered.

Her eyes widened in shock. He still had it? She'd given him the weapon back on the harvester just before she'd discovered her engagement ring.

But what good would it do? There were too many eyes on them. If they were lucky, they might be able to use it to cut themselves free later. Maybe when the Jakar were marching them back through the forest to their village.

"Not yet," Layla whispered.

Neil nodded and went back to staring at the ground.

A rattle of gunfire started up, and an animal gave a shuddering shriek. Jakar cried out in warning, their ranks shuffling toward the threat. Subsequent bursts of rifle fire joined the first and more animal screams split the air.

The Jakar erupted in chaos as thudding footfalls shook the ground like a stampede.

Layla risked looking up—

Just in time to see multiple triceratops charging through the Jakar's ranks with their heads down and horns impaling scores of them at once. The warriors assembled hastily, dropping their spears, but the triceratops were in a frenzy, terrified and trampling everything in their path.

The Jakar leader screamed something about the magic of the *sky demons* and ran into the fray with his spear. The shaman raised his hands to the sky and shook them, babbling in a cackling voice.

Rifle fire raked over the Jakar from a stone tower close to the square, sowing even more chaos and dropping soldiers in waves.

"Let's get out of here!" Cam said, struggling to his feet.

Layla and the others joined him in standing just as a triceratops came bounding through the crowd of kneeling captives. They scattered, running for their lives, but several tripped and were trampled anyway. They couldn't run with their hands bound behind their backs.

"Cut us free!" Neil cried, angling his pocket toward Layla's hands. She reached in and her fingers grazed the ribbed metal cylinder. She yanked it out and manipulated it behind her back to find the sliding switch, checking just before she activated it that the emitter was pointed at the ground and not her back.

Layla flicked the slider and the blade hummed out, sizzling on the cobblestones. She was just about to angle it into the ropes that bound her hands when someone snatched it away.

"Let me help," a familiar voice said.

Layla reeled with shock. "Bruce?" Her hands burst free and she whirled around to see—

A floating sword.

Of course, he'd cloaked himself. The blade flicked across Cam's wrists next, and then the air shimmered and Bruce appeared standing in their midst. He cut the others free next and pointed to a nearby alleyway with the glowing sword. "This way!"

They tore after him, dodging terrified abductees. The Jakar soldiers were fleeing the square to get away from the combination of rampaging triceratops and the unknown shooter busy slaughtering them from above.

This particular alley was relatively empty, with only a handful of soldiers regrouping there. Layla saw the glint of arrows being drawn seconds before the first one shattered on Bruce's armor.

"Look out!" she cried.

Bruce flicked the sword off and fired back with a flickering pulse of lasers from his rifle.

The roar of gunfire paused, and they kept running, darting and zagging between buildings like rats in a maze. Layla raced through another turn to see the city walls looming at the end of the alley up ahead. They burst out and ran along the perimeter to the breach, but long before they arrived, hordes of Jakar reserves came rushing through the gap.

Bruce skidded to a stop on the grassy cobblestones. "We'll have to find another way. Come on!"

They ran the other way, following the walls deeper into the city.

"We're not going to make it," Bruce huffed.

Layla stared hard at him. "What do you mean?"

"The lander. It's going to take off without us."

"They'll get shot down!" Layla cried.

"Maybe not," Bruce replied. "We've got ten minutes to get there if we want to join them."

"But we don't even have a way out of the city!" Jess screamed.

"There," Bruce pointed to a shallow stone ditch up ahead. It led to what looked like a drain in the bottom of the wall.

Before Layla could say anything about it, someone burst out of an adjoining alley, slamming into Bruce and knocking him off his feet. The hilt of the plasma sword went flying and rolled toward the ditch.

Bruce began picking himself up, only to have a hulking Jakar warrior land on his back and begin wrestling for control of his rifle.

Layla recognized the feathered hat with a crown of spikes and realized that it was the barbarians' leader. She cast about frantically for the plasma sword and spotted it a dozen feet away. She sprinted for the weapon just as Bruce's rifle went off with a zapping crimson flash. He groaned and rolled over, clutching a smoking hole in his armor.

Layla seized the sword and flicked it on. The blade slid out and began glowing hotly.

"Watch out!" Cam cried just as a group of spearmen burst out of the alley.

But they weren't the threat that he was warning her about. The Jakar leader had Bruce's rifle in his hands and he was aiming it at Layla.

Cam jumped in front of her just as the weapon went off with another bloody flash of light.

Cam landed at Layla's feet. She screamed in fury and threw the sword like a knife. It flipped end over end, buzzing and humming as it whipped through the air. The blade buried itself to the hilt in the Jakar's shoulder and slid down, slicing his arm clean off. The rifle clattered to the ground, and he sank to his knees with flames licking off the furs around his shoulder.

Preston ran for the weapon, diving to reach it and snapping it up to rake fire across the stunned group of spearmen. They fell in a clattering heap of weapons and armor.

"Let's go!" Neil hissed into the silence that followed.

Layla ran back to check on Cam. She didn't even need to check his pulse to know that he was dead. One eye was open and staring up at her, while the other was a charred black hole where the laser had hit him.

Bruce stumbled to his feet and made his way over to the Jakar's leader. Layla rushed to join him, and found to her dismay that he was still alive. His teeth were gritted from the pain, and the plasma sword lay sizzling beside him, between his body and his severed arm, turning the cobblestones black.

Layla snatched up the sword, leveling the tip beneath the Jakar's chin. His skin began to blister and swell from the heat of the blade.

"What is your name?" she demanded, stalling for time while she decided whether or not to simply kill him. She had to think about the remaining captives. Maybe she could barter his life for theirs.

"Do it," the man spat blood at her. *"I am ready."*

"We don't have time for this," Bruce groaned. He pointed again to the ditch, and this time Layla saw the wrought iron grate where it intersected the wall.

"Cut a hole and we can leave!" Bruce said.

Layla cursed under her breath and ran to the grate, slicing it open.

Bruce kicked the severed section out and ducked through with Preston right behind him. Layla lingered to wave Neil and Jess through, keeping an eye on the Jakar leader as she did so, just in case he tried to stop them.

But he remained where he was, not even attempting to get up. Maybe he would die from shock. Negotiating with these people would have to wait. And besides, something told Layla that they'd rather let their leader die than give in to her demands.

She darted through the hole in the grate, and heard rifle fire start up again, a continuous roar now that suggested the shooter might be cornered at point-blank range with a group of Jakar soldiers rushing in.

Layla flicked the sword off and the blade retracted smoothly into the hilt with a subtle jolt. She ran past Neil and Jess, the long grass swishing loudly against her legs. Bruce was making good speed despite his injury, but still visibly favoring his wounded side. He might be in luck, since he'd been shot by a laser and not a bullet. The wound was probably cauterized and there would be no projectile to remove.

Preston pulled ahead, screaming, "Come on! They've already started the launch sequence!"

Layla saw that he was right. Steam was billowing from the rocket on all sides.

"Who is that shooting in the city?" Layla asked as the sound paused for a beat, then started up again.

"Tom," Bruce grunted.

"You left him?"

"Did it look like I had a choice? We barely made it out ourselves. Besides, isn't he a convicted felon? Let him pay his dues."

Layla frowned, a flicker of doubt trickling in as she wondered what kind of hardened criminal would lay down his life for a group of strangers.

Maybe the kind who deserved a second chance.

The rifle fire stopped abruptly and ice formed in Layla's veins as she realized he was probably dead.

"Two minutes!" Bruce shouted.

Preston touched his ear. "Wait! Stop the launch! Don't take off!" he screamed.

Layla saw the lander looming large before them. The Jakar were scattering from its base, scared away by the roiling clouds of steam venting from the rocket.

Then came a bright orange burst of flames as the thrusters ignited. Smoke rolled out in all directions, scattering the Jakar even further. The ear-splitting roar of its take-off reached their ears a second later.

"No!" Preston screamed.

Bruce stopped running and planted his hands on his knees. Layla, did the same, blinking stars and gasping for air.

Neil and Jess paused where they were, and they all gazed up at the vanishing silver bullet that was their last hope of making it back to Earth.

"Maybe they'll make it and send a colony ship back to rescue us," Bruce said.

"If we live long enough to be rescued," Layla added. "Look!"

The Jakar were busy re-grouping and charging toward them.

"Head for the trees!" Bruce cried.

Chapter 49

12:36 AM

Bruce gritted through the pain and ran as fast as he could, but with the searing wound in his side, it was impossible to take full advantage of the speed his armor could afford. Layla kept up with him easily, and the Jakar were gaining on them. Neil and Jess brought up the rear, each of them screaming at the other to run faster.

Their only hope of escape was that the trees were closer to them than they were to the Jakar. They would have some shelter from the arrows, at least, but what would happen after that?

The forest wasn't some magical safe zone. The Jakar would follow them in.

"They're going to catch us," Bruce said, moments before they reached the tree line.

"Just keep running!" Layla cried.

They crashed through the underbrush amidst a scattered hail of arrows and ducked behind the trees for cover. Preston fired back with the arc rifle, picking off a couple of archers.

"Is anyone hit?" Layla shouted.

Bruce glanced around to see the others shaking their heads. The Jakar were approaching more slowly now, with their shields raised in a defensive formation. Shields to the front, archers at the back. They seemed to realize that their enemy was digging in.

Preston squeezed off a couple more shots, but this time only one of the Jakar fell. The man behind him took up his shield and plugged the hole in the formation. Bruce glimpsed the number on the back of the arc rifle—7.

Preston seemed to notice it, too, and he shook his head. "We need a plan. Anyone?"

Bruce leaned around the tree trunk to count the number of Jakar approaching. Maybe twenty, but a group of about fifty more were streaming in from a few hundred feet back.

Layla still had that sword, the searing blade now curiously retracted. Bruce considered that maybe he could take the weapon and use his armor to full effect by making a stand against the approaching horde. But sooner or later they'd overpower him, just as they must have done with Tom.

Through sheer numbers they would ultimately turn his own weapon against him.

But he might be able to buy enough time for the others to escape.

"You need to keep running," Bruce decided. "Get to the river, and follow it back to the dam. Give me the sword. I'll hold them off."

"You can't!" Layla said. "They'll kill you."

"That's better than them killing all of us," Bruce replied. "I have armor. You don't."

Layla hesitated a moment longer before relinquishing the weapon. Bruce found the sliding switch, and a gleaming black blade slid out, glowing like burning coals.

"Everyone follow me!" Layla said.

A zapping shriek of laser fire sounded behind them, followed by muffled screams and the crashing thuds of something *big* approaching.

Bruce whirled around to see someone in an orange jumpsuit racing out of the forest from the direction of the river and firing blindly over his shoulder.

Fango.

Kent, the army reservist in the flannel shirt, was running behind him, screaming for Fango to wait.

Then the source of those crashing footfalls appeared with a shuddering roar. Massive jaws yawned wide and snapped Kent up. He screamed again as blood gushed from the rex's mouth. Another chomp silenced him, and then the monster swallowed Kent whole.

A moment later, it began lumbering after Fango again. He fired once more, missing and lighting a tree on fire before reaching their position. "You can't stop it!" he breathed, heaving a cloud of steam into the cold night. "I already shot it twice. It won't stop!"

Preston had his arc rifle up to his shoulder, but he was gaping at the advancing monster instead of aiming down the sights.

Another roar shattered the air, and it came stomping toward them.

"Lead it into the clearing!" Bruce said.

"What?" Fango cried. "*Estás loco!* We have to hide!"

Two more rexes appeared, peeling out from behind the first. One stood only about a meter high, but the other was an adult almost as large as the first. A family of three.

The smaller adult veered toward Layla, Neil, and Jess, while the baby angled for Preston. The billionaire snapped out of it and shot the baby. It screamed and fell back, limping. Its mother roared with outrage and pulled ahead.

"Now! Run!" Bruce cried, and Fango bolted from the trees. Bruce waved his sword in the air like a flare, shouting, "Hey! Over here!" hoping that all three would follow him.

And then he turned and ran out after Fango.

More lasers flickered from the trees as Preston fired on the female, while the male chased after Bruce and Fango.

Arrows came whistling toward them from the Jakar, plinking off Bruce's armor. Fango went down, skidding through the tall grass with a cry of pain, and then the rex crashed out of the forest, and the Jakar began shouting in alarm. Their spearmen crouched down, digging in to make a barricade. Archers aimed over their shoulders, firing a volley at the rex. The rex screamed, slowing to toss its head and snap its jaws at what it probably thought was a cloud of stinging insects.

Bruce realized that he would reach the Jakar before the rex did. He flicked off the plasma sword and dove into the grass, activating his suit's cloaking shield.

His armor and the hilt of the sword turned transparent and green, indicating that the shield still functioned, but there was a red-shaded hole in it where the arc rifle had pierced his side.

Twisting around, he saw the rex charging the Jakar formation. It hit the spearwall and barreled straight through, sending one of the Jakar flying through the air and screaming. The others held their ground, but the rex sent three more sprawling with a sweep of its tail before crushing another two in its jaws. Those warriors were all going to die, but their reinforcements had also dug in, and more arrows were busy raining on the beast from afar.

It didn't seem to be doing much other than making the rex angry.

Zapping reports drew Bruce's gaze back to the trees. He spotted a flickering crimson flash, indicating that Preston was still alive and fighting the other two rexes. Bruce pushed off the ground and ran back to where Fango was clutching a bloody leg with an arrow sticking out of it.

"We have to help them!" Bruce said.

"You see this?" Fango demanded while looking pointedly at the arrow in his leg. "I can't help anyone!"

Bruce scowled and ran for the forest. Before he even reached the trees, the others came running into the clearing. Preston was backing away steadily, firing up at the mother rex, which was now limping like its child. There was no sign of the baby.

Preston shouted in alarm as his rifle stopped firing and steam hissed out, the charge depleted. He threw the weapon aside, then turned and ran with the others. Mother rex was still coming, and he was first in line to be eaten.

Bruce sprinted toward him with the plasma sword, but quickly realized that he would never make it in time. Jaws opened wide and dropped low for the kill.

Bruce ignited his sword once more, and disabled his cloaking shield to wave it in the air, shouting for the female's attention.

But there was no deterring her from the kill.

A whistling roar and a fleeting shadow shot over the clearing just as Layla, Neil, and Jess arrived. They all looked up to see a large black spaceship firing steadily with fat red lasers. A wall of flaming grass and exploding dirt shot up in front of the rex. It screamed in terror and veered sharply away. Laser fire chased it back into the trees, and it disappeared with fading thunder.

"It's Axel!" Layla said, watching as the ship dropped down for a landing between them and the Jakar. Those warriors were still too busy with the other rex to worry about demons from the sky.

A long landing ramp dropped down. Someone in a mech suit came running out and stood waving at them from the top, at least forty feet above the clearing. Axel. It had to be.

Bruce didn't need more invitation than that. "Let's go!" he shouted, and then snapped off the energy blade to make sure he didn't accidentally cut off his own foot.

He and Layla bounded up the ramp, followed by Neil, Jess, and finally Preston, who limped along, looking terrified. His leg was bleeding profusely.

As soon as he was in, the ramp began telescoping up. In that same moment, Fango jumped up and grabbed the edge, riding the retracting ramp to the open airlock. It stopped sliding away just before he could lose his grip, and Bruce and Layla helped him in.

The arrow in Fango's thigh had been snapped off, but the head was still buried in his leg.

"Thank you," Bruce said for all of them before turning and nodding to Axel.

"You're welcome," a female voice replied. She reached up and twisted off her helmet, revealing sweat-matted blond hair, an oval face and tired brown eyes.

"Alice!" Layla erupted, and yanked the other woman into a hug. "He found you!"

"Yes," Alice replied, smiling tightly at them. She stood stiff with her arms to her sides as the detective embraced her. She seemed to be in shock. Bruce wondered what had happened to her and where she had been.

"Let's get you patched up," Alice said, pulling away as the airlock sealed with a *thump.* The inner door slid open, revealing a long corridor,

Both Tom and Preston were clutching their bloody legs, the latter with a curving horseshoe pattern of puncture marks that looked like it might be from the baby rex. He began struggling to rise and follow Alice in, but she shook her head, and said, "Stay there."

"Where were you?" Layla asked, running after her.

Bruce hurried to keep up, anxious to hear the answer.

Chapter 50

12:52 AM

WHILE ALICE TENDED TO everyone's injuries with flasks of living water, she gave a brief account of her misadventure on a planet called *Cavos*, the nearest and closest world in the night sky. Layla listened intently as she described an entirely alien biome, with higher gravity and a much thicker atmosphere. Alice claimed that she had almost died from the heat and also from several different types of carnivorous creatures that had tried to eat her—even something that sounded like a giant, flying jellyfish. Yet that wasn't the most shocking part of her story. When Bruce asked how she'd gotten there, Alice told them about the conduits that ran from the surface of the planet to its core, and about the utterly hollow vacuum beneath its crust.

At this point, Layla wasn't even surprised by that. Everything about this place was impossible. Adding one more impossibility to the pile didn't exactly tip the scales in her book.

Bruce continued to question Alice about her journey, but Layla listened with only half an ear as she glanced about the airlock, checking people over. Everyone looked as exhausted as she felt. Jess sat in a fetal position with Neil beside her. Somehow neither of them had been seriously injured, and the others were rapidly being healed by the water that Alice was pouring over them. Fango looked every bit the part of a convicted criminal, with tattoos crawling up his neck and peeking from the sleeves of his prison jumpsuit. Layla had worried about letting him on board with his arc rifle, but the weapon turned out to be depleted, so it didn't matter. She did, however, make a point of recovering the plasma sword from Bruce before Fango could swipe it. Lifers like Fango knew all about hiding shivs, and that weapon was one hell of a shiv. Layla pocketed the ribbed black cylinder, noticing Fango's eyes on her as she did so.

"Something wrong?" she asked.

His gaze slid away without a word.

"So there were *three* portals at the center of both worlds?" Bruce asked.

"Yes," Alice replied.

Bruce had his suit off and was lying on the deck beside it with his shirt pulled up so that Alice could pour water on both sides of the char-blackened laser burn below his ribs.

"Wormholes," Alice clarified. "Just like the one in the center of this solar system. Picture miniature versions of that."

"So these planets are all... hollow, artificial structures?" Preston asked. He'd removed his helmet, revealing sweaty blond hair and green eyes. "But we saw them from orbit. They're all the size of actual planets. And their gravity..." He trailed off shaking his head. His chewed-up leg was still smeared with blood, and his spacesuit looked like it had been through a meat grinder, but he was miraculously alive and well thanks to the water.

All of them were.

Except for Tom, whose fate was unknown. But maybe the Jakar had taken him hostage with the others. Layla glanced to the other end of the corridor beyond the airlock. Where was Axel taking them? Maybe he had some way of checking Tom's status. She shot to her feet and ran for the cockpit.

"Where are you going?" Neil called after her.

"To check on Tom!"

She heard clanging footsteps chasing her down the corridor and glanced back to see that both Bruce and Fango were following her there. They passed through an open door, and Layla slowed as the deck seemed to vanish beneath her feet. Transparent. *Just an illusion*, she reminded herself. Eight seats filled a big, semicircular compartment. Axel sat in the center of the deck with an empty seat beside him. Layla dropped into it, and he glanced her way. His helmet was off and tucked beneath his seat, revealing boyish features. Warm hazel eyes tightened in a smile.

"Glad to see you made it."

Layla didn't reply. Her eyes were on the city flashing beneath them, and the scattered groups of Jakar herding captives back into the square.

"Can they see us?" Layla asked.

Axel shook his head.

"Are you looking for Tom?" Bruce asked suddenly from behind them.

"Yes," Axel replied.

"Is he..." Layla couldn't finish that thought.

"No, he's alive," Axel replied.

"Where?" Layla asked sharply, her eyes on the transparent deck, searching the gathering crowd in the square for someone in a glossy black mech suit.

"Right there—" Axel pointed to the top of a high stone tower overlooking the center of the city. A crumbling balcony was crowded with Jakar spearmen. Tom was kneeling on it with his back to the edge and his hands raised, while a one-armed Jakar with a familiar, spiked and feathered hat aimed an automatic rifle at his chest.

"He *lived?*" Bruce asked.

"I know, can't catch a break," Fango muttered.

But Layla realized he wasn't talking about the Jakar leader. She shot the man a sharp look. Tom had warned them that Fango had been trying to kill him before they'd disappeared together.

Fango smiled broadly, revealing a golden tooth and a gap on the other side where another one was missing. "*Que pasó, chica? Tengo un mono en la cara?*"

Layla ignored him and looked back to the fore. "We have to help him," she whispered.

"I am," Axel said. A tiny, green-shaded sphere went shooting out and stopped to hover behind Tom. A split second later, a bright flash erupted, dazzling their eyes. When it faded, Tom was gone, leaving the Jakar bewildered in the wake of his disappearance. Their leader ran to the edge, peering over it to check if Tom had fallen.

Axel jumped out of his seat and hurried from the cockpit. Layla followed him with Bruce and Fango. A hatch in the deck slid open, and Axel started down a long access ladder. Layla hurried after him into a cavernous space with a black pedestal and a dish-like projector in the ceiling. It was identical to the transporter room aboard the other harvester, except that this one was easily big enough to hold a T-Rex. Maybe even a Brontosaurus.

Tom sat up quickly from the middle of the chamber, then reached up to remove his helmet.

"You made it," he croaked, smiling crookedly at Layla as she approached.

"Thanks to you," she said.

"You're welcome. What about the others?"

Layla nodded.

"All of them?" Tom pressed, sounding surprised.

"No." A muscle in Layla's cheek jerked as she remembered Cam throwing himself in front of a laser beam to save her. "The sergeant died. Along with a lot of others."

"But all eight minders are alive and well," Axel said, sounding pleased.

Layla scowled at him, then noticed Fango coming down the ladder.

"*He's* here?" Tom shot to his feet, his fists balling. Then he jabbed a finger at Fango's chest. "He hid like a coward while we risked our lives to save you."

Fango bristled. "So because I didn't run into battle and get myself killed like everyone else, that's somehow a crime?"

Tom strode purposefully toward him. "No, but trying to kill me is."

"You're the one who threw me over that waterfall!" Fango said.

Tom stopped with their faces mere inches apart and glared down at the shorter man.

"Get out my face, Romeo," Fango growled.

Romeo? Layla wondered. She reached for the plasma sword in her pocket, fearing that this was about to get ugly.

Axel pushed between them and said, "Whatever happened between you, it's in the past."

"Yes, one *day* in the past," Fango snorted.

"You're minders now," Axel insisted. "That means you answer to the Architects. And deliberately harming another minder could get you banished."

"Banished?" Bruce asked. "Is that what happens if you break the rules around here?"

Axel held his gaze for several seconds before replying. "Where is the lander?"

"They took off," Bruce replied.

"You *let* them leave?" Axel asked. "Didn't you warn them about what would happen?"

Bruce shrugged. "I tried, but they wouldn't listen."

Axel made an irritated sound in the back of his throat and ran for the ladder to the upper deck.

"Where are you going?" Layla called after him.

"To stop them before it's too late!"

Chapter 51

1:06 AM

THE SUN ROSE SWIFTLY above the shadowy green hills and snow-capped mountains, heralding the start of yet another local day. Alice let herself enjoy the view for a brief moment before she strapped into her seat on the bridge with the others. Only Preston didn't have a seat, but Axel folded out an extra one for him to one side of the opening of the bridge. Axel pulled straight up, and the thrusters roared, pressing them into their seats with a force only mildly stronger than the planet's gravity. Blue sky quickly faded to black, and Axel found the gleaming, missile-shaped hulk of the Eagle II in orbit. The lander and its booster were already docked to the front of the nuclear rocket. They were just in time to see its thrusters flare to life, glowing white-hot as it accelerated away from Planet B.

"Try your comms again," Axel said.

Preston placed a hand to his ear and spoke into his ear piece. "This is Preston Baylor to the *Emissary*. Come in *Emissary*."

Everyone waited anxiously for a reply from the other end.

"I've got the general," he said in a softer voice.

Alice bit her lip.

"Ryker, listen to me. You can't leave... no, I don't know that for a fact! But apparently the debris we saw in the city was the result of the last attempt to escape."

The thrusters at the back of the rocket burned brighter still.

Preston's hand fell from his ear. "He's ordering us to join them as an escort."

"Maybe we should," Bruce said.

Axel shook his head. "You know what will happen if we do. And this time we might not have such a soft landing."

Bruce frowned, and Layla's jaw slackened.

"We have to try," Alice whispered. "It's our only chance to get home!"

"*This* is your home," Axel insisted.

"Oh hell, no," Bruce said, shooting out of his chair. "I'm not spending the rest of my life in some alien zoo. Let's put it to a vote. Have the majority decide."

"No," Axel said. "I won't allow it."

"You won't *allow* it?" Bruce roared and took two long strides toward him.

Before Axel could respond, flickers of bloody light washed over them, and the *Emissary's* thrusters winked off.

"What—"

The gleaming hull of the rocket bulged, and then it burst into glittering shards. The lander went spinning end over end, and dark W-shaped black ships flitted around it, lashing it with more laser fire. Tiny white jets of escaping air burst out on all sides of the craft, and then the interceptors broke off.

"They're headed this way!" Axel warned.

He seized the flight controls and sent them diving back toward the planet. Lasers chased them down, washing the bridge in bloody hues and filling the air with the hissing reports of impacts.

"*Emissary*, come in!" Preston shouted into his comms.

Everyone watched him, waiting for the reply.

But silence reigned until orange fire plumed around the nose of their ship and the shuddering roar of atmospheric entry filled the air.

"General Ryker, Lieutenant Young, come in," Preston tried again.

Still no reply.

They were gone, taking with them any lingering hope Alice still had that she might find a way back to Earth. Back to Sean and Liam. Tears coursed hotly down Alice's cheeks.

Tom noticed and the corners of his mouth drooped. Axel saw it, too, but he smiled tightly instead. "Don't worry, Alice. I have a surprise for you. I think it might just be enough to change your opinion about Novus."

Alice blinked rapidly to clear her eyes. "Wha-what surprise? What could you possibly offer me?"

"Patience. You'll see," Axel replied.

"What about the others?" Layla asked suddenly.

"Who?" Axel asked.

"The other abductees in the city," Layla said. "We have to help them."

"We can't," Axel said. "No interference, remember?"

"But you just interfered! Again!"

"To save other minders," Axel pointed out. "That's the exception to the rule."

"What about Preston? And the others from the lander that you just tried to save?"

"They weren't brought here. They came on their own. The rules don't apply to them," Axel explained.

"So why weren't they allowed to leave?" Bruce asked. "Sounds like you're making this up as you go along."

"I wish," Axel snorted. "If I were in charge, you can bet I'd do things a lot differently."

"So who the hell *is* in charge?" Bruce demanded. "Are we ever going to meet them?"

Alice was busy wondering the same thing.

"I doubt it," Axel said. "The Architects prefer to remain hidden."

"Have you ever met them?" Layla asked.

"No," Axel replied, except he hesitated just long enough to invite doubt.

At the moment, Alice had other things on her mind. What was the surprise Axel had for her?

Chapter 52

1:29 AM

"M om?"
Alice couldn't believe her eyes.

Her husband, Liam, gaped at her and slowly shook his head as he rose from the head of the dining table.

"Mom!" Sean screamed, and knocked his chair over in his hurry to cross the room.

Alice ran to greet him. He collided with her and wrapped his arms around her armored waist.

"I missed you," he mumbled.

"Me too, sweetheart."

Liam rounded the table with a wary frown, then broke into long strides and pulled her into a crushing hug. He pulled away and grabbed her face in both hands, kissing her roughly on the lips. "You're alive," he whispered.

Alice just nodded, her mouth suddenly dry, her throat too tight to speak. Tears welled in her eyes and slipped down her cheeks once more, but this time Liam swept them away with his thumbs. "I'm here now," he said. "What happened to you? And what on earth are you wearing?"

"I never thought I'd see you again," Alice finally managed. "How did you..."

"I was putting Sean to bed, and there was this flash of light. The next thing I knew, we woke up here, in this... some kind of hydro plant?" Liam looked to the picture windows and the shimmering curtain of water rushing past them, turning the view to a blurry green haze.

Apprehension broke through Alice's joy at seeing her family again. She spun around to see the others looking on from the opening of the corridor to the bedrooms.

Axel beamed smugly at her. "You're welcome," he said.

Alice pulled sharply away from her family and stormed across the room to stop in front of him. His expression flickered, and his brow furrowed.

Alice wound back and slapped him as hard as she could. Axel's head snapped to one side, and his cheek immediately turned red in the shape of her hand.

"How could you!" she said.

"What the hell!" Axel screamed, holding a hand to his reddening cheek. "I thought this was what you wanted?"

"You told us you can't take us home. That we can't leave. But somehow you can bring my family here?"

"The woman makes a good point," Bruce said.

"It wasn't me," Axel insisted. "I just asked them if they could bring your family here. They made an exception for you! You have any idea how lucky you are? I would have killed to have my family brought here!"

"Why, so that they could go to an early grave?" Alice demanded. "This place is not safe. You *know* that, but you had my family brought here anyway."

"But you *wanted* this!" Axel replied, looking furious. "You were so desperate to go home that you almost died hitching a ride on that harvester!"

"Harvester?" her husband, Liam, asked. "You mean like a combine?"

Alice glanced back and saw him and Sean standing a few feet away, looking confused and alarmed by her outburst.

"It's a long story," Alice said.

"Well someone had better start explaining *something*," Liam said. "Where are we? And why is it so dangerous?"

Axel scowled. "Why don't you fill them in? I have business to attend to." With that, he turned and stalked back the way they'd come.

"What kind of business?" Bruce called after him.

But Axel didn't reply.

Bruce frowned and slipped his helmet back on. The air shimmered around him, and he vanished—except for a small char-blackened hole where that laser had pierced his armor.

"What... how did he?" Liam asked.

"A long story," Alice repeated.

"Where is he going?" Layla whispered. "He's not going to try to hurt Axel is he?"

"Who is that kid, anyway?" Fango muttered. "*He* runs this place?"

Tom stepped closer to Layla. "Want me to go after him?"

Layla hesitated, then nodded. "Please. We've had enough death for one day."

Tom nodded and slipped his helmet on. His armor shimmered and he vanished just as Bruce had.

"Can't Axel see them when they're cloaked?" Layla asked, looking to Alice.

She shook her head. "Not if he doesn't put his helmet on. At least... I don't think so."

Chapter 53

1:37 AM

B RUCE SLIPPED INTO THE elevator behind Axel and plastered himself to the side wall, doing his best not to even breathe to avoid being detected. His armor was damaged, so he wasn't completely invisible.

Just before the elevator door slid shut, a large, green-shaded silhouette darted through to stand beside him. He held a finger to his lips.

Bruce didn't have to wonder who it was. The difference in height between Tom and Alice was at least a foot, and she was the only other person wearing a mech suit. Somehow the suits adapted to fit the wearer, just like the jumpsuits they wore underneath—not to mention all of the eerie, mind-reading tech. Everything designed just so to accommodate the minders.

Axel reached for the control panel, and Bruce watched as he selected *S9 - Gateway* from the panel.

Bruce's suspicions kicked into high gear as the elevator raced down through the facility.

So much for 'I spent weeks trying to get in,' he thought.

The elevator opened directly into a large, octagonal chamber with glossy white walls and a black, resinous floor that was rimmed with glowing red lights. A projector dish hung from the center of the ceiling with concentric rings of red light around it. Axel walked out, and both Bruce and Tom quietly followed him to the center of the room. Axel waited there, looking annoyed and... *apprehensive?* Bruce wondered.

The rings of light in the ceiling and around the edges of the room began to flash, turning from red to green, and then searing white. The projector dish glowed brightly, and then a blinding flash tore through the chamber.

Bruce blinked and found himself standing on a matching black pedestal in the middle of a much smaller room. Axel quickly strode for the exit, and the doors parted automatically for him, revealing a long, dark hallway.

Bruce and Tom hurried out after him, and they emerged in what looked like someone's living room. High ceilings. Immaculate finishings. Elaborate crystal light fixtures.

And a startlingly familiar view—soaring skyscrapers, gleaming with lights. A vast, snow-covered rectangle of trees and grass, bedecked with Christmas lights. Central Park.

This was New York City.

On Earth.

Axel had *lied.*

Fury swelled in Bruce's chest, making it hard to think or even see straight. Not only had Axel lied, he'd lied so convincingly that Bruce had almost believed him. Almost.

"Axel!" someone called out. "To what do we owe the honor of your visit?" Bruce's gaze was drawn up to a curving stairwell where a handsome blond-haired man and a lithe, dark-haired woman were busy descending. Both of them wore pure white robes, but not terry cloth. More like silk. Axel crossed the living room to meet them at the bottom of the stairs.

"What the hell?" Tom whispered over their comms.

"Quiet," Bruce muttered back, stepping sideways to stand against the nearest wall in an attempt to stay hidden. His cloaking shield was damaged, so anyone could see him if they looked close enough.

His heart was slamming in his chest, his eyes darting for an escape. Blood roared in Bruce's ears, his pulse raging with a combination of righteous fury and terror. Something was very wrong with this situation. The penthouse apartment was massive. Its size and location screamed opulence, wealth, and power.

These people knew Axel and *he* knew them. But who were they?

Bruce was suddenly afraid to know the answer.

"They're not going to stop until they find a way home," Axel said.

"Let them try," the man said, smiling broadly. "They have no idea what they're up against. And even if they were to find a way, we'd just take them right back."

Axel nodded uneasily at that.

The woman regarded him steadily. "What's wrong, Axel?"

He blew out a breath. "What if we *let* them go? I can do it on my own. I don't *need* help."

"But you wanted it," the man pointed out.

"I didn't ask for *them*."

"Who better than people you used to know and care about? There are precious few of them still among the living."

"You brought me two convicted murderers. And on top of that, they hate each other's guts!"

"You know how it is. Sometimes accidents happen. They were standing too close together when we opened the portal, and we didn't have time to separate them. If we hadn't intervened when we did, Tom would have been killed. You can deal with Fango however you see fit. You already have eight without him now that Mr. Baylor is there."

"Just send them home, Adama." Axel insisted.

Adama? Bruce wondered. That name... why did it sound so familiar? *Agama.* That was it! The Jakar had been offering the captives to their god. His name was Agama. The similarity was too much. It couldn't be a coincidence.

"First you wanted us to reunite Alice with her family, and now you want us to bring them all back? Can you imagine the questions that would raise?"

"We're already raising those questions by abducting so many people in such a short time. And now that a ship has made it from Earth, more will follow. They sent a message back."

"We know," Adama said. "But all of this is really beside the point, isn't it, Axel? The Architects are coming to Earth. Nothing can stop that now, so the only thing you need to focus on is who else you want to help us save before they get here."

"Save?" Tom echoed in a rising voice. *"What is that supposed to mean?"*

The woman's gaze shifted fractionally from Axel, and her eyes glowed briefly, blazing bright blue as they fixed on the exact spot where Bruce and Tom were standing.

Every fiber of Bruce's being screamed for him to run.

"Axel..." the woman said slowly. "You know the rules. Why did you bring *them* with you?"

Axel spun around. "Bring who?" he demanded.

"Chava's right," Adama said. "Two of your minders followed you here."

"Reveal yourselves," the woman intoned darkly. "Now."

Rather than accede to her demand, Tom sprinted for a nearby hallway. Bruce stayed rooted to the spot, too afraid to move. The woman's hand flashed out of her robes, and a spinning black sphere left her palm and went racing after Tom.

A moment later, a second one left Adama's hand. Blinding light erupted around Tom's green-shaded silhouette, and he vanished. A split second later, another flash sucked Bruce into a fathomless void.

1:51 AM

WHEN BRUCE WOKE UP, he was lying on a black octagonal pedestal in a massive chamber with a familiar dish-like device above him, and red rings of light around it. Layla and Alice came running in, both of them looking worried.

"What happened?" Layla demanded, kneeling in front of him. "Where is Axel?"

Tom sat up beside him and groaned, holding the side of his head. Bruce noticed that both of their helmets were off and sitting beside them.

"Ow," Tom muttered.

Bruce sat up and frowned, blinking steadily and trying to sift through the fuzzy haze swirling inside his head. Everyone was there except for Axel and Alice's family. Layla, Alice, and Preston were standing closest to him, but he evaded their scrutiny, struggling to fill the gaps in his memory. Bruce remembered activating his cloaking shield and chasing Axel to the elevator. And then...

Nothing. Just a big, gaping void where his memories should have been.

"I think he knocked us out somehow," Tom said, still clutching his head.

"Knocked you out?" Layla asked. "You mean he stunned you with an arc rifle?"

"Maybe," Tom said.

"Where are we?" Bruce asked.

"In the harvester," Alice supplied. "Transporter room. We were looking for you and Axel when Layla saw a flash of light coming from down here."

Preston held out a hand and Bruce took it, springing to his feet only to sway unsteadily, his head spinning and throbbing with a sudden pounding headache.

"We need to find Axel," Bruce said, bending to snatch his helmet off the floor.

Alice hurried across the deck, leading the way up the access ladder.

Moments after they reached the landing ramp at the back of the ship, the muffled roar of an explosion shook the dam. Rock dust sifted down from the ceiling, and everyone looked up.

"What was that?" Preston asked.

"I don't know..." Bruce replied. "But it didn't sound good."

"It sounded like it came from one of the upper levels," Layla said.

Alice looked sharply to the elevator on the far side of the hangar. "My family is up there!"

She dashed down the ramp with Bruce and the others right behind her.

1:54 AM

THEY FOUND THE SOURCE of the explosion as soon as the elevator slid open and they emerged in the living room on *S2*. Soldiers in white pressure suits with blue piping and red, white, and blue-striped flags on their shoulders were busy fanning out in pairs. Two of them had Liam and Sean covered with rifles while a man with short gray hair sat on the coffee table in front of their couch, his helmet beside him, asking Liam questions in a heavy Russian accent. He looked up sharply as they entered the room, and half a dozen rifles swept into line with Alice's chest.

"Get those weapons away from my family!" she cried.

"Who are you, and how did you get here?" the gray-haired man asked, standing up from the table.

"You first," Bruce said. The air behind the Russian man shimmered, and Bruce appeared standing behind him in the mech suit. He locked an arm around the other man's throat, putting him in a choke hold before he could react.

The Russian man struggled, muttering and cursing in his language. The soldiers swung their rifles in Bruce's direction.

"Stop it!" Alice cried. "Someone is going to get hurt!"

But Bruce didn't release the man. The Russian's face was turning bright red.

One of the soldiers made hand signals, and several of the others began moving sideways to get behind Bruce.

"Bruce! You're going to kill him!" Layla said.

He gave up with a frustrated roar and raised both hands above his head. The Russian soldiers advanced steadily and took hold of him, roughly twisting his arms up behind his back.

"How did you get in here?" Tom asked. His helmet was still back in the hangar where he'd left it.

"We set charge on door and blow it open," the gray-haired man said. "How did *you* get here?"

The man's gaze shifted suddenly toward Preston and promptly widened. "Mr. Preston Baylor... we saw your rocket in orbit."

"You mean before it was destroyed," he replied.

The gray-haired man drew himself up. "Destroyed? By what? Was not us, if that is you are thinking."

"I know it wasn't you. But you shouldn't have come."

"Why we should not come? So you have planet to yourself?"

"No, because now, you're going to die here," Preston said.

The soldiers began shouting and shaking their rifles at him, as if he might have a bomb hidden inside his ragged space suit.

"Easy men. This is not a threat. Explain yourself, Mr. Baylor. What do you mean that we are going to die here? Who shot down your rocket?"

Alice glanced at him, and slowly shook her head.

Preston blew out a shaky sigh. With his next breath he began relating an impossible story about hostile alien drones, hollow planets, and the many deadly species of extinct creatures that prowled their surfaces.

Alice went to sit with her family, and the Russian soldiers slowly relaxed their guards as shock and disbelief set in.

When Preston got to the part about the *living water*, the Russian man snorted and shook his head. "Very funny, Mr. Baylor. Next time, pick a different fairy tale. Maybe we'll believe it."

"It's all true," Preston insisted.

The Russian scowled, snapping orders and gesturing to his soldiers. Two pairs stayed and raised their weapons once more, while another four followed him across the living room to the elevator and the stairwell.

"Where are you going?" Preston called after them.

"To see it for myself," the gray-haired man replied.

"Where have I heard that before?" Layla muttered.

"From me, when I arrived," Preston said, and he heaved another sigh. "This is not going to end well."

GET THE SEQUEL FOR FREE

The Series Continues With...

Worlds Collide

Coming August 2022

PRE-ORDER IT FROM AMAZON

OR

Get a FREE digital copy if you post an honest review of Planet B on Amazon https:/geni.us/reviewplanetb

And then send it to me here:

https://files.jaspertscott.com/aoa2free.htm

Thank you in advance for your feedback!

KEEP IN TOUCH

Subscribe to my Mailing List & get 2 FREE Books!

http://files.jaspertscott.com/mailinglist.html

Follow me on Bookbub:

https://www.bookbub.com/authors/jasper-t-scott

Follow me on Amazon:

https://www.amazon.com/Jasper-T-Scott/e/B00B7A2CT4

Look me up on Facebook:

https://www.facebook.com/jaspertscott/

Check out my Website:

www.JasperTscott.com

Follow me on Twitter:

@JasperTscott

Or send me an e-mail:

JasperTscott@gmail.com

JASPER T. SCOTT

OTHER BOOKS BY THE AUTHOR

Keep up with new releases and get two free books by signing up for Jasper's newsletter at www.jaspertscott.com

Note: as an Amazon Associate I earn a small commission from qualifying purchases.

Architects of the Apocalypse

Planet B | Worlds Collide | Apokalypsis

The Kyron Invasion

Arrival | New World Order | End Game

Ascension Wars

First Encounter | Occupied Earth | Fractured Earth | Second Encounter

The Cade Korbin Chronicles

The Bounty Hunter | Alien Artifacts | Paragon | The Omega Protocol

Final Days

Final Days | Colony | Escape

JASPER T. SCOTT

Scott Standalones (No Sequels, No Cliffhangers)

Under Darkness | Into the Unknown | In Time for Revenge

Rogue Star

Frozen Earth | New Worlds

Broken Worlds

The Awakening | The Revenants | Civil War

New Frontiers (Standalone Prequels to Dark Space)

Excelsior | Mindscape | Exodus

Dark Space

Dark Space | The Invisible War | Origin | Revenge | Avilon | Armageddon

Dark Space Universe

Dark Space Universe | The Enemy Within | The Last Stand

ABOUT THE AUTHOR

Jasper Scott is a USA Today bestselling author and three-time Kindle all-star. With more than thirty sci-fi novels and over a million copies sold, Jasper's work has been translated into various languages and published around the world.

Jasper writes fast-paced books with unexpected twists and flawed characters. He was born and raised in Canada by South African parents, with a British heritage on his mother's side and German on his father's. He now lives in an exotic locale with his wife, their two kids, and two Chihuahuas.

Printed in Great Britain
by Amazon